The Voice of Prophets

a novel by

Alan Simon

Alan Simon

The Voice of Prophets

Copyright © 2022 Alan Simon. All Rights Reserved.

No part of this book may be used, reproduced, stored, or transmitted in any form or by any means electronic, photocopying, recording or otherwise, without the prior written permission of the publisher, except in the case of brief quotations for reviews and critical articles.

First Print Edition

ISBN: 978-0-9994665-7-5

DISCLAIMERS

This is a work of fiction. Names, characters, businesses and enterprises, events, and incidents are the products of the author's imagination. Any resemblance to actual persons, living or dead, is coincidental. Certain historic events, long-standing institutions, governmental agencies, and public offices are mentioned, but the characters involved are wholly imaginary.

Western Pennsylvania College is a fictional higher education institution.

The American Values and Greatness Network is a fictional media company.

The Restore American Values and Greatness Party is a fictional political party.

PERMISSIONS

It's The End Of The World As We Know It
Words and Music by William Berry, Peter Buck, Michael Mills and Michael Stipe Copyright © 1989 NIGHT GARDEN MUSIC
All Rights Administered by SONGS OF UNIVERSAL, INC.
All Rights Reserved Used by Permission
Reprinted by permission of Hal Leonard LLC

American Pie
Words and Music by Don McLean
Copyright © 1971, 1972 BENNY BIRD CO., INC.
Copyright Renewed
All Rights Controlled and Administered by SONGS OF UNIVERSAL, INC. All Rights Reserved
Used by Permission
Reprinted by permission of Hal Leonard LLC

The Boxer
Words and Music by Paul Simon
Copyright © 1968 Paul Simon (BMI)
International Copyright Secured All Rights Reserved
Used by Permission
Reprinted by permission of Hal Leonard LLC

Lunatic Fringe
Words and Music by Tom Cochrane
Copyright © 1981 SKY IS FALLING ENT., INC.
All Rights in the U.S. and Canada Controlled and Administered by UNIVERSAL — POLYGRAM INTERNATIONAL PUBLISHING, INC. All Rights Reserved
Used by Permission
Reprinted by permission of Hal Leonard LLC

Night Moves
Words and Music by Bob Seger
Copyright © 1976 Gear Publishing Co. Copyright Renewed
All Rights Reserved
Used by Permission
Reprinted by permission of Hal Leonard LLC

Won't Get Fooled Again
Words and Music by Peter Townshend
Copyright © 1972 Fabulous Music Ltd.
Copyright Renewed
All Rights Administered in the USA and Canada by Spirit Four Music, Suolubaf Music and ABKCO Music Inc.
International Copyright Secured All Rights Reserved
Reprinted by permission of Hal Leonard LLC

LIFE DURING WARTIME
Words and Music by DAVID BYRNE, CHRIS FRANTZ, JERRY HARRISON and TINA WEYMOUTH
© 1979 WC MUSIC CORP and INDEX MUSIC, INC.
All Rights Administered by WC MUSIC CORP.
All Rights Reserved
Used by Permission of ALFRED MUSIC

Excerpt from **THE STAND** by Stephen King, copyright © 1978, 1990 by Stephen King. Used by permission of Doubleday, an imprint of the Knopf Doubleday Publishing Group, a division of Penguin Random House LLC. All rights reserved.

Alan Simon

*If the voice of prophets blew
on flutes made of martyred children's bones
and exhaled airs burnt with martyrs' cries;
If they built a bridge of old men's dying groans;
Ear of mankind
occupied with small sounds,
would you hear?*

- Traditional Yom Kippur reading

Prologue

This time, their false messiah arrived unencumbered by the damning baggage that opponents might repeatedly and frantically use to counter him, albeit with scant success.

No shady financial and business past, hallmarked by one outsized failure after another, rectified only through revisionist history and clandestine, Faustian recapitalization.

No readily disprovable "hyperbole" spouted day after day.

No easily discoverable affairs with an array of women over the years that had to be explained away via clumsily constructed denials; the disavowals embraced only by the truest of believers, yet the sordid tales themselves readily shunted aside by so many.

No persistent concerns about mental fitness that needed to be slapped away as "fake news" and "an attempted takedown."

No gross incompetence and blatant self-dealing, unveiled almost daily, that needed to be indignantly minimized through the de facto state media's repertoire of *1984*-ish Newspeak.

Once again, their false messiah tapped into their ugliest instincts and most vile impulses, mustering the dark armies onto the battlefield to unquestioningly do his bidding.

This time, their false messiah had risen from their own ranks, and was truly one of them.

This time, their false messiah's dark vision for immutably altering every facet of the American landscape came tightly packaged alongside competence and patience.

This time, their false messiah would prove unstoppable.

Part I
Lunatic Fringe

March–May 2033

*"Lunatic fringe, I know you're out there;
You're in hiding and you hold your meetings.
I can hear you coming and I know what you're after."*

- Red Rider, *Lunatic Fringe*

Chapter 1

The lunatic fringe was, in reality, no longer the fringe, and hadn't been for years. They had been legitimized. They had planted their flags and claimed their territory. They remained joined together as a collective voice that was perpetually amplified through the corrupt, depraved melting pot of provocative talk radio programs, televised agitprop masquerading as news, and incendiary internet sites. Social media remained the glue that connected and bound the true believers directly with one another. Conspiracy theories abounded, each one more outlandish than the last. Domination and pitiless punishment were the idols they worshipped. They comfortably led post-coherence lives, untroubled by conflicting and incompatible beliefs effortlessly coexisting inside their minds.

No longer marginalized, they had made their mark on every aspect of American life. Many from their ranks continued to ooze their way into political offices and judicial appointments at all levels of the American system, and elsewhere around the troubled world. Their influence ebbed and flowed; but as with the heartiest viruses, that influence would never be eradicated. Much like a vampire tightly shackled inside his coffin, the creature would periodically lie there for a stretch of time, waiting impatiently for the chains to be carelessly removed so he could resume wreaking havoc on those who had grown complacent or had simply forgotten.

The degree of concern from those who would oppose the once-fringe likewise ebbed and flowed. When relative stability finally returned to American life in the latter years of the 2020s, the heightened state of alarm sounded for years by the mainstream media pundits, pragmatic politicians, legal and constitutional scholars, and much of the general populace wearily deflated and dissipated. The war may not have been won, they reasoned, but at least the imminent threat had been sequestered behind the firewall of a renewed commitment to democracy.

However, even as life in America and throughout much of the world resumed some semblance of normalcy, and most people did their best to forget the absolute insanity they had endured and survived, others continued to eye the chastened yet resilient underbelly with nervous concern. The pervasive stagnation of much of the global economy, coupled with zealous resentment of "the elites" by so many among the masses, laid fears that the tamped-down ugliness of the recent past would remain dormant no longer.

Their fears were well founded. As the 2020s stumbled to their conclusion and then desolately surrendered to resurgent chaos across the American landscape, the dark forces mustered once more, culminating with the election of the Restore American Values and Greatness Party's first-ever presidential candidate, Ephraim Hollinger, to the nation's leadership in November 2032.

America had dodged the bullet of a full descent into darkness little more than a decade earlier; but now another round was in the chamber, and the hammer of hatred was cocked and on a hair trigger.

* * *

"Danny—are you ready to read?"

Daniel Jacobson's eyes shifted upward from the homemade *Megillah* booklet as his head pivoted in the direction of his mother's voice. While his father had been reading his own assigned portions, Daniel's gaze had been meandering through the booklet's text that contained selected excerpts from the Book of Esther. The lingering scent of freshly baked *hamantaschen*, the traditional Purim dessert treat, hung in the air, lulling Daniel into a near-hypnotic state as he lost himself in the Purim story. Daniel's family read from this customized, abridged *Megillah* every year when they gathered for their Purim supper, in lieu of attending synagogue services to hear a full reading of the Book of Esther, as was customary for more observant families.

This particular Jacobson family tradition had begun long before Daniel had been born. As everyone in the family knew, Daniel's great-grandfather, Nathan Jacobson, had commenced the ritual with his own parents and siblings almost ninety years earlier, shortly after returning home from the violent, climactic final year of the Second World War. Nathan had painstakingly hand-constructed that entire original set of homemade booklets during the early months of 1946: his self-prescribed therapy as he struggled to reenter civilian life. The effort and concentration that he put into each booklet helped Nathan cordon off a touch more of the war's horrors he had endured and survived.

That first set of *Megillahs* had become nearly unusable through wear and tear after three decades, and was replaced in 1976 by an unremarkable mimeographed collection. Then, twenty years later, a third generation of booklets had been constructed via computer software and brought to life courtesy of Nathan Jacobson's color laser printer. Nathan had recently retired from his state government job with Pennsylvania's Department of Transportation, having reached the age of seventy, and now had plenty of time on his hands. He meticulously replicated the colorful intricacies from that first generation of booklets in the graphics software that he quickly mastered, restoring his original hand-drawn refinement to the family's newest collection of *Megillahs*.

For almost forty years now, these were the booklets that were passed around the dining room table before each family Purim supper. Other than a few small tears here and there, not to mention minor food stains on most of them, the originals among these *Megillah* pamphlets were still as serviceable as they had been back in the 1990s, outlasting both generations of their predecessors. As the Jacobson family grew in size through births and marriages, additional copies were effortlessly printed and added to the collection. This year's family Purim gathering was on the smaller side, but some years saw close to thirty people, with dining tables dispersed across two or even three rooms in whatever home was hosting that year.

Daniel's eyes automatically shifted to his great-grandfather before realizing that, as his mother had just advised, they were all waiting on him to pick up the reading. Still, for a fraction of a second, his thoughts remained with Nathan Jacobson. Could this unbelievably old man have imagined, way back in 1946, that this far into the future he would still be alive, approaching his one hundred and seventh birthday in less than a week? That he would be sitting at the head of an oversized dining room table that now included two great-great-grandchildren among the family members? That both his overall health and mental faculties would remain more akin to those of a man twenty or even thirty years younger?

Daniel shook away the ponderings as he turned his attention to his *Megillah* reader, his eyes searching for the spot where he would pick up his assigned portion of the reading. It didn't take him long to locate the correct place, but why should it? He had read the same four paragraphs for close to twenty years now—no, make that *exactly* twenty years, Daniel realized, recalling that he had inherited this portion of the reading shortly after his bar mitzvah.

Here goes, Daniel thought, *for the twenty-first time.*

"Then were the king's scribes called in the first month," he began, "on the thirteenth day thereof, and there was written, according to all that…"

Daniel briefly paused, his eyes shifting up from his booklet to his nephew Noah and his niece Rachel, both sitting across the table, slightly off-angle from his own chair. He offered a quick nod so they knew what was coming, and then quickly resumed.

What was supposed to happen at this point was that upon Daniel mentioning the name "Haman"—the Purim story's villain, essentially the Hitler or Himmler or Eichmann of his day—the children would enthusiastically whirl their *graggers*, the noisemakers traditionally used to drown out Haman's name each time it was read from the text of the *Megillah*. The reader would pause for about ten seconds while the energetic clatter proceeded, and then resume reading the passage.

Tonight, though, ten-year-old Noah and eight-year-old Rachel Weber had quietly conspired to deliver a "special" Purim denouncement for the first encounter this evening with the hated name. The instant their Uncle Danny began to enunciate the name "Haman," the children loudly interjected, in unison, "EPHRAIM HOLLINGER!" and then immediately began to twirl their *graggers* as they giggled with guilty delight at their Purim dinner table prank.

A good two or three seconds of surprised shock passed before Marc Weber, Daniel's brother-in-law and the father of Noah and Rachel, suddenly bellowed "STOP IT! ENOUGH! BOTH OF YOU!"

Daniel was certain that his brother-in-law was about to explode: not even so much at his son's and daughter's prankish divergence from the centuries-old Purim tradition, but more in reaction to them replacing the name of the hated villain of the Queen Esther tale with that of Marc Weber's own personal "Chosen One."

Fortunately, the situation was diffused by Daniel's sister Claire, who quickly clamped her right hand onto her husband's left forearm in instant response to his overblown outburst. Claire's glaring but wordless admonition did the trick (*Was she digging her nails into her husband's forearm through his shirtsleeve?* Daniel wondered…), and nothing further was forthcoming from the man who, if anyone else present dared to ask, saw himself as the lone voice of sensibility among—and perhaps even an adversary of—his in-laws gathered around the Jacobsons' dining room table.

"Go ahead," Daniel's great-grandfather calmly commanded, nodding toward the booklet in his great-grandson's hand.

Daniel shot a quick, challenging look at his brother-in-law and then resumed his reading. He jumped back a few words but this time proceeded right over Haman's name, rather than pause for another round of *gragger* noisemaking and a possible reprise of the children's scheme.

"…according to all that Haman commanded, unto the king's satraps, and to the governors that were over every province, and to the princes of every people; to every province according to the writing thereof, and to every people after their language; in the name of King Ahasuerus was it written, and it was sealed with the king's ring."

Daniel's chest tightened as he moved ahead to the next verse. The sensation was a familiar one, and had been for twenty-one years now.

> "And letters were sent by posts into all the king's provinces, to destroy, to slay, and to cause to perish, all Jews, both young and old, little children and women, in one day…"

Daniel's eyes and mouth joined forces to continue the assigned task of reading an additional two verses, even as his mind diverged to ponder unseen—yet very real—distant storm clouds, thinking to himself that the prank concocted by his nephew and niece certainly hadn't materialized out of the proverbial thin air.

* * *

"Pop-pop?"

Nathan Jacobson's eyes were open, yet Daniel knew that his great-grandfather's mind hovered somewhere in the fuzzy-edged grayness between awake and asleep. The old man was slumped in a comfortably worn recliner that was perched on the enclosed back porch of his grandson Robert's—Daniel's father's—gracefully aging home in the southern Pittsburgh suburbs. The early March evening had turned chilly, and the forecast called for light snow flurries sometime after midnight. However, the temperature on the enclosed porch with its removable thick glass windows still in place more closely matched that of inside the house, and was the absolute perfect setting for anyone, especially someone of Nathan Jacobson's age, to drift off into a comfortable after-dinner nap. The doughy-sweet *hamantaschen* aroma had made its way to—and was now pleasantly trapped inside—the enclosed porch, bringing a slight growl of hunger to Daniel's stomach even though he was still full from dinner.

"Pop-pop?" Daniel tried again after a few seconds.

From the moment the first of Nathan's nine great-grandchildren had been born, he had been awarded the name "Pop-pop" for this newest generation of his descendants. Nathan had always been "Grandpa" to his five grandchildren, but everyone was in agreement that "Great-Grandpa" or a similar moniker sounded awkward. So he became "Pop-pop" not only to his first great-grandchild—Daniel's older sister Claire—but to all the others that followed. That term continued even into the next generation when Noah and Rachel joined the family. Who knew: If the old man could keep going for another dozen years—and perhaps old Nathan could actually pull off that feat, with a little help from modern medicine—then he could even have great-great-*great*-grandchildren likewise addressing him as "Pop-pop." Certainly nobody gave it any thought thirty-five years earlier when Claire was born, but they had fortuitously settled on a timeless, multi-generation family moniker for their ancient patriarch.

This time, the light of awareness slowly radiated from the old man's eyes. His gaze shifted imperceptibly to lock with Daniel. Without his glasses, the image before his face was fuzzily unfocused, yet he knew who was addressing him.

"Danny," the old man croaked. Whereas Daniel Jacobson preferred his given name in a professional setting, everyone in his family had called him "Danny" since he had been a boy.

"How are you feeling, Pop-pop?" Daniel decided to inquire before broaching the idea that was on his mind.

Nathan slightly shuffled his body in the recliner, a seated stretch to relax the stiffness that inevitably settled into his century-old muscles whenever he sat still for more than a few minutes. He instinctively reached to his left, feeling around the end table for his glasses. Easily finding them, he raised them to his face with a slightly quivering left hand but was still able to slip on the trifocals without poking himself with either of the temples.

Nathan didn't respond to his great-grandson's "how are you feeling" question. Perhaps he didn't think it worth the effort to enumerate a handful of minor aches and pains; or perhaps the old man already forgot that Daniel had asked the question. Nathan's faculties remained sharp for the most part, but his mind tended to dull as each day neared its conclusion. Instead, his newly focused eyes locked with Daniel's.

"A little bit of excitement during supper, huh?"

Daniel nervously looked around to see if perhaps his brother-in-law had wandered from inside the house to the porch or the doorway, and was now within earshot. The prankish moment had slid past as the selected *Megillah* readings proceeded around the table to their conclusion, followed by a more or less traditional Purim dinner. "More or less" because about half of those present in Daniel's parents' home this evening were either vegan or vegetarian, so generational Jewish dishes such as beef brisket and roasted chicken were supplemented with platters of meatless alternatives. (However, even most of the family members who habitually shunned dairy and eggs made an exception for the family's prized *hamantaschen* recipe that dated back more than a century.) Marc Weber had, fortunately, decided to sidestep the opportunity to parrot some choice Ephraim Hollinger propaganda during the dinner and dessert conversations, and apparently the Jacobson family would make it through the rest of the evening without any verbal clashes. Maybe Marc felt outnumbered around the table; but whatever the reason, the rest of dinner had been calm.

Daniel and his great-grandfather were still the only ones on the back porch. *Good,* Daniel thought, *no chance Marc heard Pop-pop, because then he would almost certainly use that slight statement as an opening for his undoubtedly pent-up recitation of the latest "Here's how President Hollinger will restore America's values and greatness" bullshit.*

"Yeah," Daniel nodded, then deliberately shifted his great-grandfather's attention in a different direction.

"Pop-pop, you remember that I'm a history professor, right?"

The sight of a man who was a tad bit short of his one-hundred-seventh birthday rolling his eyes in exasperation was a fascinating one.

"I'm old, Danny; not senile. Of course I remember that you're a history professor."

Sufficiently chastened at his impertinent opening, Daniel hurried an apology.

"Sorry, Pop-pop," he replied, his tight smile tinged with embarrassment. "I was just making sure."

Nathan Jacobson simply raised his eyebrows in a "go on; proceed" facial gesture.

"Well," Daniel continued, "you remember that article I wrote last fall? About you now being the last American soldier alive who fought in Europe during World War II?"

My God! Daniel thought to himself as he processed the sound of his own words. *That sounds so harsh when I just say it like that!*

"There's a history professor at West Point," Daniel continued after his great-grandfather nodded that indeed he remembered being the subject of the mentioned article, "who would like to interview you for an article that she's writing."

Daniel braced himself for what he was about to say next.

"It's about you being the final American soldier alive who liberated Dachau."

* * *

Corporal Nathan Jacobson's presence was injected into the Second World War in mid-August 1944, when he hit the beach in Southern France as part of *Operation Dragoon*. The much more renowned massive assault on Northern France known as *Operation Overlord*—the famed D-Day invasion—had taken place two months earlier in Normandy, and the Allied strategy called for this second set of landings to tighten the vise around the retreating Nazi forces.

Nathan Jacobson had been only eighteen years old back then, green to the horrors of combat. By the time his 45th Infantry Division arrived at the gates of the Dachau concentration camp the following April, however, he felt much the same as the unit's old-timers who had landed in Anzio and fought their way across Italy earlier in that terrible year of '44, before being redeployed to stage for *Dragoon*. That was the point at which Nathan arrived as one of numerous replacements to train for the upcoming invasion alongside what was left of the division veterans.

For years, Nathan refused to talk about what he had witnessed as the 45th liberated Dachau, and then during the aftermath. Crossing the Atlantic on the *Liberty* ship back from Europe several months later after the A-bombs ended the war, Nathan did his best to push aside the visions—some tragically genuine, others horrifically conjured—that had haunted every single night's attempt at sleep. Still, the sights and sounds and smells remained with him to this very day, periodically forcing their way into his conscious memory to instantaneously snatch Nathan Jacobson against his will back to the horrors of the war.

Most of the 45th made it back to New York by September before being sent to Camp Bowie in Texas. On the fourth anniversary of Pearl Harbor, the Army's 45th Infantry Division was deactivated. By that time Nathan had just enough points to receive his discharge, instead of being transferred to another unit. Hanukah had occurred at the beginning of December that year, and even the eighth and final day was now weeks in the past; but when Nathan's train pulled into Pittsburgh's Penn Station late that Christmas Eve afternoon, his family turned that holiday into a second Hanukah in joyous celebration of their son's safe return from the war.

* * *

That night, after returning home to his condo in the Oakland section of Pittsburgh, Daniel Jacobson contemplated what had transpired earlier that evening. He was still deeply troubled by his brother-in-law's brief outburst in response to Noah's and Rachel's mischief...some very creative mischief, Daniel still couldn't help thinking.

Daniel found his thoughts attempting to latch on to those of his sister Claire: to try and get inside her head. Daniel knew his sister well enough to be absolutely certain that she was exasperated by Marc Weber's fascination with and slavish devotion to Ephraim Hollinger. Daniel's brother-in-law had always voted his wallet; Marc made that clear to everyone. For a relatively young man, Marc had done extremely well in the rough-and-tumble commercial construction business, grabbing an outsized share of gleaming suburban office parks and urban gentrification projects when America's ever-cyclical real estate fortunes metered back over to the "booming" side once again in the mid-2020s.

While a casual observer might instantly presume jealously and resentment were in play here, Daniel truly had nothing against his brother-in-law when it came to the man's fortunes and successes. Daniel had absolutely no interest in the sometimes-murky world of construction, or most anything else from the world of commerce and business. He was perfectly content having followed his passion for history into a career in academia. Daniel lived modestly, with little need for the entrapments of wealth that seemed every bit as much a part of Marc Weber as the man's skin. *So be it,* Daniel had calmly told himself numerous times whenever the tiniest scrap of envy attempted to worm its way into his psyche. *I may not be wealthy—at least not right now, and probably I never will be—but I'm content*; that was Associate Professor Daniel Jacobson's mantra.

Nor did he begrudge his sister's entrée into a gilded lifestyle that was so far removed from how they both had grown up. Robert Jacobson—Daniel's and Claire's father—was a reasonably successful computer technology consultant, but one who had spent his entire career doing routine, moderate-compensation projects for companies in the Pittsburgh area, rather than living on the road and fanatically clawing his way up the ranks of one of the big-time global consultancies. Their father had made a comfortable living, and still did; but even in his best years he fell far short of the big bucks that he might have made had he meandered onto a different, far more aggressive—and consuming—career path.

When Claire first married Marc Weber eleven years earlier, she had been a struggling schoolteacher, living in a small studio apartment only several blocks from where Daniel now lived. Marc had been a realtor then, riding the waves of Pittsburgh's residential real estate market that gyrated between bursts of frenzied buying and selling versus, on the other side, occasional sluggish periods hallmarked by stagnant home values and relatively few transactions. Unlike his wife, though, Marc Weber was hardly content with the prospect of lifelong membership in the middle class. Initially he made some profitable forays into house flipping, doing much of the refurbishment himself. Soon he began moonlighting with a commercial construction firm and quickly learned the ropes. By 2026 he had set up shop on his own, and within two years was clearing about five million a year.

Claire had easily glided into this new world of wealth and privilege, but she had also confided in her brother several times over the years that she wasn't particularly thrilled with the accompanying changes in her husband's philosophical DNA. Like Claire and Daniel, Marc had grown up in a middle-class Jewish home that leaned slightly left of center when it came to politics and society. Now, though, Marc Weber was immutably encased in an indestructible shell of "Business Über Alles" doctrine, zealously railing against "THE LIBERALS AND SOCIALISTS WHO WON'T BE HAPPY UNTIL THEY'VE DESTROYED OUR COUNTRY!" in a manner one would never expect to hear from someone who had grown up as Marc Weber had.

For a while, Daniel presumed that his sister had likewise drifted over to the Dark Side, especially after Ephraim Hollinger leeched onto the Restore American Values and Greatness Party that had been birthed by the final, irreparable fracture of the Republican Party just before the 2030 midterm elections. Marc Weber had quickly and gleefully embraced the RAVGs, carefully maneuvering himself to land on the radar of the new party's moneyed power brokers.

Claire, however, had tipsily confided in her brother one night in the spring of '31, the two of them sitting alone in the very spot on their parents' back porch where Daniel had spoken earlier this evening with Pop-pop, that she was increasingly appalled at her husband's nascent zest for the RAVG Party, apparently choosing to ignore its openly nationalist and racist doctrine. Claire wasn't sufficiently appalled, though, she confessed to her brother when he pressed the subject, to do something severely drastic in response...such as threaten to leave if he didn't back away from his flirtation with the dark forces. At least Marc wasn't echoing the Hollinger and RAVG Party invectives against "the globalist Jews who have ruined this once-great country," she rationalized, even though her husband regularly railed against "caravans of immigrants" and "socialist Dems who are all about seizing and redistributing wealth" and the rest of the standard lineup of designated threats.

Still, Claire was, as the eye-rolling saying went, "disappointed, troubled and concerned" about this jolting rerouting onto an ominous side road detour, destination unknown for now, that her husband's politics had taken.

Daniel sighed as he retrieved an open bottle of cabernet from his refrigerator and poured himself a modest-sized nightcap. He energetically swirled the stemless wineglass, not so much for purposes of oxygenation but rather to warm the wine to a more suitable drinking temperature for a red. Claire was thirty-five; she was a grown woman. If she chose to roll her eyes and tut-tut behind her husband's back—but nothing more than that—then that was her choice. In fact, Daniel found himself smiling to himself as he took a test sip of the cab to see if it had sufficiently warmed, the prank by his niece and nephew gave him hope that Claire had successfully insulated her children at least a little bit from their father's troubling embrace of America's latest flirtation with autocracy and nationalism. Plus her swift "knock it off" silent admonishment to Marc also indicated that while she may put up with his ranting agitprop at home or in private, self-justifying whatever Marc did and thought in pursuit of construction work and other side deals because that's where the money was found, she had at least drawn the proverbial line when it came to his soapboxing and grandstanding in front of her family.

Satisfied that the chill had mostly dissipated from his wine, Daniel crossed over into the living room that adjoined his condo's kitchen. He plopped himself into a tan recliner that was almost identical to the one in which his great-grandfather had snoozed after the family's Purim dinner earlier this evening. The master control for the living room lighting was set to "late evening," with the room halfway illuminated to help transition Daniel toward the eventual darkness of his bedroom.

Daniel's thoughts instantly floated to Pop-pop; actually, to the email he had received yesterday from Major Michele Burgess, the West Point history professor Daniel had mentioned in passing to his great-grandfather. What Daniel had neglected to tell Pop-pop, though, was the specific reason that Major Burgess contacted Daniel about Nathan Jacobson.

Just as Nathan Jacobson was the final surviving American soldier who had liberated Dachau, this Major Burgess' great-grandfather, Isaac Gretz, was believed to be the final surviving prisoner of that sickening concentration camp. The Nazis had been meticulous record-keepers about their Holocaust crimes; but that paradoxical, fanatic insistence on documenting the names of their victims and the details of their crimes of humanity had been overtaken during those final chaotic months of the war.

Quite possibly, then, a few other Dachau survivors might still be alive out there somewhere, especially when one considered that "Dachau" had multiple meanings. The main camp of Dachau where Isaac

Gretz had been imprisoned eventually grew into the epicenter of a network consisting of more than thirty large satellite camps and sub-camps under its control, along with hundreds of smaller ones. Over the years, the harsh, dreaded name had been used interchangeably for the original concentration camp as well as the overall expansive network of horror.

But absent any contradictory evidence and following the deaths last month of two other known survivors, Isaac Gretz was now recognized as the final living connection to the main camp at least, and perhaps the entire Dachau network.

Major Burgess (*or would it be Professor Burgess, since she's a history professor, her Army rank notwithstanding? I'll have to ask her which she prefers,* Daniel thought) had the idea of uniting their respective great-grandfathers—or possibly reuniting them, if the two had perhaps crossed paths during that distant past spring of 1945—and documenting the solemn occasion of those two final survivors meeting eighty-eight years later. Personal memories of the Holocaust were now all but extinguished, and even the generation that followed that of the survivors and the liberators was rapidly diminishing. What Major Burgess was proposing was a final gift to history: a concluding firsthand bequest to the credo of "Never Forget."

Daniel slowly shook his head, his thoughts taking flight to snippets of a possible meeting sometime in the near future between the two old men. He tried unsuccessfully to put himself in Pop-pop's place. He could easily visualize the proposed encounter, but fell woefully short in his attempt to summon the emotions and sensations that would, no doubt, overcome Nathan Jacobson as he came face-to-face with the final Dachau survivor.

A stomach-churning chill suddenly enveloped Daniel, and he spent the next twenty minutes, off and on as he half-watched a rerun on TV, trying to wrap his thoughts around the reason for that sudden reaction. It was more than just the conjured vision of the two old men coming together; of that, Daniel was certain. He was almost finished with his nightcap glass of wine when clarity suddenly smacked him, causing an instant reprise of the same sense of dread.

Imagine that you were this Major Burgess' great-grandfather, Daniel contemplated, meeting one of the men who had liberated you from hell on earth…the *final* one of those rescuing liberators left alive. On April 29, 1945, you no doubt would have believed that your nightmare was suddenly, miraculously, finally over. Nathan Jacobson, now a buck sergeant after eight and a half months of combat, would likewise have thought the same. Total victory in Europe was just around the corner; the Nazis were finished, and the evil they had set loose on the world would soon be shoved back to the depths of hell.

Could either of these men have imagined that not only would they be alive almost ninety years later, but that they might actually come together as that very same evil bubbled far too close to the surface, threatening to be unleashed once more?

Chapter 2

"The *extremely* powerful forces who control this once-great nation's media industries are mustering every weapon they can to prevent President Hollinger and the right-minded thinkers in Congress from implementing the Truth and Accuracy in Media and Communications Act!" Toni Fowler all but screamed at the American Values and Greatness Network's broadcast camera.

"It's up to all of *us* here at AVGN," she crooked her left index finger toward her carefully wardrobed, spray-tanned cleavage, "and it's up to all of *you* loyal American patriots"—she quickly flicked that same finger directly at the camera lens—"to make *certain* that doesn't happen!"

The cameraman signaled to the AVGN star "news" anchor that they had just cut to a commercial. Toni Fowler sighed as she slumped back in her chair. Her eyes darted upward to the wall clock opposite her, behind and above the camera. Only fifteen minutes left: whew! When Toni's immense popularity resulted in AVGN doubling the duration of her previously half-hour program, her already outsized salary had likewise doubled. But wow! Summoning and maintaining the level of righteous indignation that her audience loved and expected for an entire hour was damn hard work!

If anyone could rise to the occasion, though, Toni Fowler—given name Janice Bailey—could always be counted on, five nights a week. When the American Values and Greatness Network was born out of that seismic upheaval in right-wing cable networks back in 2027, Toni was the star that Bob Platte, AVGN's power broker and programming puppet master, coveted above all others for the "hot blonde anchor" slot in his new all-star lineup. Bob Platte had been the one, in fact, who had originally hired Janice Bailey at one of those now-defunct networks and had renamed her Toni-with-an-i Fowler before wedging her into their programming. While "Janice Bailey" was far too nondescript of a name for a right-wing media star, the woman herself was straight out of central casting, as a certain former president would frequently praise someone whom he had personally selected for his entourage.

Platte's new star had been in her late twenties then: a statuesque five-nine, with a sculpted body that never failed to pivot heads. The perfectly cut blonde hair that fell below her shoulders and her stunning, precisely made-up face completed the picture. Her on-air facial gestures were perfectly fashioned at will. Toni Fowler could effortlessly gyrate between virtuous hatred for those who were steadfastly determined to ruin this nation and its culture, and seemingly genuine empathy for the plights of her loyal viewers, the Silent Majority, who suffered at the hands of those enemies. All she needed to complete the package was the right name, which Bob Platte supplied.

Toni Fowler's program followed the same inviolate formula as the rest of AVGN's hour-long broadcasts, each of which had outgrown its original half-hour format as the network soon blew past even the most wildly optimistic market share forecasts. She would begin each night with a cold open, consisting of exactly ten seconds of some precisely worded "We loyal American patriots are all under attack!" affront. Each day's portfolio of umbrages for the evening lineup was finalized during that morning's programming meeting that Toni and the rest of AVGN's evening anchors and producers attended. By that meeting's conclusion, their individual programs—each with its own distinctive angle and personality—had been orchestrated into a finely tuned, four-hour procession of aggrieved resentment for that evening's prime-time block.

After her short opening came fifteen seconds of slick graphics, swelling martial-slash-patriotic music, and a narrated voice-over intro, all choreographed to prepare the evening's battlefield, as the saying went. For the next ten minutes, Toni would expound on her topical overture through her regular concoction of pseudo-facts, questionable statistics, and unsubstantiated conclusions, swirled inside a wrapper of aggrieved wrath.

Exactly three minutes and fifteen seconds of commercials followed, and when Toni returned she would repeat the same formula, this time shifting to whatever the lead topic had been on Hayden Lafferty's (real name John Wilson) program during the preceding hour. Right-wing opinion programming had long ago discovered the sustaining power of reinforcing selected messaging at just the right intervals across multiple programs, and AVGN's sophisticated usage of data and analytics honed that practice into an art form.

A solid six minutes of commercials aired at the bottom of the hour, but AVGN's market research accurately reported that Toni Fowler's audience wasn't going anywhere. Well, perhaps to the restroom or the refrigerator, but AVGN knew that they would hurry back and remain glued to their television sets.

Toni's shtick coming back from the bottom-of-the-hour break was to open the second half of her program with some sort of urgent "This Just In!" loopback to whatever it was that she had shouted about during her opening. Sometimes she would unashamedly fabricate a quote from a sacrificial antagonist in the "lamestream media" or the "DemonRat" Party, while other times one of those designated Enemies of the State would actually oblige her with a genuine soundbite or two that she could twist to instill fresh rage in her viewers.

The last fifteen minutes of her program—and that's where she was right now—would ping-pong between three-minute blocks of sharing social media invectives submitted by her loyal viewers with patronizing commentary appended to each one, and equal-duration sets of yet more commercials. Toni Fowler had a sweet deal: Any company that wanted to land a coveted advertising slot on her program not only had to shell out top rates, but also had to kick over a percentage of their sales that came from those slots. Bob Platte made sure that not only did the network get its taste, his talent did as well. After all, a near-foolproof way to keep Toni Fowler and Hayden Lafferty and Keenan Lucas and Tristan Wyatt ensconced at the American Values and Greatness Network was to make sure each was perpetually neck-deep in cash, whether or not any of them actually bought into the toxic sewage they spewed night after night.

AVGN's overarching theme and resultant messaging had remained constant since its founding, with one big difference. Ever since Ephraim Hollinger's razor-thin election last November, AVGN had pivoted from incessantly pounding the previous administration and Congress in an attempt to drive from power both Democrats and those who had rebuilt the traditional conservatism of the Republican Party. Bob Platte, in fact, had been one of the behind-the-scenes architects of the new Restore American Values and Greatness Party, and embraced the furtive synergies between the two. "AVGN is interchangeable with RAVG," he regularly advised at staff meetings and power lunches and quiet deal-making encounters conducted in luxury airport lounges and the most exclusive private clubs.

Now, with Hollinger in the White House and more than a third each of the Senate and the House controlled by the RAVG Party, the network's messaging largely shifted to the theme that Toni Fowler had kicked off with tonight. That old bogeyman, the contemptible and disloyal Deep State, had been resurrected. A cabal consisting of traditional media, self-serving opposition politicians, disloyal "globalists," career civil servants interested only in lifetime employment while doing as little work as possible, and shadowy international moneyed interests were all conspiring to "take down" Ephraim Hollinger. ("Use the phrase 'take down' at least three times tonight!" Bob Platte would pointedly remind his anchors, producers, and scriptwriters every morning in their programming meeting.) AVGN's warning to its loyal audience that comprised the majority of Ephraim Hollinger's base was simple and unvarying: "They're coming after YOU!"

After Hollinger's election, rumors had spread that he would tap Toni Fowler and her charismatic appeal to Hollinger's followers for some role in his administration: most likely White House Press Secretary, or perhaps Communications Director. In fact, Hollinger's minions had reached out to Toni right around Thanksgiving with a "name your job" blanket offer.

The whole "center of power" aura that came with being part of President Hollinger's inner circle was a formidable lure. But why in the world would she surrender her eight-figure annual comp package for government wages, even at Executive Schedule-level pay? Bart Lawrence, Hollinger's bagman who was among those presenting the offer to her, hinted that if she came on board "we can come up with ways to make you whole." Still, Toni spent less than fifteen seconds considering the offer before declining.

Then again: Why would it have to be an either-or? If Bob Platte's ultimate designs came to fruition—and there was no reason to think that they wouldn't, later if not sooner—Toni Fowler might eventually have her cake and eat it, too.

Chapter 3

"He lives in a nursing home in Youngstown, Ohio," Michele Burgess told Daniel Jacobson, referring to Isaac Gretz, her great-grandfather. "That's only about an hour from Pittsburgh, right?"

"Correct," Daniel acknowledged.

"But I think even an hour's drive will be too hard on him," Michele interjected before Daniel could reply further. "He's been pretty frail for the past year or so."

"My Pop-p…I mean my great-grandfather should be able to make that drive," Daniel offered. "So we can meet you and him there."

"Are you sure?" The Army major's concern seemed genuine, and this time Daniel took a moment to contemplate the exercise and its possible pitfalls, rather than instantly volunteer Nathan Jacobson for his first moderate-distance round trip in…well, since before he turned one hundred, Daniel was certain.

"I think he'll be okay," Daniel finally responded, "but I'll definitely make sure that he's feeling well enough for the trip. He's pretty hearty for someone of his age. Other than a triple bypass about thirty years ago, I don't know that he's ever really been sick since he had a bad case of frostbite during the war."

Daniel watched his right hand quickly, reflexively form a fist and tap out three light knocks on his wooden office desk, as if his hand had a mind of its own. *No way am I going to let your mouth jinx Pop-pop!* the hand seemed to be silently admonishing Daniel.

"How does next Sunday look? The twentieth? Late morning or early afternoon?" Major Burgess suggested.

Daniel shook his head as he replied, even though he was alone in his small, windowless office at Western Pennsylvania College and this conversation was taking place via the college's antiquated audio-only phone system. His office was especially stuffy today, even with the door open. As soon as he was done with this call, he would phone over to the campus facilities management and see if they could do something about the staleness that permeated the building and interrupted his concentration.

Daniel forced his attention back to his phone call.

"That won't work; that's actually his birthday," he continued. "We're having a big family get-together for him."

"No problem," Michele quickly replied. "In fact, that following week is when West Point has spring break, so I wouldn't have any trouble—"

"Same for us," Daniel interrupted. "We have spring break that exact same week. How would either Tuesday or Wednesday be for you? I think that's…"

Daniel's eyes shifted to the *World War II History* calendar thumbtacked on the wall to the right side of his desk. His eyes instinctively landed on a photo of George Patton that adorned the top half of the March calendar, commemorating exactly ninety years' passage since the titanic clashes across North Africa during World War II. His gaze quickly shifted downward to the gridded calendar portion.

"…twenty-second or twenty-third."

"Let's go with Tuesday," Michele concurred. "I don't have to be back at West Point until Sunday night, so this way I can stay in Youngstown for a few days to visit."

Daniel flicked his laptop over to the calendar app and hovered the mouse above Tuesday, March 22nd.

"You were saying for that Tuesday, either late morning or early afternoon —"

This time it was Major Burgess' turn to interrupt.

"How about eleven?"

A few clicks on his laptop and Daniel had made the calendar entry.

"What exactly do you have in mind when they get together?" he asked, still uncertain exactly what this West Point history professor was seeking.

A sigh came over the phone connection.

"To be honest," she confessed, "I'm not exactly certain. I guess it's possible that neither one of them will want to even talk about what happened that day…you know, the actual liberation itself, or the aftermath. You know what happened, right? The revenge killings?"

Daniel's throat tightened as horrific conjured images of the revenge killings of S.S. guards by American soldiers and newly liberated prisoners alike translucently flashed across his field of vision.

"Uh-huh," he replied quietly, and then realized a nagging question was pricking at him.

"What does your great-grandfather think? About meeting mine?" For all Daniel knew, this Michele Burgess' great-grandfather wanted no part of dredging up whatever horrifying memories he had been able to suppress over the years. Even if the two old men did nothing but reminisce about…well, about *anything* other than the war in general and Dachau in particular, Daniel was certain that this encounter couldn't help but surface remembrances that were better left deeply buried.

"It's difficult to describe," was Major Burgess' hesitant reply. "Have you ever seen videos from any of those final gatherings of a particular group of World War II veterans? Like the Doolittle Raiders or the Tuskegee Airmen, or the Navajo Code Talkers?"

"Uh-huh."

"I think he would like the…I guess closure," Michele mused. "Not just for his own sake, but maybe the idea of my documenting it for others to see in the future. You know, 'Never forget'"?

"I can see that," Daniel nodded. "My Pop-p…I mean my great-grand—"

"It's okay, you can call him your Pop-pop," Michele Burgess interrupted. Even though they were on a voice-only line, Daniel was certain that this West Point history professor was smiling as she acknowledged the stubborn pervasiveness of Nathan Jacobson's familial nickname.

"Okay," Daniel grinned back. "Anyway, my Pop-pop feels the same way; at least I think so. He wouldn't really say too much when I asked him; you know…"

"Yeah, I know," Major Burgess indicated that she understood.

"I'll send you the nursing home's address," she changed the subject back to the forthcoming meeting. "And between now and then, I'll think of some specific ideas for how exactly the…I don't know, I guess we can call it a meeting…anyway, how it might proceed and how we can document it."

"Sounds good," Daniel replied. "Let me know if you need anything from me, or want to run anything by me before then."

"I will."

Daniel was just about to say goodbye and hang up when Michele Burgess asked:

"One other thing: Do you know if there are going to be any new faculty slots in your history department there for next fall? I'm done teaching at West Point after the end of this semester."

For a few seconds, Daniel didn't respond as his mind churned through the surprise question.

"Um…yeah, two new positions," he finally answered.

"I don't have a PhD though," Major Burgess quickly added. "At West Point, you can teach with a master's degree; you don't have to have a doctorate."

"We have some non-PhD faculty here also," Daniel responded. "In fact, one of the open slots is non-tenure track and can be for either a PhD or a master's-level lecturer."

"Would you be okay if I sent you my CV to look over and, if you're okay with it, submit it for that position?"

"Uh…sure," Daniel hesitated slightly. "But isn't the Army sending you somewhere else after your assignment at West Point is up?"

Invisible but detectable bitterness traversed the phone connection a fraction of a second ahead of Michele Burgess' voice. Daniel was suddenly certain of what she was about to say even before she uttered the defiant words.

"There's no way I'm staying in the Army and serving under *him*."

Chapter 4

June 6, 1984.

Not a morning passed that Ephraim Hollinger didn't pause and deliberately force himself to relive the nightmarish memories and wretched sensations of that day. This mental self-flagellation had shaped every action Hollinger had taken during the near half-century that had passed, and its legacy would live on long past the moment when he eventually parted company with life itself.

Most of the country's attention throughout that day was focused on Ronald Reagan's moving speech at Pointe du Hoc, in Normandy, commemorating the fortieth anniversary of the famed D-Day invasion. Reagan's speech had been precisely scheduled and timed by his advisors to be broadcast live on the morning news programs and drive-time AM radio stations back in the States, and many of those who watched or listened to the president that Wednesday morning reflected on his words throughout the day. The evening network news programs rebroadcast film and video of that morning's ceremony, highlighting Reagan's speech. The afternoon and evening newspapers that were still in print by then, even those that were typically critical of Reagan and his policies, mostly praised the president's demeanor and stirring words of remembrance from that very morning.

The commemoration in northern France and its reception here in the United States didn't come close to resonating with Josiah Hollinger or anyone else in his family, including eight-year-old Ephraim. That was the same morning that the two Jew bankers from Philadelphia arrived at Josiah's farm outside of Nuremberg, Pennsylvania, to serve him with a final notice of eviction. Three state troopers came along this time to ensure that Josiah complied with the order, unlike the previous two times Josiah had been served.

The farm crisis of the early 1980s ravaged much of the Midwest's family farms, and the troubles rippled across Ohio into Pennsylvania farm country as well. So many family farms had barely scraped by during the late '70s and early '80s when inflation and interest rates skyrocketed. The brief but brutal recession early in Reagan's first term finally tamed inflation and brought the sky-high interest rates back to earth; but the resultant severe oversupply of farm commodities, along with a significant drop in the country's agricultural exports, drove the nails into the coffins of far too many smallish farms. The big-city bankers who owned the paper called their unpaid debts and then callously arrived to steal away land, outbuildings, and farmhouses that had been owned for generations by hardworking families—that's how farmers and laborers like Josiah Hollinger saw the pitiless wave of foreclosure mercilessly rumbling toward them.

Josiah's original farm loans had been with the local agricultural bank, but one of the large Philadelphia banks had bought all of that much smaller institution's farm loans back in early 1982. These same two Jewish Yuppies who showed up on his doorstep that morning—Silver and Marcuson were their names, Ephraim would always remember—had been the ones who had contacted Josiah in the spring of '82 and convinced him to borrow an extra hundred thousand to put up a new pole barn, buy a new combine, and use the rest for a down payment on the adjoining eighty acres that had just been listed for sale. They had suckered him in, and good; and now, only two years later, they had his farm.

A sympathetic county sheriff had delivered the first two eviction notices, sitting in the Hollinger kitchen each time to commiserate with what was happening to this country, even as Reagan was setting it on a proper path once again. But the most that the sheriff could do was stall for time. "The Jews will come for their money," the sheriff morosely warned Josiah Hollinger—and his son, seated to Josiah's right at the kitchen table during that second visit—to expect the inevitable.

Josiah Hollinger moved his wife and three children—Ephraim, his older sister, and younger brother—an hour and a half southeast, taking a job in one of the Bethlehem area steel mills still clinging to life. Billy Joel had voiced the region's lament several years earlier in his hit song, but the singer's biting commentary of the then-present contrasted with bittersweet remembrances of yesteryear had only been a warm-up act. By 1984 the steel industry's troubles mirrored those of the American farmer from just several years earlier, ravaging entire communities where Big Steel had reigned for decades. Cities from Gary, Indiana, to Youngstown, Ohio, and then eastward through Pittsburgh and across Pennsylvania to the Jersey border, were all shellacked. Josiah's job lasted less than five months before he was pink-slipped.

Josiah Hollinger wound up taking a custodial job in nearby Allentown, as did his wife Emma. The Hollinger family limped along, even as they watched the Jews on Wall Street make a killing in the furious bull market of the mid-1980s. Josiah raged almost every night at the family's dinner table how "those people" sat in their offices high above Manhattan, making piles of money off the hard work of regular Americans such as the Hollingers. Even worse: Many of them pooled gigantic sums of money from their fellow Jews to use for hostile takeovers of long-standing American companies that they would then break up and sell off, pocketing millions or even billions along the way. "Arbitrage" was what the game was called, but Josiah Hollinger easily recognized a more sophisticated form of their habitual thievery.

The *coup de grâce* came just before the stock market crashed in '87 when the insider trading scandals broke. Apparently, a lot of the Jews weren't satisfied with their haul from the latest incarnations of their centuries-old tradition of scheming moneylending. Greedier than ever, the narrative went, they resorted to blatantly illegal manipulation and self-dealing in an attempt to corner even more of America's wealth for themselves.

Ephraim Hollinger grew up on a steady diet of this dinner-table bile, along with his father's regular plea to Ephraim and his siblings to somehow, someday, avenge the Hollinger family's plight:

"Never forget what they did to us."

* * *

Only days after turning twenty, Ephraim Hollinger dropped out of community college and scraped together just enough money to lease three midsized delivery trucks. The American economy was once again booming by 1996: not just in technology and finance, but also in manufacturing and physical goods that one could actually touch; goods that needed to be transported from one place to another. The swelling budget deficits of the 1980s and early 1990s were rapidly shrinking away, and within two years the nation would actually be sitting on budget surpluses. The aftermath of 9/11 would soon send the country's financial health on another downward spiral; but for the time being, the sun shone brightly on America.

Ephraim Hollinger continued to rapidly expand Hollinger Industries into a formidable nationwide trucking company. He had deliberately chosen that open-ended company name to serve as an umbrella for…well, for wherever he would be able to take his company as the years went by.

Nationwide trucking eventually expanded into global shipping and a fleet of private cargo planes, and by the mid-2010s Ephraim Hollinger was worth close to a half billion dollars. His grim determination to avenge the indignities inflicted on his family so long ago burned as fiercely as ever. If only Josiah and Emma Hollinger had lived to see what their son had been able to accomplish; that was Ephraim's only real regret. Years of bitterness had taken their toll on Josiah as well as his wife, and both had passed away in the very early 2000s, when Hollinger Industries was but a fraction of the size it eventually achieved.

Politics and commerce go hand in hand for so many, and Ephraim Hollinger was no exception. His wealth bought him access and influence. He became a commanding yet stealthy power broker in the growing world of far-right politics. Hollinger funded political campaigns and shadowy white nationalist groups alike. For a time, Ephraim Hollinger's public face as a successful industrialist and his private world of carefully deploying his "investments" remained firewalled apart.

The resurgent mainstreaming of what once would have been accurately termed the "lunatic fringe" changed everything. Funded by dark money from Ephraim Hollinger and other like-minded wealthy individuals and families, and buoyed by a new wave of sweeping, unshackled racism and xenophobic nationalism that hallmarked "the base," a sizeable segment of the American public gleefully mainlined and then vomited back a steady diet of unrepentant hatred. "America" had always been a fragile experiment. The melting pot had come into existence already in a state of advanced corrosion, and was all but destined to eventually rust out.

Then what?

* * *

The history of the Republican Party was almost always hallmarked by opposing factions, the same as the Democratic Party. Those factions had, on occasion, spawned offshoot third-party presidential candidates. Long ago, in 1872, Horace Greeley, under the banner of the new Liberal Republican Party, split from the traditional Republican Party to oppose Ulysses Grant's bid for a second term. Then, forty years later, former President Teddy Roosevelt tried for a political comeback within the party; but after losing the Republican nomination, he created and then ran as the candidate of the briefly existing Progressive Party. Other Republican politicians, such as John Anderson in 1980, would periodically run for the presidency as independents or standard-bearers of some minor political party.

The rupture of the Republican Party in the summer of 2030 eclipsed every previous rift. During the latter years of the twenties, what many termed the "traditional Republican Party" valiantly and astonishingly clawed its way back from the verge of extinction to seize control of the party leadership and doctrine, thanks to a perfect storm that slammed and then capsized the forces that had hijacked the party a decade earlier.

Conservative causes had become the veneer astride a money machine cesspool for the ages. Legions of new grifters wanted in on the act, but they realized that only so many dollars were there for the taking from the true believers and the gullible alike. No problem— all they had to do was squeeze out the current slate of grifters by discrediting "legacy" doctrine and promoting some new spin, and triggering a little character assassination here and there against the current superstars of the right. The true right feuded with the alt-right, and they both feuded with the nationalist right and also the principled right, as well as new entrants who were slippery enough not to be labeled or pinned to any particular doctrine.

Eventually, the donor class—corporate and individual alike—realized that turning on one another was bad for business, politically speaking, when it came to their own coffers. Though neither for patriotic nor altruistic reasons, they yanked their megadollar funding away from extremist causes, sitting office-holders, and wacko candidates and diverted their donations back into the campaign funds of resurgent traditional Republicans. The traditional factions again popped up their heads and seized control of the party, with some of this newer generation of party leaders tracing their roots back to the more socially liberal Rockefeller wing of the 1960s, while others were more Reaganesque in their positions. Those two resurgent wings of the Republican Party resumed their ancient doctrinal sparring over long-standing matters, from fiscal policy and taxation to same-sex marriage and abortion, so disagreements between the factions were still the order of the day; but the GOP soon looked like Act Two of its mid-to-later twentieth-century incarnation.

But make no mistake: The ugliness that had overtaken the party in the late 2010s and into the 2020s was still very much present alongside the two traditional factions, even if the advocates and practitioners of draconian far-right politics had been amazingly shunted aside as the party's minority for the time being.

The detailed history of the schism was still being written, but the end result was that those who were leftovers from the dark forces of a decade earlier, along with relative newcomers who were doctrinally aligned after coming of age during the troubled years, abruptly bailed from the Republican Party en masse during the first week of August. This time, the estrangement would lead to a political divorce with the instant formation of the Restore American Values and Greatness Party.

The new party's name sent an unmistakable message. One was either all-in on transforming the American landscape fully in accordance with the Party's doctrine, or one was a hated enemy of the American people and must be vanquished. No middle ground existed in this winner takes-all showdown that had finally arrived.

With their opponents warring against each other, the Democrats easily took sizable majorities in the House and the Senate in the 2030 midterms…much to their regret, since who would have really wanted to be in power when the Second Great Depression began in late January of the following year?

Dating back to the aftermath of 9/11, and then continuing through the Great Recession and into the brutal COVID-19 economic shutdown, the nation's financial health (or lack thereof) was nothing more than a governmental version of an individual with every credit card maxed out and a crushing debt load that couldn't possibly ever be paid off. Every financial weapon was now expended; every sleight-of-hand trick by the Fed and the Treasury Department deployed and then exhausted; every overseas savior otherwise occupied, now unable or unwilling to buy up the nation's latest several trillion dollars of debt.

A late-January stock market sell-off, triggered by the latest flare-up between the U.S. and Iran that coincided with a series of corporate earnings reports falling shockingly and dramatically short of the Street's expectations, quickly snowballed out of control. The losses were compounded by mountains of highly leveraged derivative instruments that collapsed into one another. The market indices all lost close to fifty percent in less than three months, though that initial free-fall was quickly followed by a furious three-week "bear trap" rally that recovered nearly forty percent of the market losses.

FOMO—the fear of missing out—was as potent of a siren's song as ever, and the last vestiges of prudent portfolio management were now thrown to the wind. Sidelined cash flooded the market, quickly driving the indices upward another fifteen percent during only two trading days. Social media lit up and a new rag-tag collection of so-called "meme stocks" roared to life and rocketed upward by the minute, with many of them booking dizzying ten- or even twenty-fold gains during those same two days.

This time, however, the sucker's rally betrayed the hardened believers and opportunists alike when the markets soon rolled over and resumed their downward plunge far past the previous lows, before spending the remainder of 2031 ratcheting further south without pause. The long-standing mantras of "buy the dip" and "don't get caught out of the market when stock prices come roaring back" were finally proven false. Safe havens were non-existent: U.S. and international stocks, big caps and small caps alike, corporate and government paper, gold, commodities, crypto...*everything* crashed. Even the private equity firms were burned when they came swooping in with their war chests of cash and easy credit, only to see their vulture capital investments join the free fall.

This time, the Fed, Treasury, and the rest of the government were all out of silver bullets. Housing values collapsed en masse; unemployment skyrocketed; and the dominoes of the American financial system finally tumbled onto one another, culminating in the devaluing of the American dollar, the default on a portion of the nation's debt, and the true arrival of American Carnage.

The only ones who made out were those who ran ultra-bearish hedge funds and who had fortuitously locked in existing positions against the markets before the wreckage began, as well as a handful of high-profile traders who perfectly timed the early springtime sucker's rally and were in and out of the market at just the right times. Of course, the ill-advised appearances by some of those fortunate few hedge fund titans and self-promoting, big-bet traders on the financial news programs, grimly bragging about the billions they had made from the devastation, and with so many of those financial alchemists and stock market gamblers bearing surnames like Goldstein and Feldman and Rosenbaum, played right into the hands of those in search of easily marked Enemies of the People.

The Restore American Values and Greatness Party saw its opportunity, and into the void stepped Ephraim Hollinger. Hollinger's carefully burnished reputation as an extremely successful businessman had been earned through accomplishment, rather than conjured through sleight of hand and puffery. He had created a global conglomerate out of literally nothing;

he was the personification of the self-made man. He came from humble beginnings in east-central Pennsylvania. For the sake of symbolism, Hollinger had been born during the nation's bicentennial year, two months before that glorious celebration. It was now readily apparent that America's more subdued 250th birthday in 2026 had been very much a last hurrah, and the nation had clearly jumped the shark since then. Perhaps the United States of America was unsalvageable. Or maybe, just maybe, one man alone could mean the nation's salvation.

Ephraim Hollinger easily won the RAVG Party's nomination for its presidential candidate in 2032; "easily" because he ran unopposed. As such, Hollinger was able to keep key portions of his messaging largely under wraps until after his pro forma nomination in early August, at which time he unloaded his arsenal.

America *can* be saved, he promised with grim determination, as long as we can dispense with political correctness and call out this nation's *true* enemies, so we can finally deal with all of them, for all time.

Chapter 5

Nathan Jacobson quietly snored the drive away in the front passenger seat of his great-grandson Daniel's SUV. Outside, the morning sun had finally broken through the early spring chilly grayness, and Pop-pop was enveloped in the warmish rays refracting through the passenger window. In the back seat Daniel's parents, Robert and Nancy, continued to quietly fret about whether this drive to Youngstown had been a good idea for Robert's grandfather. Several times, Daniel came close to interjecting and admonishing his parents for always being such worrywarts. He knew that their concerns weren't unfounded, though, and held his tongue. The last thing Daniel wanted was to chide his parents and then have something terrible happen to his great-grandfather. Besides, they were already well underway, so what was the use in second-guessing at this point?

Daniel's mind drifted to a mental image of the *curriculum vitae* he had finally reviewed this morning, even though Michele Burgess had emailed him the document barely an hour after they had spoken by phone to organize today's momentous meeting. What caught Daniel's attention in particular when he finally got around to reading the document wasn't the Army major's college teaching experience, which was, admittedly, somewhat limited. She was completing only her third year of teaching, though she had taught a surprisingly varied list of courses during her time in West Point's history department. She had even co-authored several papers that had been published in top-tier academic journals. Still, despite her limited college-level teaching experience, she appeared qualified for a non-PhD, non-tenure-track teaching position at an elite, private liberal arts institution such as Western Pennsylvania College, though a closer examination of her credentials and skills would be needed to definitively make that determination.

Daniel was instead visualizing the itemized list of prior assignments that had preceded the CV's entry for "Assistant Professor, United States Military Academy."

Distinguished Graduate, United States Military Academy.

Master's Degree, Harvard Kennedy School of Government.

Infantry Officer.

United States Army Airborne School.

United States Army Ranger.

United States Army Special Forces.

Apparently, teaching history was but a sideline for Major Michele Burgess: a career-broadening assignment, in military-speak. She was a warrior, at least according to her CV. From her voice, her words, and her demeanor during his phone conversation with her, Daniel couldn't possibly have imagined that he had been conversing with someone who was apparently so adept at the art of warfare. He had painted a mental picture of a nice Jewish girl, a history teacher, who just happened to be practicing that profession as an Army officer for the time being.

Daniel was instantly captivated by the aura of this woman he had yet to meet. He had debated with himself for all of five minutes before checking out the West Point website and navigating to the history department's page. Sure enough, thumbnail photos for each of the department's faculty members were posted. Daniel easily located Major Burgess' photo, and he resized the picture on his phone to take a closer look.

This Michele Burgess was pretty. She definitely conveyed a professional demeanor in her ribboned and badged uniform and pinned brunette hair, offering only a slight, tight-lipped smile. In fact, Daniel realized as he took in the image, she even looked a little bit like a slightly older Sharon Waterman, his former girlfriend from his junior and senior years at Penn State. Major Burgess looked to be in her early thirties, just about the same age as Daniel.

Thinking about that photo of her as he now approached the Pennsylvania-Ohio border, still about twenty miles outside of Youngstown, Daniel's eyes reflexively rolled upward, taking in his own image in the SUV's rear mirror. He looked tired, but otherwise wasn't entirely displeased with his own face reflecting back at him. He still retained most of his frat-boy good looks that had served him so well in college and then during grad school. Other than those two years in a mostly exclusive relationship with Sharon, Daniel's college years at Penn State and then at Western Pennsylvania College were hallmarked by a near-unbroken string of hookups and short-term relationships. His face was still unlined—mostly—he noticed, and so far his brown hair was as thick as it had always been, even though he wore it tightly cropped these days.

Abrupt sobbing shook Daniel's eyes away from his self-appraisal. His head pivoted to the right. Nathan Jacobson must have jolted awake from a nightmare. The old man was gasping—not so violently that Daniel or his parents immediately feared for Nathan's health, but in the manner of someone breaking the water's surface at the last possible second, frantically gulping life-sustaining oxygen from the suddenly present air. Daniel instinctively reached to his right, gently clasping Pop-pop's left arm, which caused the old man's entire body to shutter. Suddenly, Daniel *was* worried about his great-grandfather. Even as his parents were quickly unbuckling their seat belts and leaning forward, Daniel was vectoring the SUV to the right, headed for the westbound Pennsylvania Turnpike's shoulder. Daniel's mind raced. Where was the next turnpike toll plaza? Were there any emergency turnaround spots along the median before then? Should he continue forward and try to find a hospital way out here near the Ohio border, or try to race back into the heart of Pittsburgh?

"I'm alright," Nathan Jacobson finally choked out, still staring straight ahead. Neither Daniel nor his parents were convinced as the SUV crawled to a stop. Daniel flicked on the vehicle's emergency flashers and threw the gearshift into "Park" before unbuckling his own seat belt.

"I'm alright," Nathan repeated, this time looking first at his left at his great-grandson and then at Daniel's parents, who were anxiously leaning forward from the back seat.

The old man's sobbing had subsided, but Daniel noticed that tears still flowed from Pop-pop's eyes.

"I'm alright," he said for a third time, though this time his words seemed intended more to convince himself than the others.

"Let's turn around, Grandpa," Daniel's father grimly suggested, the concern in Robert Jacobson's voice unmistakable. "Let's get you back home, and we can maybe do this another day."

The old man immediately shook his head.

"No," he commanded, his ancient voice now almost back to normal. The gasping had subsided, and whatever demons had maliciously possessed Nathan Jacobson during his dozing had clearly been vanquished…at least for now.

"Keep driving, Danny." This time, the commanding tones of Nathan's voice were curiously intermixed with notes of pleading: *Please don't turn back toward home and take this away from me; I don't know if I'll ever have another chance to meet this survivor.*

Daniel's head pivoted to the back seat, where his parents still leaned forward, fretting over their patriarch's condition. Daniel nodded imperceptibly, signaling that unless they wanted to overrule him, he intended to comply with Pop-pop's wishes.

* * *

By the time they eased into the nursing home's parking lot, Pop-pop seemed totally back to normal. Daniel was still worried, though, as were his parents. At any moment, Daniel might decide to pull the plug (*Wow! That's TERRIBLE wording for a meeting of two centenarians!* he chastised himself) on this gathering and shuffle Pop-pop back to the Pittsburgh suburbs. They'd just have to play it by ear.

Daniel's parents and Pop-pop remained in the car while he headed inside to locate this Michele Burgess. The nursing home's lobby seemed crowded for a late Tuesday morning, with a large number of residents and—apparently—visitors mingling in the oversized lobby seating area. Daniel took in the appearance of the place. The nursing home's operators seemed to have gone out of their way to make the place seem more like a hotel than a nursing home, or even an apartment complex. Daniel presumed that the nursing home had other gathering areas and recreation rooms within the facility, but the hotel-like lobby with its seating areas, staffed coffee bar, and teakwood front desk area definitely gave the place an air of calming sophistication.

More than a dozen elderly men and women lounged on sofas and in easy chairs. Daniel immediately spotted two chessboards in use, each with several bystanders watching the players' back-and-forth moves. Another ten, maybe a dozen, other people must have been visitors, given that none of them looked to be over forty. They were interwoven with the residents, perhaps stopping by to take some of the healthier and more mobile residents away from the facility for lunch.

Then Daniel recognized her.

Michele Burgess was sitting on a two-seat sofa alongside a frail-looking man...obviously Isaac Gretz. Daniel recognized her face from her West Point website photo, but the woman fifteen yards away from him looked nothing like an Army major. In that online photo, Michele Burgess' hair had been pinned and she, of course, had been in uniform, bestowing her with a "professionally attractive" appearance. This morning, her hair flowed down to slightly above her shoulders. She was dressed in a bluish-gray knit top, stylish jeans, and calf-length dark brown boots.

Michele Burgess must have likewise recognized Daniel from a Western Penn faculty photo online, or at least presumed who he was. She rose from the sofa, spoke a few indecipherable words to her great-grandfather, and then walked toward Daniel, smiling as they came within a couple of feet of each other.

"Hi Daniel," she continued her warm smile and extended her right hand, "I'm Michele."

"Hi," Daniel took her hand, returning a quick but congenial half-smile. "It's nice to meet you."

"How was your drive? No trouble finding the place?"

Daniel blew out a light breath.

"No problem finding our way here," he said, "but we did have a bit of a scare on the way."

He briefly related the incident with Pop-pop; though as he narrated what had happened, the more Daniel began to think that Nathan Jacobson hadn't been ill at all, but rather overcome with painful emotion even before meeting Isaac Gretz. No doubt Pop-pop had been dreaming. Daniel was convinced that his great-grandfather's thoughts had traversed time and space, and he was reliving the horrors of what the 45th Infantry Division had found at Dachau.

"He seems fine now," Daniel added, as he looked past Michele Burgess to the elderly man now rising stiffly from the sofa with the assistance of a polished wooden cane.

Michele followed Daniel's eyes and saw her great-grandfather struggling to become upright.

"Here, Great-granddad," she turned and hurried back to aid the old man. Once fully standing, Isaac Gretz nodded toward his great-granddaughter.

"Thank you, Michele."

Daniel immediately took note of how the elderly man had pronounced his great-granddaughter's name: "My-KEL" with a hard "k" sound instead of a "sh" and the accent on the second syllable.

"This is Daniel Jacobson," the volume of Michele's voice rose considerably as she spoke to Isaac Gretz. "His great-grandfather is the one you'll be meeting."

"It's an honor to meet you, Mister Gretz," Daniel extended his right hand. The old man needed to shift his cane from his own right hand to his left before he could shake hands with Daniel.

"Daniel, from the Bible," the elderly man replied in a moderately accented voice. His handshake was surprisingly firm for a man who otherwise seemed rather frail, at least at first appearances.

"I'll go and get my great-grandfather and my parents," Daniel said. But as he was pivoting, Michele Burgess interjected:

"It's a nice warm morning, so why don't we all just sit outside? This way when I do the videoing, we'll have a nice background."

"Sure," Daniel quickly agreed. They all walked slowly toward the sliding glass double-front door of the nursing home, with Michele tightly gripping her great-grandfather's left arm after he shifted his cane back to his right hand. Daniel shuffled along with them; though as soon as they exited the building, he vectored toward his SUV, motioning to his parents and Pop-pop that they should now come on over toward him.

Robert Jacobson helped his grandfather slide out of the front passenger seat, and gripped Nathan's right arm as they walked much as Michele had done for Isaac Gretz. They walked slowly, deliberately toward the front of the nursing home.

Before either Daniel or Michele could introduce their great-grandfathers to each other, Isaac Gretz reached out with trembling arms and drew Nathan Jacobson into a powerful, wordless embrace that lasted for a good half-minute. The entire time, both men wept as their bodies quivered. Daniel could swear that eighty-eight years melted away, and that a sickly, emaciated twenty-one-year-old Isaac Gretz was tearfully greeting his war-weary G.I. liberator.

Daniel looked over at Michele Burgess, and saw that she had seized the moment and was already recording this tearful greeting.

She's definitely on the ball, Daniel realized. *Quick thinking to start videoing...*

Still, he noticed that her eyes were glistening, just as his were.

Funny...I would have guessed that someone with her background—career Army, Special Forces, Rangers—would be...I don't know...harder, maybe?

Eventually, the group made their way toward a whitish-gray concrete table with attached benches. A pale green umbrella was anchored into the center of the table to provide a touch of shade, depending on the sun's angle. Michele positioned herself so the old men were backlit for what she hoped would be the best exposure. She unfolded a small tripod, popped her cell phone into the clip, and resumed recording.

* * *

"Were you still there for the Shabbat?" Isaac Gretz asked.

Nathan Jacobson immediately knew what Isaac meant, even though none of the others yet did.

"I was," he nodded.

Seeing that nobody else other than Nathan Jacobson knew what the old men were discussing, Isaac Gretz explained.

"An American Army Jewish chaplain—"

"Rabbi Eichhorn," Nathan Jacobson interrupted. "A captain."

"...held Shabbat services," Isaac resumed his explanation. "Right in the center of Dachau! Can you believe it? He chanted the *Shehecheyanu* in front of the

Ark, and then held the *Torah!* In the center of Dachau!"

Daniel glanced over at Michele Burgess, his eyes narrowed. He had never heard this tale before, of a Jewish chaplain conducting Shabbat services at Dachau; and the returned look from the Army major told him that neither had she. He glanced over at his great-grandfather. Pop-pop had never mentioned having been there to witness that occasion. Then again, Pop-pop never spoke a word about Dachau.

Daniel noticed that Pop-pop's eyes were again watery as he added to the narrative.

"It was May the fifth. We liberated the camp on April the twenty-ninth, a Sunday. This was the first Shabbat, six days later. The rabbi drove into the camp on April the thirtieth, the day after the liberation. He was there with us all week helping us take care of everyone in the camp, and then on Shabbat, he led services for all of the prisoners and the Jewish American soldiers."

From the corner of his eye, Daniel noticed Michele checking to make sure her phone's video was still recording. She must have sensed that Daniel was looking in her direction, because she then shifted her gaze to catch his eye, and offer him a warm, inviting smile.

* * *

The conversation—the meeting—lasted almost two hours. Isaac Gretz shared tales of spending the next year shuttling between several Displaced Persons Camps, more commonly referred to as DP Camps.

"I was originally planning to travel to *Eretz Yisrael*," Isaac explained, referring to the thousands of Holocaust victims who made their way to British-occupied Palestine—later Israel—after the war. "I wasn't going back to Poland; everyone was gone. But the Americans who ran the DP Camps, and who liberated us"—Isaac glanced over at Nathan

Jacobson—"were such wonderful people, that I decided to come to America."

Daniel, his parents, and Michele Burgess managed to work a few questions into the occasion, but mostly the two ancient men did the talking. Occasionally one or both of them would explain a particular historical point to the others, as they had done when describing that first miraculous, surreal Shabbat service held in the midst of that horrific concentration camp. The rest of the time, though, they conversed as if they were long-lost friends who were seeing each other for the first time in almost ninety years.

The most somber moment of the afternoon came near the end, when Isaac Gretz said:

"I never would have thought that this day, of all days, would have been the one that Michele"—again, he pronounced her name as "My-KEL"—"had chosen. But maybe it was God's will."

None of the others, not even Nathan Jacobson, knew what Isaac was referring to.

"What do you mean, Great-granddad?" Michele gently asked. "Is something not right about today?"

The old man lowered his head for a brief instant, and then looked first at his great-granddaughter, and then slowly at each of the others.

"March the twenty-second, 1933."

Still no enlightenment.

"That's when Hitler and the Nazis opened Dachau. Exactly one hundred years ago."

Tears once again came to the old man's eyes.

"That's when it all began," he added, his voice again quivering. "One hundred years ago today."

Chapter 6

Ephraim Hollinger knew that for the next two years, he would largely engage in a prolonged rope-a-dope strategy. He would lob a new round of incendiaries; the mainstream media would reflexively respond by coming after him with a vengeance; and then Bob Platte's AVGN machine would bounce off the ropes with a flurry of vicious counterpunches.

Lather, rinse, and repeat.

Hollinger was perfectly at peace with this approach. Time was on his side. So what if many of his less cerebral supporters couldn't grasp his strategy? Every slam from cable news and the newspapers and opposition politicians would raise his base's collective ire, even as they grumbled that the pace of Hollinger's makeover of America was proceeding much too slowly. He didn't require any particular assistance from his disciples; he just needed them angrier than ever, eager to carry their aggrieved rage into the 2034 midterm elections.

That was the prize on which Hollinger was laser-focused: RAVG Party majorities, or better yet, supermajorities, in both the House and the Senate.

Then the real work could begin.

Until that glorious inflection point, The American Values and Greatness Network would continue to function as the de facto state-run media. Along the way, the groundswell would continue to build, the cries spreading throughout the land that AVGN's role in support of the administration needed to be codified. AVGN would continually spar with their mainstream media counterparts, and both Hollinger and Platte clearly recognized an immutable truth: The ongoing battles themselves, no matter what the topic, were what juiced right-wing media audiences every bit as much as the subjects of the clashes.

In parallel, then, the drumbeat would grow louder and louder that AVGN's all-important mission on behalf of the American people was being continually sabotaged by that tried-and-true bugaboo: the horrors and dangers of fake news spewed by the human scum in the mainstream media, in direct support of the Deep State attempting to take down a legitimately elected president. The newspapers and the cable networks, their respective websites, and the last of the old-time weekly and monthly news magazines: They were so easily branded as blatant Enemies of the State that must be stopped from spewing their ruinous propaganda, once and for all.

And that's where the Truth and Accuracy in Media and Communications Act—TAMCA—came in.

If Hollinger, the RAVG Party, and AVGN were successful, passage of the ultimate censorship law soon after the new RAVG-dominated Congress took power in January 2035, would be all but certain. Lawsuits grounded in constitutional objections would certainly be filed, but those could be dragged out through multiple levels of appeal while the new Congress swiftly packed the various courts with like-minded confederates. AVGN would, when the time was right, not only stand alone, but would function as the sanctioned—rather than de facto—media apparatus of the United States of America. Dissenting reporting and opinion would be banished. Hollinger and Platte, and the apparatus that they already controlled, would usher in a new era of American state-run media that fully supported and helped bring about the Utopian landscape that Hollinger had clearly painted for the nation's future.

Promises made; promises delivered.

Chapter 7

Daniel sensed her presence approaching his office doorway a few seconds before she appeared. He looked up from the stack of paper midterms that he was almost done grading.

"How did it go?" he asked.

"I think pretty good," Michele Burgess answered with a tight smile, halting in the doorway, waiting for Daniel to invite her in.

"Come on in," he returned the smile, motioning for her to shut the office door.

Michele nodded toward the ceiling, pausing halfway between the now-closed door and Daniel's desk, as she asked in a near-hushed voice:

"Can anyone hear us?"

Ever conscious about matters of security, the Army major wondered about sound bleed-through from one office to another.

Daniel shrugged as he responded in similarly lowered tones.

"Only if we're talking loudly."

He suppressed the volume of his voice even more as he continued, barely above a whisper now.

"I wouldn't say anything about any specific interview," he warned, shaking his head lightly to accentuate his words.

Michele nodded her understanding as Daniel quickly looked over at his students' midterms, and then back at her. He half-hesitated before posing the question.

"Do you want to go grab a quick drink before dinner and then you can give me the rundown?"

She smiled again.

"Sounds good. I can hang out somewhere near campus while you finish grading…"

Daniel shook his head as he interrupted.

"I mean now; both of us going to get a drink. I don't need to finish grading these today. They just took the midterm yesterday, and we don't have class again until next Tuesday. I'll finish grading them over the weekend, or even on Monday."

Michele Burgess had spent this entire Friday making the rounds of the history department faculty at Western Pennsylvania College. She flew into Pittsburgh from Stewart International late Thursday night, departing the West Point campus after her final class ended at five. She and Daniel hadn't crossed paths at all last night, and only briefly ran into each other today. Daniel had seen her long enough, though, to drink in her appearance. She was dressed in standard interview garb: white blouse and patterned gray blazer, steel-gray pencil skirt, and black pumps. Her hair was down, the same as when they first met in person in Youngstown, and Daniel concurred with his own earlier assessment that she looked even more attractive that way than wearing the pinned-up military regulation hairdo, as in her West Point website faculty picture.

She had been scheduled for an early breakfast interview with Diana Calloway, the department chair, and then lunch with John Lancaster, who headed up the history department's personnel search committee. The rest of the morning and afternoon saw Michele hustled on the hour from one office to the next for a seemingly endless string of interviews with every single member of the history department faculty...except Daniel, who had been designated as her final interviewer of the gauntlet, over dinner. Michele wasn't flying back to West Point until Saturday morning, so as with any out-of-town candidate staying overnight, someone from the department would play host for the evening.

Daniel had gone in person to Diana Calloway's office to request the dinnertime interview, under the premise that he had already met Major Burgess and thus could drill further into her suitability for the role beyond her scholarly qualifications. Dr. Calloway cocked an eyebrow and fought back a smirk as Daniel made his case, and then simply nodded her consent.

He flicked his computer closed after logging off and shutting down the power, and eased the laptop into his Coach briefcase. After sliding the stack of midterms into a desk drawer and locking the desk, he nodded toward the door to indicate that he was all set to leave.

Western Pennsylvania College was nestled in the midst of Pittsburgh's academic epicenter: Carnegie-Mellon and Pitt in Oakland, Duquesne close to downtown, and also Chatham. Western Penn, as the college was mostly known among locals, was a sixty-year-old private liberal arts college that had a great deal in common with schools such as Wellesley or Bowdoin or Swarthmore…just much newer, less well known, and, admittedly, less prestigious. In recent years, though, the capabilities of Western Penn had risen steadily upward, along with the quality of its faculty, the size of its student population, and its reputation. Of particular note was the school's history department, which was why Daniel joined their faculty immediately after earning his PhD there.

What was nice about Western Penn's location was that it was still within easy reach of all of the college-oriented establishments scattered around the city's Oakland section, even though the campus was slightly downriver from Pitt and Carnegie Mellon. Daniel had his rotation of favorites, including the upscale but modestly priced bistro where he had made dinner reservations tonight at six-thirty. Doing a quick bit of time calculation in his head, he figured that after the short walk there from his office, they would have a good forty-five minutes to relax over a drink or two before it would be time for their dinner reservation. By five forty-five the place would be pretty crowded, but worst case they could find a place in the restaurant's bar area to stand and enjoy a glass of wine or a scotch or whatever Michele Burgess might prefer.

Exiting the history department building, Daniel drank in the glorious late-afternoon weather of an exquisite early April Friday. Quite possibly, Michele Burgess was interviewing for teaching positions at other institutions as well; he hadn't asked yet, but would do his best to find out during their dinner conversation. But if she was, this splendid afternoon certainly was a selling point in favor of coming to Western Penn rather than some other campus next fall.

"The only interview I was uncertain about was Jim Loomis," she mused as they passed underneath the impressive stone archway that served as the main entrance to the Western Penn campus.

"You mean John Loomis," Daniel corrected.

"That's right," Michele realized. Her mistake was an easily understood one: Of the eight faculty members she had met with today, four of them were named either "Jim" or "John."

"Anyway," she continued with her blunt assessment, "I couldn't tell if he wasn't impressed with me teaching at West Point, or if it was more a matter of me not having a PhD and being a career academic. Whatever it was, he just seemed underwhelmed."

Daniel quickly looked to his left and then his right, and then pivoted his head to make sure that nobody from the college, and especially the history department, happened to be within earshot.

"Don't take it personally; he's kind of a dick," Daniel offered his take on the meeting, based on having studied under Loomis for his own PhD program and working in the same department since then.

"Honestly," he added, "nobody in the department really likes him, but he's tenured so he's not going anywhere."

"Hmmm," Michele murmured, contemplating Daniel's explanation.

"I wouldn't worry about it," he countered, detecting her concern. "He only gets one vote, and Calloway goes by a straight majority vote for new hires, so it's not like Loomis can unilaterally blackball anyone."

She shrugged.

"Okay, I guess I'll see soon enough," she replied, and then added:

"The only part that was difficult with almost everyone I met with was when they asked me why I was looking to leave the Army after fifteen years. There was no way I was going to tell them what I told you…"

Daniel immediately flashed back to Michele's—Major Burgess'—defiant and bitter declaration the first time they spoke on the phone: "There's no way I'm staying in the Army and serving under *him*."

"So what did you tell them?"

She looked over at Daniel and smiled sheepishly as they came to a red light.

"I said something like I enjoyed teaching history so much that it changed my mind about what I wanted to do for the rest of my career; that I wanted to teach college rather than go back to being a regular soldier, so that's why I was putting in for early retirement. Something like that."

She sighed as she looked upward.

"I hope God doesn't decide to punish me for lying, you know?"

Daniel half-snorted.

"Lying about Hollinger? No chance. If anything, God will make sure that you *definitely* get the position so you don't have to stay in the Army while he's president."

They shared a quick laugh that was absent even a touch of humor.

They soon arrived at the bistro and headed inside. Daniel eyed two unoccupied stools at the far end of the bar and nodded toward them. Fortunately, nobody else seemed to have done the same at that moment, so he was able to claim the spots without having to risk looking foolish by rushing in that direction, leaving Michele Burgess behind.

Daniel instinctively pulled one of the stools away from the bar and nodded toward it. Their eyes locked, and Michele offered an extremely warm smile to accompany her "Why, thank you, sir!" appreciation of his chivalry.

In the months and years that followed, Daniel would always be able to pinpoint *that* very moment, *that* shared glance, *that* smile, as the single point in time when he became certain that he wanted Michele Burgess in his life.

* * *

The first and second acts of their conversation at the bar that continued into dinner were what one might expect in this particular circumstance. Michele related everything that she could remember from each of her interview sessions, with Daniel offering running commentary on her recollections and observations. After she had exhausted her memory of the interview marathon, Daniel shared everything that he could possibly think of that might be relevant to her joining the Western Penn history department faculty. Even as he spoke, he knew that he was painting an overly rosy picture. He glossed over the less agreeable aspects of the job, such as the department's and overall college's politics. He wasn't being totally disingenuous: For the most part he very much enjoyed teaching history at Western Penn, and any of the less savory aspects of a faculty position there would no doubt be found almost anywhere else anyway.

The conversation then shifted to living in Pittsburgh. Daniel gave her the rundown of the entire metro area, including the suburbs where he had grown up. But he was careful to emphasize the merits of living in the heart of the city, close enough not only to the Western Penn campus and the resurgent day-and-night energy that defined Oakland, but also to its surrounding trendy neighborhoods such as Shadyside and Squirrel Hill and, of course, the 'Burgh's gloriously picturesque downtown area.

As he himself did.

Daniel was well aware that he was doing his damnedest to sell her on moving to Pittsburgh and teaching at Western Pennsylvania College. And he was very much at peace with what he was doing.

What Daniel didn't know, though, was that Michele Burgess was fully cognizant that he had slipped into a prolonged sales pitch...and why.

And she was perfectly fine with all of it.

* * *

The Western Penn history department had put Michele up in a boutique hotel that was located halfway between the campus and the bistro where Daniel had taken her for dinner. In fact, on their walk to the restaurant, they had passed right by the hotel.

It was only natural, then, that Daniel would walk her back to her hotel after they were done with their dinner. They had dawdled at the table for a long while after their meals were done, lingering with the remnants of the bottle of pinot noir that Daniel had ordered. To Daniel's way of thinking, he could have easily sat there for another two hours. Their discussion had long ago exhausted all matters related to Michele's interview and the college, and the ins and outs of living in Pittsburgh. The third and final act of their conversation had shifted to talking about their respective great-grandfathers; those men's life-shaping experiences so long ago during the Second World War; their respective families; and wherever else their banter took them.

Eventually, Daniel somberly knew, it was time to pay the check and leave the restaurant. The early evening air had chilled just a bit from earlier, but the weather fates were still on Daniel's side, continuing to sell the merits of living and working in Pittsburgh.

They strolled along, mostly in silence, as Daniel contemplated how he could broker a deal between Michele Burgess and Diana Calloway. What could he do to tilt the history department's hire-or-not decision in Michele's favor? Or did he even need to do so? Possibly everyone, except maybe John Loomis, was in favor of extending an offer to her.

And then: What more could he do to convince Michele Burgess that *this* was where she wanted to be? Was she considering any other schools? He still hadn't yet asked her, but maybe…

"Do you want to have another drink?" Michele's words interrupted his mental gyrations.

"There's a lobby bar," she added, nodding to her right. That's when Daniel realized that they had already arrived at her hotel. "I went downstairs to have a drink there last night after I got settled in my room, to relax after my flight and the drive from the airport."

"Sure," he quickly replied, hoping that he didn't sound overly eager. But then again, if he did…well, so what?

Daniel had never been inside this particular Oakland hotel before, and his eyes scanned the lobby area. The mood-lit bar was off to the right. Other than the bartender and one couple seated against the far wall, the entire area was unoccupied.

Michele was already headed toward one of the seating areas along the inner wall, opposite the bar, and far enough away from where the other couple was seated. A glass-top table was surrounded by four low-slung, comfortable-looking fabric seats. Daniel again pulled one of the seats away from the table for Michele, who again returned a warm smile in response to his gesture. He then plopped his briefcase and computer onto the chair opposite where Michele had just sat, reminding himself again not to forget the bag when he left. Finally, he lowered himself into the seat on Michele's left.

Wondering if he needed to order drinks at the bar, he was just about to get up and ask when he noticed the bartender headed in their direction. She plopped a bowl of mixed nuts and pretzels onto the table, along with two smallish square paper napkins.

"Slow night?" Michele pleasantly inquired. "Last night it was much more crowded."

The bartender, a college-age young woman, nodded and smiled.

"We're usually pretty busy during the week with business travelers, but not so much on Friday and Saturday nights," she confirmed.

"It'll be nice and quiet for you, though," she continued, sending a knowing smiling first to Michele and then to Daniel. They each had the same amusing thought, at the same instant: The bartender obviously thought that they were "together."

"I'll have a glass of whatever your house cab is," Michele said, and then added as she looked over at Daniel:

"I'm going to stick with wine, but you don't have to do the same. I just don't like mixing different kinds of drinks too close to each other."

Daniel nodded his understanding and then ordered the same.

"I'm like you," he offered to Michele as the bartender departed. "I don't even like mixing beer and wine at a cookout."

Michele let out a light laugh.

"A lot of the guys at West Point, and, in fact, probably most of the guys I've served with in the Army, are the exact opposite," she explained. "I can keep up with them in the field and on the obstacle course and pretty much everywhere else, just not when it comes to heavy drinking."

Michele's musing offered the opening for another question Daniel had been pondering but hadn't yet asked. The waitress returned with their wine and as soon as she departed—and after they clinked their glasses together in a wordless toast—he asked:

"I've been wondering: How did you wind up going to West Point, and then becoming an Army Ranger and a Green Beret?"

Even as he was asking the question, Daniel was again drinking in her appearance. She certainly exuded a sort of confidence one might expect from someone with "Ranger School" and "Special Forces" listed on her résumé. Yet at the same time, Michele Burgess also easily fit the profile and image of a "nice Jewish girl." He could easily see her, dressed exactly as she was now, after work at some Jewish singles happy hour, with every guy there hungrily eyeing her.

Or perhaps at Saturday morning services at B'nai Israel. Daniel suddenly imagined his mother taking notice of Michele Burgess walking down the center aisle of the synagogue's main sanctuary, past where Daniel was seated with his parents, his mother immediately elbowing him and nodding toward her, wordlessly indicating "there's a nice-looking girl for you; go talk to her during the *Kiddush* after services."

The hesitant, almost distressed look that came to Michele's face brought Daniel's meandering mind back to the here and now. She fiddled with her wine, tilting the wineglass first to the left and then to the right, her actions clearly conveying that she was contemplating how to respond. Finally, she looked back at Daniel and began with:

"Okay, here goes."

She sighed and then continued.

"About twenty years…no, it was exactly twenty years ago, I was a junior in high school. I was at synagogue services with my parents, that's when we were still living right outside of Baltimore. Anyway, it was Purim…"

At the mention of "Purim" Daniel's skin prickled.

"…and I remember Purim was early that year, at the end of February, and it was a Saturday night. They were reading the *Megillah* and they got to the part where Haman sent word to kill all of the Jews…"

Daniel's body was now a continuous sheet of goosebumps as his thoughts took flight to his own family's Purim dinner, barely more than a month earlier.

He held his tongue, though.

Michele paused to again collect her thoughts.

"I can't really explain it," she finally continued, "but something came over me…"

She halted once again, still struggling for the right words.

"I swear it was almost like I had a revelation or something; maybe a vision of a prophecy?"

She shook her head in frustration. Never before had she tried to put into words how she had felt on that late February night back in 2013, and how what she felt in that instant had shaped the next twenty years of her life.

"I can't really describe it," she finally surrendered, but the look in Daniel's eyes instantly told her that he understood what she was having so much difficulty describing.

"Anyway, I decided then that I…*needed* to be a soldier, I guess that's the best way to put it. Part of it was right at that moment looking over at my great-grandfather who was on the other side of my parents and my sisters, and he was already leaning forward and looking over at me: almost like he was expecting me to…I don't know, receive some sort of message? Definitely something to do with him being a Holocaust survivor…"

Michele sighed deeply and took a healthy gulp of her wine.

"Anyway, I applied for West Point the summer before my senior year, and wound up receiving a congressional nomination, which I accepted. I figured that since I was majoring in history that I would probably wind up in some sort of administration job when I eventually graduated and went on active duty."

She looked down at the table and once again, Daniel noticed that she was rocking her wineglass back and forth, again carefully forming the right words.

"So then five years later, when I was a First Classman—a senior—that synagogue shooting happened, right here in Pittsburgh…"

Daniel nodded grimly and, once he gained his bearings, pointed in the direction of Squirrel Hill.

"Only about three miles away," he acknowledged.

"As soon as I heard about that," Michele continued, "the exact same feeling came over me as during that Purim service when I was in high school, even stronger; and the next week I switched over to become an infantry officer candidate. After I got commissioned and then finished my first two infantry assignments, while I was still at Harvard for grad school, I put in for Ranger School, and got accepted. Then a couple of years later while I was still with the Rangers Regiment, I put in for Special Forces."

Another sigh, another gulp of wine; another determined glance shared between Michele Burgess and Daniel Jacobson.

"I can't really explain it, but I've had the strongest feeling that there has been this invisible hand steering me onto this path and then sort of shoving me further and further along it. Like someday I'll need to put everything I was learning about special operations warfare to use."

* * *

They talked until three in the morning, remaining in the lobby bar long after the bartender closed up and left them behind, alone. The conversation ventured deep into the personal. They took turns sharing narratives about and soundbites from their respective past relationships. Neither had been previously married, or engaged, or even close to matrimony. If anything, Michele Burgess' relationship history was more unconventional than Daniel's, given her frequent Army moves and her steady stream of assignments to combat-ready units. As her tale unfolded, each of her assignments seemed to Daniel to be linked to a different relationship that began soon after she arrived but seemed immutably stamped at its onset with a built-in expiration date. As if to confirm the pattern that Daniel had detected, Michele offhandedly mentioned that only a week earlier she had ended a relationship with another Army major who taught in West Point's civil engineering program.

Even as they sat there, and in the days and weeks that followed, Daniel's immediate reaction when he thought of that night and the early morning hours that followed—and he did so perhaps a dozen times each day—was that he could never have imagined forming such a deep, intimate connection with someone so quickly. As with Michele, Daniel had been in plenty of relationships dating back to high school, including a couple of serious ones. But even the most powerful physical attraction to any of those girls or women paled in comparison to the bond he built in only a single night with Michele Burgess.

Several times, as the hour slipped past one in the morning and kept clocking forward, he thought that she was about to invite him up to her room. Strangely, though, he hoped that she wouldn't. He certainly would have gone with her, and had the occasion presented itself, he absolutely would have tumbled into her bed.

But there was something about talking and talking and talking, the conversation veering into all sorts of unanticipated turns, and then parting company after sharing warm smiles and a hug—but nothing more—that made this the absolute perfect night.

Daniel was convinced that this was merely their beginning.

In what remained of the overnight hours, as Daniel struggled to fall asleep because his thoughts were consumed with images and remembrances of the past eight hours, he did his best to keep the disturbing undercurrent passage at bay (*It's only a coincidence*, he kept telling himself) of their shared reaction to that exact same *Megillah*. (*Almost any Jew would feel the same way, hearing or reading those words.*)

Deep down, especially in light of the troubled rumblings all across the broken American landscape, Daniel Jacobson was convinced otherwise.

Chapter 8

Randall Weston's breath quickened and grew ragged, and his right hand slickened an instant later. A few seconds passed before Randall exhaled with relief, as he almost always did, slumping back onto his worn sofa, his left hand reaching for the box of tissues that he always kept within reach.

On Randall's television screen, Toni Fowler was screeching about the latest caravan consisting of tens of thousands of illegals—and, of course, hundreds of card-carrying Middle Eastern terrorists stealthily intermingled among the dirty, disease-ridden masses—slithering their way north through Mexico to invade Arizona or Texas or California…somewhere along the southern border that the previous president had treasonously refused to defend. Now, the caravans were testing the newly inaugurated Ephraim Hollinger, and they would quickly learn to their great dismay that Hollinger was ten times the man than the politically impotent previous holder of the office had been!

Randall Weston *never* missed watching Toni Fowler on AVGN. He also *never* missed masturbating to her image and her voice on his television screen at least once during her program. Very often, as was the case tonight, Randall's first orgasm occurred within the first five minutes of her show, which dramatically increased the chances of that one being followed later by a second climax later in the hour, and sometimes even a third.

The derisive term "incel" might well have been invented for Randall Weston. For a long time now, for most of his life, his only outlet for sexual release was when he was alone. He had become quite an aficionado of online porn over the years; but if pressed to admit the truth, Randall would gladly confess that he preferred masturbating to the hot, angry women of

AVGN, and in years past those of earlier like-minded networks. Toni Fowler was a favorite, but by no means the only one in his rotation.

By all outer appearances, Randall Weston seemed...well, normal. His physical appearance was pleasantly average: not particularly stylish in dress or grooming, definitely on the geeky side, but nothing that screamed "social misfit" or "keep away!" He held a regular job, working as a software quality assurance tester for an insurance company. Randall was personable enough, regularly heading out with a rotating group of his co-workers for Friday happy hours somewhere along Denver's 16th Street Mall, a short walk from where he worked, celebrating the end of another humdrum workweek.

He always went home from those happy hours empty-handed and unfulfilled, though. Randall never struck up a conversation with a woman while waiting at the bar for a beer, with that initial exchange leading to the sharing of contact information and then, soon afterward, a first date. He never wound up deep in discussion with one of his female co-workers in their group after they each had two or three drinks in them, surprisingly discovering mutual interests or a shared background that neither one knew about the other, leading to new levels of friendliness the next week at work...and eventually to a relationship.

Years earlier he had tried online dating, but almost always seemed to send some ill-worded message that aborted an impending first meeting. On only a couple of occasions did Randall make it to a first date, but each of those had quickly ended without any sort of chemistry or even a hint of a second date. Eventually, he stopped trying.

Randall Weston had long ago surrendered to the life that he had convinced himself was his fate. He had found plenty of like-minded lost souls online who sympathized with his own tales of being summarily rejected by women dating back to his high school days. In fact, if not for a drunken hookup during his

The Voice of Prophets

sophomore year in college and occasional visits to illicit strip mall "massage" establishments over the years, Randall would still be a virgin at thirty-three.

One of the chat rooms where Randall spent a significant amount of time was dedicated exclusively to the exercise that he had just completed: whacking off while watching Toni Fowler on AVGN. Randall Weston was hardly alone in this endeavor, he was heartened to discover. He was a little disturbed, though—actually, more puzzled than actually disturbed—by one of the running discussion threads in the room that focused on rape fantasies for their "heroine." Toni Fowler might be hot and nasty and singing their song about the nation's ills and their cure, but she was still a woman, which meant that she was indelibly marked as one of the oppressive enemies who conspired to belittle and scorn the incel community as a whole. After all, they were *involuntary* celibates; and if not for the callousness and shallowness of women as a whole, each one would be engaged in at least some occasional non-solo sexual activity.

Occasionally Randall Weston would ponder the paradox at work here. On the one hand, so many others just like him got off—literally—at the image and even the very thought of Toni Fowler. Still, more than a few of those same men saw no contradiction with the vile fantasy of making that same Toni Fowler pay for the indignities that they were convinced an entire gender had dismissively inflicted on them.

Randall didn't give that particular paradox too much consideration, though. For one thing, the contradiction was an unsolvable enigma. He was far more focused on mustering the strength for the upcoming battles that Toni Fowler shrieked about, night after night.

These days, and for a long while now, Randall Weston was an armchair warrior. He fully bought into the impending clash of civilizations and the final, winner-take-all battle for the soul of America, brought to you by the American Values and Greatness Network. But hanging on every word uttered by Toni Fowler (when he wasn't masturbating to her) and the other AVGN talent was the limited extent of his activism...at least for now.

At one time, though, Randall Weston had been more than a couch potato combatant. Randall had marched at Charlottesville back in August of '17. Even now, more than fifteen years later, the sensations of that glorious Friday night, Randall's hand tightly clasping his torch of white American purity as he marched among so many of his brothers, instantly flooded back on command. Randall had been a young man then, a month shy of his eighteenth birthday. Yet he had been as much of a warrior as his older brethren. He had clashed with the counter-protesters, landing some damn fine blows against the enemy. He had defiantly chanted, over and over, "BLOOD AND SOIL!" and "JEWS WILL NOT REPLACE US!" the same as the older, more experienced members of the Movement.

Why had Charlottesville's promise not yet been realized? The ecstasy of Randall's recollections about that night and the glorious day of violence that followed was often quickly negated by the bitter disappointment of unfulfilled destiny. Charlottesville *should* have been the first of a rapid cadence of rallies spreading across the country, each one more populous, more violently repressive, and more decisive of a victory than its predecessors. Instead, when an encore performance of Charlottesville was scheduled for the nation's capital exactly one year later, only a handful of the truest believers were present alongside Randall, and the occasion was widely mocked.

Like so many others, Randall Weston doubled down on his online presence, spending several hours each weeknight and much of his weekend trolling social media posts and posting dozens of incendiary comments on online newspaper articles "to own the libs." He became even more glued to conservative television programming, eventually sliding over his allegiance to the new American Values and Greatness Network in 2027.

The attack on the United States Capitol at the beginning of 2021 had been another glorious occasion. Randall had been desperately ill and hospitalized in Denver with COVID-19 at the time, however, and had only been able to weakly watch the events unfold on his hospital room television. By the time Randall was released, the whole "Take back our country!" and "Stop the steal!" crescendo had retreated from violent physical confrontation along the front lines back to the bowels of the internet and the right-wing media fever swamps. Randall quickly jumped into this latest fevered front of the social media wars, but his engagement remained confined to cyberspace.

Now, though, the old saying from about fifteen years ago that had been recently resurrected had it exactly right: A storm was coming. And when the storm hit, Randall Weston vowed to get off of the sidelines and back onto the field.

* * *

Edmund and Eleanor Garfield were also dedicated fans of Toni Fowler, the same as Randall Weston. Unlike Randall and his incel comrades, however, the Garfields belonged to a very different demographic of the AVGN fan base: aging conservative baby boomers who were well along the back nine of their lives.

The Garfields had moved to Florida's largest retirement community—actually, more of a retirement city—a decade earlier, after Edmund's retirement from the cement manufacturing company job he had held for forty-one years. That job in central Indiana was the only one Edmund had ever worked, other than the six years he spent in the Army after his unremarkable K-12 academic career sputtered to a close.

By all accounts, Edmund was a competent worker over the years. Perhaps his strongest on-the-job attribute was an objective appraisal of his own self-limitations. He possessed the smarts to make it to shift supervisor, but he knew that holding any position beyond that would turn him into a living example of the Peter Principle. He was comfortable enough operating in that zone where worker-bee and first-line manager overlapped, but no further up the organization chart. He was careful not to rock any boats nor tread on any sacred lands at the plant, and he managed to hold that job until retirement beckoned.

Eleanor Garfield occasionally dabbled in the work world over the years while raising their three children. Her husband was a child of the sixties and seventies, and held no strongly chauvinistic beliefs that threatened his manhood if his wife were anywhere other than her kitchen or her backyard garden. Eleanor would occasionally take on a job as a part-time office receptionist for a year or so at a stretch, but she would quickly lose interest and quietly depart once a replacement was hired and trained.

It wasn't until after Zeke, their youngest child, finished up at the Vo-Tech in lieu of high school and took a fracking job up in North Dakota that Eleanor steeled herself to work steadily. She and Edmund had their eye on a prize, now that their children were all on their own: buying a house down in central Florida that would initially be a getaway second residence, but eventually would become their retirement home. They unloaded their timeshare (at a hefty loss, but at least it was no longer vacuuming money from their wallets every month, Edmund rationalized) and began stashing all of Eleanor's take-home pay away in their savings. None of their children had opted for college, thank heavens, so at least they didn't have big-time education expenses to worry about and to siphon their savings. In addition to avoiding those ridiculous college costs, Edmund in particular—but Eleanor as well—was equally as happy that their children's heads weren't getting filled with all of that super-liberal mush that had hallmarked American colleges and universities going back to the 1960s, if not longer.

The years slid by. Six years before Edmund's planned retirement date, they handed over a down payment on a smallish lot that would eventually contain a fifteen hundred-square foot home, tucked on a cul-de-sac in a just-opened section of that mammoth Florida retirement community. A year later, they began construction, and after another six months, the home was supposedly ready for them to occupy, even though for a while that would only be on a part-time basis while Edmund still worked. As it was, they had to spend the next five months fighting long-distance from Indiana with the builder to fix about two dozen problems, several of them significant. Eventually, though, the Garfields were the proud owners of a livable second home in the midst of more than two hundred thousand other like-minded souls. Now, all they had to do was wait impatiently for Edmund's retirement date, and then they could leave Indiana behind and move here permanently.

Perhaps the most significant attraction for Edmund and Eleanor Garfield to this particular retirement community was that it very much mirrored the demographics and politics of the Indiana town they had called home for so long...at least until recently. The cement plant eventually began hiring...well, "non-Americans" was the term that Edmund and so many of his co-workers contemptuously used. Soon, their small Indiana community looked far less homogeneous than it always had, and the Garfields couldn't wait to sell their home of forty years to one of these newcomers and make tracks for retirement in Florida.

Down here in this part of central Florida, though, these were almost all good Americans. The people who migrated here from Indiana and Illinois and upstate New York and so many other places had seen the light. Most of them were, like Edmund and Eleanor Garfield, baby boomers who had come of age in the hippie days of the late 1960s, or the disco era of the 1970s, or the preppy early 1980s. Almost all of them looked back on the slightly earlier, halcyon days of the 1950s with extreme nostalgia, even if their familiarity with that era came solely from reruns of *Father Knows Best* or *Leave It to Beaver,* or perhaps from watching *Happy Days* during their own younger years. Even the oldest residents who actually lived through the '50s were highly selective in their recall, filtering out almost everything that was at odds with their carefully curated remembrances of The Truly Good Old Days.

In their younger years, some of them had protested the Vietnam War, or marched against nukes, or rallied to save the earth from industrial pollution or overpopulation or climate change. A few of the retirees had stubbornly clung to their liberal ways and beliefs, even down here. Most, though, had come to realize that those idealistic causes of their youths had been little more than ill-informed, naïve beliefs that hadn't accounted for the hard realities and trade-offs of the real world.

Now, they grimly gathered over coffee and card games and mingled after their fitness center classes. They reinforced each other's beliefs about what was so very wrong with America these days, and batted around ideas about how those ills could be cured. They went home each night, and so many of them plopped down onto their sofas for another evening spent in the company of Toni Fowler and Hayden Lafferty and Keenan Lucas and Tristan Wyatt. They eagerly and desperately soaked in every report that President Ephraim Hollinger was hard at work, figuring out how their vastly diminished retirement funds and home values would be replenished, and how the tranquil lifestyle they had earned and come to love might be fully restored.

This was American Values and Greatness Network country.

This was RAVG Party country.

This was Ephraim Hollinger country.

* * *

Marc Weber was a master of compartmentalization, and he was increasingly angered that his wife Claire simply didn't understand how important that skill was to their success. Claire was as shortsighted and naïve as her brother and her parents and the rest of the Jacobson family. For that matter, Marc's own parents and siblings shared the Jacobsons' point of view. Sadly, he stood alone, at least when it came to family, in being able to see the forest for the trees.

Ephraim Hollinger was simply saying what he needed to say to build an unbreakable coalition of support. Right now, he only had a third of the House and an equal share of the Senate, between defections from the Republicans in 2030 and newly elected RAVGs last year. That meant that the Democrats and the few remaining traditional Republicans would easily be able to thwart his efforts to reverse the country's economic misfortunes. They were all banking on Hollinger not being able to deliver, so when 2036 came around, they could run that timeless classic from the triple-P—the Presidential Politics Playbook—and point to all the things that Hollinger was *not* able to accomplish. Never mind that both the House and the Senate would have sabotaged him at every turn, and that Congress would be truly to blame for America still being in an economic shithole. They would throw him a few crumbs to mask and deflect from their obstructionism. That was their game plan, and every Hollinger supporter with an ounce of smarts knew what was going on.

Hollinger was playing the long game, though. He wasn't looking ahead to 2036; his eye was squarely on 2034 and the midterm elections that November. He needed to build a strong enough coalition to take a majority—ideally a supermajority—in both the House and the Senate. *Then*, beginning in January of 2035, he could finally enact the bulk of the programs that were necessary to get the country back on a stable financial footing, and proceed to build from there.

Marc Weber wasn't particularly thrilled with Hollinger's regular condemnation of "the rich Jews" because, technically, that included him. But Hollinger's rhetoric was only for show, to get the juices flowing and energize his base. Marc knew this for a fact, because he was one of the biggest donation bundlers for Hollinger in Pennsylvania—one of the two largest in Pittsburgh—and had met with the man several times during campaign stops in Western Pennsylvania.

In the intimate meetings that Marc had bought his way into—unfortunately not one-on-one, but in smallish groups of twenty or so—Hollinger never gave a single indication that he actually believed the crap he was spouting. He was a businessman, and he was all about the business of executing on the new political party's namesake slogan of restoring American values and greatness. Hollinger was also a marketer and a salesman, and he knew exactly how to win over his customers and then close the deal to strengthen his hold on their loyalties.

Marc had also contributed significantly to Hollinger's inaugural committee, doing his best to stay on the new president's radar. In fact, Hollinger had already announced and formally registered his 2036 re-election campaign, meaning that Marc's fundraising and donation efforts on Hollinger's behalf could continue uninterrupted.

No explicit promises would ever be made, of course, but Marc knew how the game was played. As a bundler and through his high-ticket donations to the inaugural committee and to Hollinger-supporting PACs, he was near the beginning of the line for private sweetheart deals and no-bid contracts and all the rest of the spoils. Marc was hearing the first inklings of some pretty large federal construction deals that would be part of the forthcoming massive infrastructure spending that was the cornerstone of the administration's economic recovery plan. Hollinger would almost certainly find some way to ram at least part of his investment plan through Congress, their obstruction be damned.

And then, Marc Weber would be rewarded for what he had helped bring about.

* * *

Randall Weston, Edmund and Eleanor Garfield, and Marc Weber.

The societal underbelly.

Those who went out of their way—often literally—to surround themselves with clones, and who viewed evolutionary diversity as a mortal threat.

And those who worshipped at the altar of wealth and status, and who didn't think twice about entering into the most Faustian of bargains in the pursuit of ever-greater riches.

Ephraim Hollinger, with the help of Bob Platte and the American Values and Greatness Network, had artfully and successfully put the old band back together.

Chapter 9

Daniel's phone dinged, the ringtone indicating an incoming text. Even as he was reaching into his left pocket to retrieve the device, an overpowering sense of the message's contents enveloped him. Exactly one week had passed since Michele Burgess' interview trip; since their lengthy, intimate getting-to-know-you conversation that had lasted for hours. Daniel hadn't heard anything official from Diana Calloway one way or the other, but he had a feeling…

He was absolutely correct.

> Just heard from Dr. Calloway—I got it!

A few seconds later:

> Two-year appointment as a non-PhD lecturer, teaching 6 classes a year

Given Michele Burgess' inclusion of "I got it!" in her first message, Daniel was all but certain of the answer to the question he posed in his reply text. Still, he asked it anyway.

> Congratulations! That's great! You're going to accept?

The instantaneous all-caps reply brought a grin to Daniel's face that echoed the smiley face at the end of her text.

ALREADY DID! ☺

Which was quickly followed by:

> On my way to a graduation planning meeting —I'll call you around 7 tonight, want to discuss the video, have some great news

* * *

"West Point's graduation will be on May 27th, the Friday before Memorial Day weekend."

As promised, Michele Burgess called Daniel that evening, and she was now giving him the rundown on her upcoming timeline.

"Normally graduation is on a Saturday," she proceeded with her narrative, "but they shifted it this year to accommodate Hollinger's schedule."

"Hollinger?" Daniel's pulse quickened at the mention of the name.

An audible, agonizing groan traversed the phone line ahead of her words.

"Just announced this afternoon, at that meeting I went to. I was hoping he'd go to graduation at Annapolis or the Air Force Academy, but no such luck. He decided that he's doing West Point for his first one."

"Lucky you." The sarcasm in Daniel's response was unmistakable.

"Yeah, I know," Michele responded glumly, but then her voice immediately brightened.

"No sense in thinking about that. Today I'm celebrating! I have a new job...and it's all thanks to you!"

"My pleasure," Daniel tried to keep his voice even-keeled, but doubted that he was successful in his efforts. "I'm looking forward to having you in the department."

Daniel could almost feel a knowing smirk on the other end of their conversation.

"My last day on active duty is the following Wednesday," Michele finally continued, "so I'm thinking about coming to Pittsburgh in mid-June after I go visit my parents in Houston."

"Sounds like you'll be busy," Daniel offered.

"True, but it's workable."

"You said that you had some news about the video?" he remembered her earlier text.

"Oh, right! It's *definitely* been a day for big news!" The excitement that had infused Michele's tones since the beginning of their conversation suddenly ratcheted to a new level.

"When we were having dinner last Friday and then when we were talking afterward," a warm, fluttery feeling washed over Daniel as her words instantaneously brought back the memory and sensations of that not-too-distant night, "I don't remember if I mentioned that one of the cable news networks did a story a couple of years ago, right before I started teaching at West Point, about me still being one of only a few women in Special Forces…"

She paused to give Daniel time to reflect on her preamble.

"No, I don't think so."

"Yeah, I couldn't remember if we talked about that," she continued. "Anyway, I contacted the reporter who had interviewed me and told him about our video, and they want to debut it on the air on the twenty-ninth!"

"Wow!" was Daniel's instantaneous reaction, followed by a flurry of concerned bursts.

"That's only two weeks from now! How much more editing is there to do? Can I help you?"

"It's almost done now," Michele brushed away Daniel's concerns. "I'm planning to finish up the editing this weekend and I'll send it to you right away to take a look and let me know what you think.

"Besides," she continued, "we wanted to have it ready by the twenty-ninth anyway, so that hasn't changed."

"Yeah, that's true," Daniel found himself nodding in agreement.

April 29th, 2033.

Eighty-eight years exactly since that same date long ago in 1945.

Eighty-eight years to the day since the liberation of Dachau.

From the moment they finished shepherding the meeting between their respective great-grandfathers, Daniel Jacobson and Michele Burgess were wholly focused on having the video recording of that event in good enough shape to be posted on social media less than six weeks later. Even if only a handful of people actually viewed the video on that date, for all time it would be timestamped to commemorate the anniversary of the arrival of Nathan Jacobson's 45th Infantry Division at the gates of the main camp, and the liberating deliverance that followed. Michele had already spliced in several title cards to note that eighty-eighth anniversary, as well as the skin-tingling fact that the meeting being documented between the two ancient men less than two months earlier had occurred exactly one hundred years to the day after Dachau became the first operational Nazi concentration camp. She had also uncovered the absolutely, solemnly perfect Tchaikovsky piece to overlay the title cards and for selected segments throughout the video.

Now, with the added "oomph" coming from their video being broadcast on a major cable news network that same day...

"I hope you're okay with this next part," Michele's words interrupted Daniel's racing thoughts, "but they also want to interview both of us."

"On the air?" Daniel blurted out.

"Uh-huh," she confirmed. "The first time live, right before they show the video for the first time. And then they'll just replay that interview a couple more times when they show the video again. It's because we're both history professors, and since it's our great-grandfathers who are now the final surviving liberator and prisoner, we can talk to the historical aspects..."

"Yeah, of course!" Daniel quickly interjected. Even as he agreed, his mind resumed its frenzied contemplation, this time firing likely interview questions at him as well as offering him responses to those inquiries.

They talked for almost another full hour. They bandied about a couple of new ideas for their video of solemn commemoration and tribute. They discussed the logistics involved with Michele Burgess' impending move to Pittsburgh, including where she might consider living.

And they also talked about nothing in particular: just another round of getting-to-know-you-better conversation that Daniel hoped Michele wanted—needed—every bit as much as he did.

* * *

"We'll come back from the break directly to a five-second clip of your great-grandfathers talking," Craig Ryan ran down the list of what would soon be happening on-air. "Then we'll cut to that one sequence where your video pans across the black-and-white photo of the Dachau main gate back in the forties. That will be for another five seconds, and then we'll do the same pan with your color photo of the gate today. The video will fade and John Culverson will set up the segment, and then hand it off to me. I'll take it from there..."

The cable network reporter paused for a few seconds to check the margin notes of the script in front of him, and then continued.

"I'll go for about forty-five seconds, and then I'll introduce each of you. Michele, you'll be first, and you'll be on-screen for about ten seconds by yourself while I'm talking; and next we'll cut to Daniel for

The Voice of Prophets

about the same length of time. For both of you, just nod and smile when I introduce you; don't say anything yet. Then we'll go to split-screen with all three of us, and we'll stay that way for two and a half minutes of interview before we run the video. Remember to keep your responses to my questions on the shorter side, fifteen seconds max."

This was it.

The labor of love and eternal appreciation that had brought Daniel Jacobson and Michele Burgess together was now less than ten minutes from its debut. Craig Ryan, the network's lead national events reporter, had steadily built quite a following over the past fifteen years. As with most cable news broadcast reporters, he had spent the first couple of years of his career assigned to third- and fourth-tier stories and worked his way upward from there. His calm but commanding demeanor, coupled with his boyish good looks that almost made him appear too young for his on-air role, brought him to prominence during the whirlwind that had been 2020. Beginning with the impeachment hearings and then continuing right into the pandemic and then the midyear civil unrest, and then into the election and its surreal attack-on-democracy aftermath, Craig Ryan became known as a practiced, hard-nosed reporter who could skillfully fuse compassion and empathy with cold, hard factual reporting in a manner that instantly captured and then held a viewer's attention.

Throughout the twenties and into the early years of the current decade, Ryan took on ever-more-visible assignments. He was offered his own prime-time hour-long program a few years back, but turned down the offer to continue concentrating on outsized feature stories that he increasingly selected on his own.

When Michele Burgess contacted him several weeks back, he immediately remembered her from his earlier story about the all-too-rare presence of female soldiers with the Army's Special Forces, even years after regulatory restrictions had been lifted. Craig Ryan's on-air story, as was sometimes the case, became a catalyst of change. The United States military often moved at a glacial pace when it came to aligning the demographics of its force structure with that of the nation it served, with meaningful action often trailing far behind policies and regulations. After he reported about Michele Burgess, additional Special Forces slots were soon opened up to female enlisted soldiers and officers.

Craig Ryan's great-grandfather, like Daniel Jacobson's, had served as an enlisted soldier during World War II, landing on Omaha Beach in the first wave. Craig's dry sense of humor frequently took hold, and he often, with a deadpan face, told someone he was meeting for the first time that the 1990s classic movie *Saving Private Ryan* was actually a true story about his great-grandfather. He would keep the gag going for a while before eventually confessing to his good-natured trickery.

While working on his initial story about Michele Burgess, her own great-grandfather's imprisonment in Stutthof and Dachau had never come up. But now that Isaac Gretz was recognized as the final surviving prisoner from Dachau's main camp, Ryan instantly recognized the powerful pull of a feature story about the man while he was still alive. And to have the final living American soldier who had liberated the concentration camp also be part of the same piece? Craig Ryan's initial reflexive reaction was solely that of a skilled reporter who could sniff out a good story: jackpot! After viewing Michele and Daniel's video more than a dozen times while preparing for the upcoming segment, though, Craig could fully appreciate the solemnity of the message the two history professors had so skillfully conveyed through their homemade, highly personal documentary about their great-grandfathers' tales.

Daniel's spare bedroom in his condo had, long ago, been set up as an office, and that's where this final Friday morning of April 2033 found him. Michele had done a bit of rearranging in her own one-bedroom apartment that was about two miles outside the Thayer Gate, the main entrance to West Point. Checking the webcam on her computer, she was satisfied that her backdrop looked both professional and homey.

Craig Ryan had already warned both Michele and Daniel about making small talk or even asking a clarifying question once they were within a few minutes of their scheduled start time. There was always a chance that one of the network's broadcast engineers might press the wrong button, causing one or both of them to suddenly go live. The ticking moments of silence began to feel a touch discomforting to Michele—Daniel as well, he messaged her back after she texted him to say that just sitting there was starting to make her nervous—but she calmed herself by mentally fine-tuning some of her answers to the questions which Craig Ryan had said he would be asking.

Finally, it was time, as the network's popular morning news program returned from the bottom-of-the-hour commercial break. The short sequence of still shots and short video clips that Craig Ryan had described to Michele and Daniel appeared on-screen before cutting to John Culverson in the studio.

"As World War II fades into the past," the anchor began, "firsthand remembrances of the Holocaust are likewise fading. Today, most estimates place the number of concentration camp survivors at less than three hundred—most of them children at the time—though there's no way to know the exact number with certainty. What we do know, though, is that only one confirmed survivor of the notorious Dachau concentration camp remains alive today. Likewise, only a single American soldier who liberated that camp eighty-eight years ago today is still with us all these years later. Craig Ryan picks up the story from there."

The network's high-resolution webcam interview system displayed a small image of the actual broadcast signal in the upper right corner of both Daniel's and Michele's computer screens, and they watched the cut to Craig Ryan, standing in front of the Holocaust Memorial Museum in the nation's capital.

"Thank you, John. In early 1942, eighteen-year-old Isaac Gretz was pulled from his bed in the middle of the night and forcibly sent by the Nazis from his home outside of Warsaw to the Stutthof concentration camp, near Danzig in the northern part of Poland. For close to three years, he lived in constant fear of death from rampant disease, summary execution, or as a result of the thousands of hours of slave labor he was forced to endure. Then, in January of 1945, Isaac Gretz suddenly found himself an unwilling participant in a little-known aspect of the Holocaust as the S.S. stepped up the evacuation of some of their concentration camps ahead of the approaching Soviet Red Army. These death marches shuffled prisoners, many of them Polish Jews like Isaac Gretz who had somehow survived two or three years of brutal imprisonment and slave labor, all around the horrific Nazi concentration camp system, with tens of thousands of them dying en route."

For about five seconds, Craig Ryan's image was replaced onscreen by an ominous black-and-white photograph looking down on the expanse of Dachau.

"Isaac Gretz survived the final months of the war at Dachau, where—as John mentioned a moment ago—liberation by the American Army took place exactly eighty-eight years ago today."

A still shot of a uniformed, very young Nathan Jacobson replaced the image of Dachau as Ryan continued.

"Nathan Jacobson, from Pittsburgh, Pennsylvania, was a month past his nineteenth birthday in April of 1945. He had spent the past eight months fighting his way alongside his comrades in the 45th Infantry Division from Provence in Southern France all the way to the gates of Dachau. The war in Europe was almost over, and the horror of the Holocaust was being exposed to the world as one concentration camp after another was liberated."

The on-screen image returned to Craig Ryan.

"Today, eighty-eight years later, Isaac Gretz, now one hundred and nine years old, is the final known remaining survivor of Dachau, which had infamously been the very first concentration camp opened by the Nazis, back in 1933. And Nathan Jacobson, who celebrated his one hundred and seventh birthday last month, is likewise the final remaining liberator of Dachau, as well as the final surviving American soldier, sailor, or airman who fought in the European Theater during World War II. Their great-grandchildren, Daniel Jacobson and Michele Burgess, are both history professors, and last month arranged a meeting between their respective great-grandfathers. Professors Burgess and Jacobson have put together a remarkable video to commemorate that meeting as well as the liberation of Dachau, and both of them are here with me today."

Michele suddenly appeared on-screen.

"United States Army Major Michele Burgess currently serves as a history professor at West Point. She is a West Point graduate herself, and holds a master's degree from the Kennedy School of Government at Harvard. She also earned the fabled Green Beret and has served with both the Army's Rangers and Special Forces, and was profiled in a feature story on this very network several years back. She is one of Isaac Gretz's six great-grandchildren, and she joins us now."

A slight, professional smile came to Michele's face as she nodded a greeting to Craig Ryan and his audience, and then the on-screen image cut to Daniel.

"Daniel Jacobson teaches history at Western Pennsylvania College in Pittsburgh, where he specializes in twentieth-century American and European history. He recently wrote an article about his great-grandfather, which led to the meeting with Mister Gretz and the video that you are about to see. Professor Jacobson also joins us."

Craig Ryan artfully led Michele and then Daniel through a few background questions, and then the opening seconds of the video replaced the three of them on the news channel's broadcast screen. Michele and Daniel both fought back their own tears as they watched that first tearful hug between their great-grandfathers that they had witnessed less than six weeks earlier. They had viewed this scene dozens of times since then as they edited and reedited and reviewed the video; but both were nearly overcome by raw emotion at the realization that hundreds of thousands of people were watching this scene at this very moment, and that perhaps ten times as many would view the video either on today's replayed broadcasts or after it had been posted to social media.

Still, they both held it together as Craig Ryan brought the conversation back to them the moment the video concluded.

Later, both Michele and Daniel would each admit to the other that they remembered almost nothing from the final few minutes of their live appearance on the news network. They watched the replays and were relieved to see that they had sailed through the final round of questions and dialogue without stumbling; yet neither had more than a few wisps of recollection about what had actually transpired.

Craig Ryan's segment soon ended, and both Michele Burgess and Daniel Jacobson wondered what would come next.

If granted the proverbial million years to formulate a guess, neither would have come close to predicting what *did* occur. Within seconds after the network shared the video on social media, the firestorm began.

* * *

Randall Weston was one of the first to comment on the post that contained the video.

> Here comes the tired old holocaust story again. FAKE NEWS!!!

Randall quickly followed his initial post with a second one.

> 88 years supposedly, huh? 8 8 = H H = Heil Hitler!

And then a third:

> Arbeit Macht Frei—you so-called "history professors" might try it sometime!

Randall was gratified to see that all three of his posts quickly garnered thousands of up-votes from like-minded users. He recognized many of the screen names of those who commented on his posts; no surprise, since so many of them traveled in the same circles day after day, night after night. During the day, while at work, Randall was careful to post comments from his phone using Denver's municipal 8G system, safely walled off from his company's wireless network that they monitored. This way, he could periodically fight the good fight throughout the workday while dodging any problems that might arise from his flagrant violation of the insurance company's idiotic (in Randall's eyes, of course) policy against using corporate technology resources for "inflammatory or derogatory" purposes.

This morning, he had fortuitously stumbled on the cable network's post containing the video only seconds after they had uploaded it, and had made the first of his rebuttal posts less than twenty seconds later. Throughout the morning, Randall—and so many others just like him—firehosed the sharing of the video with thousands of contemptuous comments. Randall actually hoped that they might succeed in forcing the cable network to remove the video but no such luck, at least by the end of the workday.

Oh well; very likely Toni Fowler would take a swing at the topic tonight. Randall Weston—and his right hand—would be waiting.

* * *

For perhaps the first time since joining AVGN, Toni Fowler was uneasy about tonight's featured grievance. Her great-grandfather, Charles Bailey, had served under Patton during World War II. He had died long before she had been born, but his tales of the war had been passed down through the family's generations. Toni, therefore, knew that he had been with the Sixth Armored Division that had liberated the Buchenwald concentration camp in mid-April of 1945, just as Nathan Jacobson's unit had liberated Dachau at the end of that month. Family lore held that after his first year back in the States following the war, Charles Bailey never spoke again of that sickening place and what he had witnessed, other than to quietly acknowledge that he had been there before changing the subject, should anyone ask about his wartime experiences. Still, the whispered stories of the horrors Sergeant Charles Bailey had related before his self-imposed censorship far outlived his own years.

Consequently, if her life depended on an honest answer, Toni Fowler would be forced to admit the repulsive, horrid truthfulness of the Holocaust.

But the star AVGN anchor was a good soldier, as her great-grandfather had once been.

And a good soldier follows orders, she insisted to herself, including the verbatim recitation of the script that had been written for her and was now scrolling through the teleprompter.

"One hundred years ago," she began the first segment of this night's broadcast following her standard intro, "the German government was struggling to overcome the worst imaginable financial crisis that had crippled their entire country. However, numerous troublemakers, primarily Communists and Jews, were trying their hardest to undermine Germany's recovery, mostly because they themselves were benefiting from the woes of the German population as a whole. Sound familiar to anyone?"

The AVGN broadcast cut from Camera 1 to Camera 2 in sync with Toni pivoting her body into her customary head-on, cleavage-emphasizing position that captivated the Randall Westons and their ilk among her audience.

"As a result, the German government began creating a network of facilities where these rabble-rousers could be transported and contained to prevent their sabotaging efforts. The first of these facilities was outside of Munich and was known as Dachau. And while it's true that conditions at Dachau and so many of the other facilities were particularly harsh, it's important to remember that those housed there were true enemies of the German people."

She hesitated for a fraction of a second, and an astute viewer might have detected the briefest battle for control of Toni Fowler's soul that, with her continuation of tonight's opening monologue, was settled forever.

"Now here we are, one hundred years later, and we find the disciples—and in some cases the *DIRECT DESCENDANTS*—of those enemies of the German people doing everything they can, *RIGHT HERE IN OUR COUNTRY*, to undermine President Ephraim Hollinger's efforts to restore American values and greatness! They are trying their *DAMNEDEST* to muster sympathy for their dangerous cause by trotting out their tired old tales from so long ago; even enlisting senile old men for amateurish homemade videos, like the one some of you may have seen today, that they sell to the fake news after telling those old men exactly what to say…"

In Denver, Randall Weston was already reaching for his box of tissues, even though Toni Fowler's opening monologue hadn't even passed the one-minute mark.

Chapter 10

The ideas—disjointed, jarring fragments of ideas, to be precise—raced through Daniel Jacobson's mind from the moment he flicked off his bedside lamp until dawn peeked through the bedroom blinds the following morning. Some of the notions were fleeting offerings from unusually lucid dreams, while others sparked spontaneously in his groggy but conscious mind as he tossed and turned, chasing the elusive return to the realm of sleep.

For nearly two weeks, Daniel's psyche had been overwhelmed by the aftermath of the trolling social media attacks on the video of Nathan Jacobson and Isaac Gretz. He and Michele Burgess had, in the weeks leading up to the video's cable news debut, briefly considered the possibility of online "rebuttals" from Holocaust deniers and neo-Nazis. They steeled themselves for what they might encounter; but in their darkest nightmares, neither could have anticipated the nearly nonstop savagery that was directed their way for days after the video aired.

Eventually, the trolls moved on to a new target; but until then, Daniel and Michele could only helplessly watch as their great-grandfathers were mocked and called out as flagrant liars and tools of the Great Jewish Conspiracy.

Neither Daniel nor Michele had been born yet when a surge of Holocaust denial swept the ultra-right during the mid- and late-1990s. A new era of global person-to-person interactions had been catalyzed by the first generation of the commercialized internet, which in turn enabled those on the lunatic fringe to effortlessly connect with one another regardless of where they lived. Pseudo-scientific "analysis" of claimed impracticality of gas chambers and crematoriums as tools of mass execution was widely circulated among the deniers, much more easily than in the pre-online days. Documented confessions from concentration camp guards and even commandants were dismissed as either outright forgeries or coerced statements, with these blasphemous assertions often supported by laughably amateurish doctored images. "The testimony about the concentration camps delivered at the famed Nuremberg trials had been wholly fabricated to exact the victors' revenge on the defeated, of course"—that was the aggrieved complaint offered by the deniers. The Holocaust was, their mantra went, nothing more than a conjured tale designed to blunt opposition to the founding of a Zionist state shortly after the war.

Eventually, as the new millennium arrived, the attentions of the societal fringe were diverted from the rapidly fading mid-century past to more imminent targets, such as the dreaded "caravans of diseased illegals invading America and other civilized countries almost every day." Still, the undercurrent of denying the occurrence of the Holocaust, or at least the extent of the genocide, remained a pervasive trope of the overarching "Great Jewish Conspiracy" running theme.

For whatever reason, the video of Nathan Jacobson and Isaac Gretz and the liberation of Dachau had suddenly unchained the Holocaust denial monster. For close to a week, vile posts and comments on mainstream social media were rampant. The venom on the dark sites where so many of them writhed in the feverish orgy of hatred was even worse.

Both Daniel and Michele were consumed by an urge to fight back and defend not only their great-grandfathers but—perhaps even more so—the very essence of truth. Though tempting to simply dismiss the vicious attacks as little more than the vomitings of society's misfits, they were each obsessed with the belief that doing nothing—standing down, in the vernacular of Michele Burgess' military life—would be akin to ignoring a vast expanse of smoldering embers that was destined to ignite sooner or later.

They had to do *something*.

But what?

As the dawn's early light snaked through the shutter slats of Daniel's bedroom window, the jumbled thoughts of the previous restless night swirled through his groggy mind.

Did I dream that I was at a book burning?

In the days that followed the cable news interview, the posting of the video, and the resultant wrath from the Holocaust-denying trolls, Daniel had pored over internet content about the earliest days of Hitler's stranglehold on power a century earlier. Sparked by the dark centennial of Dachau in particular and the concentration camp system as a whole, Daniel searched for other seminal events and occurrences from Germany's slide into madness and destruction.

Yesterday, he had stumbled across an online encyclopedia article about the very first Nazi book burnings. Hitler's *Sturmabteilung*—the thuggish brownshirts of the S.A.—had sparked university students all across Germany to burn a wide array of "subversive" books in a flagrant attack on *any* beliefs that contradicted Hitlerism and Nazi Party doctrine. Though a few of the book burnings took place over a longer stretch of time, the majority of them occurred on May 10th, 1933.

One hundred years ago today.

Reading about the roaring bonfires throughout Germany's university towns that had alchemized knowledge into ashes, and knowing with the tragic certainty of hindsight what those carefully coordinated book burnings had presaged, Daniel slowly recalled that one of his nightmares had sent him back in time to bear firsthand witness to the horrors. He had been in…Berlin, he now remembered. In the dream he stood so close to the blazing bonfire that his skin prickled from the intense heat as he watched thousands of books reduced to ash.

Suddenly he heard the sharp cry of *Jüden!* Then another, and then an entire chorus.

Jüden! Jüden! Jüden!

All eyes were now on Daniel.

Throw him into the fire with the other Jews!

In the nightmare, even as the hands roughly seized Daniel's arms and began yanking and shoving him toward the flames, he found himself curiously wondering:

Why are they speaking English, not German, if we're in Berlin?

Daniel had abruptly woken at that moment— fortunately!—but must have fallen back asleep rather quickly, because he didn't recall forcing himself to stay awake long enough to prevent being pulled back into that particular nightmare.

Now, amid the safety of the early-morning light and with the clarity to distinguish between conjured nightmares and reality, Daniel pondered the true backstory to his horrifying dream. In retrospect, the Nazi Party's opening salvo against intellectualism and independent thought was hardly a surprise. Nothing gets the juices flowing among the compliant masses like a good, old-fashioned book burning, right? Hitler's Nuremberg rallies had taken place as far back as 1923; but after seizing power and after the Fatherland-wide book burnings, those from 1933 onward achieved an entirely new level of bubbling hatred. Amid the terrible whirlwind of Hitler's first months as Chancellor, the book burnings of May 10th, 1933, appeared to have been the galvanizing event that dehumanized enough of a critical mass of the German people to begin their dark descent into hell.

After finding that first encyclopedia article about the Nazi book burnings, Daniel had watched a half dozen documentary videos online yesterday that showed clips of the book burnings. No doubt those images had catalyzed his nightmare; but he was struck by the troubling similarities between the frenzied hatred that was documented in the film and images from much more recent history.

Consider the many thousands of social media comments hell-bent on discrediting a simple video of two ancient men commemorating the liberation from hell of one by the other, Daniel argued to himself. Compare that gleeful frenzy of online hatred to its earlier in-person incarnation a century earlier, as more than twenty-five thousand books declared to be "subversive" were reduced to ash.

Was there any difference at all?

As he swung his feet out of bed and gingerly stood, he knew with all the certainty in the world that a battle had recently begun. He also knew with certainty that whether he wished it or not, he was now an active combatant, and there would be no turning back.

A book: I'm going to write a book.

A novel.

A warning.

Alan Simon

Part II
The Book of Daniel

May 2033–July 2035

The Voice of Prophets

> *"I Daniel was grieved in my spirit in the midst of my body, and the visions of my head troubled me."*

- The Book of Daniel, Chapter 7, Verse 15

> *"I started having dreams two years before this plague ever fell. I've always dreamed, and sometimes my dreams have come true. Prophecy is the gift of God and everyone has a smidge of it."*

- Stephen King, *The Stand*

> *"Did you write the book of love, and do you have faith in God above, if the Bible tells you so…"*

- Don McLean, *American Pie*

Chapter 11

Major Michele Burgess' eyes shifted to the sight of Ephraim Hollinger marching into Michie Stadium, side by side with General Farrell, the three-star who served as West Point's Superintendent. They were flanked by Hollinger's Secret Service contingent and several other senior West Point leaders.

Even at a distance of fifty or sixty yards, Hollinger was a commanding presence. At close to six and a half feet in height, he was a good six inches taller than the uniformed general. Hollinger's wavy silver hair and weathered, photogenic face combined with his leanly muscled physique conferred him with the classic boardroom CEO look, especially in his custom-tailored dark suit. Michele knew that Hollinger had never served in any of the military services, yet he strode purposefully: majestically. His shoulders were pinned back and his head level, clearly conveying his constitutional role as Commander in Chief to all who watched him.

Hollinger commandingly led General Farrell and the contingent up the ramp connecting the West Point football field to the stage that had been erected for today's ceremony. Michele wondered if the general, or anyone else, would introduce Hollinger, but the president went straight to the microphone and began speaking.

"Four months and seven days ago," he began, the play on the first words of Lincoln's magnificent Gettysburg oration immediately obvious to Michele and everyone else inside the stadium, "I took an oath very similar to the one that our new graduates and second lieutenants will soon take. Shortly before I was sworn in as president, our wonderful Vice President Paul Nelson took his oath of office."

Hollinger's head pivoted to the other teleprompter, the one to his right, as he continued.

"Many of you are aware that the oath I swore, and the one that Vice President Nelson and all of our United States Army officers here today have sworn or will soon swear, are slightly different. Long ago, the Constitution established the thirty-five words that have formalized the ascendency of every American president. Yet for some reason, our founding fathers omitted the explicit recitation of a critically important aspect to the role of President of the United States."

Another head pivot brought Hollinger's eyes to the teleprompter on his left.

"Each military officer swears that he or she will defend this nation and its people against all enemies, both foreign and domestic. Yet those very words—'against all enemies, foreign and domestic'—are perplexingly absent from the oath that transforms an ordinary citizen such as me into the most powerful person not only in our great nation, but on this planet."

Michele found herself studying Ephraim Hollinger's manner of speech. Hollinger didn't roar at his crowds, as other populists of the past had notably done. He didn't gesture wildly with his arms or pound his fists to accentuate his words. Hollinger conveyed a lower-intensity, almost stealthy magnetism, spinning a hypnotic gravity that snuck up on those in his audience as it pulled them deep into his orbit.

Now Hollinger looked directly ahead. Perhaps he had memorized this portion of his speech and needed no assistance from one of the teleprompters. Or, more likely, he was now speaking extemporaneously without the need for the text of a prepared script.

"Despite the absence of those words and that phrase in my oath of office, I have committed my entire presidency to accomplishing exactly what every one of you newly minted second lieutenants are overtly vowing. For too long now, this nation has been hindered and harassed by its enemies, both foreign…"

Chills of raw fear instantly radiated through Michele Burgess.

"…and domestic. Our great nation has clearly been undermined by its *internal* enemies. I stand before you today to let each and every one of you, as well as everyone throughout this great land of ours, know that even though those words do not explicitly occur in the presidential oath of office, I am your comrade in arms. I accept the obligation to rid this country of all enemies, foreign and *especially* domestic, just as you have been called upon to do."

The president soon stepped back from his not-so-veiled threat, and spent the remainder of his fifteen-minute speech extolling the newly commissioned Army officers to live up to the glorious accomplishments of so many of their predecessors.

Hollinger was cagey enough while standing on the hallowed grounds of the United States Military Academy not to explicitly mention "thieving Wall Street Jews" or "immigrants pouring over our southern border, hell-bent on destroying traditional American values" or "multi-generational ghetto welfare families," or any of his other standard bogeymen whom he regularly targeted on the campaign trail and, even after his inauguration, at his frequent rallies in front of his frenzied supporters.

Still, *everyone* knew whom the President of the United States considered to be among the "domestic enemies" whom he vowed to vanquish.

* * *

Eleanor Garfield swelled with pride as she watched and listened to Ephraim Hollinger's West Point commencement address on television. Her visceral reaction was the same almost every time she heard Hollinger speak: It was about time! Not that long ago, real Americans like the Garfields had a champion in the White House; a man's man who was utterly fearless about calling out the pretenders who had infiltrated American society and lived to wage war on traditional American values and culture. For a short while, the Garfields' America had been led by a man who was unafraid to send the police and the military into the streets to teach the protestors and anarchists the brutally painful lessons that would send them scurrying back into hiding.

Alas, those glorious years of long-overdue reckoning had been fleeting: a shooting star that had buckled under the immense combined pressure wielded by the Deep State, the corrupt media, and their lawless agitating supporters.

Now, though…

It's only a matter of time now until our great president once again shoves all of those detestable enemies of the people back into the shadows, Eleanor Garfield thought as she continued to listen to Hollinger promise that true Americans would soon regain the upper hand.

No doubt her husband Edmund was also watching, along with the four or five other regulars from his daily card game. Every afternoon, almost immediately after lunch as Eleanor began cleaning up, Edmund wedged into their golf cart and puttered a mile and a half down the road to the closest of the massive development's fifteen full-service clubhouses. As with almost every other aspect of the Garfields' life down here in Nirvana, the card game was an immutable daily ritual. The Garfields and almost every one of their new-made friends treasured stability and routine above almost everything else. That's why they had moved here, after all. And Ephraim Hollinger's presidency meant a return to those good old days of stability and routine on a national scale.

Eleanor couldn't wait until Edmund returned home later that afternoon so they could share and relive the highlights of Hollinger's speech, and relish the budding promise of restored American values and greatness.

* * *

Michele was instantly enveloped in cold sweat as General Farrell pointed directly at her, with Ephraim Hollinger's eyes quickly tracking the direction of the general's pointed index finger. Sure enough, the two men and a small contingent of Secret Service agents began walking in her direction.

Acquiring his target, Michele's mind crazily raced.

She was standing in a small cluster of West Point faculty, about ten in all. The graduation ceremony had concluded five minutes earlier. The white service caps had been tossed high into the air in joyous celebration, and the new second lieutenants were now greeting their family and friends, or seeking their first salutes as commissioned officers. Marine One was already fired up outside Michie Stadium, and Hollinger would soon be departing.

Apparently, though, he had one more task to accomplish. Michele Burgess was not hallucinating; the President of the United States was headed directly toward her.

Hollinger was within four or five feet of Michele when his eyes glanced slightly down at her black uniform nameplate.

Confirming target.

"So you're Major Burgess."

Michele's head buzzed with nauseous cold fear, yet she still was able to take note of Hollinger's commanding tones.

"Mister President." Somehow, she mustered every ounce of strength to reply in what sounded omnisciently to Michele like a confident voice. All the while, her mind raced.

How the hell would he even know who I am?

Hollinger had halted about three feet in front of Michele. Now, though, he took another stride forward.

Locking onto target; weapons hot.

"And you're the one who made that video that's caused such a stir."

OH SHIT! MISSILE AWAY!

"I am, Mister President." How Michele was able to keep the trembling fear out of her voice was something she would ponder for a long while.

Ephraim Hollinger slowly, knowingly nodded a couple of times. Michele's nostrils were overcome with a suffocating, acrid odor.

As though Satan himself were standing in front of her.

"Interesting," Hollinger finally said, his gaze shifting toward her left shoulder to take in the prestigious insignia that indicated to one and all that Major Burgess had earned her place among the ranks of both the Special Forces and the Army Rangers.

Hollinger's eyes narrowed as if he was contemplating…something, and then he once again locked eyes with Michele for a few seconds, before wordlessly looking over to General Farrell. For those few seconds he stared down Michele, though, the look radiated by the face of the President of the United States was one of unadulterated contempt.

Michele's own gaze shifted to General Farrell, but the three-star general refused to allow his eyes to meet those of Major Michele Burgess.

Nothing else was spoken before Hollinger, General Farrell, and the Secret Service agents pivoted to head back toward the stage. As Michele watched them stride away, any remaining twinges of regretful uncertainty about putting in for early retirement from the Army were vanquished forever.

Chapter 12

Ordinarily, Daniel Jacobson was a writing machine. Each year he churned out two or three high-quality academic papers for journals or conferences, along with at least a half dozen more pedestrian articles for history magazines and their websites. Soon after joining the Western Penn history department he had found his writing groove, and was never thrown off track by writer's block or similar ails.

Through the second half of May and into the Memorial Day holiday weekend, Daniel's vision for his novel crystalized. One inspiration after another zoomed through his creative mind, and for close to three weeks he found himself dictating one note after another into his phone to capture fragmented ideas for the setting, the main characters, small and large slices of the story line, snippets of dialogue…all of it.

He would write about the here and now…but would do so in a setting fifteen or so years into the future. A fictional incarnation of Ephraim Hollinger would be elected president in, say, 2048. Whereas history was nowhere close to shutting the books on Hollinger—after all, he had only been in office for less than five months—Daniel would make some educated guesses about where the Hollinger regime would eventually end up. At least in Daniel's telling, Hollinger's dark visions that he painted for the future of the country and its population would not come to pass; he would come up short before being shunted aside by history.

Eventually, though, another Hollinger would come along, and this one would be far more successful in his willful ruination. Daniel would paint the most ominous picture of America, circa the 2050s, as a prophetic warning for what might happen if the nation and its people didn't turn away from today's seductive darkness. Perhaps at the end of the story, evil would again fall short, and the American dream would hang on—barely—and live to fight another day. Daniel wasn't certain if that's how the novel would conclude, but for now he was leaning that way.

A funny thing happened on Daniel's way to writing a novel, though. The ideas took shape and solidified easily enough. But the words and sentences and paragraphs proved difficult, almost impossible, to write; almost as if Daniel was afraid to plunge below the surface into the foreboding, icy darkness.

He struggled to trudge forward, and for the first time in his life his daily writing took the form of two steps forward followed by a step and a half in retreat.

Maybe I just need to step away from the story for a little bit and clear my head, Daniel tried to convince himself. His original intention was to write fifteen, maybe twenty second-draft-quality pages by Memorial Day, and then make it to fifty or sixty pages before Michele Burgess' arrival in Pittsburgh on the twelfth of June, knowing that for at least a couple of weeks after that he probably wouldn't make much more progress on the novel.

Now, with Memorial Day weekend directly ahead, Daniel was satisfied with the one-page Prologue he had written, and then rewritten and rewritten once again.

But that was it.

* * *

"It was the most unsettling moment of my entire life."

The West Point graduation had concluded a couple of hours earlier, and Michele promised that she would call Daniel before she bolted from the campus for the Memorial Day weekend. She paused for a brief second before elaborating.

"Actually," she clarified, "the *whole afternoon* was unsettling. The first part of his speech was horrifying. But when Hollinger was standing right in front of me..."

She hesitated, wondering if she should continue with the rest of her narrative.

I can trust him.

"...I swear it could have been Hitler; or even the devil. I've been face-to-face with the enemy a couple of times with Special Ops, on missions that I'll probably never be able to talk about. But I *never* felt like I was in the presence of pure evil the way I did with Hollinger two feet away from me."

Given his recent immersion into the earliest stages of Germany's descent into the hellscape architected by Hitler, Daniel wasn't the least bit surprised at the instantaneous shudder of dread that washed over him in response to Michele's words.

"At least it's over," Michele continued with a defeated sigh. "But I'll tell you something…"

She paused, seemingly to wait for a brief acknowledging response from Daniel Jacobson: "what?" or "go ahead" or "huh?"

Daniel opted for "What's that?"

"When he was speaking, just watching the cadets, and the faculty officers…not all of them, but enough of them…"

Daniel waited for her to proceed past a pause where Michele was apparently trying to gather her thoughts, but he was certain exactly where she was going.

"He already has them under his spell," she finally continued. "A lot of them. They were sitting there listening to him preach about defeating our dangerous internal enemies so we can restore American values and greatness, and so many of them were hanging on every word. I mean, we've seen this movie before, not that long ago."

"Yeah, I know," Daniel's tones now matched Michele's on the gloominess scale.

"At least it's over," Michele repeated, almost as if she were trying to convince herself of that fact. "I'm headed out of here in about twenty minutes. I'll be driving against rush hour, but it's still a holiday weekend Friday, so traffic is going to be heavy."

Michele had previously told Daniel that she was spending the entire Memorial Day weekend in Manhattan with two other women officers who were also on the West Point faculty. Daniel, of course, would have preferred that Michele had decided to come to Pittsburgh instead. He had held his tongue, though, resisting the overwhelming temptation to "offhandedly" suggest something along the lines of "you know, you could come down here and start looking for a house or condo, and maybe also see some more of the area..."

Nope; don't even think about saying it!

The last thing Daniel wanted to do was to come across like a lovesick high school or college kid. Manhattan was only an hour or so away from West Point—traffic permitting, as Michele had noted—and he knew that she had plenty of things to take care of as she prepared to leave Army life behind. Local, rather than longer-distance, travel certainly made sense for Michele for this weekend. She still planned to arrive in Pittsburgh in about two weeks, after flying to Houston to spend a few days with her parents.

She'll be here soon enough, he reminded himself yet again. Besides, Daniel desperately needed to recommit himself to his book project for the next two weeks. He was all but certain that after Michele arrived in Pittsburgh, he would be spending a fair bit of time helping her find a place to live, getting her settled in at Western Penn, and—he hoped, anyway—getting to know her even better than he already did.

Until then, he intended to sequester himself in his home office for hours on end, and recommit himself to transforming the still-jumbled jigsaw puzzle of characters and story lines into a solid start on his novel.

Especially after Hollinger's ominous yet cryptic words to Michele about their video, Daniel was a man on a mission.

I need to start making some real progress!

Chapter 13

Ephraim Hollinger was, as Michele Burgess had recently learned, an imposing man when he was in one's presence. Standing next to Attorney General Spencer Howell, however, even the president appeared as a secondary figure. Howell, a hulking former college football offensive lineman, stood six-ten and clocked the scale at a muscular two-ninety. A guess-your-age carny working the midway at a state fair would be right on the mark with an instantaneous first impression that Spencer Howell looked to be forty-six years old.

The two men had, for the past four months, worked under the radar on the Executive Order that they were about to announce. Only a few of Howell's trusted aides whom he had brought to Washington with him from his tenure as the Montana Attorney General were privy to what was about to be sprung on America. Those like-minded and like-spirited confidants had worked into the late-night hours almost daily since early February, hammering out the dirty details and bulletproofing the Executive Order. Neither Hollinger nor Howell gave a damn about the predictable uproar from their opponents in the Democratic and Republican parties; in fact, the louder the protests, the better. They wanted to be absolutely certain that the order would survive the inevitable court challenges. Every sentence had been parsed and challenged the proverbial six ways from Sunday, ferreting out *any* possible ambiguity or contradiction that could cause the massive reorganization of federal law enforcement to come tumbling down and be rewound.

They were ready.

The White House Press Briefing Room was packed this first Friday afternoon of June, and the press attendees buzzed among themselves as they waited for

Ephraim Hollinger to enter. All they knew was that Hollinger would soon personally make "a major reorganization announcement"—but other than that teaser from this morning, they were all in the dark. No one knew that Attorney General Howell would be part of this afternoon's performance. That factoid might well have tipped the administration's intentions, or at least have set some of the more dogged reporters onto the scent of what they were about to learn. Hollinger wanted to maintain the element of surprise to enhance the "shock and awe" of this particular announcement, yet he relished the feverish speculation throughout the morning on the mainstream cable news networks.

Bob Platte at AVGN was, of course, in the know about what was about to go down, ensuring that his afternoon news anchors all had carefully scripted programming ready to immediately join the salvo. His evening lineup talent likewise had their marching orders and their own carefully coordinated talking points. Neither Ephraim Hollinger nor Spencer Howell entertained a single worry that news might leak from the AVGN studios, though. Bob Platte's *blitzkrieg* approach to "news" and opinion shaping depended in part upon the utmost secrecy, a lesson he had drilled into Toni Fowler and Hayden Lafferty and all the others since the network's birth. None of them would dare risk the wrath of not only Bob Platte but also, in this case, the Attorney General and the president as well!

Craig Ryan, by virtue of his stature at his cable network, sometimes covered White House events if he wasn't elsewhere on assignment. For almost two years now, dating back to the summer of 2031 when Ephraim Hollinger announced his candidacy, his internal "news radar" had lit up like a Christmas tree. So many things about Hollinger's candidacy and now his presidency were a reprise of not so long ago, which was troubling enough. Yet Craig Ryan couldn't shake the feeling that this time around, the checks and balances wouldn't just be stretched to the breaking point; they could conceivably be overrun.

Thus far, four and a half months into Hollinger's presidency, the man's incendiary rhetoric had yet to be matched by action. The press release's ominous pronouncement of a "major reorganization announcement," however, was a crystal-clear tip-off—to Craig, at least—that Hollinger was about to ratchet up the "action" side of the equation, following on the heels of his divisive West Point speech. He not only wanted to personally hear Hollinger's words; he wanted to read the room as Hollinger made whatever the pronouncement would be.

One can learn a great deal from others' reactions, Craig Ryan knew.

At precisely three o'clock, Ephraim Hollinger and Spencer Howell strode into the press briefing room and headed straight for the podium microphone. Hollinger wasted no time.

"Today, Attorney General Howell and I are announcing the most sweeping change to the federal government structure since the establishment of the Office of Homeland Security long ago in 2001. America has always been a nation of law and order. In recent years, however, the contempt for law and order by too many troublemakers has not only put life, limb, and property in harm's way, it has significantly eroded traditional American values. The changes that Attorney General Howell will now announce will reverse this damaging and unfortunate trend."

Hollinger nodded to Spencer Howell as he took a small step to his right, while Howell shifted slightly to now stand directly behind the microphone. Interesting, Craig Ryan thought; apparently the Attorney General is the featured performer this afternoon, or at least a lengthy opening act.

"Thank you, Mister President," Howell nodded to Hollinger, and then faced the audience. "As the president just referenced, the Office of Homeland

Security was established by Executive Order 13228 in the immediate aftermath of 9/11. This action was taken for one timely and critical reason. At the time, the essential mission of securing the American homeland was fragmented across far too many agencies and departments throughout the federal government. Consequently, our enemy was able to exploit cracks in the overall security landscape and attack us. By fusing together the functions of these various agencies under a single leader, we were able to very quickly seal those cracks and reaffirm the federal government's commitment to protecting our American homeland from foreign threats."

Howell paused for a moment, his eyes scanning the reporters present.

"Today, and for a long while now," he continued, "we've faced the same problem with federal law enforcement protecting all of us against internal threats to traditional American values. If you go to any online encyclopedia and search for 'federal law enforcement in the United States' you'll be presented with a list of close to one hundred different organizations. Many of these organizations are housed within the Department of Justice, yet they operate far too often without central coordination among them. Further, even more of them are scattered throughout every Cabinet-level department, often with overlapping missions, but at the same time, also leaving significant gaps. Our enemies—specifically our *domestic* enemies—have been able to exploit this fragmentation."

Howell's eyes narrowed as he continued.

"Not that many years ago, in order to protect life and property in our American cities from violent and destructive anarchists, the presidential administration at the time needed to quickly cobble together an ad hoc force of federal officers from several of the aforementioned organizations. As expected, the news media and other supporters of the violence dared to criticize the responding force as illegitimate, for the sole reason that it was created on the fly, out of necessity. These claims of illegitimacy only served to embolden the anarchist protestors and prolong the violence in the streets of American cities."

Another pause; this time for effect.

"Today, that stops."

The Attorney General gave the slightest nod to an aide standing against the right-side wall of the press briefing room, a remote projector clicker in his left hand. Howell's nod wasn't even necessary, though. The presentation had been rehearsed nearly a dozen times over the past two days. At this point, Howell and his aide had the Attorney General's words and tempo flawlessly aligned with the presentation slides.

Behind Howell and Hollinger, the high-definition briefing screen bearing the seal of the office of the presidency suddenly flicked to the next slide in the presentation. This second visual displayed a subdued, watermarked seal of the Department of Justice behind three simple words. Those words were clearly intended to convey a foreboding message, and they did exactly that.

FEDERAL POLICE FORCE

A second later, an acronym was added on-screen to complete the message.

FEDERAL POLICE FORCE (FPF)

Spencer Howell proceeded to commandingly explain how he would personally oversee this new Office of the Federal Police Force, created by Executive Order, within the Department of Justice. The epicenter of this all-new FPF would be formed from existing DOJ entities—the alphabet soup of the FBI, ATF, and DEA, along with the Bureau of Prisons—but those organizations would now be reorganized into subordinate departments within a single consolidated agency and under the control of a single director, who would report directly to the Attorney General. The policing agencies within Homeland Security—border protection and immigration enforcement, in particular, Howell's eyes steeled as he made this pronouncement—would be transferred into DOJ and fused into the Federal Police Force as well.

Likewise, the Postal Inspection Service, the very first federal law enforcement organization that predated the Declaration of Independence and the nation itself, was ripped from the United States Postal Service and wedged into the FPF. The law enforcement-related missions across other federal Cabinet offices would still exist structurally in their current forms—for now—but *all* operations, Spencer Howell emphasized, would fall under the command and control of the FPF.

As Howell continued, Craig Ryan furiously tapped away at the tablet device resting in his lap, capturing the highlights of what he was hearing…even though he, the same as every other reporter present, was recording the briefing. At the same time, however, the reporter's mind insisted on multi-tasking and presented him with an ominous parallel to a century earlier. Craig Ryan had majored not only in journalism while attending the University of Illinois, but also in history, a choice inspired largely by his great-grandfather's experiences during World War II. Broadcast journalism had become Craig's chosen profession, but history remained his passion; and he *knew* his history.

In April 1933, Hermann Göring was already one of Adolf Hitler's trusted aides and confidants, serving as the newly installed German chancellor's Minister of the Interior for Prussia. One of Göring's first acts as Hitler consolidated power was to combine and consolidate several law enforcement agencies from different segments of the Prussian government into a single agency. The move was ostensibly made in the interest of efficiencies, but—as history would soon bear witness—far more sinister motives were behind Göring's actions. The World War I ace and future *Luftwaffe* leader named his newly integrated policing force the *Geheime Staatspolizei:* in English, the Secret State Police. Within a few short years, the mission and reach of the *Geheime Staatspolizei* expanded beyond Prussia to all of Germany, and eventually during the war to the entirety of occupied Europe.

The reorganized and unified *Geheime Staatspolizei* was, of course, almost always colloquially referred to as the *Gestapo*.

* * *

The questions flew from the gathered reporters. Several had the audacity to challenge the authority of the Attorney General, and even the president, to unilaterally enact such sweeping, radical change without congressional involvement.

Spencer Howell was ready.

"The FBI was created originally as the Bureau of Investigation in exactly this manner in 1908," was his smug rebuttal. "The DEA was created by President Nixon in 1973 through an executive order. The Park Police was created directly and unilaterally by President Grant, and years later Franklin Roosevelt transferred the Park Police from his own direct control to the United States Park Service. This nation has a long history of its past presidents creating new law enforcement organizations or modifying existing organizations through executive orders, and President Hollinger *will* exercise this power to fully deliver law and order throughout the land."

In response to another question asking whether the FBI, DEA, and other organizations were actually being dissolved and replaced by the ominously named Federal Police Force, Spencer Howell was ready with a response that sent chills through Craig Ryan and many of the other reporters and correspondents present.

"For a long time, using acronyms such as the FBI, or even the DEA or ATF, has been second nature for all of us. Over time, those legacy names will fade away, and the existence of the FPF will be an integral part of every American's life."

Chapter 14

"Maybe I should think about renting instead, at least at first."

A humid late June Saturday afternoon, the first truly uncomfortable day of 2033 as spring surrendered to summer, had been spent looking at six smallish houses in the Oakland neighborhood, all within two miles of the Western Penn campus. Each of the houses was older: tired. Two were definitely fixer-uppers, while the others had been restored at least to some degree within the past four or five years. All were priced on the higher side, though, especially given the still-fragile state of the country's economy. What most were now referring to as the Second Great Depression had bounced off the bottom shortly before last fall's elections. In fact, the earliest, faintest stages of recovery had almost prevented Ephraim Hollinger and his disturbing vision of America's future from winning the presidency. Enough discontent still held sway throughout the nation, however, to squeak him into office.

Now, more than five months after his inauguration, the economy still limped along and was relatively flatlined; but the worst seemed to be over. People were returning to restaurants and movie theaters. Both consumer spending and manufacturing had stopped hemorrhaging, and jobs numbers had finally steadied at around eleven percent unemployment, down from nearly twenty percent in the spring and summer of 2031. Students of American history—professional historians such as Michele Burgess and Daniel Jacobson, as well as avid readers—recognized many parallels between daily life in America, circa the 2030s, and that of a century earlier at the equivalent stage during the first Great Depression. The American economy remained in the hospital, but it had been transferred out of the ICU to a standard room, at least for the time being.

To Michele Burgess' dismay, though, nearly everyone trying to sell a house, at least in the neighborhood where she had decided to look, had priced their home as if the economy had already roared back to full health.

If a recovery is around the corner, the past-is-prologue reasoning seemed to be, apparently thinking back twenty years to the housing rebound that followed the Great Recession and then surprisingly rocketed to dizzying heights during the COVID pandemic, *then there is no way in hell that I'm going to sell out at a bargain price and let whoever buys my house make a ton of money, and quickly!*

Michele had never owned a house before, but she thought she had a good sense for distinguishing between a property that was a relative bargain, or at least priced fairly, versus one that was ridiculously overpriced. And to her dismay, everything she looked at this afternoon fell into the latter category.

"What about buying a condo?" Daniel suggested. "Like I have?"

The late afternoon sun was still high overhead, even though six o'clock was only a few minutes away. But the days were still long just on the other side of the summer solstice, and the sun wouldn't begin its downward trek for a little while longer yet. Still, despite the bright sunshine and humidity, both Daniel and Michele decided to decompress on the outdoor patio of one of the Oakland college bars. The patio's misting system made sitting outside tolerable, even though they were both sticky from an afternoon of trooping in and out of cars and houses.

Michele took a swig of her oversized draft and shook her head.

"I really want to get a house," she countered. "Every single Army assignment I had for fifteen years, I either lived on base or in a small apartment not too far away.

I never spent a lot of time in any of them, so it never really mattered. But I swore that after I retired, I would *definitely* get a house. But maybe I shouldn't buy one; maybe I should just look for one that somebody is trying to rent."

Daniel shrugged.

"Maybe," he replied non-committedly. "I guess it depends whether you're thinking about staying here for a while or not."

Daniel realized that his seemingly offhand comment was weighed down with subtext, so he hastily added:

"If you wind up going to another school somewhere else after your two-year contract is up, or if you decide that you don't want to keep teaching, then yeah, I guess you might be stuck with trying to unload a house, especially if the economy is still not that great by then."

Michele's eyes caught Daniel's as she offered the same exact warm, inviting smile that had instantly captivated him two months earlier.

"I just got here; I'm not thinking about leaving," was all she said in response as their gazes remained locked.

* * *

Summer swept by. Western Pennsylvania College started its fall semester the final week of August, which afforded Michele Burgess two full months to get ready for her classes. Daniel Jacobson helped her, of course. But why wouldn't he, given that before June had concluded, the two of them were "together" in more than just a professional sense?

Their first official date was ostensibly to celebrate Michele's offer on a house being accepted. She had dithered for a few days after that first discouraging house-hunting Saturday; but by the middle of the following week, Michele had decided to proceed with her original intentions and keep looking for a place to buy. Her salary at Western Penn, given that she was a non-PhD lecturer, wasn't overly generous; but when pooled with her fifteen-year Army retirement pay, she easily qualified for a house in the price range she had set for herself.

The trick, though, was to actually find a house that *was* for sale in that price range, and that took just a little bit more doing. The very next Saturday, at the beginning of the Fourth of July weekend, Daniel accompanied her on a reprise of her first zigzagging tour of Oakland's homes for sale. This time, a steady rain replaced bright sunshine, though the sticky humidity remained the same.

The third house Michele visited was definitely on the smallish side, slightly under 1,300 square feet. Yet the price was actually reasonable, and the place had just been remodeled by the son of the elderly woman who had lived there for more than fifty years. The old woman was moving in with that son's family, and she happened to take a liking to Michele Burgess as she insisted on personally leading this prospective buyer on the tour through the home.

A handshake deal was made on the spot. The paperwork from Michele's realtor made it to the woman's agent before five o'clock that afternoon, and was immediately accepted.

As both Michele and Daniel would often relate in the months that followed, technically she asked him out.

"We need to celebrate! What's the nicest restaurant you can think of?"

Daniel instantly responded.

"*Promettere*, in the Strip District. Upscale Italian."

Realizing that Michele hadn't yet gained her bearings for the different sections of the city, let alone the suburbs and small surrounding towns, he added:

"About two miles from here, down on the Allegheny. They're up on the fourth floor of an old produce warehouse, so you get a fantastic nighttime view of the stadiums across the river, plus downtown and the rest of the city."

Daniel caught himself before he uttered an addendum, a leading one, but Michele was a step ahead of him and pronounced exactly what he had been thinking.

"Sounds romantic," she replied, her words accompanied by an inviting smile.

* * *

They slept together for the first time that evening, back in Daniel's Oakland apartment. Before then, for nearly three hours during dinner, their gazes had rotated between the fiery Pittsburgh sunset that surrendered to the city's famous nightscape...and each other. By the time they were the final ones to leave the restaurant, Daniel and Michele both *knew* what would happen next.

For the remainder of the summer break, Daniel and Michele were nearly inseparable. They prepared for their fall courses together. Daniel accompanied her to pick out furniture and new appliances and pretty much anything else that Michele needed for her new home. They took several day trips to gloriously picturesque spots in and around the city, relishing both the scenery and the time together.

The only nagging concern that summer, at least for Daniel Jacobson, was having made absolutely no progress on the novel that had begun with such high hopes back in spring. In fact, by the time the fall semester arrived, Daniel's book was totally on the back burner of his priorities.

Maybe I'll get back to it after school begins and I get settled in, Daniel's mind provided the rationalization for his shifting priorities.

Fall classes soon began, and Daniel helped Michele settle into the routine of academic life, Western Pennsylvania College-style. Michele's apprehension about being a non-PhD lecturer proved to be for naught. Even John Loomis (who, it turned out, had voted to hire her, making Michele's approval for an appointment unanimous among the history department faculty) invited her to co-chair the department's biweekly Friday afternoon guest lecture sessions.

As 2033 edged toward its conclusion and the new year of 2034 beckoned, all seemed right with the world for Daniel Jacobson and Michele Burgess.

At least in their little corner of the world.

Chapter 15

Michele Burgess' third Army assignment, more than a decade earlier and just after she had been promoted to captain, was at Arizona's Fort Huachuca, about fifteen miles north of the Mexican border. During her two years there, Captain Burgess became personally acquainted with two of the Desert Southwest's curious weather phenomena.

Not long after arriving in Southern Arizona, Michele headed out for her daily five-mile run along a dry river wash close by her apartment. She was doing her customary warm-up stretches when she noticed what looked like a mini-twister about a quarter mile up the wash. She watched with curiosity as the miniaturized cyclone, initially rising only a few feet above the desert floor, slowly increased in both velocity and size.

The dust devil (Michele knew of the phenomenon, though she had never previously witnessed one) remained stationary for about a minute before it began slowly trekking along the wash, away from her. All the while it continued to pick up strength until, just before following the curve of the wash out of Michele's line of sight, the dust devil was a good thirty feet wide and close to a hundred feet in height.

Michele belatedly began her run in that direction, trailing the now-vanished whirling brown mini-twister. By the time she reached that same bend in the wash, however, the dust devil was nowhere to be seen. What Michele did see, though, was a long trail of downed limbs, ripped from the palo verdes and mesquites along the bank of the wash.

As she continued her run, Michele reflected on how the whirling phenomenon seemed to materialize out of nowhere and then slowly, steadily gain strength from the dirt that it drew into itself before deciding to march forward. The upheaval left in its wake was noticeable but relatively contained; yet the damage provided a clear hint of significantly broader destruction should that weather phenomenon somehow have continued to gain in size and intensity.

A couple of months later, Michele and John Garcia, the Army intelligence officer with whom she had hooked up not long after arriving at Fort Huachuca, decided that a long Fourth of July holiday weekend of cosmopolitan luxury was called for. The two captains weaved around surprisingly heavy holiday weekend highway construction and backed-up traffic for two hundred miles, driving northward to a lush resort hotel in the northern portion of Scottsdale for a few days of pool time under the blistering summer Arizona sun, relaxing dinners, and plenty of hot hotel-room sex.

Very early that Sunday afternoon, the Army officers had just plopped onto two poolside lounge chairs when both of their phones simultaneously came alive with the jarring alert sound indicating an impending weather emergency. "SEVERE DUST STORM WARNING: TAKE COVER IMMEDIATELY," the message advised when Michele checked the phone's alert screen.

Michele immediately looked skyward, and was struck by the significant contrast between the ominously worded warning related through her cell phone versus the deep blue, utterly cloudless, endless Arizona summer sky that was interrupted only by the blazing sun fire that was now directly overhead.

Strange, Michele thought; *not sure what that's all about, but for now, I'm staying right here.*

Twenty minutes passed as a half-asleep Michele soaked in the glorious Arizona sun. Soon, she decided to slip into the pool for a few minutes to cool off before flipping over and sunning her back for a little bit. When she opened her eyes, she noticed that the blue sky above her had dulled considerably. The sky was still cloudless, but now seemed to be filtered through a gauzy brownish lens.

A minute or two later, Michele noticed that the tall, lean palm trees surrounding the pool area were now swaying rhythmically. The sky's blue had now quickly and completely transformed to a surprisingly ominous dirty light brown.

"Where did everyone go?"

John Garcia's voice caused Michele to realize that they were now the only two people remaining at the pool.

Irritated that their afternoon of poolside sun was apparently being preempted, Michele threw her towels and sunscreen into her beach bag and checked to see if she might have forgotten anything.

Oh well; at least there's still hotel-room sex to pass the afternoon, she thought as they headed toward the door. The winds seemed to pick up by the second, and the palm trees were no longer rhythmically swaying; they now ferociously whipped back and forth. She looked across the pool toward the hotel room's parking lot. While visibility had definitely decreased through the brownish cloud that had descended on them, she could still see a good two hundred feet, maybe even farther; it wasn't like they were totally browned out with almost no visibility amid the dust storm that was now all around her and John Garcia.

Michele Burgess had just been personally introduced to the Mother of All Dust Storms known as the haboob. As with dust devils, Michele had previously read about this phenomenon, so she wasn't totally unfamiliar with what was occurring around her.

Well, this still doesn't seem as bad as they make haboobs out to be, she concluded as they headed inside. *It looks like a dust devil on steroids.*

Barely five minutes after making their way to the safety of their hotel room, however, three of the palm trees had been uprooted, with two of them going airborne. One of those palms took out four cars in the parking lot as it crashed to the asphalt. The other came down in the pool area, landing where Michele and

John Garcia had been sunning themselves only a few minutes earlier. The hotel suffered roof damage from the raging winds. The entire resort was without electricity—and air conditioning—until early evening because of downed power lines all around Scottsdale, leaving Michele and John to wait out a stifling, claustrophobic afternoon as the temperature in their hotel room clocked its way upward toward ninety degrees.

Later that night, while watching the local news after power was restored, both Michele and John Garcia were awestruck by the time-lapsed video being shown over and over by the news station. The haboob had risen from the desert floor to tower high above the expanse of the Phoenix metro region as it roared toward and then over civilization, steadily swallowing everything in its path.

As she watched the news, Michele was struck by the dichotomy between what she now was viewing from an omniscient, almost bystanderish point of view versus what she had witnessed in person. The timeline the newscaster related about the dust storm's path confirmed that she and John had still been dawdling outside at the pool as the worst of the haboob was beginning to hit the part of Scottsdale where they were. She had been right on the cusp of the storm. She certainly could tell at the time that *something* was happening, and she had been clearly warned via the weather alert on her phone.

She just didn't realize or appreciate how destructive the force of nature all around her actually was until it was almost too late.

* * *

Many years after her posting at Fort Huachuca had ended, when Michele Burgess looked back on the entirety of the year 2034, she would realize that the year had begun as a dust devil and had ended as a haboob.

Chapter 16

Jeremy Goldstein was the perfect villain.

Thirty-eight years old and a college dropout.

Pocketed more than two and a half billion dollars in less than three months as the stock market collapsed in early '31 through carefully positioned hedges, gleefully bragging about his prescience to one and all on every podcast and cable financial program that would book him as a guest.

Dropped nearly six hundred million dollars on the most expensive home purchase ever in the United States, with ninety mil from that amount going for the neighboring property so Jeremy could flagrantly tear down the mansion there to leave a little extra green space.

Ostentatiously jetted around the globe aboard his eighty-million-dollar Gulfstream, accompanied by a string of high-profile models and other beauties, thoroughly documenting those hedonistic adventures on social media.

And Jewish.

* * *

Jeremy Goldstein spent New Year's Day, 2034, in the French Alps swooshing down the slopes at Courchevel 1850. He had been ensconced since before Christmas Day in a three-thousand-square-foot suite that cost twelve thousand euros a night. He skied every afternoon and then partied each night all the way to dawn at one or more of the resort's ultra-exclusive clubs. Juliana Kearney, voted the world's top lingerie model each of the past three years, accompanied Jeremy on this trip and shared his suite and his oversized bed. So did Tanya Dulka, the recipient of the same honor for the previous two years before yielding her crown to Juliana.

For Jeremy Goldstein, life couldn't get any better.

New Year's Day, 2034, fell on a Sunday, which meant that this year's work calendar for privileged financiers such as Jeremy Goldstein didn't begin until the following week's Monday. That entire first week of January, all the way through Sunday the eighth, remained a continuation of letting the good times roll.

At this point in his company's life cycle, Jeremy employed a flock of talented—and ruthless—next-line directors and principals for day-to-day trading, asset allocation, and financial alchemy. Jeremy Goldstein's role these days was as the captain of his ship. His primary function was to ensure that his traders, portfolio managers, and analysts all remained hungry and merciless enough to spend every minute of every day in hot pursuit of the next kill.

On the ninth of January, Jeremy's luxury Eurocopter touched down shortly after nine a.m. on the rooftop landing pad of the midtown Manhattan building where his firm's offices were housed. His kickoff meeting for the year was scheduled to begin at nine-thirty. For the remainder of the morning, he would set the direction for the next month's trading, as well as get fully up to speed with what had happened over the holidays. He had been in touch with his executive team at least once each day while he had been in the French Alps and, after flying back to the States, for the two days he had been at his house in the Hamptons, and had already heard all the highlights; so Jeremy wasn't expecting any surprises this morning.

He couldn't have been more wrong.

Twenty minutes into his meeting, Jeremy's peripheral vision caught the lobby outside his glass-walled executive conference room suddenly fill with a mélange of helmeted, fatigue-clad and combat-booted SWAT officers wielding ominous-looking military assault weapons, together with a handful of suit-and-tie types cloaked in bulletproof vests and two-handing their .45s and nine millimeters. Within seconds, the entire posse had swarmed the conference room, multiple weapons cocked and aimed at each one of the dozen people who were stunned into terrorized silence.

"FPF! DON'T FUCKING MOVE! HANDS ON THE FUCKING TABLE! NOW! DO IT! DO IT!" the shouts rang out from all corners as the officers quickly fanned out around Jeremy's shocked executive team. Heads were brusquely slammed against the oak tabletop. Rifle barrels and pistols were pressed into temples or against necks. Inside of ten seconds, every non-FPF person in the conference room was targeted by at least two weapons as arms were yanked behind torsos and brusquely handcuffed.

Except for Jeremy Goldstein.

Two FPF SWAT officers converged on Jeremy and jerked him from his chair. They then slammed him to the ground, facedown. Each SWAT officer wrenched an arm, stomping simultaneously on Jeremy's hands. One of the suit-and-tie types, a stocky, crew-cut, cruel-looking fortyish man, knelt down and twisted Jeremy's face in his direction. The man's right knee shifted, landing with a thud on the back of Jeremy's neck.

"Welcome to the fuckin' party, Jewboy!" the stocky man sneered as he increased the pressure on his target's neck, constricting his airway and taking Jeremy, who only days before had been skiing the French Alps and living the good life, to the edge of blacking out, and then into an oxygen-starved abyss.

* * *

The raid on Jeremy Goldstein's offices was only one of more than a dozen conducted by the Federal Police Force this first business Monday of 2034. By the time the clock swept past noon on the East Coast, nearly two hundred financier types were in FPF custody. Most of the raids were conducted in either midtown Manhattan or in the Wall Street area. Two went down in the early morning hours out in California—one on Wilshire Boulevard in L.A., the other in San

Francisco's financial district—sweeping up the two largest private equity firms in that state.

At one o'clock that same afternoon, Attorney General Spencer Howell launched into his victory speech.

"Today, the Justice Department struck a blow for fairness, integrity, and honesty on behalf of law-abiding American citizens. For the past three years, a cabal of immoral individuals and firms in all corners of the financial world—hedge funds, private equity, investment banks, and brokerages—has conspired to undermine the stability of the global markets through a nonstop parade of shameless self-dealing, amid the depths of a Depression that they themselves had triggered in the first place. The forgotten American citizen has suffered long enough. As President Hollinger and I promised six months ago when we announced the formation of the Federal Police Force, today that stops."

Howell paused to gaze slowly around the Justice Department pressroom, and then continued.

"President Hollinger's wisdom in consolidating federal law enforcement into the newly formed Federal Police Force was proven today as the FPF conducted a series of raids. Almost two hundred people have been arrested and are being interrogated by the FPF. Numerous search warrants have been issued, and at this very moment, computer files and paper records and mobile phones are being searched to consolidate the mountains of evidence against these nefarious individuals. The Justice and Treasury Departments worked together to seize and freeze more than two hundred billion dollars in company and personal assets, including mansions, office buildings, private jets, helicopters, yachts and speedboats, securities, cryptocurrency, and both onshore and offshore bank accounts. Upon convictions, forfeitures of these assets will restore that stolen wealth to the rightful owners: law-abiding, loyal American patriots...our silent, forgotten majority."

Now for the coup de grâce.

"The firms that are now under indictment, and their Chief Executive Officers or Lead Managing Partners, include JBG Capital and Jeremy B. Goldstein; Deha Investments and Todd M. Silverberg; Feldman Global Holdings and Barry S. Feldman…"

* * *

Randall Weston was ready. All weekend, rumors that "something *big* is going down…and soon!" circulated on almost every murky website and social media network that he frequented. Cryptic posts instructing fanatic followers to "stand by and await specific instructions, probably on Monday" abounded.

Randall had, long ago, learned not to get his hopes up when these types of murmurings regularly popped up. After all, more than a decade ago, Randall and his ilk had been promised repeatedly that mass arrests of leading Dem politicians, ex-Republican turncoats, disloyal FBI and intelligence community leaders, Hollywood types, and fake news personalities were imminent, with either Gitmo or summary executions soon to follow. Alas, the assured detentions never came about as the goalposts were pushed time and again.

But that was then. Ephraim Hollinger, Spencer Howell, and the already ominous FPF represented an entirely new era of heavy-handed law and order. This time, justice would not be denied. Sure enough, when Howell announced the arrests of Jeremy Goldstein, Barry Feldman, and all the other thieving Jews earlier this afternoon, Randall knew with certainty that the moment had arrived. He also knew exactly what was coming next, guided by the online mind-meld that had coalesced throughout the weekend, and then the Monday afternoon posts of the promised "specific instructions," and what his role was to be, should he accept the long-awaited call to arms.

Shortly before eleven that frigid Monday evening, Randall quietly rendezvoused with a dozen other like-minded souls outside the locked gates of Denver's largest Jewish cemetery. Randall had never met any of these other men in person, though he did know most of them from social media and his frequented websites. The chained gates proved to be no problem, since several of the black-clad men had brought bolt cutters. Randall was fortunate enough to be selected to do the honors, and a couple of snips later, the gates were swung open as the men divided up into three of the cars to slowly drive, sans headlights, onto the cemetery grounds.

Along with the bolt cutters, Randall had brought a half dozen cans of black spray paint, stuffed into a camouflaged canvas shoulder bag. Everyone else was likewise equipped, as instructed. The cars proceeded about thirty yards into the cemetery until they reached pathways leading both left and right. At this point, one car peeled off to the left, another headed to the right, while the lead car continued directly ahead.

Randall was in the second car that headed to the left off of the cemetery's main road. The sedan continued for another hundred yards, and then fishtailed to a stop on the slick asphalt road. Randall and the three others quietly exited and then fanned out among the gravestones.

At this point, each man was on his own. Randall shuffled through the inch or two of snow left over from Sunday's light snowfall, searching for the headstone that would win the "honor" of becoming his first target. His eyes lit on one bearing the name "WEISSMAN" centered on the double stone, with the smaller-font names "MORRIS" and "SARAH" underneath.

He reached into the bag slung over his shoulder for one of the cans of spray paint, gave it a good shake, flicked off the plastic cap, and then took aim at the headstone. He quickly spray-painted a large swastika, end to end across the entire granite headstone. Randall's eyes had adjusted enough to the moonlit darkness to ensure that the top line of the swastika cut

The Voice of Prophets

directly through the etched "WEISSMAN" and that both "MORRIS" and "SARAH" were all but obscured by the middle line.

Randall stepped back a couple of steps to admire his handiwork for a few seconds, but then quickly moved on to the headstone directly to the left of good old Morris and Sarah Weissman's. He nailed that one quickly as well, and then defaced another, and then another. The men had agreed that twenty minutes was the most that they would spend on the cemetery grounds, and Randall was clocking three, perhaps even four, headstones a minute. They had figured that between them all, they could take care of a good six or seven hundred stones, along with the two larger structures on the cemetery grounds: the chapel where funeral services were held, and what appeared to be a maintenance building. For those larger buildings, the de facto leader of this particular mob whom the others knew only by his first name of "Kurt" had his own ideas, and had reserved both for himself.

The chapel building was floodlit, and as the allotted twenty minutes expired, the men piled back into their cars to exit the cemetery. As they drove back toward the gates, Randall admired what "Kurt" had left behind as a memento of their brief visit.

* * *

Randall was soon back in his own car and making his successful escape. Once around the corner from the cemetery grounds, he flicked on his headlights. His apartment was about twenty minutes away under normal road conditions, though with tonight's increasingly icy streets he anticipated an additional ten minutes or so of drive time.

The entire homeward trek saw Randall reliving what had just transpired. The whole night had been orgiastic! Not only the spray painting—that went without saying—but the camaraderie! For too long now, Randall's connection to similarly minded souls had been solely via the digital signals of the internet that shepherded beliefs and designs back and forth among people such as Randall. As comforting as it was to know that others, just like Randall Weston, anxiously awaited the arrival of someone like Ephraim Hollinger to once again lead them from the highest seat of power…well, it never approached the comradeship of marching side by side, chanting and with torches blazing, as Randall and the others had done at Charlottesville back in '17. Missing out on the U.S. Capitol invasion in January of '21 because of his COVID-19 hospitalization had been excruciating; Randall would have given anything to have been shoulder to shoulder with the other attackers. For so many years since that infamous January 6th, Randall Weston had wanted to actually *do* something, not just type away at a keyboard. Striking a blow on behalf of true Americans—white Christian Americans—alongside other warriors was the best of all!

Randall certainly spent plenty of time in the company of others at work and during the Friday happy hours several times each month. Yet each one of those co-workers was little more than a soulless automaton. Every so often, when someone new would join the group for happy hour, Randall would drop a couple of stealthily worded feelers to see if this newcomer might be a kindred spirit.

None ever surfaced.

But tonight, Randall's online war for an America that would soon be unchained from Jewish influence and cultural mongrelization by immigrants had fused with the interpersonal, but benign and forgettable, encounters of his "day life."

Randall Weston had been born again.

* * *

Also that night, the synagogue in Philadelphia where Jeremy Goldstein had been bar mitzvahed and where his parents still attended services was firebombed. That same night and for several more to follow, the attacks were repeated in more than a dozen other American cities and suburbs that had sizable Jewish communities, including Pittsburgh. Two synagogue buildings in Pittsburgh that dated back more than a century, to the 1920s, were targeted. The cemetery where Nathan Jacobson's wife Ida—Daniel's great-grandmother—rested was blasphemed with painted swastikas on individual gravestones as well as across buildings on the grounds. Fortunately, Ida Jacobson's gravestone was untouched; the vandals didn't make their way to the section of the cemetery where she was buried. However, more than two hundred swastikas had been hastily painted on other gravestones, the same as in Denver. The cemetery's main office that housed its prayer chapel was ominously spray-painted with "HITLER WAS RIGHT" and "ONLY THE BEGINNING, JEWS!"

Throughout the week, Pittsburghers and those in other targeted cities, as well as millions of others around the country, waited for some sort of denouncement of the violence by Ephraim Hollinger; even a halfhearted statement along the lines of "we're all Americans, and we need to coexist."

Silence.

* * *

Curiously, after exactly one week, the nightly profane vandalism against Jewish targets across America abruptly halted. No condemning pronouncement ever came forth from the president, or from the White House press secretary. Attorney General Spencer Howell likewise remained silent.

Yet the attacks suddenly ceased.

Almost as if someone behind the scenes had quietly held up a hand to signal "that's enough…for now."

Chapter 17

Phase Two quickly followed.

* * *

"Tonight we have absolutely SHOCKING breaking news captured on video," Toni Fowler began her broadcast. Behind Toni, above her right shoulder, the AVGN logo yielded to a surprisingly clear video, considering that the images had obviously been captured at night and, presumably, from a distance.

"Take a CLOSE look, Americans!" Toni's indignation redlined. On cue, the video filled the entire screen and continued rolling, showing four dark-clad, masked men exiting an older sedan that looked to be, style-wise, about twenty years old: an early or mid-2010s model. The figures blatantly strode over to what appeared to be the gates of a cemetery, making no efforts to conceal themselves or their movements. A pair of bolt cutters was produced and a few seconds later, the chain binding the cemetery gates had been cut and removed.

The surprisingly steady image followed the men inside the cemetery as they began spray-painting swastikas on gravestones.

The video shrunk back to the upper corner and paused as Toni Fowler returned onscreen.

"What do you see, America?" Toni's voice slightly—but only slightly—quivered for dramatic effect. "Supposedly this happened throughout all of last week in outraged response to the arrest of more than a dozen Jewish high-finance swindlers, all across America. *This* video was captured in a mostly Jewish suburb outside of Cleveland, Ohio. So I'll ask you again: What do you see? Purported American neo-Nazis or white supremacists or some other bogeymen attacking a Jewish cemetery and desecrating headstones with swastikas, right?"

The broadcast switched to Camera 2 as Toni shifted.

"That's what THEY want you to see!" The outrage resumed. "Let's go back to the beginning of the video and take a look at what they DON'T want you to see!"

The image, still in the upper corner of the broadcast picture, reverted to the opening frame as two highlighting ovals, one on each side of the rear license plate, drew themselves to overlay the rear bumper of the sedan.

"TAKE A LOOK!" Toni screeched as the image expanded and elongated, crowding Toni Fowler's image from the screen.

"LOOK AT THE BUMPER STICKERS!"

The wording of each was already crystal clear, but the image zoomed in toward the left sticker to leave no doubt about what Toni was highlighting. And still, despite the nighttime setting and the zoomed-in view, the characters on each bumper sticker were perfectly readable…almost as if an ultra-high-resolution, ultra-low-light camera had been used to capture this particular video.

The left-side bumper sticker read "HILLARY 2016." The letters and numerals were exceptionally crisp, showing almost no wear or fading; something one wouldn't expect after eighteen years of harsh Cleveland winters.

The image panned to the right, past the partially pixelated license plate that obscured the numbers and letters (an astute viewer could still make out the design of an Ohio plate), landing on the other bumper sticker that read "ANTIFA."

"Now look at the back window!" Toni Fowler demanded, as the zoomed-in view panned upward to a window sticker that read "BLACK LIVES MATTER."

"What we are CLEARLY looking at," Toni's incensed face was on-screen once again, "is a FALSE-

FLAG operation! We've seen this numerous times before! Leftist agitators and anarchists capitalize on a tense moment to not only cause damage and destruction, but also to pass themselves off as other groups who dare to think differently than them. And THOSE groups receive the blame! Here we have obvious radicals who weren't even smart enough to use a car without bumper and window stickers that will give themselves away! They used the arrest of swindling crooks such as Jeremy Goldstein and Barry Feldman and Todd Silverberg as an excuse for a false-flag operation to muster sympathy and cover up how broad their crimes are, and how many of their fellow globalists and anarchists are dedicated to the ruination of this once-great country!"

Time to pivot to the big finish.

"Here we have the PERFECT example of why President Hollinger's Truth and Accuracy in Media and Communications Act MUST be passed and become law! If the do-nothing, obstructionist Democrat and Republican representatives and senators cared about this once-great country, there would be a law in place to prohibit this sort of gross misinformation from being dispensed by the fake news media, trying to stir up trouble through their LIES! We may not have the votes in the House and the Senate right now, but YOU can do something about that come November!"

* * *

"I *knew* that it would turn out to be something like that," Eleanor Garfield tut-tutted to her husband as they watched Toni Fowler unmask the true perpetrators of last week's Jewish cemetery disturbances. Did those people really think that they could get away with that charade? How ignorant did they think people like the Garfields and their like-minded neighbors, and so many more people like them all around the country, really were?

Chapter 18

"How can you not be worried? They're *absolutely* going after Jews in the finance world! How can you not see that?" Claire Weber's exasperation with her husband's inflexible stance was threatening to boil over into a full-scale argument.

What a drama queen! Marc Weber thought for about the fifth time this morning. Breakfast had been an especially tense affair after Noah and Rachel had been shuttled off to school on an unusually frigid late-January morning.

She's been holding it in for a couple of weeks, but I knew this was coming.

"Come on, Claire. You sound just like your brother now. Every single thing that Hollinger does *has* to be all about hating Jews…"

"You've heard him! Ever since he began running for president!" This morning, Claire was giving no quarter to her husband. "It took a while, but eventually the Attorney General goes out and arrests every Jewish hedge fund manager and —"

"You want to exaggerate a little bit more?" Marc derisively interrupted his wife, his words dripping with condescending sarcasm. "*Every* single one, huh?"

"You know what I mean," came Claire's angry half-retraction. *Damn it! Why do I always do that? I inadvertently exaggerate something for effect, and he winds up using it to negate my entire point!*

"Look," Marc Weber reached for the key fob for his Range Rover. "I gotta get going, I have a meeting out in Cranberry, and I need to leave extra time because of the snow last night."

As Marc's eyes slid around their regal-bordering-on-pompous dining room, searching for where he had left his briefcase, he half-heartedly tried to tamp down his wife's overwrought distress. Mostly, though, Marc wanted to sufficiently extricate himself from this conversation so he wouldn't have to resume it—again!—when he returned home early this evening.

"Look, I didn't want to say anything before," he mustered the requisite soothing tones, "but I've crossed paths with a few of those guys who were arrested. I don't have any hard evidence, but I actually think they're as guilty as Howell says they are. Just because they're all Jewish...I mean, it's just a coincidence..."

"What about the cemeteries? All the swastikas?" Claire challenged.

"That's not Hollinger," Marc was ready with his defense. "Anti-Semitism is nothing new. We've always had those crazies here in the United States forever, and we always will. Every so often something really bad happens, like that synagogue shooting here fifteen years ago or whenever it was; but for the most part, they rant at each other online and then paint their swastikas, and that's it for a while. The worst thing to do is even give them any attention."

At least he didn't try to offer that bullshit story from AVGN about how it was really Jews and Blacks who actually had been the ones painting swastikas on gravestones.

"Okay, fine," Claire dejectedly surrendered.

I'm not getting anywhere with him, and I'm exhausted with this conversation anyway.

"Trust me, there's no need for you to worry over absolutely nothing," Marc Weber offered as he gave his wife a perfunctory see-you-later peck. "If Hollinger and Howell really were after every Jew who has anything at all to do with the financial world, just because they were Jewish, why would I be in consideration for a piece of several gigantic federal development deals?"

* * *

"He just doesn't see it," Claire complained to her brother.

"Oh, he sees it," Daniel contemptuously replied, almost too quickly, as if he was just waiting to unload on his brother-in-law. Michele Burgess had just begun teaching a special seminar course covering the history of Venice, and her class met during the lunchtime hour three days each week. Daniel, with the prerogative of a tenured associate professor, had his lunchtimes free. When his sister called mid-morning to see if he was free for lunch, Daniel had no problems making time for Claire, especially since today was one of Michele's lunchtime class days. Besides, Daniel wondered why Claire would brave the twenty-mile drive from the northern suburbs on the still-slick roads, all the way into the heart of the city.

"He's latched—" Daniel continued, almost using the word "leeched" instead, but he caught himself, "—onto Hollinger because he sees big bucks coming his way from all sorts of government building contracts as a reward for all of his campaign and inauguration contributions."

"Okay, fine," Claire countered. "But why won't he admit it, just to me in private, what Hollinger is clearly saying? He can play the game, but he keeps lying to me about what we're hearing with our own ears!"

Daniel had his reply locked and loaded.

"He's lying to *himself*. This way he avoids the internal conflict of putting money above principles…"

Claire's eyes shot fire, causing Daniel to abruptly halt his acidic, albeit layman's, psychoanalysis of his brother-in-law.

Daniel knew what was coming next. The whole of Claire's fuming rebuttal at the caustic characterization was contained in that single angry look. The verbal rationalization would quickly follow…as it always did.

"Maybe Marc is right," Claire quietly said, glancing down at her sandwich, avoiding her brother's eyes as she once again backed away from a principled stand. "Maybe this isn't really something to worry about."

For once, Daniel wasn't letting his sister off the hook.

"You know," he said with purposeful calm infused into his tones, "you always do that. You start to complain—and rightfully so—about something that Marc said, or did, and then as soon as I agree with you, you back off and start taking his side."

Daniel paused. Claire's eyes were still cast downward at her half-eaten grilled cheese, but Daniel's silence commanded her to again look upward. When their eyes locked, Daniel continued.

"You're not imagining things. What we're seeing *so much* parallels the early days of Nazi Germany, that you have every right to be worried. Marc can deny it all he wants, but that doesn't make it any less real."

Claire lifted her sandwich halfway toward her mouth, but then sighed and lowered it again without taking a bite.

"Yeah…"

Here comes another rationalization, Daniel knew.

"…but that's what people were saying fifteen years ago, and it all worked out. Maybe what Marc is saying is that even with a few parallels here or there, something like full-out fascism or a dictatorship can't really happen here."

Daniel snorted.

"You know that's the title of a famous book, right?"

Claire cocked her head.

"I guess 'once-famous' would be more accurate," Daniel clarified. "Anyway, back in the mid-1930s, about two years after Hitler's rise and also when Mussolini was in control of Italy, Sinclair Lewis wrote a book titled *It Can't Happen Here,* about a fascist getting elected president and then setting up concentration camps for political enemies. I read it when I was in grad school, and then reread it about a month ago. The title is obviously meant to be ironic, because that's precisely what one of the characters…"

Daniel steeled his eyes at his sister as he continued, doing his best to highlight the laser-focused relevance of what he was about to say without provoking a fight with Claire.

"…this wealthy businessman named Francis Tasbrough insists, even though paramilitary forces are already attacking protesters with bayonets, and they're holding military tribunals to send people to concentration camps. And all the while, most people in the country rationalize it away by saying 'Well, we really need to restore American prosperity and power'—remember, this was during the Depression— 'and as long as they're not coming after us…'"

Claire wanted nothing other than a rapid exit from this conversation thread.

"Speaking of books," she changed the subject, "how's your novel coming? And what's it about?"

* * *

"Wow," was Michele Burgess' response as Daniel related the substance of his unsatisfying lunchtime encounter with his sister.

"I'm not surprised, though," Michele continued. Realizing that Daniel might take her observation as a veiled attack on his sister's character, she quickly added:

"I mean that that's how most people feel. If you're not Jewish or Black or brown and a direct target of Hollinger, then…"

"But she *is* Jewish," Daniel interrupted.

"I know," Michele acknowledged with a resigned shrug. She hadn't seen Daniel this agitated since the immediate aftermath of their video and the vicious troll attacks on their great-grandfathers; and that had been more than eight months ago.

"You and I were just talking about this last week, remember?" she continued, trying to make her point and calm Daniel at the same time. "How in Germany, for almost six years up until *Kristallnacht*, way too many German Jews ignored what was happening right in front of them. It was *their* version of *It Can't Happen Here*, in real life."

Michele sighed dejectedly.

"I know how frustrating it is for you with her," she reached across the table to clasp Daniel's right hand with her own. They were once again having dinner at "their place"—the Oakland bistro where they had eaten dinner following Michele's Western Penn interview marathon, and where they had either lunch or dinner at least a couple of times most weeks since Michele's move to Pittsburgh last summer.

Daniel waited a beat or two before replying in subdued, fatalistic tones.

"She comes to me and starts complaining about Marc, and how he excuses away something terrible that Hollinger just did or said, and as soon as I agree with her, she backs off. And yeah, it's frustrating because I can't quite get her to stop rationalizing away not only Marc, but even Hollinger."

Now Daniel's voice bitterly mimicked his sister.

"Marc is probably right, everyone Hollinger had arrested just happened to be Jewish, but it's just a coincidence and got blown out of proportion, blah blah blah; and besides, it's not like Hollinger actually told anybody to spray paint swastikas all over Jewish cemeteries…"

His voice trailed off.

"Nothing I can do," he dejectedly added. "She'll either come around one of these days, or she won't. And right now, my money is on the latter."

A tight, sad smile accompanied Michele's sympathetic squeeze of Daniel's hand. At that moment, their dinners arrived. Both had ordered eggplant ravioli, the perfect entrée for a frigid January Pittsburgh evening, though Michele had asked for hers to be cooked more on the *al dente* side than the bistro usually served. The server confirmed Michele's request as she used a padded mitt to lower the plate to the table.

"Be careful, the plate is very hot," the college-aged woman warned, and then repeated the motion—and the warning—with Daniel's. The enticing aromas from their plates immediately overtook Daniel's agitation.

As had become their custom, Daniel reached for his cabernet and tilted his wineglass in Michele's direction. They always offered a toast before their first sips when the wine or beer, whatever they were drinking at any given dinner, was first served, and then repeated the ritual with a new toast before taking the first bites of their entrées.

"To enlightenment," Michele was a step ahead of Daniel in selecting this evening's toast.

"Before it's too late," Daniel rolled his eyes and offered a tight, humorless smile in return.

They abandoned conversation for a minute or two as they settled into their dinners, which were as tasty as always. Finally, Michele broke the silence, picking up the topic of Daniel's sister.

"She's one of those people who think that no matter how dangerous Hollinger sounds, the guard rails will still hold like they did, back when —"

"Guide rails," Daniel quickly, reflexively interrupted, causing Michele to tilt her head questioningly at him.

"Sorry," he actually smiled, a genuine smile for the first time this evening. "It's just…that's an instinctive reaction every time that I hear the term 'guard rail.'"

Now Michele narrowed her eyes, still not quite understanding.

"Back when I was about eight or nine," Daniel began his clarifying explanation, "we were all driving to Syracuse during the summer to visit my Uncle Mike and Aunt Sharon. Uncle Mike is my mom's brother. It was my parents, me—Claire was away at camp that summer, so she wasn't there—my grandparents before they moved to Dallas, and also Pop-pop. My parents had one of those three-row SUVs, and I was in the middle row with my grandmother. Pop-pop was in the back row with my grandfather."

Daniel paused for a quick sip of his cabernet as the recollection took shape, and then continued.

"So we were driving up I-79 toward Erie, and we were playing 'I spy,' mostly to keep me occupied. Pop-pop was asleep, which is the funny part of the story, so he wasn't playing. It was my grandfather's turn, and he goes 'I spy something beginning with a G'—"

"Isn't it 'I spy, with my little eye'?" Michele interjected with a smile that was met by an even broader smile from Daniel.

"Aha! You've played before!" he laughed.

"Hasn't everybody?" Michele laughed back.

"Anyway," Daniel picked up his story, "I was the first one to guess. So I looked out the window toward the shoulder of the highway and about a second later, I turned around to my grandfather and asked 'Is it a guard rail?' Immediately, Pop-pop—who was *asleep*, remember—mumbles 'guide rail, not guard rail.' He never opened his eyes, and to this day we're all positive that he never even woke up; he said that in his sleep."

Daniel realized that he needed to provide a touch of context to his tale.

"Remember that Pop-pop worked for PennDOT his entire career after he came home from the war. For the most part the terms 'guard rail' and 'guide rail' are used interchangeably, even though different state DOTs usually adopt one or the other for official usage. But if you think about it, the rails along the side of a highway won't absolutely prevent a car from crashing through and winding up in the woods, or maybe even over a cliff. They're more of a visual cue, especially around curves and things like that. They do provide some minimal safety, especially when you have reflectors on them at night to clue you in on where the road edges are; plus if you sideswipe one, you'll most likely bounce off rather than go off the road. So really, they *guide* you, not guard you, regardless of the terminology."

"True," Michele nodded.

"When Pop-pop worked at PennDOT," Daniel continued, "they stressed to all of the employees to use 'guide rail' rather than 'guard rail.' I heard later on that PennDOT was worried if they officially used 'guard rail' then they might have liability issues. Not sure if that's true, but it sorta makes sense."

Daniel paused for a second to smile again at the nostalgic recollection that had percolated upward from the deep recesses of his memory.

"Pop-pop was so used to correcting new employees at work who used the term 'guard rail' that I guess even though he was sleeping he still heard me say that, and instinctively corrected me. It became such an inside joke around the family over the years, and I apparently just did kind of the same thing to you."

Michele's most immediate response was to lower her fork and again reach for Daniel's left hand with her right.

"I like hearing little stories like that," she smiled.

She paused to collect her thoughts.

"We've already done a lot of 'you tell me your stories, and I'll tell you mine,' but mostly it's things from high school and college, me in the Army, both of us teaching, past relationships; those sorts of things. I hadn't thought about it before, but I honestly don't remember hearing too many stories from past boyfriends about family road trips when they were nine, or anything…I don't know, extra-personal like that."

Michele gave Daniel's hand a gentle squeeze.

"It's nice."

Warm smiles and affectionate hand squeezes now exchanged, the mood at the table considerably brightened from earlier, Michele and Daniel both settled into their dinners. A few minutes later, Michele returned to Daniel's Tale from Yesteryear.

"I never thought about that before; but legalities and usage aside, I suppose there really is a big difference between the concept of a 'guard rail' versus that of a 'guide rail.'"

The slight raising of Michele's eyes infused the air quotes into the two phrases as she continued.

"Although," she countered herself, "it's not like you would deliberately smash into one and then after you crash through, as your car is flying over a thousand-foot cliff, you're gonna be thinking on the way down, 'What the hell! I thought that was a guard rail, not a guide rail! This shouldn't be happening!'"

The epiphany slammed into Michele with the equivalent force of her hypothetical car crash, even as she was still speaking.

"*That's* what her deal is!" she immediately segued. "Your sister...Claire. You said that when she started making excuses for her husband and you called her on it, she basically said that an all-out, tyrannical dictatorship couldn't actually happen here in America; and the proof is that everything turned out okay fifteen years ago when people were worried about the same thing. Right?"

"Yeah..." Daniel's thoughts sharply vectored their way toward Michele's, though they hadn't quite yet reached the rendezvous point.

"She thinks there are actual *guard* rails out there," Michele quietly continued as a wave of nausea bubbled its way upward, instantly killing Michele's appetite. "*Political* guard rails. *Societal* guard rails. That no matter how terrifying Hollinger sounds and how deadly serious he really is about ridding this country of Jews and Blacks and immigrants, there are enough safeguards in place that he could never be successful. The system—democracy—might absorb a lot of damage, but it will still hold, just like in the past."

Daniel's mind was now fully in sync with Michele's.

"But they're *not* guard rails." Michele's hushed voice was now drenched in dread as the metaphor solidified.

"They're *guide* rails: the political checks and balances, the courts, societal norms, all of it. And there's no way they can prevent Hollinger from crashing right through them, especially if he deliberately aims for them and then hits them head-on at full speed."

Chapter 19

Daniel Jacobson's frustrating writer's block had continued through the rest of the month, and then all the way through February. Every time he opened his laptop to resume work on his novel, an impassable brick wall was quickly erected between his creativity and his fingers. Finally, in early March in the midst of this year's family Purim gathering, the turning point arrived that soon brought that wall tumbling down, as those surrounding the biblical city of Jericho supposedly crumbled long ago.

Mercifully, Marc Weber was absent from this year's gathering. Spring break for Noah's and Rachel's private school overlapped an early March Purim this year, which meant that the Weber's annual Sun Valley ski trip took precedence over *Megillah* readings and *graggers* and *hamantaschen*...and family. Claire lightly protested, but Marc remained firm: He worked hard, and this ski trip while his kids were on spring break was an annual tradition. It wasn't his fault that the alignment between the Hebrew and regular calendars fluctuated from year to year. This sort of double-booking was inevitable every so often, the same as when Hanukah occasionally came in very late December and clashed with spending the kids' Christmas-slash-winter break in the Bahamas.

Again this year, Daniel's parents hosted the family gathering. And while Claire and her family might be absent, the lost headcount was more than overcome with the arrival of Daniel's Uncle Mike and Aunt Sharon, who still lived in Syracuse, and all four of their sons and daughters. Daniel hadn't seen any of his cousins in almost five years, given that by this stage of their lives they had scattered far away to Tucson and San Diego, New Orleans and Seattle. Two of the four had married, and one of them—Daniel's cousin

Julie—had two children of her own. Months earlier, plans had been made for that entire branch of the family to come to Pittsburgh for Purim. For the first time in several years, an overflow dining table was needed, especially since Michele Burgess and her great-grandfather, Isaac Gretz, were also present.

Michele's attendance was a foregone conclusion, given her relationship with Daniel. She had, since last summer, spent a fair bit of time with Daniel's family: occasional *Shabbat* dinners, Sunday afternoon Steelers games, and last Labor Day's barbeque. No one had a single bad thing to say about Michele; she was already one of the family, or at least treated as if she was.

Isaac Gretz hadn't attended a Purim dinner for close to thirty years. The nursing home where he lived tried to cater to its moderate-sized population of Jewish residents, even though the facility was a secular one. Their efforts, however, were limited to an abridged Passover Seder each spring, as well as a small annual Hanukah party, complete with potato *latkes* for those whose dietary restrictions didn't prohibit the indulgence.

Purim, however, never made the cut. The elderly man was as frail as ever; but when his great-granddaughter made a Valentine's Day visit to Youngstown to brighten his day, and mentioned the upcoming Purim dinner at Daniel's parents', Isaac Gretz all but invited himself. Michele was immensely concerned about his ability to withstand even the relatively short drive of slightly over an hour to Pittsburgh's south suburbs, but he insisted. Finally, Michele told herself: *If that's the way he'll wind up checking out, then at least he will have had control of his own fate.*

Purim night was on a Saturday, which was perfect. Michele left for Youngstown late that morning to retrieve her great-grandfather and then circle back to Pittsburgh, with plans to arrive at Robert and Nancy Jacobson's suburban home right around four-thirty. This way, Isaac Gretz could rest from his travels, or perhaps even snooze for a bit. More likely, though, he and Daniel's Pop-pop could renew their acquaintance from almost a year earlier.

It's a shame, Michele frequently thought, *that he's not in better health to be able to bear the drive from Youngstown to Pittsburgh once in a while; he'd no doubt enjoy spending time with Nathan Jacobson.*

Following the evening of dinner and dessert and conversation, he would spend the night at his great-granddaughter's house that he had yet to see, and then sometime Sunday afternoon Michele would drive him back across the Ohio border to the nursing home. Now that Michele was ensconced in Pittsburgh, she had broached the idea to her great-grandfather that perhaps he might want to move there to be closer to her. After all, by this point, no Gretzes or Burgesses or any other family remained in Youngstown, or anywhere in eastern or central Ohio. But Isaac Gretz had flatly refused the idea. He was settled; he had friends; he had a routine.

He would, someday, die there.

* * *

The family reunion aspect of the evening was welcomed by one and all. Nathan Jacobson governed the *Megillah* reading, as usual, but the reading portions were redistributed in smaller chunks to give everyone a chance to participate. Even with Noah and Rachel absent, Julie's children were old enough to take over *gragger* duties upon each recitation of Haman's name.

Nathan and Isaac were, as expected, extremely happy to be in each other's company again. The two elderly men spent the majority of their time away from the dinner table animatedly discussing...almost everything. Isaac Gretz spent much more time than Nathan did around other elders, simply by virtue of residing in a nursing home, while Nathan lived with his grandson. Nobody else at the Youngstown nursing home, though, could rightfully be considered a true "peer" of Isaac Gretz, simply because he was at least fifteen years older than every other resident.

Beyond the age similarities for the centenarians, though, the two men had the shared experience of the war...and even Dachau. Their meeting a year ago seemed to have exorcised many of Isaac Gretz's demons of his years as a concentration camp prisoner, surrounded by constant death and vulnerable to the inhuman cruelty of his Nazi captors. Meeting one of the men who had liberated him, after the passage of almost ninety years, seemed to have blockaded many of those terrible memories that had haunted him for so long.

This evening, after the dinner plates had been cleared and the *hamantaschen* and coffee had been enjoyed, most of the Jacobson family and their guests adjourned to the oversized enclosed porch. The weather was actually warmer this year, in very early March, than it had been last year a week and a half deeper into the month. Still, Robert Jacobson left the removable windows in place for the benefit of the two centenarian great-grandfathers, even though he personally would have enjoyed the crisp, early-taste-of-spring nighttime air swirling through the porch area.

Daniel, however, remained inside to pull the first completed load from the dishwasher and put away the dishes and flatware, and then load a second round. This way, his mother could join the others on the porch now, and he would follow shortly. Daniel was about halfway done with shelving the still-warm dishes when Bob Goldman, his cousin Julie's husband, wandered into the kitchen in search of a refill for his coffee.

Daniel nodded in the direction of the recently replenished coffee pot, anticipating Bob's quest.

"Thanks," Daniel's cousin-in-law nodded as he began to pour himself another half-cup, and then turned to Daniel.

"So do you get the 'let's go kill all the Jews' portion of the *Megillah* every year?"

Daniel was instantly unsettled by Bob's abrupt, strangely worded question, but then he just as quickly reasoned that Julie's husband was simply—albeit in a peculiar manner—making small talk.

"Tradition, tradition," Daniel lightheartedly usurped the iconic *Fiddler on the Roof* verbiage.

"When you were reading that part, you sounded like you could have been sitting in a Hollinger Cabinet meeting," came the acidic response. "Amazing how so little changes throughout history."

Interesting, Daniel pondered Bob's words.

Daniel didn't know his cousin-in-law all that well. Like Marc Weber, Bob Goldman was in real estate construction. Unlike Marc Weber, Bob was satisfied with individual custom homes and partnering on the smallest-scale developments in the Seattle suburbs, and had absolutely no aspirations to become a power-wielding real estate magnate. For all Daniel knew, though, Bob Goldman might have shared Marc's insistence to excuse away the worst of Ephraim Hollinger because "he'll be good for business and the economy."

Apparently not.

"You said it," Daniel replied with a humorless smile as he extracted the last of the clean dishes from the dishwasher.

Bob Goldman apparently was in the mood to chat, since he remained standing by the kitchen doorway rather than exit in the direction of the back porch. Daniel held off any reloading the dishwasher from the stack of dirty dishes still overflowing his mother's sink, figuring that he should at least play surrogate host while Bob was still there. The food-caked dishes weren't going anywhere.

"Your girlfriend's great-grandfather is a really interesting guy," Bob quickly nodded in the direction of the porch before looking back in his cousin-in-law's direction. "It's amazing all these years later that there are still any Holocaust survivors left, let alone the very last one from Dachau."

Bob paused for a moment before continuing, seeming to Daniel as if he was collecting his thoughts.

"Can you imagine being someone who lived through the earliest days of the rise of Hitler and seeing what's going on right now with Hollinger? Listening to all of his 'blame the Jews' bullshit? It's like if someone who fought in the Revolutionary War had still been alive at the beginning of the Civil War, and saw everything that he fought for all those years ago just absolutely falling apart...I don't know if that was actually the case, but —"

"There were a few Revolutionary War veterans still alive even after the end of the Civil War, into the late 1860s," Daniel nodded as he interrupted, his extensive knowledge of American history instantly flickering to life. "So yeah, for Isaac, and for Pop-pop also, it's probably just like that."

Bob Goldman resumed his assessment.

"And then you have that dangerous asshole Howell essentially reconstructing the *Gestapo* within the Justice Department? I mean, after the war the poor guy probably figured something like 'at least the nightmare is over, and I somehow survived,' or something along those lines. And over time, I would assume, or at least hope, that all of that horror faded at least a little bit for him, even though I'm sure it never totally went away. But now, right here in the United States in 2034, it sure sounds a hell of a lot like it did in Germany a hundred years ago. And here in Pittsburgh, and for him in Youngstown, it's like 'ah, shit; it's headed our way.'"

Bob Goldman's head dropped as he sadly shook it back and forth a few times.

"The poor guy's probably thinking, 'For God's sake, we *know* where this is headed! Can't somebody do something to stop them? Or at least get the rest of the country to wake the hell up?'"

* * *

Michele Burgess had already planned to spend all of Sunday in Youngstown after she drove Isaac Gretz back to the nursing home. Partly, she wanted to spend the rest of the weekend with her great-grandfather while she had the opportunity before she returned to Pittsburgh. She even planned to take him out for a restaurant dinner, a rare treat these days for Isaac Gretz. However, Michele also wanted to closely observe him for a few more hours to make sure that the excitement and effort of the weekend didn't catch up to him all of a sudden, with resultant health problems of some type. This way, she would have some peace of mind about her great-grandfather's well-being after she got home.

Even if she had returned immediately to Pittsburgh, though, she and Daniel would most likely have spent the rest of that Sunday apart. He was now on a mission.

All night long, while tossing half-awake and then in his dreams, Daniel's mind raced, catalyzed by and swirling around Bob Goldman's words:

> "The poor guy's probably thinking 'For God's sake, we *know* where this is headed! Can't somebody do something to stop them? Or at least get the rest of the country to wake the hell up?'"

Writer's block be damned! That spontaneously erected wall that materialized each time *would* crumble. Or, in the context of Michele Burgess' former life, Daniel *would* scale and then heave himself over that wall, and then continue to overcome every other challenge awaiting him along the obstacle course until the book's completion.

If he stopped and thought about it, though, who was he—history professor Daniel Jacobson—to take it upon himself to "get the rest of the country to wake the hell up"?

But Daniel *didn't* stop and think about it. Bob Goldman's words triggered something deep inside Daniel that had been smoldering for the past ten months. The plot lines and characters and dialogue that had materialized so quickly but then frustratingly refused to gel, taking Daniel almost to the point of giving up, suddenly coalesced.

The feeling wasn't a good one, though. The solidified visions were terrifying! Perhaps the vignettes he constructed in his mind were so horrifying that his fingers had been rebelling against being asked to form the sentences and paragraphs that would give them substance and permanence; maybe that's what was behind his frustrating writer's block.

No matter. The barrier, whatever it had been, was now vanquished. Daniel wrote fifteen pages that Purim Sunday of 2034, and ten more the next day. By Monday night, when he met Michele for dinner at "their place," Daniel's novel—*The Twilight's Last Gleaming*—was finally underway.

Chapter 20

Officially, Bart Lawrence's job title was the highly generalized "Special Assistant to the President of the United States." Unofficially, Bart Lawrence's role was much more specific. If Ephraim Hollinger had been, say, an organized crime kingpin rather than president, Lawrence's picture would be pinned up on a law enforcement task-force bulletin board somewhere, underneath—but with a directly drawn line to—the boss', with the words "Enforcer/Bagman" attached to his name.

Bart Lawrence had worked for Hollinger for more than thirty years. Initially, Lawrence's shifting responsibilities were constrained to matters related to the trucking business. Hints of labor union problems? No problem: Bart Lawrence made the deals happen to give everyone a little taste of the overall pie and make the troubles go away, including stealthily shuffling payoffs to wherever they needed to wind up. A Hollinger Industries long-haul driver got out of line and busted up some small-town bar or a highway truck stop, or was arrested by a county sheriff somewhere for dealing? Lawrence would quietly take care of the damages, and then exact substantial punitive tribute from the offender for besmirching the Hollinger name.

Eventually, Bart Lawrence's talents were redirected to aid Ephraim Hollinger's efforts in political influence. He was invariably at Hollinger's side at surreptitious meetings where deals were hammered out. Afterward, Lawrence took care of making payments on behalf of Hollinger, as well as ensuring that the agreed-to quid pro quos were honored. As Hollinger began his shadowy dalliances with white nationalists and others on the fringe, Bart Lawrence treated and enforced those agreements and arrangements the same as any other political deal.

On the campaign trail, Lawrence was chiefly responsible for keeping the money flowing from both public and off-the-books top-dollar contributors. The PACs, the bundlers, the advocacy groups: all of them went through Bart Lawrence. He had developed an innate talent to discover and track the weaknesses and clandestine peccadilloes of those with whom Ephraim Hollinger dealt. Lawrence had become an expert at obtaining maximum value from those compromised individuals without exposing either himself or Hollinger through explicit threats or sketchy promises that might be recorded. Blackmail, extortion, bribery, or simple charm—all were readily accessible arrows in Bart Lawrence's well-stocked quiver.

Unlike his boss, who had adopted the perplexing habit of remaining faithful to his wife, Bart Lawrence saw no reason for such restrictions when it came to his own marriage. In another life, in another time, he would have been like so many other wiseguys, with Friday nights reserved for the girlfriend and Saturdays slotted for the wife. As it was, Bart Lawrence's rugged good looks had no fear of going to waste: short- and longer-duration mistresses, hotel bar hookups, unfaithful wives of other powerful men, and "invitation-only group parties" were plentiful.

Approaching fifty, he looked a good ten years younger. The gray was creeping into his hair, especially at the temples; but his hair remained thick, and still showed no signs of receding. He stood a couple inches shorter than Hollinger, but that still put him at a good six-three with a lean but noticeably muscled torso, the same as his boss. A photo of the two of them—just Ephraim Hollinger and Bart Lawrence—quietly conversing could be overlaid onto a grainy black-and-white image of a Brooklyn or Queens neighborhood, circa the mid-1970s, and one would swear that the two were the Don and a trusted *capo* of an old-time mob family.

The winter of '34 had passed and with spring now speeding to its conclusion, the timeline that Ephraim Hollinger had established to bring about RAVG Party domination of the United States Congress now called for the talents of Bart Lawrence.

* * *

For the most part, Ephraim Hollinger had stocked his initial Cabinet with highly competent Secretaries. Given that the RAVG Party came into existence only two years earlier, the newly inaugurated president didn't exactly have a deep bench of accomplished, long-time party loyalists to tap for key administration posts. The most critical Cabinet roles—Defense and State in particular—went to two stalwarts who had stayed with the Republican Party after the schism with the RAVGs, but who were highly respected both at home and abroad. Hollinger wasn't stupid; he knew that he couldn't afford any blowups on the international front, which meant that extremely qualified and skilled Secretaries running Defense and State were a must. Besides, he picked up a few brownie points, even from his enemies in the mainstream media, for "reaching across party lines in the interest of the country."

If they only knew...

For Health, Veteran's Affairs, Agriculture, and most of the other domestically focused positions—even Education—Hollinger went with a mixture of somewhat more moderate RAVGs, traditional Republicans, and even a token Democrat who was given the Housing and Urban Development role.

All were white Christian men of Western European ancestry, of course.

Five positions, however, had been designated for special treatment. One was Attorney General Spencer Howell, who was dedicated to permanently reshaping the structure and culture of the entire federal law enforcement machine. Next was the Secretary of the Treasury, Tom Buckner, who controlled the power of the Internal Revenue Service. Buckner would, upon instruction from Bart Lawrence as a cutout proxy for Ephraim Hollinger, set the IRS on the trail of...well, anyone. Buckner had been a fiery congressman who bolted the Republicans along with the rest of the RAVGs, and he despised Jews, minorities, and especially immigrants perhaps even more than Hollinger.

Homeland Security Secretary Braxton Knox was, in most ways, a Tom Buckner clone. Hollinger's chief difficulty with Knox, at least thus far, was restraining him from going overboard with mass immigration raids, forced detainments, expulsions from the United States, and other weapons in his war chest. "The time will come," Hollinger promised, and what the president permitted Knox to get away with to this point absolutely fed the proverbial raw meat to the RAVG Party base. Family separations—always a fan favorite —were quickly revived once Knox took over DHS to keep the venom flowing among the base, though Hollinger ordered Knox to pump the brakes and keep that whole effort on a slow burn. A totally unleashed Braxton Knox would be, at this juncture, a liability in the long game that Hollinger was playing, and the president occasionally required assistance from Spencer Howell to reign in his impatient and impulsive Homeland Security Secretary.

Those three Cabinet positions—Attorney General, Homeland Security, and Treasury—were critically important to Hollinger's intentions for his first two years in office, and thus the special treatment. Labor Secretary Stephen Channing and Commerce Secretary Jim Wiley were interesting cases, however. Both had come over to the RAVGs during the 2030 political party divorce, but neither one had made a name during his time in Congress as an ultra-right firebrand. Both Channing and Wiley had long business careers before running for their House seats, and, in fact, had done some business together.

And that was the critical piece to the puzzle.

Twenty-five years earlier, Stephen Channing and Jim Wiley had been executives at a Miami-based hedge fund. The details would require a team of forensic accountants to decipher and then patiently diagram for the layman. The upshot was that Channing, Wiley, and another partner had secretly siphoned off close to eighty million dollars during the most panicky and chaotic days of the Great Recession's financial system meltdown, and then sequestered their haul in a maze of offshore bank accounts under the cover of their hedge fund spiraling downward in flames to its death.

While the aforementioned team of forensic accountants never appeared on the scene to discover the conspiracy, the scheme was, in fact, known to a small number of "interested parties"—including Ephraim Hollinger, who uncovered the machinations when first Channing's wife, and then Wiley's, engaged in brief liaisons with Bart Lawrence. Each wife independently and indiscreetly gossiped about her husband's financial transgressions during pillow talk, and Lawrence vacuumed up the details that he conveyed to his boss.

Two of the earliest congressional campaigns that Ephraim Hollinger bankrolled were, in fact, Stephen Channing's and Jim Wiley's. Neither man was privy to Hollinger's awareness of their financial indiscretions. Likewise, for a long while neither knew that his wife had slept with the bagman-slash-enforcer of the man who had been instrumental in making their congressional aspirations a reality and then later bestowed them with Cabinet posts.

In the spirit of history repeating itself, Bart Lawrence had recently renewed his acquaintance with Lori Wiley and then, three days later, with Blythe Channing. Now, with the summer of 2034 soon arriving and the all-important midterm elections peeking over the horizon, the time had arrived to make some changes in who knew what.

* * *

Stephen Channing's experience with what was happening right now in his mahogany-paneled Labor Department office was limited to movies, television, and the occasional novel that he read to pass the time while flying. In his frame of reference, one man wordlessly sliding an unmarked, letter-sized manila envelope across a desk to a second man meant one of two possibilities: either that second man was a private investigator who was receiving a packet of essential background information as he was being hired for an investigation, or the first man was about to unveil extremely compromising and damaging information just before making a set of demands that would otherwise be rebuffed.

Stephen Channing, of course, was not a private investigator, which ruled out the first scenario.

His heart pounding, sweat now pouring down his chubby face, Channing looked away from Bart Lawrence's condescending stare and, with a trembling hand, managed to open the envelope. He was fairly certain what he would find, and he was partially correct. He didn't need to look at the details on the financial statements or offshore banking records to know that a flock of quarter-century-old chickens had belatedly come home to roost. He did, however, eject a shocked gasp at the first of the three crisp color pictures, this one exhibiting his kneeling wife with her head buried between the legs of a seated, leanly muscled nude man whose head and face had been cropped from the top of the photo.

"Let's discuss Paul Miller and Hal Steele," Bart Lawrence quietly said, referring to Channing's two senior deputies who were responsible for pulling together and validating the myriad of underlying data that went into the monthly unemployment figure that economists, the markets, and the general populace watched so carefully.

Upon Lawrence's recitation of those two names, belated clarity slammed into Stephen Channing. Something that Channing had occasionally puzzled over—why the White House had insisted on those two individuals being appointed to their respective positions last year, while they showed no interest in any other patronage throughout the Labor Department—suddenly made sense, even though he had yet to learn the sordid stories that were doubtlessly attached to those names.

* * *

An hour after departing Stephen Channing's office, after describing Paul Miller's role in an unsolved hit-and-run fatality a decade earlier and then detailing the undiscovered-thus-far massive tax fraud scheme that involved not only Hal Steele but also both of his brothers and their parents, Bart Lawrence delivered an encore performance at the Commerce Department for an audience of one: Secretary Jim Wiley. The financial documents were identical to those that had been delivered to Stephen Channing, but the first of this sequence of photos featured Lori Wiley on her back, her stocking-clad legs locked around a leanly muscled naked man on top of her, a look of ecstasy on her face that was sadly unfamiliar to Jim Wiley. As with the photos delivered to Stephen Channing, the man's head and face had been cropped from the edges of these pictures.

"Let's discuss Kyle Oliver and Jack Westfield," Bart Lawrence commanded, referring to—no surprise here—two more individuals whom the White House had long ago insisted be installed in key deputy positions, this time in the Commerce Department.

* * *

At Ephraim Hollinger's explicit direction, Bart Lawrence made his visits to the Labor and Commerce Departments on Tuesday, the sixth of June, the same day that marked the ninetieth anniversary of the D-Day invasion. Today was also the first significant milestone anniversary of D-Day in which not a single one of the Allied liberators who fought that day remained alive, and one might have expected the President of the United States to have made the pilgrimage to the Normandy beaches to mark the solemn passing of an era alongside today's European leaders.

Not Ephraim Hollinger. Victoria Baker, the White House Press Secretary, had proclaimed a month earlier that the ongoing struggle to lead the nation's economic recovery would, unfortunately, prevent the president from making the trip in person…though he would, of course, "be there in spirit" to mark the occasion.

In reality, Ephraim Hollinger couldn't care less about the D-Day invasion or the climactic drive across Europe into Germany that destroyed the Third Reich. Hitler had been on a mission to rid Europe of its Jews, but sadly had been thwarted. D-Day marked the beginning of the end of Nazi Germany, and was hardly a day for solemn, appreciative commemoration on the part of *this* President of the United States.

Hollinger's attention was instead laser-focused on another momentous anniversary.

Exactly fifty years ago, the Jew bankers came for Josiah Hollinger's farm.

Exactly fifty years ago, the greedy thieves heartlessly forced eight-year-old Ephraim Hollinger from his own home.

Exactly fifty years ago, Josiah Hollinger first ordered his son to swear that someday, Ephraim would find a way to deliver the most punishing revenge on behalf of their entire displaced family.

The President of the United States couldn't think of a more perfect date to have Bart Lawrence catalyze the all-important next phase of honoring a vow that had been made five decades earlier.

* * *

The stock market exploded on Friday, July 7th, when the Labor Department announced a shocking two-and-a-half percentage-point drop in the unemployment number, all the way down to just over eight percent. For months, unemployment had stubbornly pivoted back and forth around the ten percent mark: up a little, or down a little. In fact, the consensus of economists had been for a sizable uptick with this latest number, back up to the eleven percent mark where it had been a year earlier.

A few eyebrows were raised as the financial network talking heads and their guests dove into the numbers that didn't seem to sync up with underlying state-level data coming out of large employment hubs such as California or New York or Texas. Nevertheless, the numbers were what they were. The checks and balances were in place within the Labor Department to prevent anyone from fudging the numbers, the story went. Sometimes our forecasts turn out to be way off target, the talking heads concluded by the end of the day, and the official numbers turn out better—even much better—than we think they'll be. No sense in looking the proverbial economic gift horse in the mouth, right?

Three weeks later, another bombshell report rocketed the markets upward again when the second quarter gross domestic product number came in at a blistering four percent increase. Similar to expectations for the unemployment stats at the beginning of the month, economists had been anticipating anemic GDP growth of less than half a percent…or possibly even slipping back into negative territory. But here it was: the second extremely positive shock-and-awe report of the month!

On August 4th, unemployment ticked down another three-quarters of a percentage point, to slightly over seven and a quarter percent. Immediately following Labor Day, the slightly delayed September unemployment number dove further, to six and a half percent. By this time, tongues were wagging that something was amiss. Ephraim Hollinger had, of course, anticipated the inevitable claims by his political and media adversaries that the books weren't only cooked, they had been turned into a gourmet banquet. That second Thursday of September was the occasion for a morning press conference at the Justice Department, where Attorney General Spencer Howell, flanked by three of his trusted aides, proclaimed that he had already taken it upon himself to launch an investigation into the integrity of the financial numbers coming out of the Labor and Commerce Departments.

"I am fully satisfied," came Howell's proclamation, "that the checks and balances are firmly in place to prevent not only willful manipulation of these all-important economic statistics, but even accidental error. My senior team from the Justice Department"—he nodded to the three men standing sternly to his right—"has fully and independently audited the work being performed by the Secretary of Labor, Stephen Channing, and also his two top deputies, Mister Paul Miller and Mister Hal Steele, who are responsible for consolidating and verifying the unemployment numbers and then finalizing them with Secretary Channing. Likewise, the work of Secretary Wiley at Commerce and his two top deputies, Mister Kyle Oliver and Mister Jack Westfield, have also been thoroughly audited and found to be infallible."

* * *

"This is what our great President Hollinger has been able to accomplish, even with the obstructionist Democrats and Republicans doing everything they can to TAKE HIM DOWN!" Toni Fowler shrieked later that night, hours after the Attorney General huffily cleared the Hollinger administration of even a hint of economic reporting chicanery. "Imagine how much MORE President Hollinger will be able to do with a Congress that is on his side, rather than working to destroy not only him but also YOU, the Silent Majority! Remember ALL of this in November, when we ALL get our chance to save our great country's history and culture and RESTORE AMERICAN VALUES AND GREATNESS!"

In Denver, Randall Weston expressed his appreciation for Toni Fowler's vehement testimonial to Ephraim Hollinger in his usual manner.

In Florida, Eleanor and Edmund Garfield relished their favorite AVGN anchor's recitation of the president's latest victory over the entrenched Deep State and their evil designs to undermine everything that was good and true about America.

In suburban Pittsburgh, Marc Weber was still suspicious about the unemployment and GDP reports over the past couple of months; they *really* didn't feel right. Marc was suspicious…but not bothered. Even if Hollinger's guys at Labor and Commerce were cooking the books, the resultant boost in consumer and business confidence would likely make those statistics a self-fulfilling prophecy, sooner or later. And that, of course, would be a great thing for Marc Weber's fortunes.

Chapter 21

For many, October of 2034 was a heartbreaking vigil, mournfully awaiting the inescapable beginning of the end of American democracy. For others, that same month was the jubilant fourth quarter of a blowout championship football game, exuberantly and drunkenly counting down to the inevitable moment when the lopsided final score in favor of their team was in the record books for all eternity.

Depending on one's perspective, the evening of November 7th, 2034, marked either the time of death or the moment of vengeful, supreme triumph.

* * *

"The only remaining question at this point is exactly how many Senate and House seats President Hollinger's party will capture," John Culverson opined to his election night co-anchor, Craig Ryan. Culverson's voice remained steadily professional, which was a notable accomplishment, given that in his mind, the sixty-four-year-old man was channeling the rage-filled, iconic "I'm mad as hell…" on-air rant from the classic 1970s movie *Network*. John Culverson's tirade, though, would have been more along the lines of "WHAT THE ALMIGHTY FUCK IS WRONG WITH ALL OF YOU PEOPLE! LOOK AT WHAT YOU'VE DONE!"

Craig Ryan's own morose thoughts were fully synchronized with those of his co-anchor. As of this moment, Hollinger's party held thirty-five seats in the Senate, a substantial minority. In slightly less than two months, on January 3rd, the United States Senate would become the home to at least sixty-two RAVG Party members, with only a handful of senatorial races remaining to be called—all of which were tilting to RAVG victories. Hollinger's party would also more than double their presence in the House, from the current 153 to at least 310.

Hollinger was on the verge of possessing and wielding untethered power, with the coronation soon to follow.

"We have to go back almost a hundred and eighty years," Craig Ryan chimed in, trying his best to dispassionately add a little historical context and color commentary to the glum broadcast, "to the elections in the second half of the 1850s, to find anything even close to equivalent in American history. The election two years ago was very similar to that of 1854, when the Whig Party collapsed and the Republican Party came into existence. The Democrats maintained a strong advantage in the Senate amid all the chaotic shuffling between the Whigs and Republicans. But over the next three elections, the new Republican Party kept making gains in both the Senate and the House until finally, in 1860, they had control of both branches of Congress."

"And that, of course, was immediately before the Civil War," John Culverson couldn't fully keep the bitter irony from invading his words.

"That's absolutely correct, John." This time, Craig Ryan's mournful voice likewise left viewers with no illusions about his reaction to the night's election results.

* * *

The AVGN election night broadcast, of course, was far more jubilant than any of those offered by—in Toni Fowler's vindictively triumphant word salad—"the lamestream media enablers of the detestable, loser Deep State and their despicable supporters who hate this country and its patriots." AVGN scripts in general were stuffed with sentences that overdosed on pejoratives, but Toni Fowler's lead writer was in a class by himself, even among the many right-wing media veterans who staffed the network's writing teams.

"Now we'll see our magnificent President Hollinger bring out the big guns," Keenan Lucas sneered. Ordinarily, Lucas was third in the AVGN pecking order, underneath Hayden Lafferty but above Tristan Wyatt. In recent months, however, Lucas' ratings had skyrocketed, thanks in no small part to having passionately taken up the cause of United States Army Major General Frank Douglas.

Earlier this year, charges had been brought against General Douglas, accusing him of having perpetrated and then covered up a horrific massacre of civilians during the darkest days of the Iraq War, almost three decades earlier when Douglas had been a first lieutenant platoon leader. Rumors occasionally surfaced within Army circles over the years that Douglas "had done something," but not until the early 2031 suicide of one of the now-general's former platoon members—and the suicide-note-slash-confession the tortured man left behind that accused Douglas—did the Army begin a formal investigation of the man and the incident. The passage of so many years presented a significant challenge to the Army's criminal investigators, but they doggedly pursued the matter. Three years later, a court-martial was convened to try the now-two-star general on twenty counts of premeditated murder, along with a host of associated war crimes.

General Douglas was convicted. His team of military and civilian lawyers immediately requested clemency from the court-martial convening authority, which was denied. Next came the Army Court of Criminal Appeals, and this is where the American Values and Greatness Network came into the picture.

Right-wing media had learned long ago that one of the best ways to inject the masses with a fresh dose of outrage was to take up the cause of a supposedly wronged "American military hero," suffering mightily at the hands of the "libs and Dems who hate their country and its military." And while all of AVGN's prime-time programs played a role in advancing the cause of a presidential pardon for General Frank Douglas, Keenan Lucas quickly became the most vocal advocate of the convicted war criminal.

The pardon from Hollinger, along with the presidential order to award Major General Douglas a third star and once again assign him to lead a combat command, was issued on Labor Day. To the American Values and Greatness Network and RAVG Party crowds—which were essentially one and the same—Keenan Lucas became almost as much of a hero as the pardoned general. Toni Fowler still had a death grip on the "hot blonde anchor" slot at the American Values and Greatness Network and for now remained Bob Platte's go-to broadcast personality; but Lucas had made his move and was galloping up on the outside in the race for the wire that signified supremacy within the AVGN ranks. As a result, Keenan Lucas—not Hayden Lafferty—shared election night anchor duties with Toni Fowler.

"That's exactly right," Toni Fowler sneered at her co-anchor. To the AVGN audience, Fowler's hate-filled look was, of course, intended for their common enemies: the defeated Democrats and Republicans, traditional broadcast and print media, Hollywood, the Deep State military leaders who weren't true warriors...all of them. Toni Fowler and her spray-tanned cleavage just happened to be facing Keenan Lucas at that moment.

In fact, Toni Fowler had grown to despise Keenan Lucas, and her narrowed eyes and triumphantly ugly facial expression were also directed at him. His newfound stature at AVGN in the aftermath of the now-Lieutenant General Frank Douglas matter marked a clear and present danger to her own position in the pecking order. To their audiences, Bob Platte's prime-time anchors were portrayed as a tight-knit group of selfless team players, fanatical in their combined efforts to advance Ephraim Hollinger's agenda and help restore American values and greatness.

The four AVGN prime-time anchors were, in reality, the proverbial nest of vipers, nervously eyeing each other and awaiting the inevitable strike.

* * *

Tonight's AVGN programming was structured differently than normal to deliver the election results, meaning that Toni Fowler's regularly scheduled hour-long program was preempted. Consequently, Randall Weston engaged in a bit of multitasking this evening. He certainly kept an eye on Toni's and Keenan Lucas's elated recitation of RAVG Party victories not only in the Senate and the House, but in state and local elections across the country. Governors and mayors, state senators and legislators, judges, county sheriffs— especially sheriffs!—all rode the RAVG Party wave. Many who had cut their teeth in state legislatures more than a decade earlier, with waves of vindictive voter suppression laws and repeated demands to recount their states' 2020 presidential election ballots over and over, were now headed to Congress. No worries: Like-minded confederates were easily elected to those state-level seats, along with local school boards and other bodies to maintain the American Values and Greatness movement's stranglehold on so much of the political apparatus across the country.

The elitist liberal enclaves on both coasts appeared to have held at the state levels, but they were broadly speckled internally with victorious RAVG Party incursions. Across the rest of the nation, RAVG Party brown erased almost all of the last vestiges of Democratic Party blue and Republican Party red, except for offices not up for re-election this year.

For those Democratic and Republican officeholders who would continue into 2035 solely by the grace of their respective election calendars, their reckonings were coming sooner or later. Two years earlier, with the American economy down for the count, Ephraim Hollinger had vowed to restore American values and greatness. The vastly improved unemployment and GDP numbers over the past several months were the

The Voice of Prophets

proof that whatever Hollinger was doing was working. Ephraim Hollinger had earned the trust of a relieved and grateful nation, and now deserved the broad support across the rest of the governmental landscape to finish the job; that's how AVGN framed where tonight's inarguable election night verdict would lead next.

However, while Randall watched the election results and relished in the triumphant commentary, he also bounced around his favored internet sites and social media platforms, celebrating in the virtual company of his comrades in arms. He posted frequently, both original entries as well as numerous replies and comments on existing threads. He trolled the defeated libs at every opportunity, warning via all-caps posts that "WE'RE COMING FOR YOU NOW!" and "MAYBE YOU SHOULD LEAVE THE COUNTRY RIGHT NOW WHILE YOU STILL CAN!"

As the night progressed, Randall Weston's thoughts headed in the direction of the night at the Jewish cemetery, back in January. The sensation of camaraderie he had experienced that night was now a painful ache—the only damper on this triumphant evening. In another life, Randall Weston would have rendezvoused tonight with "Kurt" and the others, and they would be wildly celebrating the RAVG victories in each other's company at an overflowing, decibel-crushing Denver bar. No doubt some mouthy Jew or Jew-lover would make some snide comment, causing Randall and the others to stomp the absolute shit out of him, along with anyone else stupid enough to interfere with the beat-down. Conjured images of grainy, hundred-year-old newsreel films of Hitler's brownshirts violently taking control of the streets of Berlin and Munich and Nuremberg rolled through the theater of Randall Weston's mind. He saw himself in their midst, much as he once marched in the company of their spiritual descendants at Charlottesville.

Maybe soon, Randall thought. *Maybe very soon.*

* * *

"They still got the courts to deal with," Duncan Heltefer mused to his wife Darlene, Edmund and Eleanor Garfield, and more than two dozen others ensconced in the community clubhouse who had gathered to watch the election returns on AVGN.

"Those courts still got a bunch of those…whada they call 'em, activist judges," the transplant from South Dakota continued, his words even more slurred than they were ten minutes earlier. "And a lotta 'em are Jews. Hollinger needs to clear 'em all outta there and get real Americans in those judge jobs. Otherwise, every time Congress tries to get somethin' done about the economy and the immigrants and everything else, the Jews and the other liberals are gonna block 'em, just like we seen before."

"He will," Edmund Garfield confidently proclaimed.

"Yeah," Clyde Carver seconded Edmund's opinion. "Might take a little while, but I'll bet before the next election the whole court system will look a shitload different than it does today. Ain't no liberal judges getting through all those RAVG Party senators…not that Hollinger would nominate any libs, anyway. But now the DemonRats can't block him no more, so we can get some *real* hard-ass judges in there. Just wait!"

To a man, Edmund Garfield, Duncan Heltefer, and the others wouldn't have traded the camaraderie of relishing these glorious election night returns in each other's company. The paradox of the American Values and Greatness movement was that while its credo was a defiant "Individualism Trumps Society," the true power of the movement was drawn from the steely bonds of tribalism.

"Looks like Hollinger's kickin' up the swamp drainin' a coupla notches tonight," Duncan Heltefer slur-snorted as he reached for his quarter-full bottle of big-box-store house-brand bourbon that he had freshly cracked barely three hours ago. Another House race, this one a surprisingly close contest out in

Oregon, had just been called for the RAVGs: time for another celebratory refill! He knew that a monster hangover would be waiting for him tomorrow morning, and probably some puking later tonight; but the rushing stream of victorious news delivered by Toni Fowler and Keenan Lucas sure as hell made it worthwhile.

Darlene Heltefer and Eleanor Garfield and Judy Carver and the other wives mostly just listened to their husbands ruminate about how tonight's election results would soon reshape politics and society. Occasionally one of the women would interject a touch of commentary, but for the most part their contributions were of the "uh-huh" and "that's right" variety. The wives seemed satisfied silently savoring the victorious evening and leaving the talking to their men, and allowing their minds to invoke soothing images of the not-so-distant future when the rest of the country would mirror the compliant tranquility of their own daily lives down here in American Values and Greatness Network country.

* * *

Claire Weber went to bed early on election night. Alone.

Marc Weber was prescient enough to avoid his wife for the rest of the evening, and probably all of tomorrow…and maybe the following day or two as well. He remained downstairs, watching the election returns as the background portion of his mind went to work contemplating what the magnitude of the RAVG Party conquest might mean to his business. He had spread his money around to numerous Senate and House and state races, using every possible vehicle available to him. Certainly his continued loyalty to Hollinger's party would be amply rewarded.

Upstairs, Claire had no interest in watching any more of the election night broadcast. John Culverson's look of despair had deepened by the minute, and Craig Ryan's prognostication about what January 2035 might bring with an unleashed Ephraim Hollinger dragged her to the verge of throwing up.

She flicked off the television, but against her better judgment, grabbed her phone to thumb through a couple of social media sites. Misery loves company, and the only source of sympathetic mourning tonight for Claire Weber would have to come from outside her house.

Ten minutes later, Claire dejectedly shut her phone. Interwoven with angst-filled "the end is nigh" posts were endless hate-filled warning shots and outright threats: anything from "EAT IT LIBS!" to "MAYBE YOU SHOULD LEAVE THE COUNTRY RIGHT NOW WHILE YOU STILL CAN!" to "WARM UP THE OVENS FOR THE JEWS—HERE WE COME!" American Jews certainly weren't the only ones targeted; posts abounded that threatened both documented and undocumented immigrants ("CAGES FIRST, THEN SEND THEM ALL BACK") and, of course, African-Americans ("BLACK LIVES DON'T MEAN SHIT NOW!").

Mercifully, Claire was asleep when Marc finally came to bed. Even the nightmares that haunted her sleep the entire night were preferable to looking her husband in the eye.

* * *

Neither Michele Burgess nor Daniel Jacobson could bear to be inside either her house or his condo tonight. They needed to be outside, under the sky. They needed to be able to look heavenward and do their best to convince themselves that somewhere up there, God—or any supreme being, at the moment they weren't being picky—had some divine plan that perversely included the American electorate moving en masse to the Dark Side.

Michele had told Daniel the night of her Western Penn interview, as they arrived at her hotel's bar for a nightcap after that first dinner together, that she wasn't much of a drinker. She knew by now that neither was Daniel; each of them almost always stopped after two glasses of wine or a couple of beers. On a rare occasion and with enough available post-dinner time to sit and relax, a third might be called for…but never more than that.

Tonight proved to be the exception to the rule for Michele Burgess. She was on her fifth beer, with a strong possibility that at least one more would be in order. Yet she gave absolutely no indication that she was anywhere near drunk. She wasn't slurring her words, and the three times—so far—that she had made a restroom trip, she didn't come close to staggering or even hesitating for a beat or two.

They grimly talked, and as the night went on, Michele Burgess no longer looked much like the "nice Jewish girl" whom Daniel's mother once might have pointed out during Saturday morning services as a possible match for her still-single son. She no longer radiated the scholarly-yet-approachable appearance of a popular history professor at Western Pennsylvania University, or even at West Point. She was once again Major Michele Burgess: Infantry, Army Rangers, Special Forces Green Beret. Small arms expert, combat zone sniper, and skilled practitioner of special operations. Her eyes had hardened as they coldly awaited a visual on the enemy that she knew was now in position just over the horizon.

* * *

Isaac Gretz was frightened: but strangely, not for himself. He feared for his great-granddaughter Michele. He feared for Michele's parents—his own granddaughter and her husband—down in Houston. Isaac's own children and their spouses—an entire family generation—had all passed, and mercifully they would be spared what lay ahead. But he feared for every other one of his descendants who were scattered around the country.

Isaac Gretz had been here before. He hadn't heard Bob Goldman muse to Daniel Jacobson this past

Purim that "The poor guy's probably thinking, 'For God's sake, we *know* where this is headed!'" but those conjectured thoughts exactly matched what the centenarian had resignedly pondered since the first election results became official earlier this evening.

His own brothers and sisters had perished in the ghetto or the camps long ago, as did their parents. Isaac was the only one of them granted a second chance at life. *I survived and lived to become a very old man,* he reminded himself. *After Dachau, I've had a very long, blessed, and content life. They can't take that away from me.*

His heart ached for all of his descendants whom, he was sadly certain, would not be able to declare those same words about a blessed and content life.

Chapter 22

Political shock tends to wear off and surrender to an anesthetizing amalgamation of the triple-Rs: resignation, retrenching, and rationalization. What Michele Burgess and Daniel Jacobson had come to think of as "the guard-rail theory" takes over, largely because to contemplate the alternative is to acknowledge that "civilization" is little more than the thinnest, flimsiest veneer overlaying a societal cesspool of callous and brutal selfishness.

Things can't get too bad, right? After all, this is the United States of America, and we go back a long, long time; we even survived a Civil War, right? Even the attempted insurrection at the Capitol fizzled out.

Hollinger and the RAVGs will make life miserable for illegal aliens; but for American citizens, will there really be any difference in our day-to-day lives?

You'll probably see a rise in local police and the FPF using excessive force, especially in the major cities against Black people; but as long as you stay out of trouble, it won't affect you personally.

The media—other than AVGN—will hold him to account; and besides, there's only so much the courts, especially the Supreme Court, will let the RAVGs get away with.

The American electorate is notoriously fickle; if the RAVGs get too extreme, they'll pay for it in the '36 election, so that should constrain them...at least a little.

Worst case, we take to the streets and make our collective voice heard.

* * *

The morning of Election Day, Daniel was, by his estimate, slightly more than halfway finished with his novel. One month later, as Hanukah arrived, he was nearly finished. He wrote with a renewed purpose. Daniel Jacobson was definitely not a subscriber to "the guard-rail theory" that had settled over much of the country in the month following the election. The dystopian America that had solidified in his mind and which had taken form in his novel was frighteningly real.

Why bother, he had argued with himself in the days immediately following the election. *Hollinger now has a stranglehold on Congress, and God knows what they'll do.*

The other side of Daniel's mind countered with this assertion: *We have one final chance to set things right, in two years. Maybe they'll overreach, and the country will wake up and realize that we don't actually want the reincarnation of Hitler in the White House and today's version of the Nazi Party with a stranglehold on Congress.*

Writing the novel had become a cathartic exercise. Daniel had created the most horrifying apocalyptic world that he could imagine, and maybe—just maybe—the picture he had painted would shock a few people here and there back into sensibility before the next election. Daniel harbored no grandiose illusions that his novel, if it was to be published and wound up selling some copies, would become any sort of inflection point, or *the* catalyst for some broad anti-Hollinger movement. He simply wanted to avoid the feeling of utter helplessness that came with being totally sidelined and out of the fight. His novel had become his weapon.

An acquaintance of Daniel's from his undergrad days worked at a public relations firm, and she had a friend who had a friend…everybody knows how the relationship chain sometimes goes when seeking out someone, anyone who might help turn aspiration into reality. In Daniel's case, that friend of a friend of a friend had been an established literary agent for more than a decade. Upon hearing thirdhand about the premise of Daniel's novel, she sent word back through the chain to Daniel, asking to read the manuscript. Daniel still had about fifty pages remaining to write out of an estimated five hundred total, and he was still a bit fuzzy about *exactly* how the story would conclude.

Nevertheless, he certainly was not going to pass up this opportunity, so he emailed a copy of his nearly complete manuscript, along with a synopsis, on a Thursday afternoon in mid-December.

That Saturday afternoon, the agent—Paula Fontana—emailed Daniel: "Fantastic! I want to shop it for you!" along with a representation agreement, which he quickly signed.

The following Tuesday morning, Daniel thumbed open his email on his phone, and the index line for the first unread message jumped off his screen.

Paula Fontana 7:29 a.m.
Great news!!!!

Daniel hesitated for a few seconds before opening the message.

From: **Paula Fontana >**
To: **Daniel Jacobson**

Great news!!!!
Today at 7:29 a.m.

Dan—I already have 2 publishers who want your novel! I'm going to put it to auction this week. There's a chance we might hear something even before the end of the year, seems like almost every publisher is looking for Hollinger dystopia right now after the election. Stay tuned!

Two days after Christmas, in the middle of what would normally be the quietest week of the year in publishing, Daniel's phone dinged to indicate an incoming text message.

CHECK YOUR EMAIL ASAP!
GREAT NEWS!

The email message that followed the all-caps text:

From: **Paula Fontana >**
To: **Daniel Jacobson**

Sold!!!!
Today at 2:22 p.m.

Dan—Congratulations, you're about to be a published novelist! Here's the details:

* * *

"I still can't shake the feeling that I'm only tilting at windmills," Daniel half-smiled at Michele as they did their best to celebrate the sale of his novel and the end of a manic 2034 and usher in the uncertain new year.

Michele reached across the restaurant table to take Daniel's hand in hers, tuning out the boisterous commotion surrounding them.

"Maybe if enough people read your novel, it'll become part of the backlash after Hollinger and the new RAVG Congress really go out onto the lunatic fringe. Right now, it's all theoretical what they will or won't actually do, but we know it's coming. Once they start, though, maybe people will *really* start coming together against them. And you never know, maybe your book will be one of the ones that they read for inspiration, especially since it's going to end with Americans coming to their senses. You can contact

Craig Ryan and line up a bunch of interviews on his network, and then leverage that..."

The distant look in Daniel's eyes instantly caught Michele's attention, and she interrupted herself.

"That's still how you're going to end the story, right?" Daniel had written about thirty pages since receiving word that Paula Fontana had sold his novel, but still had another fifteen or twenty pages remaining to complete. Also, he intended to circle back for an additional deep editing pass on the final third, or maybe even more, of his manuscript.

"Uh-huh," he finally responded after a long hesitation.

A deep sigh preceded what he said next.

"I guess so. But I don't really believe it anymore."

Chapter 23

Sometimes, one's momentous undertaking calls for moving slowly; methodically. Other times, a person on a mission moves at light speed.

The first two years of Ephraim Hollinger's presidency constituted the former. Now arrived the occasion for the latter.

Administration shake-ups following midterm elections were nothing new in American history; but the tsunami that was January 2035 and which continued through the winter months was unprecedented.

* * *

The changing of the guard in both the House and the Senate took place on Wednesday, January 3rd. Two days later, shortly after noon, Ephraim Hollinger launched his first salvo in the White House Press Briefing Room.

"Today I am announcing the following changes in my Cabinet," Hollinger began, his expression and his voice both more tersely matter-of-fact than usual.

"I am immediately relieving the following Cabinet officials from their respective positions, and likewise immediately replacing each one with an acting Secretary who will serve in that capacity until their confirmations in the Senate…"

Hollinger apparently wasn't giving anyone the opportunity to play the "submitting my resignation to spend more time with my family" game, Craig Ryan grimly realized as he eyed and listened to the president. Anyone being replaced was being summarily—and publicly—fired. Not one of them was thanked by Hollinger for his service. They were being wiped from existence, at least in terms of their political futures.

By the time ninety seconds had passed, ten Secretaries—a full two-thirds of Hollinger's Cabinet—no longer held their positions. Three of the holdovers whose names were not announced were hardly a surprise to Ryan, or to any other press member present to witness the executions. Spencer Howell would remain Attorney General; Braxton Knox would still helm Homeland Security; and Tom Buckner stayed on as the Secretary of the Treasury.

The two others who survived the purge—Commerce Secretary Jim Wiley and Labor Secretary Stephen Channing—were somewhat unexpected, considering that the other traditionalists in the Cabinet who most closely mirrored these two in background, temperament, and doctrine were being shown the door. Upon realizing that both Wiley and Channing would continue on, and reflexively thinking back to the shockingly positive economic reports that began in lockstep last July and which proved to be rocket fuel for the RAVG November victories, Craig Ryan's news radar again lit up.

Were Channing and Wiley being kept around because they had somehow "proven useful" and could continue to do so? There's a story here…

The incoming acting Secretaries, to a man (and every one of them was, of course, a middle-aged, white Christian man), resembled Howell and Buckner and Knox far more closely than the men they were replacing had. All of the newcomers were RAVG loyalists; all were firebrands when it came to far-right political and societal stances; and all had been staunchly aboard the Hollinger train since the earliest days of his candidacy back in 2031. Almost all of them were veterans of the whole "Stop the Steal" bullshit almost a decade and a half ago, either in Congress or at the state level. All had spent the first two years of the Hollinger administration in either the Senate or the House, doing their best to frustrate the designs of the Democrats and traditional Republicans through constant destabilization and outright sabotage. Each was also from a state with an existing or newly elected RAVG Party governor, who would now appoint a clone to any newly vacated Senate seat. In the case of suddenly vacated House seats, special elections for successors would easily be won by up-and-comers among the RAVG-controlled state legislatures. In all cases, the RAVG Party would maintain their embryonic overwhelming party majorities on both sides of Congress.

All were fully aligned with Hollinger and Howell and Knox and Buckner when it came to their dark vision of a permanently altered America that they would soon make a reality.

And now, all of them were about to be unleashed.

* * *

The next blow was landed exactly three weeks later, on another Friday afternoon. Gil Reed, the unapologetic white nationalist former Missouri congressman confirmed by the Senate as the new Secretary of Defense four days earlier, stepped to the podium in the Defense Department briefing room to deliver his bombshell.

"As Secretary of Defense, I serve the president as his principal adviser and policy maker in all matters related to the defense of the United States of America. I am responsible for carrying out the president's orders and wishes regarding the structure and leadership of all branches of the military. Accordingly, today I am announcing the following changes in the composition of the Joint Chiefs of Staff in accordance with the president's directions…"

When the dust had settled, less than two minutes later, each of the four-star generals currently serving as the chief of staff for his respective service had been relieved of that responsibility and forced into retirement. Each newly announced replacement had, during the past two years, cultivated favor with influential RAVG Party leaders, and was widely known to be significantly more partisan in word and deed than the traditional apolitical stance of the United States military and its leadership. All would require Senate confirmation, which naturally would be little more than a formality.

A new Chairman of the Joint Chiefs of Staff was also announced. To many, the elevation of AVGN idol Frank Douglas, abruptly bestowed with an additional star for the second time in less than five months, to the JCS Chairman position was the single most shocking nomination of January's unprecedented reshaping of the Cabinet and the joint chiefs. If one took a step back, though, a convicted-but-now-pardoned war criminal speedily rising from the ashes—with more than a little help from Bob Platte's American Values and Greatness Network—to become the nation's top uniformed military officer should hardly have been a surprise in the opening moments of the Ephraim Hollinger era's second act.

By the conclusion of January 2035, the executive branch of the federal government had been transformed beyond recognition. The United States Congress was also now under new ownership, and so far had been busy confirming Hollinger's new Cabinet and military appointees as fast as the names could be sent to the Hill…as well as rapidly and quietly drafting Hollinger's long-desired legislation that would soon be unveiled.

Ephraim Hollinger was far from finished, of course, as he now shifted his attention to the courts.

Chapter 24

Back in the autumn of 2033, during Michele Burgess' first semester teaching at Western Penn, one of her assigned courses was "The History of the United States Federal Government." The course was dual-listed with the school's political science department, meaning that out of Michele's forty students that semester, about half were from Michele's new home in the history department while the rest were poli sci majors.

Michele's syllabus listed a short introductory overview chapter in the textbook as an assigned reading before the first class. Daniel had warned her, though, that many of the students would show up for that first session without having done the reading. Rather than give the class a graded pop quiz during their very first class, Daniel suggested that a no-credit, round-robin series of quiz-show-style questions, thrown out to the students with the implied warning that "Ahem: This was *all* in your assigned reading" would be a better approach. Michele had originally planned to go the graded pop quiz route, as she had frequently done while teaching the Army cadets at West Point. Daniel knew the Western Penn culture much better than she did, though, so she yielded to his suggestion.

"Okay, first question," Michele began once the class introduction formalities had been concluded and she informed them that the "quiz show" was about to commence, "how many justices sit on the United States Supreme Court?"

"Nine," came the answer from at least a dozen students in the class.

"Correct," Michele nodded. "That was a really easy warm-up question, so here's the second one. True or false: That number of Supreme Court justices—nine—is specified in the United States Constitution."

Dueling "true" and "false" answers were quickly shouted by a handful of her students…but far fewer students than those who quickly answered her first question. A few stragglers threw out their answers—each one of the laggards offered "true"—and then silence fell.

"Okay, let's take a vote," Michele replied. "Show of hands: How many of you are answering 'true,' that the Constitution specifies the number of Supreme Court justices? And everyone has to vote on this question: either true or false."

A large number of hands were raised quickly, again followed by some stragglers. After Michele called for any final votes and no others appeared, she did a quick visual: about thirty students had answered "true."

"Okay, just to be official here, how many of you think the answer to that question is 'false'"?

Only about half of the remaining students raised their hands, and after a few more seconds passed, Michele gently prodded: "Everyone has to vote; so by default, anyone who hasn't raised a hand is voting 'false'—so you might as well raise your hand now."

The remaining five hands were reluctantly raised, yielding exactly ten "false" votes.

"And the ten of you who answered 'false' have answered that question correctly. Even though the Supreme Court itself is specified in Article III of the Constitution, the number of Supreme Court justices is not. Which brings us to question number three: Where or how *is* that number specified?"

"By Congress," a female student in the front row quickly replied.

"That's correct," Michele nodded as she gazed at the student's cardboard name tent, which read "Jeri Kraft."

"Jeri, not to put you on the spot, but can you give us a quick rundown from the reading of significant milestones regarding the size of the Supreme Court?"

Michele then added, addressing the class as a whole:

"Oh, and by the way, you can consider this as a pretty good example of the type of essay question that you might see on a quiz or exam...hint, hint."

A few of the students chuckled.

Jeri Kraft had obviously done her reading, since she began her synopsized narrative with the Judiciary Act of 1789 that established a six-member Supreme Court, and proceeded through the congressional machinations in the immediate aftermath of the Civil War that jumped the number of justices all over the place, eventually settling at the current number of nine.

"Very good job," Michele nodded approvingly. "Here's another follow-up question: Who can tell the rest of us what 'court-packing' means in the context of the Supreme Court?"

Crickets from the majority of the class, though Jeri Kraft offered a tight smile that signaled to Michele that she knew this answer as well.

"Okay, Jeri—would you like to answer this one as well?"

Jeri Kraft ran through another concise narrative, this one describing Franklin D. Roosevelt's frustration with the Supreme Court finding portions of his New Deal legislation to be unconstitutional. In response, after being re-elected president in 1936, FDR attempted to "pack" the Supreme Court by adding additional justices to tilt the balance in favor of his upcoming New Deal efforts. Roosevelt's congressional allies introduced the legislation in early 1937, but Congress as a whole refused to go along with the president's plan, even though FDR's Democratic Party held majorities in both the House and the Senate.

"Professor Burgess?" The raised hand came from the back row.

Michele strained slightly to read the student's name tent, especially since he had used a thin ballpoint pen.

"Does that say Cleon?"

"Uh-huh."

Apparently Michele Burgess' eyesight was still as sharp as when she went through Army sniper training a while back.

"Okay, Cleon: You have a question?"

"Um, yeah. So let's say Hollinger decided that he wanted, like, five more justices on the Supreme Court…let's say a bunch of, like, really crazy far-right ones. You're saying that he could actually try to do that?"

Michele resisted the urge to chide Cleon for obviously having not read the assigned chapter before class. If he had, he would know the answer to his own question.

"That's correct."

"So," Cleon added, "what's to stop him from doing that?"

"Well, for one thing," came Michele's reply, "the Democratic majority in both the House and Senate right now, here in 2033, would *never* pass legislation to give him and his party that amount of power over the courts."

Cleon wasn't giving up.

"But what if the RAVGs had control of Congress? Like, in the midterms next year, they win both the Senate and the House. What about then?"

Michele was about to answer, but decided to spur a touch more class participation.

"Who would like to answer Cleon's question?"

Silence and diverted eyes, except for—once again—Jeri Kraft in the front row.

"Jeri?" Michele figured that if this student wanted to get the semester off to a roaring start, then hey: more power to her.

"Sure," Jeri grimly answered. "It could definitely happen exactly like that, and then Hollinger would be in total control of all three branches of government."

* * *

After Hollinger's shock-and-awe January, few were surprised when the Judiciary Act of 2035 was introduced in Congress in early February; was quickly passed by both the House and the Senate; and immediately signed into law with a flourish by Ephraim Hollinger on Monday, February 20th, which served as President's Day this year. As with the various Judiciary Acts and Circuits Acts of the eighteenth and nineteenth centuries, the number of justices sitting on the Supreme Court was once again changed. This time, instead of the number going up or down by one or two, six—*six!*—justices would soon be added to the Supreme Court.

Six new justices, each one all but certain to be philosophically aligned with the nationalist and authoritarian views of the RAVG Party, would be named by President Ephraim Hollinger and then summarily confirmed by his like-minded confederates in the United States Senate.

And then, as Michele Burgess' star student Jeri Kraft had mused to the rest of her Western Penn class a year and a half earlier, Ephraim Hollinger would have unencumbered control over all three branches of the United States Government.

* * *

With the Judiciary Act now signed into law, the nominations came swiftly; so did the Senate confirmations. Voilà!

Brandon Wilson, Roger Stanton, and Adam Danvers; Peter Tannen, Owen Murphy, and Earl Moore.

All white Christian males, none older than forty-nine.

Each awarded the highest marks for his track record of rulings on the federal bench from every influential conservative legal watchdog organization.

Each energetically endorsed by a broad constituency of "traditional American values" advocacy groups.

Each vehemently opposed by numerous advocacy organizations chartered to advance the causes of civil liberties, environmental and ecological concerns, reproductive rights, religious freedoms, immigration reform, and other "progressive" stances…not that any of those oppositions, for any of the nominees, mattered in the least.

Each closely aligned for years with a critical mass of politicians who were now RAVG Party heavyweights.

And by the end of the first quarter of 2035, justices number ten through fifteen sitting on the United States Supreme Court.

Chapter 25

The administration, their congressional allies, and the American Values and Greatness Network—especially AVGN!—had been beating the TAMCA drum since the earliest days of Ephraim Hollinger's presidency.

The moment had finally arrived.

The opposing sides had mustered their ammunition for the inevitable battle for the ages.

In this corner: the First Amendment of the United States Constitution, weighing in at the ripe old age of two hundred and forty-three years, and bearing the ostensibly sacrosanct verbiage that Congress shall make no law abridging the freedom of speech or of the press.

In the other corner: the United States Supreme Court, circa 1919, with Chief Justice Oliver Wendell Holmes' often-misquoted opinion that "falsely shouting fire in a theater and causing a panic" does not constitute protected speech under the First Amendment.

Wait a minute, folks! Pairing up with the 1919 restrictions on unrestrained, so-called free speech is the Communications Act of 1934, which permitted content restrictions on radio broadcasts irrespective of the First Amendment! It looks like we're going to have a lopsided two-on-one tag-team match here tonight, with precedences from the courts and from Congress ready to pound away at that tired old heavyweight, the First Amendment! What a match!

* * *

Passage of the Truth and Accuracy in Media and Communications Act of 2035 within the RAVG Party-controlled Congress was a foregone conclusion. Civil libertarians, constitutional scholars, and many in the general public—not to mention the mainstream media that would bear the brunt of a highly restrictive TAMCA—had been fighting against the very idea of

TAMCA since Ephraim Hollinger first floated the idea during his inaugural address.

Hollinger was both methodical and crafty. He knew that until the RAVGs achieved numerical superiority in both houses of Congress, and then were able to rig the Supreme Court to do their bidding and that of the president, the best strategy was to spur as much bitter conflict as possible between the world of AVGN and the RAVGs and their designated enemies. Hollinger relished the mainstream media's nonstop doom-and-gloom warnings of what a post-TAMCA America might look like. Day after day, night after night, both sides duked it out on the cable news airwaves.

The president, Attorney General Spencer Howell, and Homeland Security Secretary Braxton Knox all were students of recent history. Trigger words such as "sedition" and "treason" were welcome raw meat for the ravenous base, and were guaranteed to spark the reflexive reactions from their political opponents and the media. But the rhetoric only went so far without the force of law to carry through with the incendiary accusations.

Enter TAMCA.

But wait: The rights of free speech and a free press are GUARANTEED IN WRITING in the First Amendment—full stop! This was the crux of the argument—ostensibly, the *only* argument—needed to argue the illegitimacy of the governmental censorship that would be sanctioned should TAMCA become law.

Not so fast, the TAMCA proponents countered. Right-wing attorneys and others flooded their frequent AVGN talking-head appearances with huffy assertions citing *Schenck v. United States*, *Brandenburg v. Ohio*, and a few other landmark cases; and then these positions in favor of weakening First Amendment protections were parroted and magnified through social media. If not for the severity of the consequences, one might be highly amused how many under-educated, not-quite-cerebral, cultish partisans seamlessly morphed into social media-credentialed legal and constitutional scholars through their posts and trolling comments.

The upshot of the pro-TAMCA argument was simple: Fine, we'll concede that the First Amendment does provide for free speech and a free press. However—and this is an elephant-sized "however"—the courts have ruled time and again that limitations on the *unrestrained* free speech of individuals as well as that of the press were definitely, positively, *absolutely* permissible! In fact, the Supreme Court's famous-but-misquoted "fire in a crowded theater" contention back in 1919, courtesy of Oliver Wendell Holmes, was that the concept of "free speech" certainly did not extend to that which was *both* false and dangerous. And then, fifty years later, *Brandenburg v. Ohio* affirmed that free speech could certainly be curtailed if such speech was likely to produce or incite—and this is a direct quote here, you libs—"imminent lawless action."

And then, they brought the argument home.

One of the primary drivers of TAMCA, at least according to the cover story, was to prevent the rabble-rousing mainstream media from trotting out their tired old mainstays to incite and defend lawlessness. Remember all of those slanted videos back in 2020 from D.C., Portland, and other cities where federal law enforcement was unfairly portrayed as a brutish force of aggressors, versus those supposedly peaceful protestors who were all, in fact, card-carrying violent anarchists? The reporting, the still images, and the videos were precisely crafted to *falsely* portray what was really happening in the streets of those cities to spur additional—get ready—"*imminent lawless action*" by spreading the violence to additional cities around the country.

In other words, the sin of sedition.

That's our story, and we're sticking to it.

Oh, and by the way: What about the century-old mission of the Federal Communications Commission?

As far back as the 1930s the Supreme Court has upheld the FCC's power and right to govern—*to censor*—content based on public interest.

Ba-boom! Double tap!

With that, the case for passage of TAMCA in Congress and then winning the inevitable fight in the courts rests.

None of that matters, came the counter-counter arguments. We all *know* what Hollinger will do if he gains the power to shut down the media—other than his sycophantic confederates at AVGN, obviously—and to restrict what had always been presumed to be a fundamental right for all Americans. Who's to determine what speech or press reporting is "false" and thus needs to be curtailed? Ephraim Hollinger? His minions in Congress, or others who are planted into some new censorship agency? Look at Hollinger's intent! For two years now, he's resuscitated and led the War on Truth, and he's winning.

* * *

January had seen the reshaping of the executive branch, and the next two months heralded the reformation of the Supreme Court. Hollinger now held all the cards. As March drew to a close, with the highest court in the land firmly secured, Senate Majority Leader Tal Chadwick and House Speaker Lowell Irvine shepherded the TAMCA bill through Congress.

The bill passed both the House and the Senate along party lines: every RAVG voting in favor, versus every Democrat, Republican, and Independent opposed. President Hollinger reprised his triumphant signing ceremony from February—the one for the Judiciary Act—less than two months later, and presto: TAMCA was the law of the land.

Even before any TAMCA-produced action occurred, the battle moved to the courts. Stays were immediately issued at the lower courts where Hollinger's influence hadn't yet fully taken hold; the counter-punches in the form of appeals came just as quickly. A month later, the matter went before the newly restructured Supreme Court, which wasted no time in upholding TAMCA in a nine-to-six decision.

Not that anyone was surprised, but without the six new justices whom Hollinger and the RAVG Party-led Congress had strong-armed onto the Court, TAMCA would have been struck down in a six-to-three decision.

"The Congress of the United States is a solemn institution," the recently appointed Chief Justice wrote in the Court's majority opinion, "and is entrusted to enact legislation on behalf of the nation and its citizens. The Court's responsibility is solely to determine the constitutionality of any such legislation, rather than inject political or societal factors or beliefs…"

* * *

The nation held its collective breath, but the most ominous of the predictions curiously failed to materialize. "Curiously" because the TAMCA drumbeat during the past two years unmistakably led one to believe that the days were numbered for any cable news network not bearing the initials "A-V-G-N," and for Hollinger's other "fake news" media targets. Summer arrived, though, and none of the news-focused cable networks had been abruptly shut down. The major newspapers and their websites still operated, serving as fodder for AVGN. Was it possible that what most took for Hollinger's and the RAVG Party's disingenuous cover story—that the Truth and Accuracy in Media and Communications Act really *was* all about truth and accuracy, rather than crushing the First Amendment—was a reality?

Even though the "free press" was left alone in the immediate aftermath of TAMCA becoming law, Hollinger's pet legislation still quickly made its mark on the country. The same nation that had long embraced the transformative power of books, that had largely facilitated the publication and dissemination of Thomas Paine's *Common Sense* even before the American Revolution, would soon learn the impact of the innocuous-sounding Federal Literature Commission.

Ostensibly patterned after the century-old Federal Communication Commission (or so the story went), the FLC was chartered by TAMCA to "promote traditional American values through published books, and to prevent published books from fomenting civil unrest and sedition." The FLC was placed under the auspices of the Commerce Department and the always-malleable leadership of Jim Wiley. In reality, Bart Lawrence's personal portfolio took on a new assignment with the passage of TAMCA, and he pulled the strings and called the shots when it came to action taken by the FLC.

Part of the whole new alphabet soup to which American citizens would soon become accustomed was the LRB: the Literature Review Board, which functioned as the FLC's epicenter. The LRB's structure and mission were eponymous: a governmental board of "editors" responsible for reviewing and approving *every* new book that would be published and sold in the United States.

One might have thought that the sheer volume of published works every year would make this proposed censorship process not only unwieldy, but logistically impossible. However, the FLC adopted a model similar to that which the Transportation Security Administration had been using for years with its suite of various Trusted Traveler programs. Every book publisher in the United States, large and small, was now required to apply for a publishing license. The major traditional publishers had their applications expedited, while smaller publishing houses wound up waiting months for theirs to be approved.

A licensed publisher was required to submit any potentially "problematic" title to the FLC's Literature Review Board for approval...but only those titles. A non-fiction title about, say, scrapbooking or vegan cooking or dieting could be safely published in the same manner as always, without involving the LRB. Political works that fawned over Ephraim Hollinger, his administration, and the RAVG Party's political doctrine were, of course, greased to bypass the LRB. Fiction was a bit murkier, but steamy romances and mysteries and other titles that steered clear of espousing controversial, anti-government views in plot and dialogue were in the clear.

The catch was, though, that if *any* citizen or business or any other entity filed a complaint to the Federal Literature Commission about a book that had not been submitted for LRB review, and if that book was subsequently determined to violate the FLC's standards, then not only would the book be immediately yanked from both physical and digital shelves, the publisher was also in danger of having its license pulled.

Because self-published books, both in print and eBook, had shared shelf space with traditionally published works for the past quarter century, the LRB made provisions to control these titles as well. All of the major online retailers that supported self-publishing were also required to hold an FLC-granted license to operate. Each retailer already had its own approval process for submitted self-published works, though the checks were usually limited to quality-related issues with uploaded manuscript files and covers. Now, though, the retailers were required to take on content approval as well. A complaint filed against a self-published work that was found to be warranted would result in drastic blowback for the online retailer, possibly leading to having their FLC license revoked and thus being shut down and forced out of business. Therefore, it would now be a matter of survival for an online book retailer to heavily curate—in every sense of the word—all submitted self-published works, and decline the publication and listing of any work that might lead to the FLC death penalty.

A sibling organization to the LRB—the Existing Works Board, or EWB—would soon be similarly responsible for proactively and reactively culling the existing body of published works to remove subversive and inflammatory books whose publication predated TAMCA, the FLC, the LRB, and the rest of the alphabet soup. The mechanics were still being worked, but any already-published book that was subsequently flagged and censored by the EWB would soon be pulled from physical and online bookstores, but without penalties foisted on the publisher. American citizens would be expected to voluntarily surrender these banned works upon notification, with harsh penalties proposed and making their way through Congress for retaining a copy of a banned book. Online bookstores would be required to automatically purge copies of disavowed titles from their customers' eReader devices, bypassing any necessity for voluntary cooperation when it came to eBooks.

The EWB side of reshaping American literature would come soon enough. At the outset of the existence of the Federal Literature Commission, the focus was squarely on preventing newly published titles that took aim at Ephraim Hollinger's post-midterms *blitzkrieg*. Not that long ago, another American president facing re-election had faced a barrage of unflattering and potentially damaging titles authored by pundits, dismissed administration officials, allies-turned-enemies, and others. The snowball effect of so many damning exposés during such a short period of time may have contributed at least a little bit to that president's electoral defeat, and Ephraim Hollinger had no intention of allowing that sort of disruptive, provocative bullshit—that was for certain!

And so, the dubious honor of becoming the Literature Review Board's inaugural banned book fell to Daniel Jacobson and his tome of veneered Hollinger dystopia, *The Twilight's Last Gleaming*.

* * *

"I don't know what to say." Paula Fontana's voice shook when she delivered the ominous news to her client, only minutes after receiving word from the publisher that *The Twilight's Last Gleaming* had been banned from publication by the LRB.

Daniel had finished the book in early February, and a final round of edits and minor revisions was rushed by Daniel and the publisher's editorial team, finishing up in early April. By then, though, TAMCA had been passed and was being fought in the courts. The publisher rushed Daniel's novel into their production schedule, realizing that they were all racing the clock. The mechanisms of the Literature Review Board had yet to be unveiled, but everyone involved in the book's publication knew that censorship was a very real possibility.

The book went to press in early May, with a respectable forty-thousand-copy print run at the publisher's facility in south-central Indiana. By the time copies rolled off the presses and into shipping boxes, though, an injunction against publishing Daniel's novel had been granted by a RAVG-friendly federal judge, pending the book's formal LRB hearing. For the time being, forty thousand books sat in cardboard boxes on pallets inside the printer's warehouse, awaiting their fate.

"I'm so sorry," Paula Fontana continued as she delivered the news to Daniel. "I don't know, maybe there will be some sort of appeal process…"

The agent's voice trailed off; and other than a quiet "uh-huh…bye" Daniel Jacobson was speechless during the brief phone call.

* * *

Jesse Stewart had worked as a shift supervisor at this south-central Indiana printing house for more than twenty years. Other than dealing with a sudden machinery breakdown or supply shortage, not too many surprises broke up the typical workday in his line of business.

The appearance of more than a dozen midnight-black semis on the humid, overcast morning of Friday, June 29th, each truck emblazoned with the ominous Federal Police Force emblem, definitely signaled a departure from more than twenty years of daily "same old, same old" for Jesse Stewart. A beefy, surly plainclothes FPFer smacked a warrant against Jesse's chest, a split second before barreling into and then past the nearly sixty-year-old man. Jesse's bad left hip and equally bad left knee almost gave out from the abrupt shove, and he barely kept his balance and remained on his feet...which was a good thing, because two heavily armed FPF SWAT teams were right behind the plainclothes guy, and Jesse was all but certain they would have stomped right over him if he had fallen.

The SWAT teams and their assault weapons were definitely overkill for serving a warrant at a book printer; but this was the menacing Federal Police Force that the public had come to know and fear for just over two years now, trafficking every bit as much in domination and dread as law enforcement. In addition to the heavily armed SWAT officers, a couple dozen other camo-clad, sidearmed FPFers marched purposefully past Jesse Stewart.

Within minutes, the first half dozen of them were already on their way back out of the building. Each of the men carried two boxes, which were then expediently stacked inside the nearest semi before heading back inside for another load, reminding Jesse Stewart of those endless lines of ants scurrying past each other as they labored on behalf of the collective. As each truck was filled, its driver quickly departed and was just as quickly replaced by the next one. Once fully loaded, each semi departed the printing plant's parking lot, destination unknown to Jesse Stewart or anyone else who worked there, and was replaced at the loading dock by the next in line.

Gotta say, Jesse Stewart mused, *these Feds sure are efficient...*

Jesse stood to the side of the doorway, occasionally rubbing the sore spots on his body, and watched as the warehouse was emptied of every copy of *The Twilight's Last Gleaming* in less than one hour.

Not my problem, Jesse reminded himself later as he again kneaded his still-sore left side and watched the last of the trucks pull out onto the state highway access road and then soon fade from sight.

Not my problem.

* * *

The trucks rendezvoused in a large open field, about five miles down the road from the plant. Their drivers headed to their pre-assigned spots around the open area. Just as efficiently as the semis had been loaded, they were unloaded with the copies of *The Twilight's Last Gleaming* dumped from their boxes and spread out along several shallow trenched lines that had been roughly dug into the field by a couple of backhoes a few days earlier.

No summer Indiana thunderstorm or crop-friendly gentle rainfall was expected over the next couple of days, but a stack of tarps lay off to the side should they be needed to keep the books dry. For now, the rows of books would sadly lay there for the next few days, awaiting the fate to which they had been consigned.

* * *

Seventeen years earlier, after dark on the Fourth of July, Bob Harris had found himself on a flight out of Cleveland to Houston. Harris was a tech consultant with one of the big firms, and his attendance had been demanded at an eight o'clock meeting the next morning at a client site. Bob Harris traveled almost every week for his consulting work, but he had never before been forced to skip watching Fourth of July fireworks with Katie and their two kids. Normally he took vacation around the Fourth every year; but this project was one of those "all hands on deck" ones, meaning that an early July vacation was off the table.

Not that it was much consolation, but for the duration of the three-hour flight, Bob was able to watch dozens of fireworks displays from his window seat. At one point, probably somewhere over the southern tip of Illinois, he could see at least ten different vibrant displays at the same time dancing in the darkness below.

In the years since then, Bob and Katie Harris had adopted a curious annual early summer ritual: flying on Fourth of July night to watch fireworks exhibits from the air. For the first couple of years, the kids, of course, went with their parents. As they went off to college, however, the annual ritual had evolved into a sort of "extreme date night" for Bob and Katie. They would fly to Houston or Dallas or Denver—any place that was right around three hours away from Cleveland—and spend the night at a Marriott or a Hilton or some other upper-quality chain hotel, somewhere close to the destination airport. Along the way, they would watch for fireworks displays; and just like Bob's first Fourth of July flight, they would see dozens from the air.

Once they landed and shuttled to their hotel, they would enjoy a late supper in the hotel restaurant that was usually holiday-quiet, have a few more drinks, and then adjourn to their room where they would remind themselves how much in love they still were, even after so many years of marriage. The next morning—not too early—they would fly back to Cleveland.

This year, their flight out of Cleveland was delayed for an hour, and they weren't wheels-up until after it was already dark. Chances were that their tally of displays would be on the lower side this year, but they should still see enough fireworks during the early part of their trip, and perhaps a few late stragglers as they skirted over the edges of Illinois and Missouri and into Arkansas.

So what if our flight was delayed, Bob Harris reminded himself once they were in the air and soon spotted their first display of the night. *Nothing can spoil the evening for us.*

In south-central Indiana, twenty-five thousand feet below where the Harris' plane would soon be, a cadre of uniformed FPF officers dispersed along the rows of seized and discarded copies of *The Twilight's Last Gleaming*. The books had been doused in gasoline twenty minutes earlier, giving the fuel time to soak in, and each FPF officer carried an unlit torch as he stood and awaited the command for what would come next.

Surrounding the FPFers was a crowd that Bart Lawrence—on hand to oversee what was about to occur—estimated at right around five thousand, though Attorney General Spencer Howell's official report would—ahem—"tweak" that number by a factor of four. Five thousand hearty souls turning out on the Fourth of July for tonight's festivities was nothing to sneeze at. Still, Bart Lawrence reckoned that a reported tally of twenty thousand loyal followers better served Ephraim Hollinger's purposes.

Nothing gets the juices flowing among the compliant masses like a good, old-fashioned book burning, right?

At nine-thirty, Bart Lawrence gave the signal to the FPF commander, who relayed the "let's go" order to his scattered troops via police-band radio. En masse, each of the FPF officers flicked a lighter which was used to light his torch. For close to a minute, the FPF contingent stood in place, each one wielding a flaming torch as the backdrop for the now-mostly drunk crowd to holler in lusty, nostalgic appreciation:

BLOOD AND SOIL!

BLOOD AND SOIL!

JEWS WILL NOT REPLACE US!

JEWS WILL NOT REPLACE US!

Hundreds among the crowd livestreamed the images onto social media, and a thousand more videoed the event for subsequent posts.

A second police-band command—this one a simple statement of "do it"—resulted in more than one hundred Federal Police Force officers tilting their torches forward and downward, each torch making contact with a point along the track of gasoline-soaked books. A hot WHOOSH arose all along the lines of books, causing almost all of the FPFers to instinctively drop back a couple of steps because of the sudden intense heat and wildly gyrating flames.

The conflagration rapidly spread from the touch points, up and down the rows of books, until forty thousand copies of *The Twilight's Last Gleaming* were now nothing but fuel for the hellfire of Ephraim Hollinger's hatred.

Twenty-five thousand feet above, Katie Harris, still searching for new fireworks displays, saw something off the plane's three o'clock position, maybe twenty miles away. She blinked, and her head executed a classic TV sitcom double take. What she saw down on the ground, though, was far from humorous.

She furiously elbowed her husband, who was in the middle seat scanning the farther-out nighttime horizon over Katie's shoulder. Instantly alarmed at the wide-eyed horror in his wife's eyes, Bob Harris leaned into Katie, his face now flush against the plane's age-etched window, and then looked downward where she was pointing. They wouldn't know until two days later exactly what was burning beneath them. For now, that knowledge was unnecessary. The terrifying shape of the abomination rising from the darkness below as the plane lazily slid southward was what mattered.

Alan Simon

Part III
For the Good of the Nation

Summer 2035–October 2036

"Team by team, reporters baffled, trumped, tethered, cropped…"

- R.E.M., *It's the End Of The World As We Know It*

―――――――

"It may happen, at some future day, that he will establish a monarchy, and destroy the republic."

- George Mason, cited in "Debate in Virginia Ratifying Convention," June 18, 1788

―――――――

"I'll tip my hat to the new constitution, Take a bow for the new revolution, Smile and grin at the change all around…"

- The Who, *Won't Get Fooled Again*

Chapter 26

Near-constant polling throughout the remainder of July 2035 revealed an ominous trend.

In the immediate aftermath of the Federal Police Force's swastika-shaped incineration of forty thousand copies of *The Twilight's Last Gleaming*, 48 percent of adult Americans polled stated that they were in favor of the book burning as a means for the government to send the strongest possible message about TAMCA's "censorship in the public interest" provisions, while 40 percent were opposed and 12 percent either expressed no strong opinion either way, or claimed to be unfamiliar with the incident.

By the end of the month, however, a follow-up poll using the same methodology and questions already showed a jump to 63 percent in favor, with only 31 percent now stating their opposition. Weeks of nonstop, carefully scripted drumbeating by Toni Fowler, Keenan Lucas, and the others at AVGN, which was then amplified through the dark arts of social media influencing—both cognizant and subliminal—had done the trick, exactly as Bob Platte's messaging strategists and analytics wizards had predicted.

Even more troubling: Only 14 percent of those in favor tempered their support with "mild or significant concern" about the swastika shape being deliberately used to light the nighttime Midwestern blackness. The rest either didn't care, or blatantly and shockingly relished the symbolism, to the horror of the pollsters and then the newscasters on networks other than AVGN who solemnly reported and then discussed the poll results.

The pundits shouldn't have been surprised. In the midst of the dystopia that had been the year 2020, a survey of then-younger American adults under the age of forty revealed that almost two-thirds were unaware that six million Jews had been murdered by the Nazis. Nearly half of those polled couldn't name a single concentration camp—the names "Auschwitz" and "Dachau" and "Bergen-Belsen" meant absolutely nothing to them—and eleven percent of them actually believed that Europe's Jews themselves had somehow been responsible for the Holocaust!

The terrifying, dismaying statistics from that survey had only worsened during the past sixteen years. Far too many Americans were either unaware of the evils of the Third Reich, or believed that history had given Hitler and the Nazis a bum rap. They viewed grainy films of the masses gathered for the monstrous Nazi rallies and torch-lit night marches with yearning eyes and a perverse nostalgia for a time and place that they had never known. (*Triumph of the Will,* the infamous Nazi propaganda documentary that commandingly depicted the massive 1934 Nuremberg Rally and its seven hundred thousand participants, was a fan favorite.) Leaving all of that unpleasant starting-a-world-war business aside, Hitler had unified a nation; wasn't that obvious by these many images documenting hundreds of thousands of good German citizens united in their fanatical passion toward their leader, and against a common enemy?

And wasn't that what this country, fractured for too many years now, genuinely needed: its own charismatic leader to once again unite *this* nation by whatever means were necessary, and then lead it forward?

The United States had test-driven autocratic fascism not that many years earlier, and far too many Americans discovered that they actually enjoyed the ride. For several harrowing years they had willingly surrendered the wearisome exertions of independent thought and critical thinking, along with any sense of social justice, in exchange for the lobotomized simplicity of cult-of-personality authoritarianism and the belongingness of tribalism. For many, the titillating excitement of bizarre conspiracy theories trumped the dullness and disappointments of real life. Normalcy was dulling; constant baiting and warring instilled a sense of euphoric daily purpose in many. Still, the resuscitation of democratic norms and institutions leading into the late 2020s was believed by many to have pulled the nation out of the darkness, just in time. But now, the pendulum appeared to have again reversed direction, and was accelerating at an alarming pace.

"The American Experiment" wasn't just a throwaway phrase; a nation governed by democratic values and ideals for longer than just a sprinkle in time is a frustrating, exhausting proposition, seemingly unnatural to the human condition. The return to the paternalistic, trickle-down patronage of autocracy promised by President Hollinger and the RAVG Party was again viewed by so many as the preferred path for the future legs of the American journey. Philosopher George Santanaya's often-misquoted passage had posited that "those who cannot remember the past are condemned to repeat it." Hollinger's America, however, was populated by tens of millions who *did* remember the past—the recent past, specifically—and yearned for its return.

The many layers of the American Values and Greatness movement had been painstakingly constructed and wrapped around a single core proposition: that neither government nor society nor the word of God could force one to accept those who were uncomfortably different from the whitewashed profile of "A Loyal, True American Patriot."

And if some books wound up being incinerated along the journey toward that utopian homogeneous state, and if a few dark ghosts of genocide and ruin were dredged up in concert with the effort...well, "it is what it is."

Chapter 27

"I need to finish up my last syllabus this morning," Michele Burgess told Daniel Jacobson over the phone, "but this afternoon I think I'm going to go to that new indoor shooting range over in East Liberty. Want to come with me?"

This overcast, already sticky early August mid-morning followed one of the nights that neither Michele nor Daniel spent at the other's place. The routine that they had adopted nearly two years earlier still held: sort of a two-by-two-by-two pattern, divided more or less equally with nights together at Daniel's condo, other nights together at Michele's, but also nights spent apart. They were closer than ever, especially after bearing witness to the online images and videos of every existing copy of Daniel's book fueling the horrific burning swastika that lit the south-central Indiana night. Still, a night or two apart from each other, every couple of days, proved to be just the right amount of cushion to keep their relationship at exactly the level that worked for both of them.

"Um…I've never fired a gun before," Daniel replied after a brief hesitation, his mind still digesting Michele's surprise suggestion. He knew that Michele owned a couple of handguns, one of the final remaining legacies of her Army days. To the best of his knowledge, however, those weapons had remained unused and under lock and key for the past two years, ever since she moved to Pittsburgh. Daniel knew that over the years she had qualified as "Expert" with many different weapons, but she seemed to have left that part of her life behind after retiring from the Army.

"That's okay," Michele replied. "I haven't done any shooting myself since I was at West Point," confirming Daniel's supposition about her handguns remaining unfired for the past two years.

"Why the sudden interest?" Daniel blurted out before he could check his words.

Michele hesitated a fraction of a second before answering.

"Oh," she blandly replied, "I just feel like doing a little target shooting. It always used to force me to really concentrate and forget about problems for a little while."

Silence hung on the connection for a couple of seconds.

"So do you want to come with me?" Michele repeated her original question.

In a split second, Daniel made his decision. He had never previously fired a handgun, or any other type of firearm, as he had told Michele. Truthfully, the whole idea of pistols and rifles made him nervous. In his family, other than his great-grandfather (and only during World War II for Pop-pop), nobody else had ever even handled a weapon to the best of his knowledge.

Still, above all else, the opportunity to do something together with Michele that was different than the usual had appeal.

"Sure," he replied.

"Good—I'll be over to pick you up," Michele replied with a tight smile, and then added in a deliberately offhand manner:

"Oh, also—leave your cell phone at home, I'm doing the same."

* * *

The next morning, after spending the night together at Michele's house, Daniel and Michele were sitting in her sun-drenched breakfast nook, each working on a second cup of coffee while individually skimming various newspaper websites on their phones.

"I'm going running later," Michele turned to Daniel and said in what seemed to him as a deliberate, almost forced "oh, by the way…" manner. "Want to come along?"

Daniel was in decent enough shape overall for a somewhat sedentary college professor. He was sort of active, but his "exercise" mostly consisted of long, leisurely, contemplative walks around the Oakland section of Pittsburgh, combined with one or two days each week of moderate stretching. Two or three times each week Daniel would remember to do fifteen or twenty pushups. But that was about it.

Michele's own workout regimen was now nothing like it had been during her Army days, but she ran circles around Daniel—literally—with a six- or seven-mile run almost every day, not to mention using weights and machines at least two days each week at the Western Penn campus fitness center. Daniel had long felt a bit uneasy with the imbalance between their respective exercise routines, especially because his predecessors in relationships with Michele had all been Army officers with a similar fanaticism for working out as her own. Michele didn't seem bothered by this disparity, though, so Daniel did his best not to let any sense of inadequacy pollute their relationship.

"I don't know about six miles," Daniel countered her suggestion. "Occasionally I'll walk that far, but I haven't done much running for a long time, since way back when I ran track and cross-country in high school."

"No problem," Michele quickly replied. "We can run for a mile or two together, at whatever pace is comfortable for you, and then I'll continue on for a couple more afterward."

"Sure," Daniel shrugged. "I'm game."

* * *

The next week, with two weeks still remaining on their summer schedule until the fall semester began, they again went shooting at the indoor range. They continued to do short runs together. That week, Michele also suggested that Daniel join her at the campus fitness center, which he agreed to do.

The pattern continued past Labor Day and through the rest of the summer, and then into the fall: running, working out, and shooting lessons. At times, it felt like Michele had stealthily maneuvered herself into becoming Daniel's personal trainer. She wasn't too obvious, but Daniel could tell that she was gently pushing him, week after week. Soon he was running the full six or seven miles, side by side with Michele, at a brisk pace. He had reluctantly done some weight lifting back in high school when he was on the track and cross-country teams, but now he actually enjoyed working out in the campus fitness center at least three times each week without fail.

They made an effort to visit the shooting range at least once each week. Daniel's marksmanship with both the .45 and the nine-millimeter dramatically improved from the first time they went, when he had missed the paper target more than he had hit it. Now, he could cluster his shots pretty much where he wanted them on the target, even when he emptied most or all of Michele's 10-clip .45 in a rapid burst.

All the while, Daniel couldn't shake the feeling that Michele had something in mind that she wasn't sharing with him; that his fitness and even his marksmanship had become some sort of a "cause" for her.

And when he had asked her that first time, when she arrived to pick him up, why he should leave his cell phone at home, Michele's eyes instantly went cold as she bluntly answered:

"Just because; you need to trust me."

The next time they went to the shooting range, and every other time after that, when Michele invariably reminded Daniel not to bring his cell phone, he complied with her order—her words were unquestionably exactly that—and didn't bother asking why.

Chapter 28

Bart Lawrence grunted twice as he spasmed inside Toni Fowler. As always with Toni, and with almost any other woman, for Lawrence the sensation was more expulsive relief than ecstasy; domination rather than connection. For Toni Fowler, her own rapture was solely a by-product of bedding a powerful man.

They had been sleeping together every week or two for more than nine months, after first drunkenly hooking up at the orgiastic White House celebration last New Year's Eve. The aftermath of the RAVG Party's election night conquest of America, along with the countdown to their hostile takeover of Congress coming up in only a few short days, had provided the perfect backdrop of victorious debauchery for those attendees who wished to partake—Caligula would have been proud.

Bart Lawrence had eased Toni out of the crowded East Room and then led her upstairs to the Lincoln Bedroom, where he brusquely shoved her onto the bed only seconds before wordlessly unzipping and mounting her, neither of them shedding a single item of clothing. That first encounter had lasted less than five minutes before they slipped back out of the famed room and then separately made their way back into the East Room to rejoin the celebration. Lawrence's wife was still engaged in discussion with two of the on-deck future Cabinet Secretaries who would soon be unveiled in the opening salvo of Hollinger's *blitzkrieg*. She hadn't noticed her husband's absence; but even if she had, Kristen Lawrence knew the score, and she turned a blind eye to her husband's numerous indiscretions in exchange for her own ready access to the halls of power and the trappings of wealth.

By October, Toni Fowler had graduated from short-term fling to longer-term mistress. Long ago, Bob

Seger had sung about the nostalgic recollection of a star-crossed young romance where "I used her, she used me, but neither one cared; we were gettin' our share." The encounters between Bart Lawrence and Toni Fowler perfectly mirrored those words, though they were utterly devoid of any sepia-tinged, adolescent romanticism or bittersweet remembrances of lost innocence. Their "relationship" was purely transactional, and suited both their needs.

Toni Fowler had a problem: specifically, a Keenan Lucas problem. Lucas was still riding the Frank Douglas horse, and he was now neck-and-neck with Toni into the home stretch of the AVGN Derby. Lucas had successfully lobbied Bob Platte that Keenan's program should be the only one in the AVGN prime-time lineup that would regularly headline the new JCS Chairman's makeover of the entire United States military. Toni Fowler and Hayden Lafferty and Tristan Wyatt would be permitted to cover the ongoing flag officer purges and overall shifts in culture and doctrine, but only secondarily to Keenan Lucas. Lucas' program was the one on AVGN where General Frank Douglas frequently appeared live to announce that Confederate battle flags were once again permitted to be proudly flown on military bases, or that white supremacist tattoos were no longer *verboten* on either incoming recruits or veteran soldiers, or that women were once again banned from certain military specialization codes such as the Army's Special Forces.

The loyally fanatic Hollinger base not only relished the messages, they elevated the stature of the messenger himself. Keenan Lucas now hosted a weekly Sunday-night bonus program, for his fans who couldn't get enough of him during his weeknight shows.

And all the while, the other AVGN prime-time anchors seethed.

And plotted.

* * *

"So what do you think? I gotta tell Hollinger something soon."

Toni Fowler's fingers lightly traced Bart Lawrence's lower body as she contemplated the latest incarnation of his long-standing proposition. In another setting, with different people, her actions might have been an intimate way to maintain a connection between the conclusion of one sex act and the commencement of another. For Toni, though, her finger-wandering was little more than absent-minded filler as she coldly calculated the cost-benefit trade-offs of becoming Ephraim Hollinger's White House Press Secretary *and* retaining her big-bucks AVGN programming slot.

More than two years ago, Bart Lawrence had approached Toni about becoming the new president's press secretary. The whole "seat of power" was an overwhelming aphrodisiac, but in the end the AVGN money did the talking. She didn't know Bart Lawrence very well at the time, and his slippery hints of "we might have ways to make you whole" should she join the administration didn't resonate at all with her back then. Besides, for the first year or so of Hollinger's reign, the true seat of power for the nascent American Values and Greatness movement remained the AVGN studios.

Now, though, Hollinger was firmly in control of all three branches of the federal government, and truly had crossed the threshold leading to absolutely unchecked power. Bob Platte might have been the man behind the throne between the 2032 election and the midterms, and he still wielded significant sway over the RAVG Party's doctrine and agenda. But those first three months of 2035 had immutably shifted the epicenter of power from AVGN to the White House.

Bart Lawrence's proposition was straightforward. Toni would immediately replace Victoria Baker, who would shuffle over to become the "Hollinger-Nelson

2036" campaign press secretary. Victoria's experienced team of five deputy and assistant press secretaries would remain in place in the White House, underneath Toni.

Whenever her travel schedule and other press secretary duties permitted, Toni would put on her other hat in the evenings and do her regular hour from the AVGN studio, which was fortuitously only a few blocks from the White House. Bob Platte had already agreed to beef up the staff for Toni's show. She would only need about twenty minutes of prep immediately before each show, because her scripts would already be fully edited and in the can, ready for that time-tested, summoned-at-will Toni Fowler outrage to bring the day's grievances to life, even without a preliminary table read and some final tweaks.

And most important: Toni would still bring home the *big* bucks by remaining on the AVGN payroll, the same as right now. She would retain her sweetheart deal with the payoffs from AVGN advertisers on her program. In Ephraim Hollinger's government, petty little nuisances such as the Hatch Act and all of the government ethics regulations relating to conflicts of interest were easily swatted away.

For days when she was on the road with Hollinger through the evening hours, she would attempt to do her show remotely from wherever she was, if she could make the schedule work. If not—say, during an overseas trip where the time zone difference was a problem, or if she was by Hollinger's side as part of an honored state dinner guest party—one of several AVGN second-tier players would fill in for Toni and guest-host her program.

She knew that what Bart Lawrence was proposing was going to be a ballbuster workload. Yet the seduction of double-dipping between the White House and AVGN—having her cake and eating it too—was overpowering.

"I already decided…I'll do it," she answered his question, leering at him as her fingers traveled upward, clearly letting him know that she was ready for an encore.

Toni Fowler still had a Keenan Lucas problem, though. No doubt Lucas would attempt to turn Toni's double-dipping against her, perhaps leading a smear campaign within the halls of AVGN that she was no longer fully on board and committed to the network's quest for power and dollars.

Bart Lawrence must have been reading her mind. A hard look came to his face as he told her:

"Just leave Lucas to me; I'll take care of it."

Toni had begun shifting her head and upper torso downward, heading toward and then slightly past Bart Lawrence's waistline, but his words froze her in place. She rotated her lust-filled face toward his.

"You just need to be patient for a little while and trust me," Bart Lawrence added as his right hand nudged Toni Fowler's head back toward where it had been headed.

Chapter 29

Shortly after 9:00 p.m., Randall Weston made a right turn off of the main four-lane road, slowing his car to about fifteen as he rolled past the floodlit development entryway sign that read "Bellamy Oaks." He flicked his phone to "on" and quickly double-checked the list that he had downloaded. Bellamy Oaks was definitely one of the suburban Denver neighborhoods listed, he confirmed. No monitored public surveillance cameras on these residential streets: time to go to work.

He executed a couple of quick turns and then paralleled his car in between two SUVs near the end of one of the streets, being certain that he left enough room to his front in case he had to race back to the car and execute a quick getaway. He had already unrolled the obscuring film layer over his license plate, so hopefully there was no chance of his car being precisely identified through someone's home surveillance system, or possibly someone sprinting after him as he made his escape while videoing him on their cell phone.

As he exited his car into the unseasonably icy Colorado night air, thick Phillips-head screwdriver in hand, he quickly glanced at the luxury SUV in front of him. No bumper or window stickers of any kind: Perfect, this Ford would be his final target before he made his escape.

On this side of this street alone, at least a dozen cars were parked either along the curb or in driveways. Bellamy Oaks was a sizable development, built back in the mid-2010s, but there was no way Randall could safely cover more than a single street anyway. No matter; volume wasn't the goal here. Someone else could come back another night and take care of a different street, perhaps. After that, it would be time to move on to another neighborhood.

Randall eased the handle of the screwdriver upward, past his left wrist and tucked into his jacket sleeve while resting on his fingers, safely keeping it out of sight should someone spot him on the sidewalk. Exactly one week from now, these same streets would likely be packed with trick-or-treaters; but for now, the sidewalks were void of anyone other than Randall Weston. Even on the sidewalk, he would likely trip at least a few home surveillance systems merely by walking by. However, Randall was dressed in drab, dark clothing with a tightly pulled hood obscuring his facial features. The whole idea was to do his work quickly, before anyone became wise to what he had done, and then make his escape. After the fact, when the night's handiwork was discovered, there would be little likelihood of identifying Randall Weston as the culprit, even from one or more doorbell camera recordings that revealed a faceless stranger in nondescript clothing strolling up and down this particular street. For now, though, Randall was primed to fleet-foot it back to his car at any given instant and peel away in escape, if necessary.

He slowed his pace as he came upon his first target: someone's pricey BMW crossover. Even before his eyes began their scan, Randall was certain there was no way this vehicle would have any type of "Hollinger-Nelson 2036" sticker or decal. His eyes ratcheted over the bumper, the back of the car, and then the back window, confirming his supposition. Glancing around the street once again, this time ensuring that nobody happened to be looking out a nearby front window at the moment, he lowered the screwdriver just as he reached the back right side of the BMW. Tightening his grip, he torqued the screwdriver to be parallel with the ground and then jammed it into the charcoal gray hindquarter of the vehicle. The orgasmic sensation of forged steel gouging into paint and sheet metal traversed Randall's left hand and arm as he quickened his pace. About five seconds later he was past the BMW and eyeing his next target, about fifteen yards ahead.

This next one was perfect: an all-electric vehicle with a "Willis 2036" bumper sticker. No doubt the vehicle's owner was some Hollinger-hating, pussy lib; after all, who else would be backing that America-hating congressman Paul Willis in the Democratic Party primary?

This one was worthy of more than just an industrial-strength keying, Randall quickly decided. As with the BMW, Randall began digging the screwdriver into the paint as soon as he reached the back right of this one. He skipped over the back right tire to keep the screwdriver at work, but when he reached the front right tire, he suddenly dropped into a squatting position, drew back his left arm, and then thrust the screwdriver into the front tire's sidewall. Satisfied that he had cleanly punctured the rubber, he jerked the screwdriver back in a single motion, smoothly rose to his feet again, and resumed his stroll. He waited anxiously for a few seconds for someone to come racing out of the two-story house to his left, meaning that his actions had been picked up on a home surveillance system.

Nothing.

Randall decided, though, on the spot, that tonight he would stick to the cars parked in the street, along the curb, and bypass the ones in driveways. Those ones were always riskier, with a highly increased likelihood of being picked up on someone's door or home surveillance and then winding up in a face-to-face confrontation, possibly with a gun-wielding homeowner. Sometimes, though, the sheer thrill of stepping right up to the brink was worth the risk, at least to Randall.

But not tonight.

This was Randall Weston's fourth such venture over the past two weeks. To the best of his knowledge, at least ten others had fanned out over other parts of metro Denver, down into Colorado Springs, and north into Fort Collins. Word was just starting to trickle back via dark web social media and chat rooms that other cities and towns across the country were in the crosshairs of like-minded patriots. So far, no local or national news had picked up the story of a wave of seemingly politically motivated vehicle vandalism.

Randall finished his handiwork on this side of the street, crossed over to the other sidewalk, and then repeated his efforts as he headed back in the direction of his own car. He bypassed the first three cars, since each was adorned with a Hollinger-Nelson sticker. The next five, though, all fell victim to his screwdriver. One of those—another all-electric vehicle, this one a full-sized SUV—had a sticker that read "HOLLINGER FOR PRISON 2036." Randall not only screwdrivered both sides of this vehicle, he punctured all four tires.

Because he spent so much time on this blasphemous SUV, Randall decided to call it a night and not attempt an encore performance in some other nearby development. He remembered to take care of the Ford SUV in front of him, this time on the street side on his way back to his own driver's side door. He slipped into his own car and eased into the street, executed a quick U-turn, and then departed Bellamy Oaks.

Mission accomplished.

* * *

Josh Stein had the perfect job.

As Chief Analytics Officer for the Colorado Bureau of Investigation, he had a proverbial "seat at the table" in the bureau's leadership tier. Josh had joined the bureau shortly after earning his PhD in artificial intelligence-enabled analytics from CU—the University of Colorado's main campus in Boulder—and had now worked at CBI for fifteen years, holding his current position for the past three years.

Josh's formal job description was a lengthy one, but it could easily have been summarized in a single sentence: "Go dig through mountains of data and pull out interesting and important insights—some that we would otherwise never know, or even think to ask the questions—about which we need to do something." Even though he headed a staff of ten other data analysts and analytics specialists, at various levels of the CBI hierarchy, Josh spent much of his own workday getting his hands dirty, chasing an endless trail of "what if..." and "okay, then what about..." and "what does that really mean?" types of questions.

Armed with his PhD, Josh could probably make double his current salary—at least—out in Silicon Valley, or even fifteen or so miles to the southeast down in the heart of Denver's technology center complexes...especially with the economy now showing signs of life. He truly enjoyed his job at the CBI, though, and made decent enough money perched in the upper echelon of the state's pay grade system. Plus, with the economic turmoil of the past several years, the security and stability of a government job had a great deal of appeal—especially a job with reasonable working hours rather than the killer schedule and lousy work-life balance that was still so prevalent in the tech industry. He worked from his Boulder home at least two days each week, avoiding the frustrating and sometimes weather-treacherous commute into and then back from Denver's Lakewood suburb, where the CBI building was, on those days.

Sometimes the CBI's director would specifically ask him to dig into a time-sensitive matter, as quickly as possible. The idea was that if Josh and his team could glean and then validate a few critical insights, CBI might possibly interdict some existing and problematic situations before more damage occurred.

Such was the case this morning. The rash of vehicle vandalism all around metro Denver, and even up and down I-25 to include Fort Collins and Colorado

Springs, had finally lit up the CBI's radar. Now, the thinking was that this wasn't just a burst of teenage vandalism or even gang-driven destruction. So many areas had been consistently hit over the past four weeks that…well, *something* was amiss here.

And that's what Josh Stein was asked to find out.

The era of "big data" was now at the quarter-century mark, but the powerful new analytical tools developed over the past five years or so gave experts such as Josh Stein unprecedented power at their fingertips to dive into mountains of all kinds of data. In particular, the application of the latest wave of artificial intelligence technology to the analysis of images and video had reached a new zenith.

Today was one of Josh's work-at-home days, which meant that he participated in the daily CBI morning stand-up via videoconference. After receiving his marching orders, he made a fresh pot of coffee, told his wife Kara that he would be locked in his first-floor home office for at least the next two hours, and then went to work.

Josh had been analyzing data for so many years now that he had his regimen down to a science. He spent about twenty minutes browsing through CBI's vast master catalogs of their own data resources as well as those from elsewhere, deciding which pieces of data he wanted to use for his initial efforts. Next, he set up a suite of sophisticated "data mining" algorithms and models designed to discover if any hidden patterns in the data might emerge. Then he put his models to work while he took a quick lunch break and braved the still unseasonably chilly late October weather to walk his black Lab Otis. This time of the year along the front range of the Rockies was always a crapshoot, weather-wise. Sometimes the mercury topped off in the seventies, seeming much more like spring or early summer, but other days saw the thermometer steadily remain below freezing. Occasionally the temperature would whipsaw throughout a given day, starting off in the sixties or even the seventies and ending up in the teens. Today was one of those extra-cold ones, so Josh donned the full Colorado outdoors getup—parka, gloves, ski cap—for his fifteen minutes outside with Otis.

Josh had barely settled back into his home office when he was already digesting the early results of his analytics. The first one: Every report of multiple instances of vandalism had occurred in a residential neighborhood, rather than in an office parking lot or garage, at a sporting event, or in some other business-type setting. Additionally, every occurrence happened after dark, which one would have expected for neighborhoods, the idea likely being to avoid face-to-face confrontation with residents.

So far, nothing earth-shattering: just simplistic data filtering and matching that could have been gleaned from far less sophisticated analytics than what Josh had put to work. The next insight, however, was a bit more telling: Every single neighborhood hit, even down in Colorado Springs and up in Fort Collins, was one that did *not* have any sort of street-level public video surveillance system. As with most metro areas, Denver had steadily blanketed its streets, parking lots and garages, and even the interiors of high-traffic buildings with a variety of reconnaissance capabilities. Privacy advocates had protested for years, but all levels of Colorado's government had remained resolute in their stance that the role of videos and images in preventing and solving crimes trumped privacy concerns. Colorado's state, county, and local policing agencies went out of their way to protect their enormous libraries of videos and images from hacking; and to date, at least, they had successfully fought any and all legal challenges to their data collection and harvesting efforts.

Though reconnaissance capabilities had steadily spread throughout metro Denver and elsewhere in Colorado, the coverage was by no means universal. Plenty of neighborhoods in particular were absent any sort of public surveillance.

The salient point here immediately jumped out at Josh. Surveillance technology had advanced so far during the latter years of the 2020s and the first half of the 2030s that it was now extremely difficult to detect the surveillance camera equipment. Perps couldn't just drive into a neighborhood, especially after dark, and readily determine whether or not they were being recorded.

They knew.

Whoever was doing the vandalism *knew* with absolute certainty which neighborhoods to hit where they would be safe from public surveillance, much of which was monitored live by various policing agencies around the metro Denver area. Josh immediately knew that pointing his analytics software at CBI's surveillance video library covering the last month would be an exercise in futility.

They probably had inside knowledge.

Were the offenders cops, with access to the closely held list of surveillance sites all around the metro area? Given the geographic dispersal of the vandalism, and especially with several clusters occurring simultaneously miles apart from each other, more than one person was involved. A question to be addressed later…

With this first round of insights in the books, Josh began round two of his analysis. He grabbed the collection of online incident reports, most of which included digital photos of the marred vehicles and each one's specific damages. He selected several of his favorite photo analysis models, each one equipped with artificial intelligence-powered image recognition, and linked those models to the incident reports.

Time for an afternoon cup of coffee, Josh decided as he headed into the dated farmhouse-style kitchen that was at the top of Kara's wish list for a home makeover. Given that their house had dropped nearly fifty percent in value during the crash a couple of years earlier, and had only recovered about half of that so far, Josh and Kara had reluctantly put the brakes on the top-to-bottom home makeover for their forty-year-old house that would easily hit six figures when everything was paid for.

Someday…

By the time Josh was back in his office and seated behind his desk, this second round of models had completed its work. *Not surprising*, he thought to himself. Even with a month-long vandalism spree, only about a thousand vehicles had been targeted. The sophisticated image recognition software made short work of analyzing the police incident report photos, cross-referencing the results with the rest of the police report data, and then spitting out a few interesting findings.

Josh scanned the top five insights, and one in particular jumped out at him:

VEHICLES WITH BUMPER STICKERS: 542
VEHICLES WITH WINDOW DECALS: 149
VEHICLES WITHOUT STICKERS OR DECALS: 397

At first glance and to the untrained eye, these three data points might seem meaningless. Still, well over half of the vehicles targeted did have some sort of bumper sticker or window decal…an oddity, Josh thought, because these days, most people no longer pasted either to their vehicles.

Unless it's during political season.

Realizing that he had to make some adjustments to one of his algorithms and rerun that model, Josh did so, but he first needed to do an internet search to extract a complete list of all of the current presidential candidates in the three major political parties…even including Ephraim Hollinger, the sole RAVG Party candidate. He fed that list into his model, reran it, and his results came back in less than thirty seconds. Josh quickly scanned the output.

Just as I thought.

Of the targeted vehicles that had bumper stickers or window decals, almost every single one was for a Democratic or Republican Party presidential candidate. Only three bore the name "Hollinger," according to the results.

I wonder...

Josh clicked on the underlined "Hollinger" name in his results list, which immediately brought up multiple thumbnails for each of those three incidents. He clicked one of the thumbnails for the first one, and the image instantly expanded into the upper right corner of his screen.

I was right.

The photo of the back of the car, taken by the responding Denver police officer, showed a bumper sticker that read "HOLLINGER FOR PRISON 2036." To confirm his suspicions, Josh viewed photos from the other two. One of those vehicles, an SUV, had the exact same bumper sticker, while the final one—a battered sedan that had seen better days—had a window decal with the same wording.

A few drags and clicks later, Josh was able to determine that each of these three vehicles had been hit especially hard: multiple tire punctures instead of one, or both sides keyed instead of just one side.

They're targeting supporters of the president's political opponents: Republicans, Democrats, and anyone who has something on his or her vehicle indicating opposition to Hollinger.

Josh's thoughts raced.

But what about the vandalized vehicles that didn't have any stickers or decals?

Josh Stein had been in the analytics game for a long time. Sometimes, the *absence* of certain data tells a story every bit as important as the presence of other data.

He *knew* there was a story here.

He just couldn't yet put his finger on what that story was.

* * *

Kurt Stobel, the de facto leader of Colorado's white nationalist movement—the same Kurt who had accompanied Randall Weston on the Jewish cemetery desecrations, and who had personally defaced the targeted cemetery's buildings with huge swastikas and "Jüden Verboten" blasphemy—had been the one to come up with the idea.

The first primaries and caucuses were less than four months away, meaning that more than twenty Democrats were vying for their party's nomination to face off against Ephraim Hollinger. Likewise, eight Republicans were doing the same over on their side. Anyone who backed any of these non-RAVG Party candidates was obviously someone who hated the country, Kurt had argued on the secure chat room for his like-minded Denver-area patriots. Therefore, these scum should be made to pay for their treasonous behavior.

Better yet: Not only should any car with a bumper sticker or decal promoting a Dem or Republican candidate become a target, so, too, should any car that *didn't* have an emblem professing support for the re-election of Ephraim Hollinger and Paul Nelson.

Either someone was fully on board the RAVG Party train, and clearly made that support known, or that person was a traitor; there was no in-between anymore.

Kurt's like-minded brother Lucas was a Denver cop, and had access to a comprehensive, confidential list of metro Denver neighborhoods that indicated what sort of street video surveillance, if any, was present. Lucas Stobel slipped his brother a copy of the list, and then Kurt shared with his followers a subset from the master list that indicated all neighborhoods that were sans cameras. His message to Randall Weston and the others:

Have at it!

* * *

In years past, Josh Stein would have immediately been on the phone to his counterpart at the FBI, sharing his findings and suppositions, and seeing what the Bureau might have from other states. The absorption of the FBI into the Federal Police Force more than two years earlier had been an inflection point, however. Josh's own politics tended to run right down the middle. He had been a registered Republican in his younger years, but in the later years of the 2010s he had switched over to the Democrats. He was the classic moderate: fiscally conservative, a believer in the nation projecting a strong global presence —militarily and diplomatically—but fairly liberal when it came to societal issues.

He was an increasing rarity these days.

Consequently, Josh Stein harbored a deep distrust of the FPF. He saw Spencer Howell's masterpiece for exactly what it was: an increasingly brutal enforcement arm of RAVG Party doctrine, rather than any sort of dispassionate, measured national policing agency. Being Jewish, Josh was appalled not only by the nauseating images of that swastika-shaped book burning last Fourth of July over in Indiana, but also by FPF's unrepentant role in the whole sickening business.

Odds were that reporting his findings of apparent politically motivated vandalism—admittedly only a hypothesis at this point, but a substantial one worthy of immediate follow-on analysis—to the FPF in order to spur them into applying Josh's work to similar vandalism clusters now being reported in other states, would only result in the whole matter vanishing from the radar.

Instead, Josh spent the rest of the afternoon and the early evening working the phones, contacting his counterparts in four other states where similar vandalism outbreaks were known to CBI to have occurred. Tara Hernandez, the Director of Data Analysis for the New Jersey State Police, was Josh's first call.

"Great minds think alike," Tara replied dryly after Josh summarized his findings so far. "We've had clusters from up in Mahwah all the way down to Cape May; almost five thousand vehicles. I ran a bunch of models against the data yesterday, and wouldn't you know it, I came up with the same thing you did."

"Did you contact the FPF?" Josh asked.

"Shit no!" Tara's voice was pure disgust. "For all we know, they're the ones behind it!"

"You think so?" Josh's tones were skeptical; fearful.

A short pause.

"Probably not," Tara Hernandez admitted. "I mean, it's not an impossibility; but I guess not. But maybe it's the same degenerates who did all that Jewish cemetery and synagogue damage early last year. Hollinger definitely has all corners of the lunatic fringe out in force."

She gathered her thoughts.

"Still, I don't see the FPF doing anything about it—especially after that swastika book burning."

A shiver ran through Josh Stein at Tara's words.

"Any thoughts about the cars without bumper stickers that got hit?"

A longer pause this time.

"Not sure," she seemed to be thinking out loud. "I think there's something there, but I'm not sure what."

"Exact same with me," Josh replied.

They talked for a few more minutes, changing the subject to different matters. Josh was just about to hang up, having already said his goodbyes, when Tara Hernandez interjected:

"I just had a thought," she blurted out, again seeming to be thinking in real time. "It's a safe bet that whoever is doing the vandalism are fanatical Hollinger supporters, right?"

"Most likely," Josh agreed.

"I wonder if there's a way to find out if there were cars on those streets that didn't get hit, and if those ones had some kind of Hollinger sticker or decal...not 'Hollinger for Prison' but an actual 'Hollinger 2036' or 'Hollinger-Nelson 2036' one."

What's she getting at?

The epiphany came to Josh, just as Tara continued her real-time contemplation.

"Could it be that they left alone all of the Hollinger cars to not only hit the ones whose owners supported someone else, but also decided to damage other ones that *didn't* show support for Hollinger? Sort of extortion through vandalism?"

* * *

Mike Lewis in Washington State hadn't yet begun his own data and image analysis, but after Josh presented the Reader's Digest version of what both he and Tara Hernandez in New Jersey had discovered thus far, Mike promised that he would run some preliminary analytics later this afternoon or early this evening, and let Josh know what he found.

Stephen Heinz in Georgia confirmed that in Atlanta, Savannah, and Macon—the three cities in that state hit hardest so far—he was seeing the same patterns as in New Jersey and Colorado. Even before Josh had a chance to prompt him about Tara's hypothesis about the un-stickered and un-decaled vehicles, Heinz offered the same proposition.

Maya Garcia in Arizona had gone even further.

"We already sent state troopers out to do walk-throughs of about a quarter of the streets that were hit all over metro Phoenix and down in Tucson; maybe a little less than a quarter. They went around the same time that the vandalism had occurred, after dark, to approximate the same cars parked on the street. Sure enough, almost every street had at least two or three vehicles with some sort of "Re-Elect Hollinger" sticker or decal, and not a single one of them had been vandalized. Who was it that said they thought the perps were bypassing Hollinger vehicles?"

"Tara," Josh answered.

"In Jersey; Tara Hernandez," he added, even though he was fairly certain that Maya Garcia and Tara Hernandez knew one another.

"I know Tara," Maya confirmed. "Yeah, she's definitely onto something."

"I'll get CBI to send investigators out to our streets, and I'll let Tara know that she should request some NJ troopers to do the same thing there."

"This is batshit crazy, huh?" Maya Garcia mused as they said their goodbyes.

Josh Stein hesitated a moment before replying.

"Honestly, it scares the hell out of me."

A short pause preceded Maya's response.

"Me too."

* * *

The next morning at the CBI stand-up, Josh presented not only his findings, but the concurrence of his counterparts in four other states. (An email from Mike Lewis in Washington State was waiting for Josh that morning, confirming the same attack patterns in Seattle, Tacoma, and Spokane.)

That evening, shortly after nightfall, CBI investigators fanned out over a sizable subset of impacted streets in metro Denver, and also in Fort Collins and Colorado Springs. Within a half hour, the final missing piece to the puzzle had been slotted. The conclusions were unmistakable. A vehicle that had any sort of sticker or decal supporting Hollinger's re-election effectively had a protective bubble surrounding it, because not a single one had suffered any damage during the attacks on that particular street. The CBI investigators confirmed with the various vehicle owners that their cars and SUVs and trucks had indeed been parked on the street on whatever night that neighborhood's vandalism had taken place. But absent a pro-Hollinger sticker or decal, a car or truck or SUV was almost certain to have been hit—even one *without* any sort of political messaging.

The next morning, Josh Stein quickly wrote up his findings and then submitted them to the FPF's LIRP (Local Incident Reporting Portal) interface. By noon, Josh confirmed that Mike Lewis, Tara Hernandez, Maya Garcia, and Stephen Heinz had all done the same. Certainly, with the analytics leads from five states all simultaneously reporting the same findings, the FPF would be spurred to action, political allegiances aside.

* * *

A week passed.

Then another week went by.

Josh pinged the FPF multiple times for a status update on the matter. Or, more accurately, Josh Stein *attempted* to ping the FPF. Every outreach to the FPF got exactly nowhere. Even more state-level analytics leaders had jumped onto the bandwagon in the meantime: Michigan, New York, Massachusetts, Pennsylvania, and a number of others.

Along with the deafening silence from FPF, another significant roadblock emerged. Those states with RAVG Party governors abruptly and decisively shut down the investigations in their respective states when they became aware of what their state police and investigation bureaus were tracking. Stephen Heinz in Georgia was summarily and brusquely fired, with no explanation. So was Tyler Blake in Alabama; and likewise Kendra Goldberg in Florida.

Clearly, the RAVG Party stakeholders at the state level wanted to bury the entire matter. That was hardly surprising. What was extremely disheartening, though, was that the agency that should have pursued the matter under a doctrine of "justice is not only blind, it doesn't belong to a political party"—the Federal Police Force—might as well have been called the RAVG Party Police Force.

* * *

"This is bullshit," Tara Hernandez fumed to Josh and several others during a video chat that had been surreptitiously organized after they all realized that the RAVG Party machine had successfully blockaded their efforts.

"I have an idea, though," Tara added. Everyone on the call, including Josh, could sense the hesitation that suddenly permeated her words.

"My husband Quincy went to college with Craig Ryan...you know, the cable news reporter?"

Nods and murmured uh-huhs came from most of the others on the video call.

"We'll be sticking our necks out," she continued, "but Quincy can feed Craig the story, and I'm sure he'll run with it."

A collective look of dread spread across the faces of the attendees.

"We can leave out the FPF stonewalling," Tara suggested. "Same with Stephen and the others getting fired. We can just stick to the story itself: how this vehicle vandalism is happening all around the country, and how the exact same pattern keeps showing up. This way, once it's out in the public, maybe the FPF will be forced to act."

"Or at least pretend to act," a skeptical Mike Lewis mused.

"Maybe," Tara added. "But otherwise, I can't think of anything else to try."

* * *

"Political bumper stickers for presidential races date back to the early 1950s," John Culverson opened as he came back from commercial, "and have long been a popular way for Americans to show support for their favored candidates in both primary and general elections. But in our hyper-partisan political climate of the 2030s, bumper stickers—and car window decals as well—can also make your vehicle a vandalism target. And, as Craig Ryan has found, even the *absence* of a sticker or decal can have the same result."

Cut to Craig Ryan, live on location in Colorado.

"Five weeks ago, this street in Littleton, a suburb of Denver, saw a vandalism spree that targeted cars parked along the curb. But this vandalism wasn't the work of juvenile delinquents or even street gangs. It was politically motivated."

The camera lens slowly backed away from the reporter, revealing an attractive, fortyish blonde woman and her athletic-looking husband of about the same age standing alongside Ryan.

"Melissa and Todd Helms were home that evening, but were unaware until the next morning that their two-month-old Honda Accord had been damaged. Melissa, can you tell us what happened?"

"Well," the woman began, "the entire right-side length had been gouged by some sort of knife or screwdriver or something, and also the front right tire had been punctured through the sidewall."

"Any idea why your car might have been targeted?" Craig Ryan looked at Todd Helms as he asked the leading question.

"Well," Todd replied, "based on a bunch of other vandalism that same night on our street, we think it's because we had a 'Paul Willis for President' sticker on the back left bumper."

"And why do you say 'based on a bunch of other vandalism'?" Craig continued to prompt.

"From what the police told us," Melissa chimed in, "pretty much every car on the street that had a bumper sticker for a Democratic or Republican presidential candidate was vandalized."

"Or window decal," her husband interjected.

"What the Colorado Bureau of Investigation has discovered is even more alarming," Craig Ryan resumed his story narrative as the camera again zoomed in tight on just him. "Not only were cars on this quiet street with Democratic or Republican candidate stickers and decals attacked, but so, too, were vehicles that had *no* political statements of any kind. The alarming part of the story is the only undamaged cars were those that displayed some sort of emblem in favor of President Hollinger's re-election."

In the network control room, the lead technician cut to a sequence of clips of other vandalized neighborhood streets, each one three or four seconds in length, as Ryan continued.

"The Helms' street was only one of hundreds here in metro Denver and also up and down the front range with *exactly* the same pattern of damaged versus undamaged vehicles. And to make matters worse, our investigations have uncovered the same exact situation all across the country."

Craig Ryan proceeded with the remainder of his report, covering another two and a half minutes, and then John Culverson took the story back to the studio where he led a roundtable discussion for another five minutes with three of the network's regular contributing analysts.

During that time, secure text messages were already flying.

* * *

"Craig Ryan?"

The reporter was on his way into the network's headquarters building when a plainclothes FPF officer intercepted him, stepping aggressively and threateningly into Ryan's path. Accompanying that officer—who apparently made the extra effort to dress like a stereotypical Gestapo agent in a 1940s war movie, with the whole black trench coat and brimmed fedora resting low on his forehead getup—were three heavily armed, camo-clad FPFers. Their appearance was identical to those who had stormed Josh Goldstein's conference room almost two years earlier, or those who had provided the "DON'T EVEN THINK ABOUT FUCKING WITH US!" fear factor as forty thousand copies of Daniel Jacobson's *The Twilight's Last Gleaming* were ferried from the printer's warehouse to their demise.

Ryan's crowded flight had landed at Hollinger National (until earlier in the year, Reagan National) shortly after seven on Tuesday, the twentieth of November. Washington's late-November weather had been balmy, almost summerlike, for the past two weeks. Craig had originally intended to grab a rideshare directly home, but at the last minute remembered that he needed to swing by the network building to retrieve the birthday gift he had bought for his mother that he would give to her when the entire Ryan family gathered for Thanksgiving in a couple of days. But even if Craig Ryan had headed home, he would still have wound up spending this night—and quite a few more—detained in FPF lockup at their main downtown facility, since another crew of FPF agents was staking out his Georgetown brownstone.

The plainclothes FPFer flashed his badge. Instead of confirming his own identity as demanded—they all knew exactly who he was anyway, formalities aside—Craig Ryan attempted a disarming:

"What can I help you with?"

Apparently, these particular Federal Police Force agents were in no mood for pleasantries. One of the camo-clad agents rifle-butted Ryan in his left shoulder blade, knocking him off-balance just as another one grabbed Craig's right arm and shoved him to his knees. Within seconds he was handcuffed behind his back, and then the same two who had manhandled him jerked him to his feet. Once again off-balance, the reporter was shoved into the back right side of a jet-black, oversized SUV with opaquely tinted windows that screamed "the Feds" in its appearance.

The ten-minute drive to FPF headquarters was done in total silence. Craig Ryan's anger threatened to boil over, but he held his temper in check. He had a quick flash of the government vehicle diverting to a deserted portion of Rock Creek Park, where they would yank him out of the car and make a severe beating look like a mugging before they dumped his near-lifeless body…

He shook away the terrifying thoughts and conjured images, instead concentrating on his plan of action once he was unloaded into an FPF interview room. He would immediately demand a lawyer, and refuse to utter a word until his representation arrived.

* * *

"You're no doubt familiar with the provisions of the Truth and Accuracy in Media and Communications Act," Chase Dylan, recently appointed as Deputy Director of the Federal Police Force, glared at Craig Ryan. The reporter had spent three hours alone in the cramped, over-lit interview room, his repeated requests—demands—for an attorney unheeded, before the Deputy Director finally commandingly strode into the room.

"I'm not answering any questions, or saying anything, until I have an attorney with me," Ryan decided to counter Dylan's obvious attempt to take early command of the interview, or interrogation, or whatever the FPF had in store for Craig.

"TAMCA expressly prohibits the dissemination of false information that is intended to trigger social unrest," Dylan continued, swatting away Ryan's latest demand for his Sixth Amendment rights. Chase Dylan was leaving no doubt that not only was he in charge here, but also that he was manifestly pissing all over Craig Ryan's constitutionally guaranteed rights.

"Your live segment on the afternoon of Wednesday, November 14th, from Littleton, Colorado, blatantly included false information with the express —"

"What false information?" Craig Ryan demanded.

"— intention of causing social and political turmoil," Chase Dylan ignored the interruption, stomping right over the reporter's words.

"What false information?" Ryan demanded again.

This time, the FPF Deputy Director offered the details behind the accusation.

"Your report stated that unless a vehicle had a President Hollinger re-election sticker or decal, it would inevitably be vandalized. You falsely accused the President of the United States and his campaign of targeting —"

"I never said a word about Hollinger or his campaign!" Ryan was now enraged. "I reported *exactly* what the Colorado Bureau of Investigation found by analyzing their vandalism data. That's a *fact!*"

"You falsely accused the President of the United States and his campaign," Chase Dylan backtracked, the look on his face a curious combination of smugness and disgust, "of extorting citizens of the United States to place a particular type of political bumper sticker or decal on their cars, or otherwise be subject to vandalism and damage of their personal property."

Is this guy for real? Craig Ryan couldn't believe what he was hearing. Talk about twisting a few factoids into an entirely unsupportable conclusion!

"You are being charged with one count of 'Sedition through Media Content and Transmission' as specified by Section 2203 of the Truth and Accuracy in Media and Communications Act."

"I WANT A FUCKING LAWYER! NOW!" Craig Ryan lost any remaining self-control.

"You will be provided with an attorney at the appropriate time before your trial," Chase Dylan pronounced, his tone clearly communicating his disinterest in Craig Ryan's right to representation. "Until then, you will remain in custody as a designated Enemy of the United States of America under Section 1104 of the Federal Police Force Reorganization Act."

So much for Thanksgiving at my parents' house was, crazily, Craig Ryan's reflexive reaction to being coldly informed that not only did Ephraim Hollinger regularly refer to Ryan and his ilk as "Enemies of the State" and "Enemies of the People" during his press conferences and modern-day Nuremberg Rallies, he was now legally designated as such.

* * *

That same day, the FPF came for Josh Stein. They also came for Tara Hernandez and her husband Quincy. They took Maya Garcia. They came for Stephen Heinz and Mike Lewis and nearly a dozen of their counterparts in other states.

They came for the directors of the Colorado Bureau of Investigation, and the New Jersey State Police, and other state-level policing and investigation agencies who had failed to muzzle their analytics leaders and data scientists, and bury the whole matter.

They came for John Culverson, since he had anchored the program where Craig Ryan's segment had aired, and had provided the lead-in to Ryan's report. They dragged away Brad Scott, the network's broadcast engineer that afternoon, since he had been the in-studio lead technician for the segment that brought Ryan's words to the airwaves.

By the time the arrests were concluded, thirty individuals were in detention at FPF facilities all around the country. A few days later, attorneys were finally permitted to consult with their imprisoned clients. To a person, each attorney vowed to fight the charges on constitutional grounds. But also, to a person, each attorney privately feared that in Ephraim Hollinger's America, constitutional grounds meant little or nothing.

* * *

The combined trial for all of the defendants together began on Monday, December 10th, at the Federal Courthouse in downtown Denver. Apparently, in the reshaped judicial system of Ephraim Hollinger, justice moved extremely swiftly when it suited the purposes of the president, his Attorney General, and their Justice Department. Since Craig Ryan's summary offense had occurred in the Denver suburbs and had relied on data provided by Josh Stein of the Colorado Bureau of Investigation, Spencer Howell decided that Denver was the ideal location to unveil the consequences of defying Ephraim Hollinger's post-midterms stranglehold on America.

It's like a scene right out of the Nuremberg trials, Craig Ryan—ever the historian—thought to himself when he and the others were led into a single large area, consisting of three rows of uncomfortable-looking wooden benches, each one with room for ten defendants. Instead of Göring, Hess, Jodl, Ribbentrop, and most of the other surviving upper echelon war criminals of the Third Reich, however, today's defendants were two reporters, a cable news broadcast engineer, thirteen analytics geeks (along with the husband of one of them), and also their unfortunate state government bosses—some of them career civil servants, others political appointees—who suffered the misfortune of having allowed their subordinates to actually do their jobs.

Spencer Howell, as a proxy for Ephraim Hollinger, personally selected Thomas Shawnessy as the federal judge for this trial. Shawnessy was originally from Colorado's Western Slope on the other side of the Rockies. Plainly, Thomas Shawnessy was a hateful man, though this distinguishing characteristic had hardly been a hindrance in his advancement through first Colorado's and then the federal judicial system. Shawnessy's hallmark was "law and order," even though he had no qualms about, say, locking up peaceful protesters for a few years despite having been brutalized by marauding police and having broken no laws. Unbeknownst to all but a handful of others, Shawnessy had grown rich via a scheme to hand down sentences far in excess of what defendants' offenses warranted in exchange for kickbacks from the privately run, for-profit state and federal prisons where he ordered the convicted offenders to be confined.

The all-white jury of eleven men and one woman listened to Erik Donaldson, the United States Attorney for the District of Colorado, make his opening arguments that the evidence these jurors were about to hear constituted an open-and-shut, slam dunk case for conviction. And by the way, the U.S. Attorney added with a patronizing smile directed to the jurors, not to worry—this should all be over in time for any procrastinators among you to be out of here and then still get your Christmas shopping done.

Exactly one week later, following three and a half days of testimony, a day and a half of deliberation, and then a weekend recess to build the suspense for the Big Reveal, the jury did precisely what Erik Donaldson had advocated. They delivered guilty verdicts on all charges, for every one of the defendants. Sentencing took place three days later, just in time for the judge to cross the Rockies back to his Western Slope home—by way of a private jet provided by the Justice Department—and settle in for a good old-fashioned Shawnessy family Christmas. The sentences ranged from five years in federal prison for a few of those deemed to have been only ancillary participants in the seditious acts, to fifteen years each with no possibility of parole for Craig Ryan, Josh Stein, Tara and Quincy Hernandez, and Mike Lewis, and also Maya Garcia, and also…

Appeals for every one of the defendant's convictions were filed before the end of the year, under a myriad of constitutional grounds. Ephraim Hollinger and Spencer Howell wanted these particular wheels of justice to move swiftly, and so the appeals arrived en masse at the doors of the Supreme Court before the end of February 2036. Within days, the Court returned its decisions for all of the cases, upholding each conviction and sentence by the same nine-to-six decision that had upheld TAMCA in the first place.

And, as with TAMCA itself, absent Ephraim Hollinger's court packing a year earlier, each conviction and sentence would have been overturned by a six-to-three margin.

Personal assets of most of the convicted offenders were also seized as the monetary fine portion of Shawnessy's sentences. About a hundred thousand dollars from the total would trickle into Shawnessy's offshore bank accounts as the judge's cut; Hollinger's bagman Bart Lawrence, now doing double duty for Spencer Howell as well, would see to the surreptitious transfers.

Consequently, some stranger would soon be making those long-overdue renovations to Kara Stein's dated farmhouse kitchen and the rest of the house in Boulder that was no longer her home.

Chapter 30

"I need you to do something for me."

Daniel Jacobson's pulse quickened in reflexive response to Michele Burgess' out-of-left-field statement. They had just finished a six-mile, quick-paced run through Pittsburgh's Schenley Park, down Forbes Avenue, and into nearby Frick Park. Even though the calendar had slid past Christmas Day, the thermometer held at a pleasant fifty degrees for the mid-afternoon—the absolute perfect weather for an earliest-days-of-winter outdoors run. The trees had shed the last of their crinkled, washed-out brown hangers-on during a brisk windstorm on Christmas Eve day. But despite the barren oaks and their brethren trees, the day had the feel of early autumn rather than the beginning of winter; all that was missing were the surrounding swirling brushstrokes of reds and yellows and oranges.

Daniel's brisk cool-down stroll instantly slowed, as did Michele's. They both continued walking as Daniel's brain frenziedly processed her peculiar request.

Michele looked over at Daniel, locking eyes. She was still slightly winded from exerting herself during their run, and her breathy words reflected that she hadn't yet fully recovered as she continued.

"I can't tell you…um, I actually can't tell you anything at all, but you have to trust me."

Daniel's confusion yielded to apprehension. In his experience, the only time a statement with this phrasing was ever uttered between two people in a relationship was when someone had just done, or was about to do, something dicey that could possibly threaten the stability of said relationship.

And there she was again: *Trust me.*

"I need to go out of town for two or three days," Michele continued. "This weekend. But I can't tell you where I'm going, and you won't be able to get in touch with me because I'm not taking my phone with me. I will be back by New Year's Eve, though; actually a day earlier, probably late Sunday, but I don't know exactly when."

What the...

"I also need you to cover for me when I'm gone, to make it seem like I'm still in Pittsburgh. I can't just leave my phone at my house the whole time I'm gone."

Daniel's confusion shifted into high gear.

"Are you going to Youngstown to see your great-grandfather?" For some reason, that idea popped into Daniel's head. Hanukah was exceptionally late this year—the first night had actually been on Christmas, and the eighth night wouldn't be until New Year's Day...next year!

That makes sense—she's going to visit Isaac Gretz for Hanukah.

But why the cloak-and-dagger business? That doesn't make sense...

No response from Michele to Daniel's question.

"Okay, seriously," he finally insisted, his mind still trying to solve this puzzle without any clues, "where are you going?"

Michele halted, and Daniel did likewise.

"I can't tell you," she repeated her earlier assertion. Not only had she fully recovered her wind, her voice now held a hard note that clearly issued an order to Daniel: *Stop asking me that!*

Apparently realizing that she needed to throw him at least a small bone, she reached with her right hand to take his left one as they both began walking again.

"I'm not involved with anyone else," she half-smiled as she looked over at him, "if that's what you're worried about. I'm not sneaking away to some resort with some other guy, or anything like that."

"That's not what I was thinking," Daniel's response was too quick; his tones too disbelieving.

"I'm *not*," Michele repeated emphatically.

"I don't understand why you can't tell me where you're going," Daniel sighed.

"And why aren't you taking your phone with you?" he added. "I really don't get that. This isn't like going to the shooting range for an hour; you're talking about a couple of days! And what's this about me covering for you? To make it look like you're still in Pittsburgh? Seriously—what's that all about?"

"At some point," Michele followed Daniel's sigh with one of her own, "I'll probably have to tell you what's going on. Maybe not; I really hope not. I promise you that *when* you need to know, I'll tell you everything."

Michele Burgess looked away from Daniel, upward at the top branches of what was probably a hundred-year-old oak that they were passing, and then back at him.

"But not now. I need to be totally off the grid for a couple of days, but I need to look like I'm not; and I need your help." The hardness instantly returned to her voice.

"Yeah…okay," Daniel finally conceded. "Just let me know what you need me to do."

A sad smile came to Michele's face.

"I have a list back at my house," she said. "I'll go over it with you when we get back."

Her words, her commanding tone, now became those of retired United States Army Major Michele Burgess, Special Forces.

"But you can't let *anyone* see the list, or even know that it exists. Don't go and visit anyone in your family while I'm gone, and they can't come and see you and wind up disrupting the schedule. Just follow *exactly* what the list tells you what to do, step by step with absolutely no deviation. If it says to use your car for something, make sure that you don't use mine instead. *Everything* exactly as it's written, okay?"

Daniel could only offer an uneasy, wordless nod in reply.

Her eyes narrowed.

"And when you finish the final item on that list," she added, "you need to burn it."

* * *

Michele Burgess' handwritten list of precise instructions for Daniel Jacobson:

#1: Friday morning: At around 8:30 AM, text <u>MY PHONE</u> from <u>YOUR PHONE</u> at your condo and say that you're coming over in about a half hour, and that you're bringing bagels and coffee

#2: Buy a half dozen bagels and <u>TWO</u> large coffees, <u>make sure that you pay with a credit card</u>, and then drive over to my house

#3: Wait another three hours, and make sure that you don't text or call anybody. Then drive MY CAR back to your condo <u>but take MY PHONE with you — DON'T FORGET TO TAKE IT!</u>

#4: At around 4:00 PM go drive around for about 45 minutes, and <u>make sure you take MY PHONE with you</u>

#5: Spend the rest of the evening at your condo, keep my phone next to you; but a couple of times <u>take MY PHONE into the bathroom for a couple of minutes</u> while you leave YOUR PHONE in the living room

#6: Saturday morning: <u>leave YOUR PHONE at your condo</u>, and drive to my house with MY PHONE. Text YOUR PHONE from MINE that we'll go running today around 2:00. <u>Then leave MY PHONE in my bedroom</u>; drive YOUR CAR back to your condo

The list of cryptic, explicit, unnerving instructions continued from there for another three extremely detailed pages…

Chapter 31

"This is by far the largest contract I've ever received! By far! Nothing has ever even been close!" Marc Weber's elation was enough for both his wife and him together—which was a good thing, since Claire wasn't displaying anywhere near the jubilation one might have expected upon being informed that her husband's company had just been awarded a four-hundred-million-dollar federal building contract.

"I told you it would all pay off!" Marc Weber couldn't help adding, with the "it" in his condescending addendum referring to buying his way into the graces of the RAVG Party's reign, the swastika-shaped book burnings (a dozen more had taken place around the country since that first one the previous Fourth of July) and stepped-up Jew-baiting notwithstanding.

Earlier that morning, just after arriving at his office, Marc Weber received the not-unexpected news. True, some sort of curveball might have derailed the contract award at the eleventh hour. After all, Marc Weber wasn't the only construction industry wannabe-mogul throwing around money at the RAVGs. And especially since the midterms, even those builders who had been squeamish about the vicious RAVG Party messaging realized that unless they got on board, they would be coldly cut out of consideration for about a quarter trillion dollars of federal building contracts at the epicenter of the next wave of Hollinger's economic recovery agenda.

Marc Weber's firm was actually the beneficiary of two different awards this morning: one directly to his firm and his chosen subcontractors, and the other to a syndicate comprised of Weber's firm and a half dozen other similar-sized construction companies. The much larger syndicate award was for down the road:

probably breaking ground in mid-summer of 2037, timed perfectly for when Marc would be finishing up this first solo award that was scheduled to take a year and a half to complete. This first award also included more than ten million dollars in performance bonuses for finishing on schedule and on budget, so Marc Weber had every incentive in the world to be ready to go in mid-2037 when the mega-deal commenced.

"You hadn't mentioned anything at all about this," Claire reminded her husband when he returned home for dinner and shared the news.

"At least I don't remember you telling me," she added.

"I didn't," Marc admitted as he helped himself to a generous pour of Macallan single malt to commence the celebration.

"It's actually a top-secret project," he added. "I don't even know too much, other than the overall specs the government provided and what we proposed. But during the bidding process, we weren't allowed to even talk about it. Even now, there's only so much that I can say, and there's still plenty that I don't even know."

Claire cocked her head, confused.

"All of the bidders had to pass top-secret security clearance checks," Marc continued. "I know what government agency is issuing the contract, but I don't know exactly what they will be using the facility for once it's completed."

Claire Weber stared expectantly at her husband, obviously expecting him to expand on what he had just shared. Perhaps he would walk over to the oversized front window, pull the plush cinnamon-colored drapes to close them, and then lower his voice to a near-whisper as he brought his wife into his confidence.

Nothing doing. All Claire would know—all she *could* know—was that he had just been awarded a hush-hush building contract that would clear about seventy-two million dollars in profit for Marc's firm, out of the total four hundred million. Then, Marc's piece of the follow-on syndicate deal would push his total contract revenue above a billion dollars and profits to almost a quarter billion, just from these two deals! Marc reasoned that she could certainly brag about her husband's success to her parents and her brother, and to her friends at both of their country clubs; and she should absolutely drop the "b" word—billion—into the conversation. But the details? That was all "need to know," and Claire had just been informed of everything—which wasn't much at all—that she needed to know to carry out her role in touting Marc Weber's successes.

* * *

What Marc hadn't shared with his wife was that the contract came out of the Department of Homeland Security; that much Marc certainly knew. He had even surreptitiously met twice with Braxton Knox in the Secretary's plush downtown D.C. office. The first time had obviously been for Knox to feel out Marc Weber: not so much qualifications and capabilities of the man and his firm, but more Marc's attitude and appetite for DHS work that might make some people squeamish. The second meeting had been for Knox to let Marc know that this particular contract was being greased for him, and also that the follow-on one was being earmarked for the seven-firm syndicate in which Marc's firm had a slot. Even in Ephraim Hollinger's pay-to-play government, nothing was guaranteed until the contracts were actually signed; but Marc had walked away from that second meeting all but certain that his payoff was on its way.

Nothing in DHS' RFP—the formal Request for Proposals document that was part of the veneer of a fair competition in accordance with federal contracting practices—specified exactly how the sprawling facility would be put to use, once it had been completed. Marc Weber could certainly venture an educated guess, though.

Two hundred three-story, barracks-style buildings, each one with a capacity of one hundred and fifty people.

Two more two-story barracks-style buildings labeled on the layout map within the RFP as "open-bay guard sleeping facilities."

Six oversized, prison-style dining facilities.

A motor pool and fully stocked vehicle maintenance facility; a fire station; two helicopter landing pads; a three-story medical clinic containing rudimentary hospital facilities.

Surrounding the entire eighty-acre facility, a thirty-foot-high, seven-feet-thick block wall with observation posts every fifty yards.

The facility's location: in the empty, bleak desert 22 miles due east of the minuscule town of Wikieup, Arizona (population all of 125 souls), literally out in the middle of nowhere.

If the contract had been coming out of the Department of Defense, Marc Weber's educated guess would have been that he would be building the shell and infrastructure of some sort of top-secret military installation. He might joke that the Air Force had run out of room for aliens and their spacecraft at Area 51, and they now needed to expand to an equally desolate overflow facility.

But since DHS was running the show, and given the location, and even with nothing more precise to go on other than the facility's specifications, Marc was all but certain that his masterpiece would serve as some sort of super-sized detention center for undocumented immigrants on their way out of Ephraim Hollinger's America: illegal aliens (sans political correctness) rather than outer-space aliens.

Marc Weber was perfectly at peace with that proposition.

Chapter 32

"Grandpa?"

Ephraim Hollinger's head pivoted in the direction of his grandson Zachary's voice, his eyes signaling "go ahead" when they locked with little Zach's.

"You really lived here when you were my age?" the six-year-old questioned, again peering around the farmhouse's kitchen to take in the restored old-fashioned cook stove, the newly repainted glass-front cabinets filled with stacked antique dishes and cups, and the pleasantly weathered, free-standing kitchen pantry that dated back to the 1950s. Other than a single wispy memory of playing in the front yard of his grandparents' getaway lakefront cabin in southern Missouri, back when Zachary Hollinger was three and a half years old, every other recollection of his grandfather swirling around the boy's memory placed Ephraim Hollinger at the White House. Could Grandpa have actually lived in this small house at one time, as Zach's father had insisted?

The farmhouse's west-side wall chattered in response to a strong gust of frigid, late-January wind. The sound instantly flooded Ephraim Hollinger's mind with remembrances of the icy east-central Pennsylvania winters of his youth…or, more accurately, a few of the earliest years of his youth, given the family's eviction from this place when young Ephraim was only eight. Still, those couple of years in the early 1980s had acquired a mythology of their own in The Ephraim Hollinger Story, particularly in comparison to the extremely difficult ones that followed in Bethlehem and Allentown that had been hallmarked by one disheartening disappointment after another.

Three years earlier, shortly before his inauguration, a pro-Hollinger PAC forked over slightly more than seven hundred thousand dollars to acquire the soon-to-be president's boyhood home. Given Ephraim Hollinger's own massive wealth, he certainly could have easily bought the acreage and buildings where he had once lived, long ago, without any outside involvement. Hell, he could have purchased every surrounding farm within sight—even overpaying as much as necessary to secure every single one of those properties, and barely make a dent in his liquid assets. But something about the idea of paying his own money to reacquire something that rightfully should have been his anyway…well, it was a matter of principle to Hollinger.

The PAC that purchased the land and buildings that once belonged to Josiah Hollinger initially placed the entire property in a trust. They then executed a dizzying series of edgy financial and legal maneuvers that ended up transferring ownership of the property to the new president…not only without Hollinger forking over a dime, but also magically with no tax implications. Not that Tom Buckner's IRS posed any sort of threat to Ephraim Hollinger anyway, but this way the prying eyes and fingers and mouths of investigative journalists and broadcasters would come up empty as they frantically looked for something, *anything*, to pin on Hollinger during their futile attempts to roadblock his agenda.

Over the past three years, Ephraim Hollinger did spend about a hundred fifty thousand dollars in total to restore the farmhouse exterior and interior, and also the outbuildings, to an idealized version of their 1984-era state. He certainly could have bulldozed the creaky old house and replaced it with a far more elegant home, turning the outskirts of Nuremberg, Pennsylvania, into a presidential weekend retreat.

No.

Ephraim Hollinger wanted a highly accurate—albeit romanticized—reminder of those handfuls of his early years when his father and mother labored from before dawn to after nightfall almost every day; that too-brief blip in the universe's timeline before the Jew bankers ripped away those rewarding daily hardships. He was a busy man, especially so given that he was now the President of the United States, and didn't envision making his way to the property more than once or twice a year for the foreseeable future. But when he did have the opportunity to come here, and especially when he could bring his children or grandchildren—or sometimes both, as was the case now—Ephraim Hollinger relished the opportunity to shepherd his family back in time to reconstituted images of earlier, supposedly happier days. He even relocated his parents' graves from the cemetery outside Allentown, and reburied Josiah and Emma in a small clearing in the midst of an expanse of trees about five hundred yards from the farmhouse. His parents had been coldly evicted from this land that they loved, but Ephraim Hollinger had the last laugh: They would now be at rest here for eternity.

Hollinger had invited his son Hans along on this trip, along with Hans' wife Phoebe and their children, six-year-old Zachary and five-year-old Claudia. The president's wife Abigail also flew on Air Force One from Andrews to the Lehigh Valley Airport outside of Allentown, and then they all helicoptered to her husband's boyhood home, where they were met by the rest of the president's secret service contingent who had arrived earlier to set up the security perimeter and make other necessary arrangements. The agents all remained outside while Hollinger shuffled his family into the farmhouse.

This particular trip had no political or governmental purpose. In fact, young Zachary Hollinger was the primary reason for gathering part of his family at this particular location. Now that Zach was six, the boy's parents and grandparents knew the time was right to begin easing the youngster into the realities of a sometimes-harsh world.

"Would you like to know why Grandpa had to move from here?" Hans Hollinger squatted so he was now face-to-face with his six-year-old.

Before the boy had a chance to answer, Hans shifted his head to his daughter Claudia, standing a few feet away from her brother, and asked her the same question: "And would you like to know?"

At only five years old, chances were that Claudia wouldn't fully understand the intricacies of the upcoming lesson; in fact, she might not even remember this day. No worries: This would be only the first of countless times during the forthcoming years that Hans and Phoebe Hollinger, and also Hans' parents, would share their worldview with the children, the same as was already occurring with the three slightly older children of Hans' sister Holly.

Zachary and Claudia answered in unison with an enthusiastic "uh-huh" at the same instant, upon which Hans tilted his head upward at his father.

"Come on up here," Ephraim Hollinger told his grandchildren as he eased himself into one of the lath-style wooden kitchen chairs, clapping his hands in unison on each of his thighs. Each of his grandchildren approached him, and he simultaneously scooped up each of them and deposited Claudia on his left leg, and Zachary on his right.

"A long, long time ago," Ephraim Hollinger began his tale, "on this one morning when I was just a little bit older than Zachary is right now, I was helping my father—your great-grandfather—out in his workshop that's in the back of the closest barn. I'll take both of you out there later to show you. Anyway, on this one morning, these two Jew bankers drove up to the house with three policemen, and told my father that we all had to move away."

Ephraim Hollinger continued with his grim once-upon-a-time tale of foreclosure and eviction, his family's transient aftermath, and the comedown that sent Josiah and Emma Hollinger to their early graves.

He carried his story into the larger world of the mid- and late-1980s, making sure to weave into the tale the thieving Wall Street Jews and their money-grabbing foreign brethren who controlled the global financial system.

The entire time, Hans Hollinger stood nearby listening to this latest recitation of the tale that he knew by heart. Hans had heard his father's personal narrative perhaps two hundred times while growing up. Ephraim Hollinger had faithfully carried out his father's wishes to not only "never forget what they did to us," but to also make certain that the next generation of Hollingers, and now the next generation after them, fully understood the deceptive destruction that had been laid on this family by the greedy Jew bankers. Specifically, Ephraim Hollinger—his like-minded wife Abigail, as well—needed their children, and now their grandchildren, to understand the harsh reality that honest, hard-working people were constantly at a disadvantage because of the moneyed elite in this country and around the world. The powerful globalists could be beaten at their own game—Ephraim Hollinger was the living personification of having triumphed over the Jews who had stolen his father's farm—but righteous, vengeful victory required clear-eyed, unwavering acknowledgment of the enemy.

Perhaps his grandfather's mention early in the tale of "policemen" triggered young Zachary Hollinger's two-part question about these "Jews" that sounded so awful.

"Are there still Jews today, Grandpa?"

The President of the United States grimly nodded.

"Yes there are, Zach."

"Then since you're the president, can you arrest them for doing bad things?"

A sense of fear pervaded the boy's question, as if he had just finished hearing a frightening ghost story for the first time, and he was now asking if his grandfather could protect his sister and him from those scary ghouls.

A half-smile came to Ephraim Hollinger's face, but it was his son Hans who answered Zachary's question.

"Grandpa will arrest all of them. Don't worry, you and Claudia will be safe; the Jews won't be able to hurt you."

Chapter 33

From the moment Ephraim Hollinger announced his initial quest for the presidency back in 2031, he drew massive crowds of frenzied supporters to his many rallies. They loudly hailed every call to restore American values and greatness. They jeered every pronouncement of the names of the hated enemies in government: the mainstream media, Hollywood, and every other haven for their enemies. They savagely beat any protester who dared invade a Hollinger rally and make his—or her—presence known, drawing cheers from the others who were present as well as praise from the man himself.

They also revived several unsettling hallmarks from the 2020 presidential campaign; though once the 2032 election had been settled, the grandiose, in-your-face parades of boats and hulking pickup trucks and retirement community golf carts faded for a while.

Now, with the calendar having flipped to 2036 and the next presidential contest heating up, the parades were back.

* * *

Saturday, February 9, 2036.

Interstate 8, westbound from Yuma to El Centro and then back to Yuma, saw more than eight hundred vehicles—almost all of them pickup trucks, and the majority of them oversized—filling both lanes as they drove in formation, tooling along at forty-five most of the way. The vehicles were decked out with the standard collection of American flags, RAVG Party banners, and more than a few Confederate battle flags. Most also displayed homemade signs or custom-printed flags professing their undying allegiance to Ephraim Hollinger.

As each vehicle skirted the U.S.-Mexico border about seventeen miles west of Yuma, obscenities were hurled south against the invisible invaders who perpetually threatened their peace of mind and way of life. A few assault rifle and semi-automatic handgun rounds were fired in that same direction now and then, though most shooters were careful to aim high above the former border patrol outpost stations—now subsumed into the dark star of the FPF—that dotted the American side of the border.

Still, an "unfortunate incident" (in the words of a Sunday morning AVGN anchor, the only time the matter made the network's airwaves) occurred when the too-drunk truck bed occupants of a one-and-a-half-ton black pickup, a Confederate flag bolted to one side of the cab and a Hollinger flag to the other, passed a small group of four Hispanic men who were most likely in their late teens or early twenties, walking along the side of the highway.

Until that moment, the young men had been targeted by shouted insults, wrappered food trash, and even a couple of hurled beer bottles from the occupants of almost every other vehicle that passed them. When these truck bed occupants decided to unload a salvo of more than a dozen bottles en masse at the pedestrians, one of the men responded with two defiant middle fingers, displayed in tandem. He was rewarded with a burst of .223s from one of the assault rifles, and also with four nine-millimeter bullets sent his way from one of the handguns as punctuation on the matter.

"They're all illegals anyway," one of the shooters shrugged as they observed the other three young men futilely attempt to aid their suddenly dead friend. Realizing that eyewitnesses were not exactly what one wanted to leave behind at a shooting, all five of the heavily armed Hollinger supporters then opened fire on the cluster of Hispanic men.

Since no witnesses came forward from other participants in the truck parade, and none of the

Hispanic men—who happened to be on their way home from their Saturday trade school classes when their car broke down two miles back along Interstate 8—were left alive to give any kind of statement, the whole matter was quickly filed under "Unsolved."

* * *

In early March, about twenty-five miles east of Scranton, Pennsylvania on Lake Wallenpaupack, a Hollinger Boat Parade was scheduled to welcome the transition from winter to spring. Nearly two hundred vessels of all sizes formed up as their occupants hooted their support for the Hollinger-Nelson ticket, and their vow to continue to restore American values and greatness.

Andy Friedman was a hotshot partner in a Philadelphia law firm that specialized in securities law. Ten years earlier, when his mother passed away, Andy inherited the lakeside vacation home that his parents had built back in the 1980s. At least once a month, usually twice, he made the two-and-a-half-hour drive north from Philly to spend most of the weekend in the Poconos. Even in the winter, Andy would take his wife Cheryl and their three children away from the city. Lake Wallenpaupack didn't freeze solid during the heart of winter as it once had—thank you, climate change—but the tranquility of the wintertime forested mountains was a welcome, calming change from the often insufferable clients his firm took on to help them beat insider trading charges, or skirt taxes through dizzying financial and legal alchemy.

Other than that one glacial winter back in 2014, the calendar turning to March signaled the annual return of boaters to the lake. The water was still frigid, but at least the ever-thinning layer of ice had melted. The air temperatures were usually pleasant, especially on a cloudless day with the sun's rays refracting off of the water.

Andy's father—Jerome Friedman, also an attorney, though one who had worked as a government prosecutor his entire career, specializing in civil rights violations—had purchased a burled wood speedboat more than thirty years earlier. Jerome Friedman loved that boat, and so did his only child. Taking the speedboat out onto the lake for the first run of the season always felt to Andy like a connection to his deceased father: that shared passion that traversed not only the passage of time, but the barrier between the living and the departed.

This morning, as the Hollinger boat parade was forming up, Andy was already on the lake, enjoying the crisp but pleasant weather. Seeing the myriad of Hollinger flags interspersed with American flags—and, of course, the inevitable stars and bars of the Confederacy—Andy's face morphed into an ugly scowl. He steered his boat back to the dock that adjoined his house, tied it, and quickly went inside.

Andy Friedman was a bundler for Jack Bancroft, the Virginia senator who had been victorious in more than half of the Democratic Party primaries a few days earlier on Super Tuesday. Bancroft still had a fight ahead of him, but he now looked to be on his way to an insurmountable lead for the party's presidential nomination.

In the back of his SUV, Andy had a box of Democrat-blue "BANCROFT 2036" flags that would be used at a rally next week over in Wilkes-Barre. His plans were that sometime later today, he would make the quick drive over to Scranton and then down I-81 to Wilkes-Barre to deliver the flags, along with other Bancroft paraphernalia, to the campaign office on Market Street. On the way back, he would grab a couple of slices at his favorite pizza place in all of Pennsylvania in nearby Forty Fort, and then be back here just in time for dinner with Cheryl and the kids.

He grabbed one of the Bancroft flags from the box, shut the tailgate, and returned to the speedboat. Long ago, his father had fashioned a retractable telescoping rod to the right side of the windshield—sort of like an old-fashioned retracting aerial on an antique car—that could be used to display Jerome Friedman's support for his Penn State alma mater, or his diehard backing for one of Philly's sports teams.

Andy raised the telescoping rod and clipped off some snips of wire from the spool that he retrieved from the utility box area underneath the boat's padded seat. Now displaying his anti-Hollinger support for Jack Bancroft, Andy eased the speedboat back out of his dock and lazily headed back onto the lake.

By this time, the Hollinger boat parade was underway. Andy made sure to give them a wide berth. He wasn't intent on direct confrontation, but at the same time, Hollinger's insistence on channeling Adolf Hitler turned Andy's stomach. He steered clear of the procession—figuratively and literally—but knew that his boat and its Democratic blue "BANCROFT 2036" flag were easily visible, should anyone in one of the parade boats glance his way.

And that's exactly what happened.

A sport yacht, decked out with two oversized "American Values and Greatness" banners and a Confederate battle flag (but interestingly no American flag), peeled off from the left side of the procession and vectored in Andy's direction. Andy coolly observed this yacht, wondering how close it would actually come. Close enough for its occupants to be heard when they hurled the usual insults and curses at this obviously liberal Democrat? Closer, perhaps even whooshing close by Andy's boat in a threatening and dangerous maneuver?

Worrying a little bit about the latter possibility, Andy flicked his cell phone camera to "Video" mode and began recording the sport yacht picking up speed as it headed straight toward him. The other vessel was now only about fifty yards away, showing no signs of slowing. Part of Andy's brain insisted that he should show no fear; that he should remain in place, puttering along at his present speed, even if this boat peeled off only at the last moment, its pilot intent on throwing a good scare into this lib who dared to be in the proximity of their Hollinger boat parade.

Don't give them the satisfaction!

Another part of Andy's brain argued for a different course of action. *You're in a speedboat, and you can easily outrun them. If they don't slow down, or peel off—NOW—drop your camera, hit the throttle, and get the hell out of here!*

Andy, unfortunately, went with the first option, which became the proverbial last great act of defiance.

The sport yacht closed on the speedboat—the burled wood vessel that his late father had loved so much—and only began to swerve at the last possible second. Perhaps the pilot's spatial judgment was faulty because he was impaired, or possibly his intent was indeed to ram the speedboat; no one else would ever know for certain. The speedboat splintered under the crushing velocity of the larger vessel at the moment of impact. Andy went flying under the force of the sport yacht slamming into him. He was instantly concussed from the blow, but still conscious as he sank deep into the icy waters of Lake Wallenpaupack.

A county sheriff who was a zealous supporter of Ephraim Hollinger and the RAVG Party recorded the death of Andy Friedman as "accidental drowning secondary to the collision of two water vessels, with contributory negligence on the part of the deceased through reckless speedboat operation and maneuvering."

* * *

The same day of the Hollinger boat parade on Lake Wallenpaupack, a massive golf cart procession was scheduled for the pro-Hollinger supermajority in the Florida development where Edmund and Eleanor Garfield lived. Naturally, Edmund planned to participate in not only the parade, but the daylong festivities. Eleanor would be watching the parade in front of the closest clubhouse, in the company of Darlene Heltefer, Judy Carver, and many of their other friends and neighbors. Edmund would drive his own cart, with Duncan Heltefer as his passenger. Duncan was already half-finished with the bottle of bourbon he had brought to the pre-parade barbecue, so it was a damn good thing that he wasn't driving—even a golf cart.

The parade got underway at one-thirty in the afternoon. Edmund's cart, displaying the obligatory pairing of a Hollinger flag with that of the country, was about a quarter of the way back in the procession, which meant a good twenty minutes longer until he began moving. In the meantime, Duncan Heltefer finished off the rest of that bottle of bourbon before cracking open a beer that he retrieved from the ice chest resting on the cart's caged carrying tray behind the seats.

Soon, Edmund and Duncan were underway. The parade route had the golf carts traversing both main roads and residential ones, covering a broad selection of the massive development over the next hour and a half. For Edmund, navigation was ridiculously easy; he only had to follow the carts in front of him.

While most of the two hundred thousand residents of the massive development were Hollinger supporters, some were not. These others had largely moved here for the climate and the charm of the overall community, rather than to be with like-minded "American Values and Greatness" types. Most had coexisted for years with their more conservative neighbors back home in Ohio and Pennsylvania and Illinois; but that was before tribalism roared in the late-2010s. But almost all of the retirees who leaned Democratic or moderate Republican were among the earliest residents who had been here before the schism, and they had no intention of being forced away by the intolerance of Hollinger's fervent senior supporters.

For the most part, the non-RAVG Party residents kept to themselves these days. Today, though, the golf cart parade route had been specifically architected to weave onto several streets where known Democrats and Republicans lived. Perhaps those lovers of high taxes and Jews and immigrants, not to mention coddlers of minority criminals roaming freely on American streets as they plotted their next rounds of heinous crimes, couldn't be legally forced away from this mega-community steeped in traditional American values; but a show of golf cart force, shoved right down their throats on a tranquil Saturday afternoon, should at least ruin the rest of their day.

Sharon Kaplan was a transplant from Philadelphia, along with her husband Richard. Sharon was a retired law partner who occasionally did a little family law down here in Florida, while Richard had taught organic chemistry at the University of Pennsylvania, retiring as a full professor. As fate would have it, Sharon Kaplan had once worked with Andy Friedman, for about two years back when they were both fresh out of law school, at a different firm from the ones where they each eventually settled and spent their respective careers. Over the years, they occasionally ran into each other at Philadelphia Bar Association events. Early next week, when Sharon would learn of Andy Friedman's untimely death on Lake Wallenpaupack, she would think back to those long-ago days, remembering a couple of nights when they and several other newbies had worked sixteen-hour days and then still went out to drink and decompress amid the Center City nightlife for a couple more hours.

Knowing that the golf cart parade route would pass by their house, Sharon made certain that her two "WILLIS FOR PRESIDENT" signs were secured into the front lawn. Paul Willis had won two primaries on Super Tuesday, but Jack Bancroft looked to have built an insurmountable lead. Oh well; Bancroft might be a bit too much for Sharon Kaplan's taste with his career military background and too-centrist views on so many issues, but he was infinitely preferable to Ephraim Hollinger. If and when Bancroft became the

Democratic nominee, she would switch over her signs; but not until then.

Her campaign signs secured, Sharon Kaplan eased herself into the wooden rocking chair on their house-length front porch. The porch had actually been *the* selling point for this house when Sharon and Richard began seriously thinking about buying a second home—and an eventual retirement home—in Florida twenty-five years earlier. In concert with the pastel-blue clapboard siding and the bright white, thickly framed country windows, just gazing at their house every time she pulled into the driveway immediately enveloped Sharon in serenity. And given that her blood pressure tended to be on the high side, calming forces of any kind were most welcome.

Today, though, Sharon's blood pressure would surely be redlining, even with her meds, if she were to take a moment to check it on her home BP monitor. The invasiveness of this whole golf cart parade was infuriating! Fine; this whole development had become infested with narrow-minded, bigoted "American Values and Greatness" types. Everyone was entitled to his or her own political preferences; no argument there. But the incursion of cultish, tribal "it's us or them!" dogma into American politics that took hold twenty years ago had vanquished almost all civility, in Sharon Kaplan's experience.

Today, she would gain a tiny bit of satisfaction from the display of her Paul Willis signs directly along the route of this moronic display of support for the re-election of that dangerous, disgusting man. Most of those who lived down here should know better. They mostly weren't the vile racists and white nationalists who made up a sizable portion of Hollinger's base. However, so very many of these mega-development residents were the classic low-information types who lazily lobotomized themselves through hours of AVGN agitprop every day and night, and then reinforced those injected views through their clubhouse groupthink sessions. Sharon Kaplan leaned left, but she had respect for traditional conservative views—her own father had voted Republican for years, all the way back to Eisenhower—and the trial lawyer in her relished a healthy debate about immigration rights, race relations, or pretty much anything.

These people were too much, though.

But there was no way that she was going anywhere; she was here first.

At around two-thirty, Edmund Garfield's cart rolled up the street toward Sharon and Richard Kaplan's house. Starting with the first cart that had driven by, a few semi-good-natured jeers had been tossed her way in response to her Paul Willis yard signs, but nothing more concerning than that.

When Duncan Heltefer spotted the Willis signs, though, something snapped in his alcohol-fogged mind. He had just finished his third beer after that entire bottle of bourbon, and old Duncan Heltefer was feeling no pain—at least not yet.

"TAKE THAT FUCKING WILLIS SIGN DOWN! BOTH OF THEM!" Heltefer bellowed the moment he spotted the signs in the Kaplans' front yard.

Sharon was taken aback for a second or two at this man's vileness. She didn't recognize him, but even from fifty yards away she could tell that he was shitfaced, so she decided on the spot to just ignore him. In ten or fifteen seconds, he would be past her house; and that would be that.

"HEY, BITCH!" Duncan Heltefer yelled again. "I SAID TO TAKE DOWN THOSE FUCKING SIGNS!"

He then added:

"GET OFF YOUR FAT ASS AND DO IT! NOW!"

At this point, Heltefer's fellow golf cart paraders, in front of Edmund's cart and also those following behind, were appalled at what they were hearing. Even Edmund Garfield, who usually enjoyed Duncan

Heltefer's "commentary" on political matters, was taken aback.

"Duncan!" Edmund reached with his right hand in an attempt to clasp his friend's left arm, but Duncan jerked away.

He's going to rip those signs out himself, Edmund realized. *Oh well—as long as he doesn't do something stupid like throw a rock through her window, or anything like that. What can they really do to him for yanking up a couple of political signs from someone else's front yard?*

The question that Edmund Garfield silently pondered turned out to be an academic one. Duncan Heltefer was so drunk that when his right foot grazed the golf cart step as he attempted to dismount, he was thrown drastically off balance. His right foot then landed awkwardly on the street's surface, instantly rolling his ankle into a severe sprain. The jolt of intense pain from the sprain then caused Duncan's right leg to collapse, sending him crashing. His head bounced off the asphalt. And then he was motionless.

At Duncan Heltefer's funeral four days later, the pastor at one of the community's mega-churches eulogized him as "a man of extreme passions, even up to the moment of his death."

* * *

And so it went, during the first months of 2036 in Ephraim Hollinger's America.

Chapter 34

"Then were the king's scribes called in the first month," Daniel Jacobson read, "on the thirteenth day thereof, and there was written, according to all that..."—a slight pause—"Haman..."

At the anticipated sound of the villain's name, Noah and Rachel Weber energetically twirled their *graggers* for the first time this evening. Thirteen-year-old Noah's bar mitzvah was fast approaching, yet his childlike enthusiasm for the Purim ritual remained every bit as strong as ever.

Erev Purim for 2036 landed on the evening of March 12th, a Wednesday. Both Daniel and Michele had been assigned late-afternoon Monday-Wednesday classes for this spring semester. By the time they left campus and crawled their way through Oakland, along the accident-strewn Parkway, and then across the Monongahela, close to an hour had passed—and they still had another forty-five minutes through heavy rush hour traffic until they arrived at Daniel's parents' house. Nancy Jacobson wasn't worried, though—she would hold dinner as long as necessary for her son and Michele to arrive.

This year's Purim dinner was once again on the smaller side. Claire and her two children were again in attendance after a two-year absence, but Marc Weber was "somewhere out West" overseeing his hush-hush government construction project. Marc's landmark deal even preempted the previously sacrosanct Weber family ski trip to Sun Valley this year, which said as much as anything possibly could about how important of a contract this was.

"He can't tell me exactly where he is, or what they're building," Claire had hesitatingly explained to her mother when Nancy Jacobson was finalizing the guest list. Neither Nancy nor her husband dared say anything to Claire, but once again they were secretly relieved that they wouldn't be subject to their son-in-law's presence, especially given the unsettling parallels between the Purim story and the near-daily, gloves-off frightful rhetoric vomited by Ephraim Hollinger, his mouthpieces, and the AVGN talking heads. Marc Weber's willingness to line his pockets with Hollinger administration blood money put him at odds with his wife's family—that was an immutable, inarguable fact. However, neither Robert nor Nancy Jacobson had the stomach to nervously wait to see if several hours of unspoken tension might abruptly boil over into open hostilities.

Isaac Gretz was also absent this year. Two years earlier, Michele Burgess had driven her great-grandfather from Youngstown for the Saturday night dinner at this same location, in the company of much of the Jacobson extended family. Last year's *Erev Purim* had also landed on a Saturday night, meaning that Michele was able to make the same back-and-forth trek between Pittsburgh and Youngstown to retrieve and then return her great-grandfather.

The issue this year wasn't even the Wednesday night timing versus a weekend. Michele was now established enough at Western Penn to have arranged for a fill-in instructor, or switched just this one afternoon's late class to some sort of online, self-study variation. She then could have departed Pittsburgh early enough in the afternoon to retrieve her great-grandfather from Youngstown.

Isaac Gretz hadn't been feeling well for the past month, however. The past two years had been somewhat of a rejuvenation for the ancient man. He had relished the periodic visits to the Pittsburgh suburbs, to spend time with Nathan Jacobson in particular. Sharing stories and memories with one of Isaac Gretz's very few contemporaries remaining on the planet had effectively shaved away a couple decades' passage.

Alas, that reprieve from the march of time was destined to slow and eventually reverse. When Michele Burgess had first made contact with Daniel Jacobson, and when they had arranged for the first meeting between their great-grandfathers, Isaac Gretz had been too frail to travel more than a couple of miles from the nursing home where he lived—thus the necessity of meeting in Youngstown. Once again, unfortunately, the elderly man's condition prevented him from trekking to the Pittsburgh suburbs to celebrate Purim with the Jacobsons. Beyond the physical toll, the somber realization that his overall health had regressed so markedly, so rapidly, had crushed Isaac Gretz's spirits.

Then again, Isaac Gretz was now one hundred and twelve years old. He was now listed among the top one hundred oldest men who had ever lived. He was currently the fifth-oldest man alive in the world, and the third-oldest in the United States. The number of his remaining days was dwindling, he knew.

As for Nathan Jacobson, his milestone one hundred and tenth birthday was fast approaching: only eight days from now. Unlike tonight's subdued Purim ceremony, a blowout, all-family celebration was planned for next Thursday. Marc Weber had reluctantly agreed to fly back to Pittsburgh earlier that day, though he did his best to hide his agitation from his wife. Marc was now typically staying out West for two- or three-week stretches, especially since he was spending many of his evenings and nights in the bed of a twenty-five-year-old woman named Dalia Travers, who lived in a trailer just outside Wikieup.

The two had met about a week after Marc arrived onsite, in a country bar an hour north of Wikieup, in Kingman. He had grabbed a barstool only minutes before a woman plopped herself on the empty adjoining seat to Marc's right and immediately tried to sell him crystal meth, or oxy, or perhaps something else that might interest him. He passed on the drugs, but began talking with Dalia. A few minutes later, they adjourned to a nearby table.

Marc was pleasantly surprised to learn that this sexuality-oozing woman lived far closer to his construction site than where she was now fondling his blue-jeaned crotch under the table with her bare right foot. He drove her back to her trailer that night, leaving her car back in Kingman, since she was far drunker than he was. From that night on, being surrounded by the empty Arizona desert was hardly a hardship for Marc Weber.

Sex with Dalia Travers was an energizing rush of freaky and kinky, especially when she was wasted, but also exhausting. A few days back in Pittsburgh, with only one or two mundane, obligatory encounters with his wife, would be a much-needed break, and perfectly timed for Claire's great-grandfather's milestone birthday party.

Beyond being graced with Marc Weber's presence, every living descendant of Nathan Jacobson would be present: more than sixty people, when spouses (and former spouses, in some cases) were included. Robert Jacobson had taken the lead on planning his grandfather's party, given that he was now on some downtime between consulting contracts. A half dozen other Jacobson family members elsewhere in the Pittsburgh area also helped out.

But Nathan Jacobson's celebration was still eight days away; tonight saw the latest installment in an unbroken annual tradition dating back exactly ninety years, to that first post-war Purim in March 1946.

* * *

"I saw on the news about the Jewish military purges," Nathan Jacobson sighed. As had become his tradition for Purim and most any other family gathering hosted at Robert and Nancy Jacobson's home, after supper Nathan adjourned to the enclosed back porch and eased himself into the recliner that he had long ago congenially claimed for himself. He quickly fell asleep while his great-grandson Daniel and Michele Burgess quietly chatted, seated on a nearby sofa. What usually happened was that the old man remained asleep for no more than a half hour, and tonight was no exception. After his brief nap, he awoke and began talking with his great-grandson and the woman who had become his constant companion.

"I know," Michele grimly nodded. "I heard about it from several Army officers I served with, all the way up to Colonel, and the Army isn't even attempting to hide what they're doing. The same with the other services also."

Michele paused to sip her coffee before continuing.

"Normally, unless you sell secrets to the Russians or something along those lines, getting promoted from first lieutenant to captain is automatic. I heard that with this last promotion board, every single Jewish first lieutenant was passed over. Not that there were that many of them, but between the Army and the other services, it was something like a hundred and fifty officers."

Michele's eyes narrowed.

"Every single one," she reiterated. "Out of the military now."

"It was almost the same with Black and Hispanic officers," Daniel chimed in. "Not a one hundred percent 'failure to promote' rate, but pretty close."

"At the senior ranks," Michele added, "I don't think there's a single Jewish colonel or general left in any of the services."

"The mark of Frank Douglas," Daniel shook his head, referring to the joint chiefs' chairman who was still reshaping the United States military in the image of Ephraim Hollinger's white nationalist wet dream.

"When I was going through training at Camp Croft," Nathan suddenly reminisced, referring to the long-closed World War II-era Army post in South Carolina, "I was one of…"

The old man hesitated as he frustratingly tried to recall a factoid from more than ninety years earlier.

"...I don't remember, but there were only a few of us Jews there," he finally surrendered to the toll of time on one's memory. "Even then, in the middle of the war with all of us getting ready to fight, some of the others who had never been around a Jew would give us a really bad time. Even some of the drill sergeants were like that. And it wasn't just the Southern boys, either. There was this one fellow, I don't remember his name, but he was from Chicago, and he was about the worst of anyone. I don't remember anymore exactly what he did, but he was..."

Nathan halted and rapidly shook his head, and Daniel couldn't tell if his great-grandfather was frustrated that he couldn't recall these long-ago (and probably better-forgotten) details, or if he was trying to actually shake away long-dormant disturbing images that had just resurfaced.

"Guess what, Pop-pop," Daniel instantly attempted to change the subject. Nathan Jacobson shouldn't have to relive past unpleasantness. "Michele has been taking me to a laser-tag place out in Monroeville, and she's been teaching me a bunch of stuff that she learned in Special Forces and the Rangers."

A thin smile came to Daniel's face as he related the highlights of their most recent session. They usually drove the twenty-five minutes out to the converted warehouse in Monroeville on Saturday or Sunday afternoons now, and had been making the trip at least three times each month since late December. They would join in an all-comers session that usually had somewhere between five or ten others. The first couple of visits, Daniel had plainly sucked at every aspect of the game: individual and coordinated maneuvering, taking cover, instantaneously identifying a potential target as comrade or enemy: all of it.

Now, though, under the painstaking tutelage of Michele Burgess, Daniel Jacobson actually believed that if dropped into an actual combat situation, he might not be channeling Rambo but he would have a decent chance of surviving. She had taught him battlefield hand signals, and they now effortlessly communicated back and forth during the one-hour sessions. Daniel now instinctively and continually scanned every possible angle of attack against him, even while plotting his next offensive moves in tandem with Michele. He had absorbed more than a dozen tactical maneuvers, both offensive and defensive, and knew how to assess the scenarios in which each might be applied.

Daniel continued describing some of what he had learned to Pop-pop, hoping to take the old man's mind away from the troubling memories of being singled out for Army training abuse simply because he was Jewish. True, he was venturing into suspect territory here, describing mock combat situations to a very old man who had survived a war; but hopefully Pop-pop would be grateful that someone else in the Jacobson family finally had something approximating a firsthand appreciation for the intricate tactics that had kept Nathan Jacobson alive while fighting his way across France and into Germany all those years ago.

Daniel heard a noise from behind him, and halted his narrative to turn around and see his father making his way to the back porch to join the gathering.

While Daniel was looking away, Nathan Jacobson locked eyes with Michele Burgess, quickly and wordlessly communicating his crystal-clear understanding of exactly what this retired Special Forces and Ranger officer was attempting to do.

* * *

Daniel and his father had returned to the house, leaving only Pop-pop and Michele Burgess on the back porch.

"I'm sorry that your great-grandfather wasn't able to come," Nathan Jacobson mentioned for the third time this evening. Michele wondered if the old man had forgotten expressing the same sentiment, using the exact same words, twice already.

"I know," Michele again replied as if she were hearing Nathan's words for the first time. "He just hasn't been feeling that well lately."

Nathan Jacobson sighed.

"I know," he nodded, though Michele was certain that his "I know" was also about himself, not only her own great-grandfather.

Nathan looked over at his great-grandson's girlfriend, or "significant other," or whatever the appropriate term was, through cloudy eyes.

"He's seen and endured so much," Nathan continued, and Michele was certain that the image in front of his eyes this very moment were those of the past, not the present. If Michele Burgess could transfer the images from Nathan Jacobson's mind into hers, she knew that she would now be in the midst of Dachau.

She waited for him to continue, but nothing else was forthcoming, at least immediately. They sat in silence for almost a minute before Nathan spoke again.

"Moses was one hundred and twenty years old when God showed him the Promised Land from the top of Mount Nebo, right before he died," Nathan murmured. At first, Michele was certain that the old man's neurons were now firing wildly, resulting in a perplexing non-sequitur. As Nathan continued speaking, however, her thought process vectored into his.

"And the children of Israel wept for Moses in the plains of Moab thirty days; so the days of weeping in the mourning for Moses were ended," Nathan Jacobson now recited verbatim two of the final verses from Deuteronomy. "And Joshua the son of Nun was full of the spirit of wisdom; for Moses had laid his hands upon him; and the children of Israel hearkened unto him, and did as the Lord commanded Moses."

Nathan Jacobson's trembling left hand reached forward toward the end of the sofa, and gently but firmly clasped Michele Burgess' right forearm as their eyes met.

* * *

The large family gathering planned for Nathan Jacobson's one hundred tenth birthday would instead be for his memorial service and burial. Very early that next morning after Purim Eve, right around five-fifteen, Michele wasn't surprised at all when Daniel groggily answered his cell phone to learn that Pop-pop had quietly and—apparently—peacefully passed away sometime during the night.

"I'm so sorry," Michele felt the tears come to her own eyes as she hugged Daniel.

"I'm going to grab a quick shower before I go back," he mechanically answered, referring to his parents' house.

"Do you want me to go with you, or would you rather be alone?" Michele asked.

Daniel was puzzled why she was even asking this question, at this point in their relationship.

"Definitely, come with me."

Fate had other plans.

A half hour later, as Daniel was finishing getting dressed, Michele's own cell phone rang. The clock still hadn't swept past six on a Sunday morning, and she knew with all the certainty in the world that something else had happened.

"My great-grandfather is in a coma," she told Daniel the second she hung up with the nursing home's medical director, even though Daniel had pieced together what had happened from listening to Michele's side of the conversation.

"He's not going to make it," her voice broke.

"I'm so sorry," Daniel echoed Michele's own words from less than half an hour earlier back to her as he hugged her tightly. His thoughts raced even while they were still in each other's arms.

Sunday morning—shouldn't be much traffic getting out to the highway.

I'll drive; I really don't want her behind the wheel.

We can get there in an hour, faster if I floor it.

Unless Michele needs to grab anything from her house first.

But she may want to go straight to Youngstown, because who knows how much longer he has; maybe that extra twenty minutes would make a difference for her getting there while he's still alive.

Then it hit him:

Pop-pop just died, and I'm supposed to be on my way to my parents' house!

Daniel took a step back, and then two steps to his left, halted, then a step to his right—a GIF of him at the moment would be perfect for "running in circles," minus all humor.

Michele instantly realized what his quandary was—and hers as well.

"You go to your parents', I'm fine going to Youngstown by myself. I'll either catch up with you at your parents' or you'll come later to Youngstown, or we both meet back here."

Her voice was collected; her "stay calm and execute smartly" instincts had already kicked in.

Daniel detoured slightly on his way to the south suburbs to drop Michele at her house so she could pick up her car; and then they headed to their respective great-grandfathers.

* * *

"Just a little while longer, most likely," was the matter-of-fact answer by the nursing home's medical director to Michele's question of "how long does he have?" She made it to Youngstown in slightly under an hour. The nursing home had full hospice care capabilities, and equipment had been rolled into Isaac Gretz's room for the final hours of his life. He would pass away in the same room where he had lived for so many years now.

Michele was alone with him early that afternoon. Her parents were already on their way from Houston, but they wouldn't arrive until a few more hours had passed. Isaac Gretz was hooked up to a morphine drip to alleviate pain while he slipped away, but no breathing tube nor any type of life-sustaining or life-extending measures. She sat in a chair to her great-grandfather's left. His left arm lay loosely at his side, and the only-slightly-faded tattooed concentration camp number cruelly imposed on him at Stutthof, and which accompanied him to Dachau and then through the rest of his long life, glared back at Michele.

She thought back to when she was in fourth grade, the year that her parents began sending her to both Hebrew School and Sunday School at Beth Shalom. That one Sunday in late October of 2006 suddenly came to life. Mister Green, her Sunday School teacher, had spent the morning discussing the Holocaust. Michele had the faintest understanding of the Holocaust from the time two years earlier when she had asked her mother about the greenish-gray numbers on her great-grandfather's left forearm. Michele's mother had rendered a hazy "it's from the war, a long time ago; bad men did that to him" response but apparently decided that was as much as a six-year-old could—or should—process.

Now, at the age of eight, the Beth Shalom Sunday School curriculum pulled no punches in describing what the ancestors of many of these Jewish children had endured, and the horrific toll on not only those murdered during the Holocaust, but also those who miraculously survived.

That Sunday afternoon, then-eighty-one-year-old Isaac Gretz was spending the day with his granddaughter and her family. After lunch, the elderly man who would still live for thirty-one more years was reading the *Sunday Plain Dealer* sports section and looking forward to the start of the Cavaliers' season, only a week away now. From the corner of his eye he noticed his eight-year-old great-granddaughter silently staring at his left arm that was holding the newspaper. He instantly knew what specifically had engrossed her.

"Do you know what this is from?" he asked, lowering the paper and pointing with his right index finger at his tattooed number.

For a flash of a second, Michele was afraid to answer, but the trepidation quickly passed.

"Uh-huh," she nodded. "We learned today in Sunday School about the Holocaust. Is that why you have that number on your arm?"

"It is," Isaac Gretz answered the question in even tones. "What did you learn today?"

Michele offered a one-minute synopsis of a third-grade description of the Holocaust, at least as described by Mister Green that morning.

"That's all correct," Isaac nodded somberly.

Michele couldn't help blurting out the question on her mind since this morning.

"Did you know anyone who the Nazis killed?"

Tears instantly formed in Isaac Gretz's eyes as he sadly nodded with the images of nearly every member of his family slowly, wretchedly clocking before him.

Michele jumped. She was suddenly back in the present day; in a nursing home, in Youngstown, Ohio, in her great-grandfather's room. That same left arm that had propelled her thoughts off for a melancholy journey to the past had moved past the edge of the bed. Isaac Gretz's left hand was now lightly clasping her own right forearm. With all the certainty in the world, Michele knew that if she had traced the outline of Nathan Jacobson's hand last night when he had made the same gesture, her own great-grandfather's hand would exactly overlay that tracing.

He didn't say anything—his power of speech had abandoned him for the final moments of his life—but words were unnecessary. Isaac Gretz had willed his arm to connect with his great-granddaughter as he left this world for whatever came next.

His wordless message was the same as the one conveyed by Nathan Jacobson less than twenty-four hours earlier, and the same one that Moses had delivered to Joshua long ago:

My days at long last have come to their end, and the torch is being passed to you for the battle that lies ahead.

Chapter 35

Everything about Jack Bancroft, even his name, shouted "Presidential!" In normal times past, closer to either side of the turn of the last century and facing off head-to-head against almost any Republican, Bancroft would have been the odds-on favorite to win the presidency. He expertly and uniquely straddled the line between the traditional conservatism of military strength, fiscal responsibility, global leadership, and the world of commerce, coexisting alongside the liberalism of social and racial justice, insistence on corporate accountability, dedication to combat climate change, and commitment to revitalizing the nation's infrastructure. In a different era, the retired Air Force three-star general and second-term senator from Virginia would likely lose those on both the left and right extremes of the political spectrum; but for a healthy majority, he would be a highly appealing choice to lead the nation. In some ways, Jack Bancroft seemed a throwback to Dwight Eisenhower when it came to straddling that political no-man's-land. At an overly energetic, extremely fit sixty-four, Bancroft also settled into that sweet spot between the idealism of youth and the beneficiary of experience.

Bancroft's bio was a political handler's dream. At eighteen, the high school valedictorian from the Virginia beltway stunningly detoured from his parents' college plans for him and enlisted in the Air Force. A year and a half later, Airman First Class Bancroft was in the thick of the first Gulf War, heading off for SR—special reconnaissance—missions mostly behind enemy lines, and earning a Silver Star for heroism during a particularly harrowing mission in the earliest days of Desert Storm.

After the war, Jack Bancroft was admitted to the Air Force Academy, graduating third in his class.

Following pilot training and his assignment as an F-16 fighter pilot, he served a total of four tours in the quagmire of the nation's longest wars. Bancroft also flew with the Air Force's Thunderbirds before moving into a series of senior command positions, leading up to his retirement in 2024. Along the way, he earned a master's degree in American history from Georgetown and a PhD in Public Policy from Harvard's Kennedy School of Government.

Two years later, Bancroft easily won a Senate seat in his home state of Virginia, and emerged victorious again in that tumultuous year of 2032 that slipped Ephraim Hollinger into the White House. If Jack Bancroft didn't capture the presidency himself in 2036, he still had two years remaining on his second Senate term. What might 2038 bring? He had no idea, nor did Jack Bancroft give the matter a thought. He was focused at the moment on a single proposition: rescuing the nation and democracy itself from its deep entanglement with tyranny.

Senator Bancroft's personal life was blemish-free, at least in a political baggage context. He met his wife Chelsea while he was a cadet at the Air Force Academy, and married her exactly two weeks after his graduation and commissioning. Not that marital transgressions disqualified one from the White House anymore, but neither of the Bancrofts had strayed over the years. Their three adult children had all graduated with honors from top-tier universities and were now in the earliest stages of their professional lives. The Bancrofts' finances were squeaky clean—about three million dollars in index mutual funds and government bonds stashed away for their retirement thanks to prudent investing and constrained family spending for almost forty years, but no shady business ventures or anything even close to problematic.

Even in the ruptured, down-is-up politics of 2036, Jack Bancroft still had an outside shot against Ephraim Hollinger and Asher Clayton, the outgoing Texas governor and presumptive Republican nominee. Three weeks out from the Democratic Convention, his nomination awaiting only the official delegate count, Bancroft steadily polled in the low to mid-thirties in the three-way race. And when it came to the Electoral College, the Democrat was the leader or within striking distance in the elector-rich states of California, New York, New Jersey, Virginia, and possibly even Florida. Jack Bancroft might have to draw the perfect three cards to fill the ultimate inside straight, but he was still seated at the table and the cards were still being dealt.

Muddying the picture even more: The Republican Party might be an empty shell of its former self, but just enough Republican traditionalists still existed who hadn't defected to the RAVGs to give Asher Clayton a steady ten to twelve percentage points, poll after poll.

As long as the 2036 campaign remained a three-way race, though, the smart money and even most of the stupid money was on Hollinger's re-election. Short of Hollinger's sudden unexpected death or some sort of political miracle, this race was OVER even though the calendar had yet to flip to August.

But as a long-ago sportscaster once spontaneously blurted, "DO YOU BELIEVE IN MIRACLES? YES!"

* * *

Michele Burgess sat across from Daniel Jacobson on the patio of a newly opened upscale Italian restaurant in Pittsburgh's East Liberty neighborhood. Every night during the past week had been exceptionally sticky, but tonight was a reprieve, especially for a late-July Friday that had hosted an hour of ferocious thunderstorms earlier in the afternoon. But climate change equaled climate weirdness, and both the temperature and humidity had nosedived over the past couple hours, making patio dining and sunset gazing a must for the start of the weekend.

They were each about a quarter of the way into their entrées—gnocchi for Michele, while Daniel had ordered the tortellini—as they reminisced about Pop-pop and Isaac Gretz. Four months had now passed since their great-grandfathers' deaths within hours of each other. They had reminded themselves dozens of times during the spring and into the heart of summer that both men had lived their lives to the fullest, especially considering what they had each endured so many years ago during that horrific world war.

Still, their absence had instantly created an outsized void for both Michele and Daniel. The emptiness existed largely because their great-grandfathers' lives had been the personification of such a broad expanse of American and world history, lasting right up to the present day, and now that lengthy chapter was shuttered for all eternity. Turning the page on history was also accompanied by an overpowering sense of dread, given the ominous state of the nation in the earliest months of its next chapter.

God or fate had seen fit to fleetingly place those two men in the vicinity of the other more than ninety years ago, at Dachau; and the reason that Michele Burgess and Daniel Jacobson were sitting here this very evening and had been together for more than three years was linked back to that moment in history.

Even during brief stretches of dinnertime silence tonight, Michele's mind—Daniel's as well—pondered the invisible but very real cosmic threads traversing both time and space, from the here and now back to Dachau. Especially in the context of watching the American Experiment disintegrate right before their eyes as the nation became more like 1930s Nazi Germany each day...

Maybe none of this is coincidental...

Daniel's eyes suddenly widened in astonishment, and Michele immediately took notice. She followed the trajectory of his gaze, slightly above her head, and pivoted to see what had caught his attention. The oversized television screen on the other side of the patio was tuned to one of the mainstream cable news networks—an increasing rarity in Hollinger's America was to find a public TV not tuned to AVGN—displaying a red-and-white "BREAKING NEWS" banner across the lower portion of the screen. The wording on the banner:

CLAYTON DROPS OUT, WILL BE BANCROFT VP NOMINEE; REPUBLICANS OUT OF RACE

The television's closed captioning was on, but at this distance the scrolling words were slightly too small for either Michele or Daniel to read legibly. Daniel quickly reached for his phone at the same instant that Michele grabbed hers. They each flicked to this cable station's website and absorbed the stunning, absolutely unprecedented turn of events.

The seven words of the network's breaking news banner said it all, though the lead website story fleshed out the details. Asher Clayton acknowledged that he had exactly zero chance of being elected president slightly more than three months from now. Jack Bancroft only had the slightest chance, but "slightest" trumped "zero." The Republican Party, circa 2036, might be a hollowed-out incarnation of its former self, but its tattered remnants were light-years closer to today's Democrats than they were to the RAVG Party. Maybe—just maybe—the combined forces of America's two traditional political parties could unite the dwindling ranks of moderates, and even pull just enough uneasy RAVG Party members who didn't fully buy into Hollinger's totalitarian vision.

Bancroft hadn't yet announced his selection for a running mate, even though the Democratic Party convention scheduled for Chicago was fast approaching. The Republicans had been scheduled to gather two weeks later, and Clayton likewise hadn't announced his vice presidential nominee. Over the next few days, the behind-the-scenes details would trickle out through the inevitable leaks. Asher Clayton had approached Jack Bancroft with this wild idea a week earlier, and Bancroft was "intrigued and receptive." Bancroft was significantly out-polling Clayton at the moment and thus would be at the top of the unified ticket, and they would do so under the Democratic banner rather than as Republicans: Nothing more complex than a couple of data points went into the who-does-what-and-where calculus behind this unprecedented political Hail Mary.

This was the ultimate expression of "Country before Party." This was 2020's "Republicans for Biden" on mega-steroids. This was teaming up to fight for the soul of the nation while salvation was still a possibility.

* * *

Throughout August, past Labor Day, and into mid-September, what was now a two-way race told a very different story than the summer's polls. The Hollinger-Nelson ticket still had the lead in every single poll, but the Bancroft-Clayton pairing was almost always within striking distance, especially given margins of error. An interesting (though possibly Pollyannaish) theory swirled into existence: the "shy Bancroft voter." Hollinger and the RAVG Party were such an ominous force, the theory went, that some or possibly many of those corralled for the various polls were reticent or even fearful of declaring their support for the Bancroft-Clayton ticket. Quite possibly, the theory went, they feared that their stated preferences weren't anonymous; in fact, the pollsters themselves might actually be RAVG Party or even Federal Police Force operatives who were literally "taking names." Therefore, the safest answer to the question of "Hollinger or Bancroft?" was "Ephraim Hollinger, of course! Restore American Values and Greatness!" even if the respondent intended, or at least contemplated, a vote for Jack Bancroft.

The Electoral College factor made the race even more interesting. A couple of long-shot scenarios showed Bancroft losing the popular vote but squeaking ever-so-slightly past the two hundred seventy votes needed to win, thanks to increasingly strong support in the few remaining blue or red states—but mostly large, populous states, each carrying sizable Electoral College vote counts and which were all but immune from scheming state legislature manipulation—amid the sea of RAVG Party brown. And if Asher Clayton could somehow deliver his home state of Texas, well just maybe…

The RAVG Party ticket was still in the driver's seat, but the question for the ages was whether they would run out of fuel before they crossed the finish line.

* * *

Amid all of the historic political drama unfolding in the summer and autumn of 2036, Ephraim Hollinger wasn't worried in the least. Neither was Spencer Howell nor Braxton Knox nor Bart Lawrence nor Bob Platte, nor anyone else among the American Values and Greatness movement's inner circle.

Chapter 36

Keenan Lucas looked up from his copy of tonight's opening monologue to catch Bob Platte's eye. Lucas' eyebrows raised, his eyes wordlessly indicating:

THIS is what I'm supposed to go with on the air? Really?

The AVGN favorite son of the past two years had never been one to shy away from fact-free bomb throwing during his program, in his books, via his blog posts, or during fire-breathing speeches that commanded six-figure appearance fees. Keenan Lucas was a platinum-level member of The Ongoing Big Lie Club and had been substantially rewarded for his efforts. Now, though, his self-defense radar was lighting up. His eyes went back to the paper script and he reread what were supposed to be his opening words.

> Jack Bancroft and Asher Clayton share much in common, including their allegiance to the global conspiracy of Jewish moneyed interests. In a shocking revelation, one that is exclusive to our program, I will detail for you tonight how billions of dollars of illicit global banking money has been funneled from the dark shadows into this perverse, anti-American combined Democrat-Republican ticket with the intention of surrendering the sovereignty of the United States to Israel and the globalist Jewish bankers if they somehow win the upcoming election.
>
> Even more shocking, tonight we have exclusive details how the America-

> hating Dems intend to win. We have just learned that Jewish hackers from Israel have penetrated the voting systems in at least seven RAVG Party-controlled states, and they intend to change votes cast for President Hollinger and Vice President Nelson to Bancroft and Clayton. Homeland Security Secretary Braxton Knox and Attorney General Spencer Howell have promised a full investigation, and have vowed to maintain electoral integrity and not let the Dems steal this election!
>
> And even worse, if you can believe anything could actually be worse, we have also learned...

This time, when Keenan Lucas looked up from his script to lock eyes with his boss, he did more than just raise his eyebrows.

"This is...I mean, this is really over the top," Lucas contemplated aloud, struggling for the right words. "I mean, wouldn't it be better to, you know, space this stuff out over the next couple of weeks? Or maybe, I don't know..."

Bob Platte cut off his anchor.

"Just read it the way it's written," he coolly commanded. "This comes straight from the White House. I met with Bart Lawrence this morning and this is what they want. And they want it from you."

Platte leaned back; that power gesture of dismissive authority he had mastered long ago.

"Unless you'd rather I give this to Toni," he added, knowing exactly what buttons to push to abruptly shelve this rare pushback from a man who had proven that he would literally say or write anything in hot pursuit of adoration and riches.

* * *

Keenan Lucas' anti-Jewish, anti-Bancroft diatribes became more hateful by the broadcast—a stunning feat of achievement by both writer and anchor, considering that the inaugural salvo of the sequence had redlined on the outrage meter. By the beginning of the following week, Lucas had angrily informed his viewers that Jack Bancroft was, in fact, three-quarters Jewish, and that dozens of his *Jüden* ancestors had been traitorous Nazi collaborators during World War II. Lucas truly walked a fine line with this particular thread of lies, given that being a Nazi collaborator wasn't exactly a badge of shame in Ephraim Hollinger's America. Still, "um, wait…hold on a minute…" critical thinking wasn't quite a strong suit of the tribalized masses, so he was on safe ground here. (Absolutely none of what Lucas claimed was true. Jack Bancroft was a practicing Presbyterian from his father's family, and via his mother's side he was fully half-Episcopalian.)

Jews, Jews, Jews. Keenan Lucas' program suddenly became "All Jews, All the Time." The other AVGN anchors—Hayden Lafferty in particular—bristled at this latest favoritism from the American Values and Greatness leadership hierarchy bestowed on Lucas, especially after Keenan made it widely known that the White House had explicitly tagged him for this all-important messaging in the home stretch of the election.

Toni Fowler, Keenan Lucas' self-appointed bitter rival, felt the same as Lafferty and Tristan Wyatt, and even the network's daytime supposed-straight news teams. She certainly had her plate full enough as the White House Press Secretary in the home stretch of a re-election effort, plus doing her AVGN program at least three evenings each week at the moment. But watching helplessly as Bob Platte steered this patronage to Lucas was infuriating! More than once, she contemplated going rogue in the midst of her own broadcast and ad-libbing her own versions of "It's the

Jews!" She certainly had enough material, dating back to her "exclusive false-flag exposé" of the synagogue and Jewish cemetery desecrations at the beginning of 2034.

Just let it ride, Toni told herself each time the temptation to freelance bubbled. *Just let it ride.*

And there was something else.

The fact that Bart Lawrence had been the one who supposedly had delivered these orders to Keenan Lucas by way of Bob Platte made her think back almost a year, to that night when she had agreed to accept the press secretary position.

Just leave Lucas to me; I'll take care of it.

You just need to be patient for a little while and trust me.

She hadn't been in bed with Bart Lawrence for nearly three weeks, nor had they even been in each other's presence during that stretch. He was off doing "special tasks" on Hollinger's behalf, while Toni was tethered to the president as he flew Air Force One from one fever swamp campaign rally to the next. Normally, their paths would cross at least once each week, even if they didn't manage to hook up. But Bart Lawrence seemed to be avoiding her at the moment; and though she didn't know exactly why, Toni Fowler trusted that it was in her best interest to just go with the flow.

* * *

Tuesday, September 30th, 2036; late afternoon outside the AVGN headquarters and broadcast building in Washington.

Yom Kippur Eve would begin at sundown.

Keenan Lucas had finished his table read for tonight's broadcast an hour ago. He was sitting in his luxurious office when Bob Platte stuck his head through the open doorway.

"Bart Lawrence wants you at the White House."

Lucas cocked his head.

"Now?"

"Yeah, now."

Platte flicked his wrist to sneak a look at his Patek Philippe.

"You have plenty of time to get over there and back before makeup."

"Any idea what he wants?"

Bob Platte shook his head.

"No idea."

Lucas shrugged and reached for his suit jacket that he had slung over the chair that was astride his over-the-top mahogany desk. He almost asked Bob Platte if he knew why Hollinger's hatchet man wanted to meet in person, rather than talk over the phone. But then he reasoned that whatever it might be, the subject was so sensitive that Lawrence didn't want to take even the remotest chance of a phone conversation being overheard or recorded.

"I'll be back later," Keenan Lucas said indifferently as he strolled past Bob Platte.

* * *

Outside the AVGN building, three men waited. Two of the men stood together, about thirty feet away from the imposing glass-front entrance. The afternoon sun had a direct bead on them, and they were both perspiring lightly. Still, they both wore full-length camel-colored raincoats.

And both men wore yarmulkes.

The third man was offset from the other two, about fifteen feet away, leaning back against a parked car along the curb. He was inconspicuously dressed, in an open-necked white shirt and gray wool dress pants. An oversized cell phone was clasped in his left hand that dangled loosely next to his torso.

Keenan Lucas appeared about ten minutes after the three men moved into position. He should have been there a few minutes earlier, but Lucas had stopped to use the executive restroom that was reserved for AVGN's top talent. At the White House, the anchor would be afforded no such perks; he'd have to use the standard public men's room that the run-of-the-mill staff and reporters all used. Why not make a stop now, even though he probably could have waited?

The brief delay was of no consequence to the three men outside. They were in position; they were patient.

Keenan Lucas strode commandingly through the AVGN building front door. His eyes scanned left and then right, searching for the AVGN black car that would ferry him the short distance to the White House. Curiously, the car wasn't to be seen.

His first reaction: *That's odd.*

His second reaction: *How dare they keep me—AVGN's Keenan Lucas—waiting. I'm wanted at the White House!*

The man leaning against the car straightened when he spotted Lucas. He flicked his cell phone into video mode, directed the lens at Keenan Lucas, zoomed the view, and then double-checked to make sure the phone was recording. He gave a quick nod that the other two men were watching for.

They briskly walked in Keenan Lucas' direction, and had cut the distance in half when the AVGN anchor noticed them. His first reaction was that these were two of his many fans who wanted his autograph, or perhaps wanted to share a moment or two of fawning dialogue with their favorite anchor.

Then he noticed the two yarmulkes.

Keenan Lucas froze in place as each man withdrew his right hand from his oversized raincoat pocket, revealing a flat black, nine-millimeter semi-automatic handgun. The man videoing the scene had begun slowly, evenly walking in the direction of the unfolding confrontation. He made sure that he was capturing the images of the handguns, which were the same model and distinct style that the Israeli Special Forces had recently adapted.

"This is in defense of Israel and all the Jews!" one of the two shooters loudly enunciated.

"This is for what you have said on the air about us Jews!" the second shooter then added, also carefully enunciating his words.

The two men opened fire as their confederate documented the violent death of Keenan Lucas.

* * *

Neither of the shooters was ever captured or tried for the cold-blooded murder of Keenan Lucas on the streets of the nation's capital, despite the crystal-clear video and accompanying audio that was broadcast over and over and over on AVGN. They both seemingly vanished from the face of the earth within minutes of the shooting, as did the third man who had carefully recorded the shocking moments.

Questions abounded as to the shooters' identities, as well as the identity of the mystery man who—the story went—just happened to have his cell phone handy to record those fateful moments. Neither of the shooters, nor the third man, was in fact Israeli or even Jewish. Eventually all three would surface in the bowels of authoritarian Eastern Europe after enough extensive plastic surgery to ensure that even the most advanced facial recognition technology couldn't link them to Keenan Lucas' murder.

The only salient outcome of the assassination of Keenan Lucas was that the American Values and Greatness movement now had its martyr.

Chapter 37

The Jewish cemetery and synagogue desecrations of January 2034 provided the starting blueprint for Yom Kippur Eve, 2036, and the days that immediately followed. So many swastikas were spray-painted on and gouged into gravestones, businesses and homes, and vehicles with even the faintest connection to "being Jewish" that one would be excused for thinking that the hated symbol was now the official emblem of the United States.

Some of the attacks would have been laughable if not for the terrifying implications of what was occurring. Tony Gustoso, the owner of Gustoso Bagels (literal translation from Italian: "Tasty Bagels") in Minneapolis, drove up to his shop at 4:30 a.m. on the morning of October 2nd to find his plate glass front window smashed and the stucco walls on both sides of his storefront spray-painted with swastikas and the obligatory "JÜDEN VERBOTEN" threat.

"I'm fifth-generation Italian-American," Mister Gustoso angrily complained to a reporter from one of the local Minneapolis television stations who had been dispatched to report on damage thus far in the metro area. "I mean, they're such stupid f…"—since the live field broadcast was on a seven-second tape delay, the rest of Tony Gustoso's acidic assessment of the rioters' collective intellect wound up being dumped back in the station's control room.

Angry mobs surrounded and attacked numerous American Jews who dared attempt to attend synagogue services that night and the following day, shrieking their vengeance for the martyred Keenan Lucas. The ghastly scenes captured on video and broadcast on most of the cable news stations—sans AVGN—were sadly and eerily reminiscent of the few remaining grainy films of the horrors of *Kristallnacht* nearly one hundred years earlier.

Bob Platte's American Values and Greatness Network chose instead to repeatedly air the pristine footage of Keenan Lucas being shot to death. Toni Fowler had been rushed to the AVGN studios less than fifteen minutes after the bullets had been fired, and she captained the entire night's special AVGN programming, sharing airtime with Hayden Lafferty much as she had with Lucas himself the night of the triumphant 2034 midterm elections. She summoned her trademarked outrage at the two "murdering Jews"—Bob Platte had fed Toni that must-use phrase during a hurried consultation before she was rushed onto the air.

For her part, Toni Fowler could smell "false flag" all over this whole business. The oddly worded yet crystal clear enunciation of "This is in defense of Israel and all the Jews!" by one of the shooters and then, just as clearly, the equally peculiar "This is for what you have said on the air about us Jews!" by the other? The rock-steady, professional-quality video footage of the entire encounter, versus the jumpy, hastily-captured amateurish images one would expect from someone stumbling onto the horrific scene purely by happenstance and then scrambling and fumbling to record what was happening? That same footage making its way onto the AVGN broadcast barely ten minutes after the shooting itself?

So this is what Bart meant when he told me to be patient, and that I should just leave Keenan to him.

Even while Toni Fowler was screeching on-air about the brazen audacity of these Enemies of the People who had been hell-bent on silencing Keenan Lucas for calling out their treachery, she was periodically enveloped by sudden chills of sheer terror. She had always suspected that Bart Lawrence was capable of anything—anything!—on behalf of Ephraim Hollinger. Now she knew that "anything" included staging a cold-blooded murder—of an unwavering media ally no less!—with the express purpose of sparking massive civil unrest and rioting...toward what specific end Toni wasn't quite sure yet, though she could definitely conjure a few unnerving ideas on the matter.

Over on the other cable news stations, their broadcasters interspersed the scenes of nationwide violence with their own suspicions about "the story behind the story." Toni Fowler might have been pleased to know that she wasn't the only cable news personality for whom the shooters' bizarre utterances were the clearest indication possible that Keenan Lucas had been coldly sacrificed by the inner circle of the movement he had championed on the air, night after night. The difference was, though, that whereas Toni Fowler wisely kept her suspicions to herself, the anchors and guest commentators on the other networks dared to voice their skepticism on the air.

As the brain trust of the American Values and Greatness movement—Spencer Howell and Braxton Knox in particular, along with the four-star Joint Chiefs Chairman, General Frank Douglas—expected they would.

* * *

After the shock of the initial Yom Kippur mob attacks across the nation wore off, millions of people in New York City, Los Angeles, Seattle, Portland, Pittsburgh, Miami, and nearly every other large and midsized city took to the streets in outrage. Following on the heels of mainstream cable news analysis and social media speculation, the false-flag nature of the AVGN anchor's murder couldn't be more obvious. The shooting had so obviously been orchestrated to fire up the entire American Values and Greatness population in the home stretch of the presidential election, by channeling their outrage against a concocted common enemy! More than that: Hollinger, Spencer Howell, Braxton Knox, and the others clearly wanted to catalyze a nationwide orgy of violent retaliation against this supposed attack on their movement. As of sundown, October 1st—the conclusion of Yom Kippur—more than twenty American Jews had been reported killed by the many mobs, and thousands had been sent to hospitals throughout the country from the numerous attacks.

Enough!

The lessons of 2020 and the years that followed were burned into the memories and souls of many across the nation.

Take to the streets!
Be outraged!
Fight back!
Be fearless!

The mobs of lawless, heavily armed militias—so many militias!—carrying out their rampages of destruction against American Jews required those who were sickened by these actions to unite in defense of the force of law. If local and state police forces largely stood down as the attacks progressed, and if the Federal Police Force showed no interest in enforcing their codified mission of "protecting the people and the property of the United States of America" that they invariably fell back on to excuse away their own excesses, then it was up to the masses themselves to face off against the vicious attackers.

* * *

"Do you believe this shit?" Clyde Carver spat in disgust as the usual suspects gathered in the clubhouse to eagerly ingest AVGN's coverage of the socialist anarchists attempting to overthrow the government of the United States, as their beloved Toni Fowler put it, versus the countering defense of hardworking true Americans loyal to Ephraim Hollinger and the RAVG Party.

"I know," Edmund Garfield shook his head, likewise sickened by what he was watching. All of these America-hating damn protestors!

"I don't know what the FPF is waiting for," Edmund added. "They should be in there cracking heads, that'll stop this bullshit."

"Damn straight," Clyde Carver nodded approvingly at his friend's assessment of the situation. Nothing would send these vermin scurrying back to the shadows faster than some good old police brutality. What in the world were Hollinger and Spencer Howell waiting for?

"It's a tragedy what they can get away with," Eleanor Garfield chimed in.

"That's for sure," Clyde's wife Judy seconded.

Darlene Heltefer didn't feel the need to offer yet another affirmation of the consensus. Though, she knew, if Duncan were still alive, by now he would be staring at the bottom of an empty bottle of bourbon and would have some choice words of his own to add.

Darlene found herself wondering if, perhaps, that horrid Sharon Kaplan woman was over in Orlando, or maybe down in Miami with all the other Jews, stirring up trouble in the streets. If so, Darlene hoped that some loyal American took an assault rifle butt to the Kaplan woman's face. She had been responsible for Duncan's death seven months back, with her obnoxious "Paul Willis for President" signs in her front yard. If Sharon Kaplan hadn't been an America-hating Jew, she would have had a Hollinger-Nelson sign like almost everyone else down here. Her beloved husband had only been trying to defend traditional American values when that bitch from Philadelphia baited him into falling out of Edmund Garfield's golf cart and smacking his head on the concrete.

She'll get hers, Darlene Heltefer thought to herself. *Maybe not tonight or tomorrow, but soon enough...*

* * *

For three days and long nights, the streets of America erupted in nearly nonstop conflagration. Police presence was still frustratingly lacking in most cities as the two sides viciously and repeatedly clashed.

Mainstream cable news and AVGN alike documented the increasingly violent confrontations, with each broadcast camp adding its expected commentary. The mainstream anchors and commentators, and their brethren in the print media, called out not only that the rampaging nationalist militias were largely the aggressors in one clash after another—facts plainly documented through plentiful video and accompanying audio—but that the policing entities appeared to be giving the assailants a clear field of attack by remaining largely out of the pictures.

Over on AVGN, in contrast, the running commentary lauded the "brave defenders of American Values and Greatness against the lawless and Godless anarchists." Every recorded image of an anti-Hollinger protestor spray-painting a wall or helping to overturn a vehicle was given outsized airtime. The tried-and-true right-wing media tricks of interspersing still images and video from years-old protests in other countries with actual footage of the here and now were dusted off, all in an attempt to portray the massive civil unrest throughout the country as the doings of supposed left-wing anarchists intent on destroying this great nation, once and for all.

After three days and nights of unrelenting violence, along with no actions nor even statements from the federal government or the leadership of RAVG Party-controlled states and cities, the ominous feeling began spreading to those on both sides of the numerous clashes, and to at-home observers alike:

Something's coming.

* * *

Act II.

Edmund Garfield was far from the only American Values and Greatness supporter who was royally pissed off by the absence of law enforcement to shut down the counter-protestors. All across the country, frustrations were voiced in living rooms, bars, apartment and retirement community clubhouses, and nearly every other place where RAVG Party voyeurs gathered to eagerly drink in the scenes of unfolding violence, delivered directly to them thanks to the loyal sponsors of AVGN programming.

Some AVGN viewers were now so perturbed that they took up arms themselves and banded together with the nationalist militias who were already in the streets. Randall Weston was one of them, bringing along his assault rifle and two handguns when he headed to downtown Denver as night fell on Friday, October 3rd. His blood furiously pumping and his heart racing, Randall went to a prearranged rendezvous point slightly northwest of the Capitol Building. Kurt Stobel was there, along with six others who had already arrived. Four of them Randall "knew" only via social media and the dark web chat rooms, while the other two, like Kurt, had been among the avenging posse the night of spray painting swastikas in the Jewish cemetery.

The eight men were soon joined by a dozen others and were just beginning to plan their line of assault against tonight's Marxist protestors, when the most beautifully terrifying sounds Randall had ever heard reached his ears. Quickly swiveling his head to peer down East Colfax Avenue, Randall gazed lovingly at the shimmering images of an equally glorious sight headed in the direction of the city's central downtown area: an endless stream of armored vehicles. Most of the vehicles were personnel carriers, but Randall could soon pick out at least a half dozen tanks and mobile artillery pieces, all intermingled with what looked like a thousand or more camo-clad, heavily armed soldiers...or possibly Federal Police Force officers...or maybe militia reinforcements to their brethren who were already fighting in the streets? And could some of them be "private contractors"—the polite-company term for mercenaries?

As Randall Weston, Kurt Stobel, and pretty much the entire country would soon learn, the correct answer was "E—All of the Above." Spencer Howell, Braxton Knox, and General Frank Douglas had chosen the night of Friday, October the 3rd, for the commencement of their all-out final assault on the Constitution of the United States. A hideous amalgamation of regular active duty military—the Posse Comitatus Act be damned!—alongside federalized National Guard troops, the highly militarized Federal Police Force, "contractors" from several army-for-hire firms owned by friends of the administration, and hundreds of heavily armed white nationalist militia members were headed directly into the battle here in Denver, and doing likewise throughout the country's cities.

"We gotta get out of the way," Randall heard Kurt Stobel shout above the ever-growing noise from the armor-led show of force. Randall realized that Kurt was absolutely right: The last thing they needed was to be mistaken for the leftist anarchist protestors, and wind up on the receiving end of this overpowering show of force!

Kurt Stobel nodded in the direction of Denver's Civic Center Park, just to the south of where they were perched, and all twenty members of this ad hoc militia ducked into the park to get out of the way of the oncoming firepower. Chances are that they would have been okay where they were, Randall belatedly realized as they headed deep enough into the park, even if they had stayed put. Right now, the leftist protestors were all up near the 16th Street Mall, a half mile away, not down here on Colfax. Further: Randall's appearance, and Kurt's, and that of nearly every other member of this rag-tag band, was indistinguishable from those in the militarized horde that was soon to pass where they had just been standing. Randall and the others were all decked out in full camo fatigues and pattern-matching camo combat helmets, with their faces fully covered up to their eyes with olive drab or black facemasks. Every man carried an assault rifle, along with at least one visibly holstered sidearm. They could have easily met the oncoming force, quickly signaled that they were also there to kick some anarchist ass, and simply vectored their way into the ranks.

Which was what happened anyway, just a little bit farther down Colfax, after Kurt and Randall and the others realized that they were perfectly and fortuitously geared up. Randall wordlessly fell in between two beefy men as his eyes scanned each one's uniform for some sort of rank, or an identifying unit patch, or a name tape, or anything at all that might give Randall a clue about the men with whom he was marching into battle.

Nothing.

* * *

The assault on Denver was echoed in Seattle, and in Portland, and in Dallas, and in Los Angeles, and independently in each borough of New York City…and in every other city across the United States where protestors had taken to the streets to counter the vicious right-wing attacks. As Randall Weston had noticed in Denver, the camo combat fatigues or black assault uniforms or whatever else the members of this nationwide assault force might be wearing were all absent anything that could identify a given individual. To the naked eye, regular military and National Guard soldiers were indistinguishable from FPF officers, the mercenaries, and most of the militia. Tomorrow, on cable news and on social media, astute observers would point out that some of the assault force troops were wearing commercial logo-emblazoned black athletic T-shirts, or helmets with slightly different dimensions than official military or police gear, or camo patterns that appeared to have come from the hunting gear section of a big-box sporting goods chain rather than issued by some supply sergeant. Most likely, those were the nationalist militia members who didn't quite get the idea of uniforms being fully...well, uniform.

For all intents and purposes, the Chairman of the Joint Chiefs of Staff, together with the Attorney General of the United States and the Secretary of Homeland Security, had artfully constructed a hellish fusion that was ominously reminiscent of the regular German Army—the *Wehrmacht*—fighting alongside the Waffen-SS and the *Ordnungspolizei* (the militarized and uniformed "Order Police") during much of World War II. Throw in the homegrown right-wing militias, and this nightmare of an "army" was primed for conquest.

* * *

Sixty-six years earlier, a handful of somber numbers had been burned into the collective American psyche, at least for a little while.

Thirteen seconds.

Sixty-seven shots.

Nine wounded.

And the most infamous number of all: four dead on an American college campus in Ohio.

The cold numbers, and even remembrance of the Kent State tragedy itself, faded soon enough, like so much else for a people increasingly hallmarked by an appalling apathy toward its own history.

This time, the numbers would never be known and would be, in fact, incalculable; but the synopsized version of the events of the first weekend of October 2036, would live on as a highlight in the glorious history of Ephraim Hollinger's reign.

In Denver, the armored caravan turned northwest on 15th Street off of Colfax at the entry to Civic Center Park, made a quick right onto Cleveland followed by a quick left, and then rolled up 16th Street into its place in the overhauled American history books that would soon document the restoration of the nation's greatness, thanks to the RAVG Party and its loyal minions.

Word had quickly spread to nearly sixty-five thousand protesters that the confrontation landscape was about to be radically altered. They were no longer facing off against militias and individual right-wing nationalists; this was the real deal coming right at them.

No matter. Even in Ephraim Hollinger's America, they had justice and the strength of their convictions on their side. The clashes might get bloody, and some of them would almost certainly be seriously hurt; but this was a battle for the soul of the nation.

Fight back!

The lead militarized vehicles and the accompanying armed men were now within sight and closing threateningly.

Be fearless!

The protesters steeled themselves to remain in place, scattering only when the approaching armed men opened fire on the defenseless protesters. Unlike the summer and autumn clashes of 2020, the chosen weaponry of this assault force wasn't rapidly spitting out "less than lethal" ammunition: rubber bullets, beanbag rounds, pepper spray canisters, and the like.

These ammunition rounds were fully lethal; they were the real thing.

* * *

The cable news networks—all except AVGN, curiously enough—and numerous local television stations showed one shocking video after another of murderous rampages by the militarized assault forces, in city after city across the country. Some of the attacks were captured live, to the horror of viewing audiences as they watched protesters gunned down by the masked and uniformed attackers. Newspapers, news magazines, and their websites all covered the murderous assaults as well.

America's deep chasm ruptured even further. Those who normally lived and died by AVGN and wouldn't be caught dead watching one of the "lamestream media cable news networks" had to sneak a peek to bear witness to the glorious show of force against the anarchist enemies who threatened their way of life, even as they wondered why in the world AVGN wasn't airing these images. Many other Americans—one would hope many *more* Americans, but one could no longer be certain—were nauseated and repulsed by what they were helplessly watching, hour after hour.

This wasn't the United States of America! This wasn't a democracy! This was *by far* the most outrageous, sickening occurrence in this nation's history! Countless people—some estimates were as many as four thousand killed, and three times that amount wounded—had been brutally and cold-bloodedly attacked by…well, by someone bearing the full authority of the federal government. The cable news anchors and commentators repeatedly called viewers' attention to the lack of any identifying artifacts on the uniforms of the assault troops. Was this the work of Spencer Howell's Federal Police Force, now plunging to unprecedented depths of hellish immorality? Was this Frank Douglas' restructured and darkly transformed United States military, turning its weapons of war on its own people? The nationalist militias, embarking on wild killing sprees under the protective umbrella of the federal government? All of them?

The confrontations ceased after three days and long nights, largely because the protestors eventually scattered to the winds with their lives in unprecedented mortal danger. Protesting injustice was instinctive for many; they themselves, or their friends and parents, had taken to the streets during the long, terrible summer of 2020. They viewed the here and now as the resumption of those long-ago street protests—at least at first. But when faced with a high probability of being mercilessly gunned down—not clubbed and beaten, but shot in cold blood—the instinct to protest can quickly fade away.

Which was exactly what Spencer Howell and Frank Douglas had calculated when they unleashed their forces.

* * *

The video evidence of the numerous atrocities continued for days longer on cable news as Democratic and Republican current and retired politicians, retired military leaders, and many others conveyed their outrage at what they had all just witnessed.

What could be done? Any and every option, no matter how extreme, was offered up for consideration.

Reach out to foreign countries for assistance against the monster in the White House and his murderous administration.

Find some way for those who are horrified by what had happened to secede from the United States, because this is NOT our country!

Perhaps individual citizens—not only Jews, but Blacks, Hispanics, and others clearly targeted and threatened by Hollinger and the RAVG Party—should flee the country now, while they still can.

Ephraim Hollinger had engineered his Reichstag Fire.

Chapter 38

Section 2203 of the Truth and Accuracy in Media and Communications Act was titled "Sedition through Media Content and Transmission."

Checkmate.

* * *

Saturday morning, October 11th, 2036.

Robert and Nancy Jacobson, Daniel's parents, watched in captivated horror as five masked and military-uniformed men mercilessly beat a young, twentyish Black woman with a combination of riot batons and the butts of their assault rifles. This particular attack in the Century City area of Los Angeles had been replayed dozens of times on the mainstream cable networks. Perhaps even more than the plentiful video of the cold-blooded shootings, this one assault came to symbolize the soulless brutality of what was taking place in American streets across the country.

Suddenly, the Jacobsons' television set flickered to black. Nancy's eyes shifted slightly to the cable box, which still indicated that it was set to the news station they had been watching. She reached for the remote that was resting on the smallish coffee table that rested between their two recliners, and flipped to the other news station that she and Robert regularly watched. That other station was just switching over at the top of the hour from one anchor's program to the next when suddenly the Jacobsons' TV image again blacked out.

"What's going on?" Robert Jacobson mused aloud as Nancy switched back to the news station they had originally been watching.

Still a blacked-out television screen.

"Let me see that," Robert reached for the remote, but Nancy yanked her arm away from his reach.

"I know how to change channels," she retorted in angry tones that she immediately regretted. Nancy Jacobson was fully aware that the tensions of the past week and a half had taken a terrible toll on her own disposition, as well as that of her husband. On Yom Kippur Eve, the attacks against synagogues in Pittsburgh occurred within the city limits and in the northern and northeastern suburbs, so they had been fortunate to make it to services and then back home again without personally encountering danger. They were both worried about their son's well-being, given that he lived in the heart of the city and normally attended services where the attacks had occurred. When they reached Daniel by phone, however, he only offered a quick "we're both fine"—referring to Michele Burgess as well—along with a cryptic "we didn't go to services, we were…we just didn't go. Don't go tomorrow; you need to stay home."

By the next morning, however, the attacks had spread to the south suburbs, and following Daniel's advice, they remained tightly locked inside at home and away from the confrontations. For days, the oscillation between fear and outrage had pervaded every second of Nancy and Robert Jacobsons' lives, and tempers were now overheating at the slightest perceived provocation.

Retaining control of the remote, Nancy flipped back and forth between the two cable news networks several times, to no avail. Her eyes narrowed as she steeled herself to suppress her gag reflex, and then flicked over to AVGN to see if they were likewise absent. This time, they were "rewarded" with what appeared to be their normal Saturday morning warm-up programming, architected along with the rest of AVGN's weekend lineup to keep the righteous indignation of the American Values and Greatness movement on a low boil through the weekend, until a fresh round of agitprop could be delivered when the new week began.

After barely more than five seconds, Nancy tried to go back to the cable news station they had been watching, hoping that perhaps their cable provider had been the cause of the outage.

Still nothing.

Back to the other mainstream cable news network: *nada*.

Back to AVGN, just in case: Sadly, they were still broadcasting.

"Let me," Robert Jacobson tried once again. This time, Nancy decided to pacify her husband, and she handed him the remote.

Robert Jacobson repeated the same sequencing that his wife had just attempted, with exactly the same results. He then tried one of the basic cable networks whose lineup was filled with reruns of ancient programs from the early days of television, sometimes even dating back to the late 1940s and early 1950s. Sure enough, an eighty-five-year-old episode of *I Love Lucy* from the show's first season filled the television screen. Short on cash, Lucy had mischievously conned her way onto a radio quiz show, as if nothing was amiss over in the world of cable news or in the modern world at large.

A few more buttons on the remote were pressed, and the TV switched over to one of the history channels that their college professor son frequently watched. Grim black-and-white images of what appeared to be a huge Nazi gathering were being shown—most likely one of Hitler's monstrous Nuremberg Rallies. Robert Jacobson quickly flicked the remote again. If he wanted to watch Nazis, he could just turn on the news; he didn't need to take a televised trip into the past, they were here now!

But wait: Could he really "just turn on the news"? Other than AVGN, no news seemed accessible at the moment.

He rotated through the sequence several more times, still with the same results: Other than AVGN, the broadcasts of the other cable news stations weren't to be found.

* * *

Spencer Howell's Federal Police Force operated swiftly and with an overpowering show of force that Saturday morning. They stormed into the headquarters' facilities and remote locations of all of the cable news networks. Workers were slammed against walls and onto hard floors as Howell's storm troopers cut the feeds of the broadcasts that were then underway. They were careful not to destroy any of the equipment, since it would all soon be transferred to AVGN for Bob Platte to use as he saw fit. Every employee, in each location, who happened to be at work that Saturday morning was hauled outside and shoved into one of the dozens of prison vans that had been dispersed to the FPF's targeted locations.

The FPF raids also hit the news centers of the traditional major television networks, as well as many of their local affiliates. They went after and shut down the major newspapers in Washington, New York City, Los Angeles, Chicago, and nearly every city across the country.

The only local broadcast affiliates and newspapers that were spared were those owned by either of the two major conglomerates run by shadowy right-wing "industrialists" and who had bought favor with, and demonstrated fealty to, Hollinger and the RAVG Party. They would survive to carry the fight forward, philosophically and politically aligned with Bob Platte's American Values and Greatness Network, much as they already were.

The government went after the major and even the minor social media sites, using the advanced technology of the Federal Police Force's hacking unit to blockade their server farms and networks from the world at large. From this day forward, social media was a thing of the past—other than the AVGN-run site that came online later that same day.

Not that Ephraim Hollinger and Spencer Howell felt the need to stand on legalities at this point, but they certainly had their ducks in a row to help grease the results of the inevitable court challenges. The cable news stations, the news divisions of the traditional broadcast networks, newspapers and magazines, social media sites…all of them had blatantly and repeatedly violated the spirit and the letter of the law during the past week and a half, the charges read.

Specifically, they had fomented rioting in the streets and outright sedition through their unending live broadcasts and videos in support of violent anarchists who were dedicated to the overthrow of the United States government. They had solicited incendiary, seditious opining from current and former politicians, former military and intelligence officials, self-appointed legal "scholars," and others that threatened the stability of the nation itself. Hadn't a former Democratic senator proclaimed that those opposed to the administration needed to "reach out to foreign countries for assistance against the monster in the White House and his murderous administration"? A retired Army general and former intelligence community leader angrily contended on the air that it wasn't out of the question to "find some way for those who are horrified by what had happened to secede from the United States, because this is NOT our country!" Could anything be more seditious than those statements?

And what about all the outrageous, incendiary on-air and in-print speculation that President Hollinger, or Spencer Howell, or others in the leadership of the American Values and Greatness movement had been behind the cold-blooded assassination of Keenan Lucas? Was that not an incitement toward violence against governmental targets? An unmistakable provocation for insurrection, offered up by the mainstream media?

As with the TAMCA Act itself back in early 2035, and as with much of what Ephraim Hollinger and the

RAVG Party had brazenly carried out over the past two years, the court challenges came flying from all corners. By this time, not only was the Supreme Court handily in Hollinger's pocket, so, too, was enough of the judiciary system as a whole that nothing even reached the Supreme Court.

Freedom of the press? Freedom of speech? The battle had already been decided when TAMCA became law; neither was wholly immutable when the fate of the nation and the welfare of its people were at risk, as determined and then declared by the Hollinger administration. Just because Ephraim Hollinger had initially chosen to keep his powder dry and only fight a border skirmish or two, such as book publishing censorship delivered through the Federal Literature Commission, didn't mean that the war wouldn't begin soon enough, with the odds tilted heavily in Hollinger's favor. Hitler had spent about a year and a half probing into Czechoslovakia and Austria and the Sudetenland, gathering modest victories at first, before launching all-out warfare; Ephraim Hollinger essentially followed the same playbook.

The *blitzkrieg* on behalf of the President of the United States, Ephraim Hollinger, was now fully in motion and prosecuting all-out warfare.

* * *

For almost four years, dating back even before Hollinger's inauguration to the ill-omened night in early November 2032, that saw him capture the presidency, Bob Platte's American Values and Greatness Network was acidly referred to as "state-run television" because of the echo chamber operating among AVGN headquarters, the RAVG Party, and the White House.

As of October 11th, 2036, AVGN's role as the official—and only—media voice throughout the United States, communicating on behalf of its government, was now codified.

Chapter 39

Sixteen years earlier, during that dystopian year of 2020, much of the nation became obsessed with what a sitting president might do to steal an election.

Foreboding allegations of renewed foreign interference.

Brazen court challenges attempting to hinder voting by mail in the midst of a raging global pandemic.

Complicit state electoral officials closing polling locations and severely limiting drop-off ballot locations, and then subsequently concocting alternative slates of electors.

Defiant pre-election threats to disregard "rigged" election results that were indeed carried through after the election in the legal courts and especially in the court of public opinion, to the bitter end.

And, of course, the storming of the United States Capitol that took democracy itself to the brink, followed by the stunning revelations that followed over the next couple of years which detailed that the fears leading up to the 2020 election had not only been well-founded, but actually hadn't been sufficiently imaginative!

Then, in the aftermath of the early 2020s, concern and alarm shifted to the possibility that come 2024 or 2028, swing state legislatures whose members valued party and cult over constitution and democracy would blatantly and gleefully ignore the will of their states' voters and—this time successfully—submit loaded-dice slates of electoral votes to effectively hijack a presidential election.

All of those and much more turned "Is this the end of American democracy?" from a theoretical political science exercise into a chilling, real-world possibility.

Along the way, and all but forgotten in light of the tsunami that had followed, another scenario briefly posited by the incumbent president himself in mid-2020 was that the election might be postponed because of supposed public safety implications related to the ongoing global pandemic. The rebuttals to this particular "suggestion" came fast and furious as constitutional scholars and other law professors, former Justice Department officials, opposing politicians, and pundits all quickly pointed out that the President of the United States has absolutely no authority to delay or postpone—or cancel, just to cover all bases—a presidential election. The Constitution of the United States clearly vests the power to control presidential election dates in Congress. Further, the states themselves control the mechanics of their respective elections, and the president has no direct authority over governors, the state-level secretaries of state and election supervisors, and state legislatures.

The dialog quickly shifted from "can the president actually postpone or cancel an election to remain in power?" to "how can we safeguard this crucial election from outside interference, malevolent manipulation, and outright cheating?"

However, that was 2020. Democracy might have been teetering, but just enough cards remained out of reach (if only slightly) of those who might have been intent on fulfilling the ominous prophecy offered by George Mason, long ago in 1788:

> "It may happen, at some future day, that he will establish a monarchy, and destroy the republic."

Most Americans had mistakenly believed for years, before 2020 and even after that year's close call, that the guard rails were in place to protect democracy itself from crumbling, no matter how much stress was applied. But as Michele Burgess had suddenly and shockingly realized several years earlier, "they're not guard rails, they're *guide* rails: the political checks and balances, societal norms, all of it. And they can't actually prevent Hollinger from crashing right through them, especially if he hits them head-on at full speed."

Michele Burgess was, unfortunately, both prescient and correct. Recent history proved that even a strongman president who was worshipped literally to death by his cult followers, a strongman who then pulled out all stops to overturn election results and the will of the American people, could still be turned out of office through the power of the ballot and the rule of law. Hollinger was leaving nothing to chance.

Sixteen years after America had stepped back from the abyss at the final moment, the President of the United States, Ephraim Hollinger, held all the cards.

* * *

Friday, October 17, 2036.

One o'clock in the afternoon, Eastern Permanent Daylight Time.

The Oval Office.

The American Values and Greatness Network had, earlier in the week, taken over the channel slots for each of its now-departed mainstream news competitors on all of the nation's cable and satellite providers. AVGN's social media site had come into existence only six days earlier, with automatically created accounts for every email address on all of the major electronic mail service providers. The URL internet addresses that had belonged to the web presences of every now-disbanded mainstream newspaper, magazine, and also those of the cable news networks were now all redirected to AVGN.

The United States had suddenly become "All AVGN, all the time" for anyone who wanted any sort of news. Many Americans steadfastly refused to play the game; even if this AVGN takeover of the entire news media continuum lasted for more than just the near-term, there was no way in hell that they would bend to the will of Ephraim Hollinger, Spencer Howell, Bob Platte, and the others.

Still, many—even most—of those holdouts who stood on principle reluctantly tuned into one of the now-numerous AVGN outlets for this unprecedented announcement by Ephraim Hollinger.

They had to hear the abomination with their own ears.

"My fellow Americans," Hollinger began with the tried-and-true opening of thousands of previous presidential addresses, "we live in unprecedented and dangerous times. Never before in the history of this country have our values and institutions come under attack from within this nation's borders. We have all seen the violence in the streets over the past several weeks, and we have seen how the combined forces of the nation's military and the Federal Police Force have been needed to prevent the violence from spreading."

Hollinger's head pivoted to his right, to the rightmost teleprompter, as the AVGN control center switched active cameras.

"Because of the ever-present danger, and for the good of the nation and its patriots, I have asked Congress to postpone the presidential election from its scheduled date on November the fourth of this year— less than three weeks from now—until a to-be-determined later date, to a date when the safety of our citizens can be guaranteed when they venture to their designated voting locations. Senate Majority Leader Tal Chadwick and House Speaker Lowell Irvine have both assured me that Congress will act immediately and affirmatively on my request, in accordance with their constitutional powers and obligations."

Another head pivot, this time back to center.

"Until such time that a safe and secure presidential election can occur, I will safeguard the office of the presidency and continue to carry out the duties and obligations invested in the Executive who occupies that office. Each and every loyal American patriot has the obligation to fully and unquestionably comply with the laws of this nation to help bring about order and safety, and help this administration restore American values and greatness."

* * *

In the main AVGN broadcast studio, already seated in preparation for her special coverage of this historic announcement, Toni Fowler listened carefully to Ephraim Hollinger's announcement. Even though she had skillfully maneuvered herself to be on the winning side of the history that was being written in real time, Toni couldn't shake the menacing thoughts and images that clocked through her head alongside Hollinger's words.

It doesn't matter, Toni Fowler reminded herself. *Your soul is already forfeit, so you might as well be at peace with wherever this jarring journey takes you until then.*

Part IV
The Twilight's Last Gleaming

November 2036–March 2037

Alan Simon

"*Lunatic fringe, in the twilight's last gleaming,
…We're on guard this time against your final solution.*"

- Red Rider, *Lunatic Fringe*

"*Heard about Houston? Heard about Detroit?
Heard about Pittsburgh, PA?
You oughta know not to stand by the window,
Somebody see you up there…*"

- Talking Heads, *Life During Wartime*

Chapter 40

Ephraim Hollinger shrewdly and skillfully walked the finest of lines for the remainder of 2036, and then into the new year.

"If you've got 'em by the balls, their hearts and minds will follow" aptly described Hollinger's shock-and-awe opening strike, but was not a sustainable strategy in the long-term for those beyond his cult following. He understood the importance of affixing a veneer of constitutionality onto his coup. The DNA of the American spirit instinctively rebels against naked power grabs and draconian authority. Hollinger *needed* to shift the collective mindset to not just temporarily tolerate under duress the current state of the nation, but rather permanently accept or even embrace a new reality that the electoral public would no longer be permitted a say at the ballot box, whether they chose to exercise that right or not.

Hollinger's quandary was that on the one hand, he had informed the nation that Congress was *postponing* the election at his request, not canceling it, which meant that for at least a while, he needed to maintain an unyielding tension of "an ongoing, extremely dangerous time unlike any other in this nation's history." Otherwise, shouldn't the election belatedly be scheduled and held once the crisis passed?

Spencer Howell's Federal Police Force officers and General Douglas' military troops flooded the nation's streets—not just in major cities, but also in middle-sized ones and in numerous small towns across the country. Day after day, one would inevitably encounter numerous small squads of helmeted, camo-clad, weapons-of-war-carrying soldiers and federal officers, carefully eyeing everyone who passed them—and stopping more than a few for probing, intimidating questioning. Roadblocks spontaneously sprung up, causing lengthy delays as soldiers and FPFers searched for...something, perhaps; or possibly the barricades and the menacing, intrusive vehicle searches were solely for effect.

The segment of the nation's population that saw Hollinger's murderous power grab as the ultimate affront to American values was quickly and largely cowed into submission. Taking to the streets was no longer a matter of strength in numbers. The foul coalition of Spencer Howell's Federal Police Force thugs, the darkly transformed military, and the heavily armed militias and government-hired mercenaries had transformed the nation's long tradition of civil unrest into a deadly proposition. Those who would normally mass outside the White House gates, or in Times Square or Washington Square Park, or in other traditional protest areas around the country now had to ask themselves the ultimate question:

Is taking to the streets worth losing my life?

Still, the FPF permitted just enough outraged protests against Hollinger's brute seizure of absolute power to spark and take form before powering in to squelch the latest unrest. Every one of those angry demonstrations was, of course, fully captured on video, aired on AVGN, and held up as the latest proof that America was still a nation in peril. Spencer Howell's special operations strike teams seeded the protests with violent actors—literally—who flamboyantly torched buildings and vehicles, and did their best to incite others to follow their lead. The nationalist militias were on the spot to trade blows with the protestors and escalate the viciousness of the clashes. Unlike the original October unrest that saw the FPF shockingly gun down so many protestors and which led to the near-universal TAMCA-authorized censorship, however, the FPF and the military stopped short of opening fire on the massed civilians...as far as anyone knew, given that only AVGN was now available for news.

The threat of additional cold-blooded massacres was ever-present, however.

* * *

On the other hand, simultaneously with maintaining this ongoing aura of unprecedented danger, Ephraim Hollinger somehow needed to convey that this "new normal" wasn't really all that different than what loyal American citizens were used to in their daily lives, *at least when it came to the things that really mattered.*

So what if American streets were teeming with heavily armed soldiers and federal police officers, eerily reminiscent of Hitler-era Germany and occupied wartime Europe?

So what if nobody had the foggiest idea if another free and fair American election—presidential or otherwise—would ever be held again?

Did any of that really matter, if Ephraim Hollinger could navigate this unprecedented constitutional crisis to a soft landing?

Talk about a high-wire act!

Fortunately for Hollinger, America's collective memory was as short-lived as ever. Surprisingly—or perhaps not—the death of democracy soon caused little disruption to, or even unpleasantness in, the life of the average person. Schools reopened after Thanksgiving and again operated as normal; and people still commuted to and from work, seemingly coexisting with the stifling FPF presence. Bob Platte's rapidly expanding AVGN empire had abruptly seized operational and financial control of the numerous dating and hookup websites and apps during their massive media grab; and people still used those sites and apps, arranging dates or hooking up as much as ever. Restaurants and bars soon grew crowded; and despite the national chaos, the 2036 holiday shopping season was surprisingly looking to be the best in years. As 2037 rang in, the college football bowl games were held, and the professional football season entered the playoffs and clocked toward its own championship game.

Unemployment statistics continued to ratchet downward, thanks to the continued "assistance" of Labor Secretary Stephen Channing. The stock market was roaring, and by Christmas of 2036, the major averages were within striking distance of their pre-crash early 2031 highs. Without the annoyance of an inquisitive free press, disquieting rumors that Hollinger loyalists in the investment world were furiously gaming the markets may have been prevalent in certain circles, but never reached the general populace. AVGN hammered the message that Wall Street was signaling its confidence in Ephraim Hollinger and the RAVG Party to bring life back to some semblance of normalcy!

Truthfully, even if people knew that the nation's new oligarch class—the uber-wealthy RAVG Party intimates—were gleefully pouring billions of dollars into the markets with the express intent of driving up the stock prices across the board, and were doing so with backroom assurances that Tom Buckner's Treasury Department would quietly backstop any and all trading losses…well, as long as some of the largesse was trickling down to the little guys, so what?

American citizens, increasingly desensitized to the reality of a police state, submissively acceded to that proposition; after all, what other choice did they have? They forced their focus away from heinous actuality to Pollyannish faith that this new reality of an imperial presidency wasn't really that bad, after all.

* * *

Still, much of the nation held out hope, even if subconsciously, that the "old normal" would eventually return.

They'll hold the election on Thanksgiving; that's only three and a half weeks later than it would have been. Just wait.

Someone at work heard that the election is gonna be by Christmas at the latest.

My friend out in Phoenix said that if we get to vote no later than New Year's Eve, then everything goes back to normal next year.

Too many others believed differently; that "American spirit" and "free and fair elections" and even "democracy" were just heinous, deceptive crap propagated by the all-controlling Deep State to deceive and control the masses. AVGN and its predecessors had hammered the point home for years.

Look what happened when the Dems rigged the election back in 2020. Millions of fake mail-in ballots, fixed machines switching votes; all of that. You can't trust those crooked DemonRats in an election—we learned that the hard way. The best thing to do is get the right guy in there, and then don't give nobody a chance to steal the presidency from him. And Hollinger is definitely the right guy!

On AVGN's new social platform, only the most foolhardy dared challenge Hollinger's destruction of democracy. Given the ongoing brutal FPF crackdowns, not too many people were dauntless enough to consider voicing opposition to Hollinger's gambit, even online. But for those who did summon the courage to make the attempt, AVGN's highly sophisticated software expertly and instantly applied "sentiment analytics" to *every* attempted post before allowing the words to make their way online. If the AVGN filtering software determined that a user was endeavoring to post something critical about Hollinger, his administration, the RAVG Party, AVGN itself, or the American Values and Greatness movement as a whole, the entry was censored and rerouted to the Great Cybertrash Dump rather than making it online for others to see and comment on.

And, of course, *every* fragment of data about that offending individual—user ID and full name, IP address and device information, along with database cross-references to determine where that person lived and worked and who their family members were, bank account and retirement fund information, voting history, religion and ethnicity, sexual activity history, and much more—was recorded and channeled over to the Federal Police Force's rapidly growing "big data" pool.

Truthfully, the most significant source of discontent on the now-one-and-only AVGN social media platform was the tedium of rebuilding one's network of connections and online friends. AVGN had abruptly routed the entire online world its way, but they left it up to individuals themselves to reestablish connections. (AVGN and the FPF, working in tandem, did, however, preserve existing connections on the now-defunct legacy platforms as part of their ever-widening surveillance net.)

The legions of social media influencers, in particular, were the angriest about losing all of their existing connections. Few had any heartburn about now reaching their followers via an AVGN-run network of sites, versus whatever platforms they had previously used; but they were collectively outraged that tens or hundreds of thousands, or sometimes even millions, of their followers had to be reacquired! This was costing some serious money!

Most everyone adjusted soon enough, though.

* * *

As an unprecedentedly mild-weathered January progressed, Inauguration Day—the 20th—neared; and Ephraim Hollinger's quest for uncontested power faced one more obstacle, courtesy of the United States Constitution.

Chapter 41

The Twentieth Amendment of the United States Constitution was adopted a little over one hundred years earlier, in January of 1933, and was best known for shaving about six weeks off of the "lame duck" period between Election Day and the inauguration that followed. The amendment also addressed the line of presidential succession, including provisions for how to handle the death of a president-elect before Inauguration Day.

Beyond these better-known aspects of the amendment, its opening words presented Ephraim Hollinger with his final hurdle:

> The terms of the President and the Vice President shall end at noon on the 20th day of January...

To accentuate the point, the amendment's authors added at the end of the same section:

> ...and the terms of their successors shall then begin.

The significance of the wording was unmistakable: Even though Hollinger's Congressional co-conspirators had gamed the Constitution, subverted democracy itself, and managed to—ahem—"postpone" the 2036 election, come January 20th, 2037, Ephraim Hollinger and Paul Nelson would no longer hold their respective offices, according to that very same United States Constitution. If they had won the 2036 presidential election, they essentially would be sworn in to replace themselves; otherwise, Jack Bancroft and Asher Clayton would receive the honors.

But what if there were no successors?

That's exactly the situation that the country now faced, given that neither the Hollinger/Nelson ticket nor Bancroft/Clayton had received the voters' mandate nor the stamp of the electoral college in the election that never was.

Could electors be appointed by state legislatures anyway, and then cast their votes? Possibly, though "the first Monday after the second Wednesday in December"—the head-scratching legislated meeting date for the Electoral College—had already slid by. Perhaps the RAVG-dominated Congress could quickly pass legislation to enact a special Electoral College date and procedures for this election cycle that was like none other?

The same Twentieth Amendment that was Hollinger's final hurdle, however, also provided the solution.

* * *

Section 3 of the amendment was a prime example of a word salad. Tracing the flow of that section's provisions was an exercise for a graduate-level logic class, or perhaps an experienced computer programmer steeped in the machinations of multiple nested "IF…OR IF…" conditional statements.

Ephraim Hollinger frankly didn't care about the logic flow of that critical section, nor the intent of its authors. With the assistance of his crafty White House counsel, Travis Whitman, the president laser-focused instead on the phrasing that he would use to conclude this electoral and constitutional no-man's-land, and permit him to proceed with his reshaping of the country.

> ...and the Congress may by law provide for the case wherein neither a President-elect nor a Vice President shall have qualified, declaring who shall then act as President, or the manner in which one who is to act shall be selected, and such person shall act accordingly until a President or Vice President shall have qualified.

Michele Burgess' "The History of the United States Federal Government" course at Western Penn spent two full classes covering the surprisingly sticky topic of presidential succession: the Twentieth and Twenty-fifth Amendments, the Presidential Succession Act of 1947 and its predecessors through the years...all if it. Michele borrowed from her own graduate school days some of the most on-target, succinct phrasing about the United States Constitution to describe the Twentieth Amendment as a whole, and in particular, its third section: "It predefines a *process* to follow if everything goes to hell and we wind up in uncharted territory." That "process" meant, however, that a sycophantic Congress was handed the mother of all loopholes to conspire with a rogue president to subvert the electoral process, should they wish to sanction the end of the American Experiment.

No president-elect?

No vice president-elect?

No problem!

The same men who had saluted smartly and maneuvered Congress into "postponing" the election—Senate Majority Leader Tal Chadwick and

House Speaker Lowell Irvine—would now simply "declare who shall then act as President."

For how long? Thanks to the Twentieth Amendment, "until a President or Vice President shall have qualified."

Legislation was rushed through both houses of Congress on Monday, the 12th of January. Hollinger signed the bill the next day. Ephraim Hollinger was named to act as President of the United States, "indefinitely and until such time that an election is held to qualify a successor."

The legal challenges instantaneously followed, and were immediately struck down by Hollinger's loyal and trusted Supreme Court.

The American public had, by now, largely and flaccidly come to terms with the sobering reality that the American Experiment had been extinguished.

All hail King Ephraim the First.

Chapter 42

Only minor lineup changes occurred in the opening days of what technically could be called Ephraim Hollinger's second term as President of the United States. Mike Jeffries, the Secretary of the Interior, left to become Chairman and Chief Executive Officer of an energy exploration company that had been awarded substantial lucrative drilling rights leases in national parks throughout the western continental United States and Alaska during his tenure. Now, it was time to cash in.

James Clark, the Secretary of Veterans Affairs, departed to become the CEO of a company that had—big surprise—received a contract worth more than nine billion dollars to develop and install an all-new integrated medical records system at every VA and Department of Defense hospital and clinic. Clark's new annual salary and target bonus peaked past the eight-figure mark, but his package of stock options and restricted stock shares—the big score—could conceivably hit nine figures within the next four years.

Other than Jeffries and Clark, however, the rest of Hollinger's Cabinet stayed in place. They all had important work ahead of them—Spencer Howell, Braxton Knox at DHS, and Tom Buckner at Treasury, in particular.

And Toni Fowler remained in place as the White House Press Secretary, still double-dipping at AVGN. Now, though, given AVGN's codified role as state-run media, Toni hosted her official White House press briefings as part of AVGN's regular programmed lineup. Each weekday, between one and two o'clock eastern time, Toni would adjourn to either the White House press room or Studio Number One in the AVGN building—both sets were now identical—and convey the latest round of *1984*-ish Newspeak to her viewers. This televised and webcast afternoon press session even had built-in commercial breaks, and of course, Toni got her cut from the proceeds that came into the American Values and Greatness movement-friendly merchants.

Two or three times each week, several of her AVGN underlings would be seeded in her "audience" with pre-approved, carefully worded questions to prompt Toni's next round of utterances. The rest of the time, the official press briefing was sometimes difficult to distinguish from her regular evening hours AVGN program. The wording of Toni's scripts tended to be different, though. During her official press briefings, she would often open with a recitation along the lines of "The Hollinger administration has issued the following official statement regarding…" or "President Hollinger met this morning with the following foreign leaders…" Other times, though, she would begin by shrieking about illegal immigration and the borders, or the latest anarchist protests that needed to be stomped by the FPF and the military, much as she did on her evening AVGN program.

Today's broadcast was one of those for which stoic formality was called for.

"Good afternoon, America. I will now read an official United States government statement from President Hollinger," Toni began.

"In accordance with Article I, Section 5 of the United States Constitution, the United States Senate this morning expelled Virginia Senator Jack Bancroft on charges of sedition against the lawful government of the United States of America, and conspiracy to incite civil unrest. Bancroft unsuccessfully attempted to enlist the Supreme Court of the land to overturn the efforts of the executive and legislative branches to maintain law and order in the streets of American cities and towns."

Toni Fowler shifted her head to Camera 2, complying with her producer's directive piping through her earpiece.

"Bancroft has been detained by the Federal Police Force and will soon face formal charges commensurate with the seriousness of his efforts to undermine this nation and bring harm to its citizens. Additional co-conspirators are being rounded up by the Federal Police Force, based on evidence seized during the former senator's arrest. Bancroft is being held without bail in a secure, undisclosed location."

Another head shift, this time back to Camera 1.

"That is the conclusion of our president's statement. Speaking on behalf of the president and the entire Hollinger administration, I am authorized to share my OUTRAGE at this TREASONOUS behavior!"

Toni Fowler had expertly and obviously shifted into her AVGN persona, even though her afternoon White House press briefing "show" had barely begun.

* * *

"Fuck yeah!" Kyler Becker fist-pumped in the direction of the FPF Academy lecture room screen.

"Fuckin' Bancroft's off to Gitmo!" Randall Weston nodded as he echoed Becker's gesture.

Randall Weston and Kyler Becker were two of more than four dozen FPF trainees clustered in the sixty-seat room. Each weekday afternoon, following lunch, this cohort was ushered into this room for the mandatory viewing of Toni Fowler's press briefing. For Randall, the only downside to an extra hour spent gazing at his favorite nasty, hot AVGN personality was that he was doing so in the company of his entire training class—which meant, of course, that expressing his "appreciation" for Toni Fowler in his usual way was out of the question!

Last November, in the aftermath of the massive protests and civil unrest that had prompted Ephraim Hollinger's power grab and election postponement, the call went out from the Federal Police Force for new recruits by the thousands. That early October night in downtown Denver, marching among the menacing FPFers and soldiers and militia members—and using his semi-auto rifle to mow down protestors himself, just as the "professionals" had done—had given Randall Weston the taste of blood that would never be satiated.

Randall Weston applied online, and much to his surprise he was immediately accepted into the training program. No interview required, no psychological evaluation, no background check...nothing more than checking the box in the online form that read:

> I swear that upon the completion of my training, I will unfailingly and unquestioningly obey all orders issued to me directly by, or on the behalf of, Ephraim Hollinger and Spencer Howell.

The FPF Academy training program lasted twelve weeks. Randall was assigned to Class 36-45, which was scheduled to begin on November 30th, the conclusion of Thanksgiving weekend. Since Randall had disavowed his liberal-leaning family years earlier, the timing of his flying from Denver to Hollinger National that Saturday was hardly an imposition on the holiday weekend. No way would he have ventured up to Boulder anyway, except perhaps to screwdriver some more cars or, perhaps, brutally squash another protest by those antifa anarchist scumbags.

Most of his new comrades in Class 36-45 were strikingly similar to Randall in both background and beliefs: white nationalist aficionados loosely affiliated with one another via social media. Some were card-carrying members of heavily armed militias with avowed missions to overthrow the last vestiges of state and local governments that remained outside of

RAVG Party control. These weren't the college-educated professionals, many of them already lawyers and accountants, who would have attended a much earlier incarnation of this training program back when the FBI still existed.

The FPF training program was somewhat challenging, though nothing approaching the difficulty of, say, military basic training or the old FBI Academy. Still, more than a few enrollees washed out within the first couple of weeks—most of them leaving voluntarily rather than being dismissed.

Three weeks ago, at the halfway point in the training course, those still enrolled in Class 36-45 received their assignments for where they would be headed following graduation. Randall learned that he would soon become a Transportation and Detention Officer, assigned to the newly formed FPF Special Services Division…emphasis on the word "special."

"We can't tell you the details yet," his TO—Training Officer—smirked at Randall and the forty-nine others who had received the same assignment, and had been split off from their overall class of two hundred for the remainder of their time at the Academy.

"But I *can* tell you," the TO continued, "that you'll soon be the pointy tip of the spear of the FPF's mission to restore American values and greatness."

* * *

"I knew that Bancroft asshole was up to no good," Clyde Carver snorted as he killed the rest of his bourbon and refilled his glass from the near-empty bottle. In recent months, Carver had eased his way into the departed Duncan Heltefer's role when he and his wife Judy, the Garfields, and others gathered to bask in the latest glorious news, delivered to them by AVGN. Duncan had been the heavy drinker in the group, but Clyde apparently felt obliged to now fill the gap and offer the running stream of alcohol-tinged bile.

Never mind that Jack Bancroft had been a three-star general who served in the United States Air Force for more than thirty years, or that he had served nearly two full terms with an earned reputation as one of the Senate's most collegial, results-oriented members in years. Daring to run for president against Ephraim Hollinger was bad enough. Then Bancroft went and filed suit alongside all of those libtard groups to try and overturn Hollinger's emergency measures, and put the entire country at risk?

"Maybe they're sending him to Gitmo," Edmund Garfield mused, echoing the same thoughts, at the same exact moment, as those of Randall Weston, eight hundred miles to the north.

"I sure as hell hope so," Darlene Heltefer chimed in, apparently channeling her late husband. "And maybe they'll execute him there. Good riddance to a filthy traitor who commits treason—that's what I say!"

"Amen," Eleanor Garfield added, smiling at the thought that very soon, all of their great president's enemies would be defeated; and then, loyal American citizens such as all of those gathered here in the clubhouse, in the midst of their utopia, would no longer be in danger from the anarchist outsiders.

* * *

Michele Burgess and Daniel Jacobson were perched on a bench on the south side of the Western Penn campus, watching the opening moments of Toni Fowler's White House press briefing. Each had a class starting at one-twenty this afternoon, but they made sure to tune into any and all news as part of Michele's intelligence-gathering mission that had been underway for a while now.

Upon hearing Toni Fowler's vindictive announcement of Jack Bancroft's arrest, Michele soberly, coldly locked eyes with Daniel.

"It's starting," was all she needed to say to elicit a solemn, acknowledging nod from Daniel in response.

Chapter 43

"I heard a rumor that your prison out there in the desert isn't gonna be for illegal aliens," Dalia Travers probed, her eyes dancing with salacious eagerness in anticipation of Marc's confessional answer.

Marc Weber's eyes narrowed as his left hand froze, suspended halfway between the table and his mouth, watery salsa threatening to cascade downward from the two soggy, melted cheese-slathered tortilla chips.

"Whaddya mean?" he cocked his head as he answered.

"I think you know," Dalia challenged with her trademarked infuriating smirk.

Marc ignored the look on her face and simply shook his head in response. He truthfully had no idea what she was referring to.

Damn it! She really pisses me off sometimes, he thought for at least the third time tonight as his hand—and the nachos—resumed their upward trajectory. As with each of the previous times, however, Marc's mind immediately gravitated to the images and sensations of what would take place later, during the drive from here in Kingman back to Wikieup and then at length in her trailer. Dalia was wired tonight, and that's when she was at her wildest.

It doesn't matter, Marc repeated his mantra. *She's only around for stress relief while I'm out West.*

One thing was for certain: Marc Weber definitely needed stress relief these days!

Two weeks earlier, the original completion date for his "project" had been abruptly moved up three months, from mid-June to mid-March. Marc certainly wasn't privy to the reasoning of DHS Secretary Braxton Knox, nor was he consulted about the viability of the schedule acceleration. He had been coldly and tersely informed of the change by one of Knox's underlings, and immediately had to scramble to hire more than a hundred additional workers to begin work on the final section that hadn't been scheduled to be started until late February, since all of his crews were already working overtime.

Truthfully, Marc still wasn't certain if the mid-March date could be met; but if not, he knew that he would be damn close, maybe a week late at the most. Worst case, he was confident he could talk his way past a few days' delay, especially after they abruptly shaved three months off of his schedule at this late date!

But even then, the intense pressure would be far from over. Marc's piece of the significantly larger encampment that was supposed to have begun in mid-June, right after this solo project was finished, would now commence in mid-March: another three-month acceleration!

"Seriously," Dalia continued probing, this time lifting her bare right foot under the table into Marc's crotch, as she often did when she wanted something.

Tired of this back-and-forth dialogue—but not her back-and-forth bare foot grinding into him, of course—Marc replied:

"No, really; I don't know what you're talking about. What have *you* heard?"

Dalia stopped massaging Marc's groin with her toes, but kept her foot pressed there as she answered.

"I heard that they're going to start rounding up Jews and sending them there," she replied in a near-whisper, her eyes locking with Marc's as if she could suck the truth out of him through a penetrating stare.

Marc was speechless for a moment, but he recovered quickly.

"Where did you hear that?" he asked.

"Aha! You're not denying it!" Dalia replied in accusatory, "gotcha!" tones.

"No…yes, I am denying it," Marc stumbled over his words. "I mean, I have no idea, I've never heard anything like that. Seriously, where did you hear that?"

"From Jack."

"Figures," Marc blurted out, immediately regretting the utterance. Jack Keller was Dalia's other "regular" and also her connection for meth, oxy, and pretty much everything that she sold up here in Kingman or sometimes farther up the highway, in and around Vegas. Marc intensely disliked Jack Keller, not the least because Keller absolutely hated all Jews, including Marc Weber. How absurd! Marc was the farthest thing from the stereotypical East Coast Jew that this hick bartender-slash-drug-dealer automatically assumed him to be.

Now she'll think that I'm jealous of that asshole, or something like that.

Truthfully, Marc Weber didn't give two flying you-know-whats about Jack Keller, or whatever the specifics of his liaisons with Dalia might be. Marc unfailingly used a condom with her, so he wasn't all that worried about who else was doing her. If anything, Dalia was starting to get on Marc's nerves—Exhibit A occurring at this very moment—so any sort of divided time on Dalia's part was perfectly okay for him. As long as she was around for an occasional dinner to squelch the early-evening loneliness, a weekend jaunt up to Vegas here and there, and for slightly more frequent stress relief, Marc had no complaints.

"That's crazy," Marc changed the subject—or at least the train of his own thoughts—back to this strange assertion.

"Where the hell did he hear that?"

Dalia shrugged.

"I dunno," she answered. "But he said that it's all tied back to the Jews killing that AVGN news guy last fall and starting all the riots. Supposedly, Hollinger is gonna round 'em all up so they can't start any more trouble."

"That's crazy," Marc repeated his retort from a moment earlier.

"Aren't *you* worried?" Dalia actually seemed concerned, at least from the sudden change in her voice. She obviously knew—but didn't care, unlike her drug dealer "friend"—that Marc was Jewish.

Marc had told her that he was, for the most part, a non-practicing Jew. One time, though, he had slipped and mentioned something about celebrating Purim at Claire's parents' house…the slip being accidentally injecting his wife into the conversation, rather than anything related to the Jewish holiday. Maybe Dalia had extrapolated that passing reference into an assumption that Marc was actually more observant than he admitted, or that he had an affinity of sorts for Jewish cultural traditions and the religion itself.

If so, then that was on her. Marc Weber definitely hadn't said or done anything to make Dalia Travers believe with any certainty that he was anything other than Jewish by birth. He enjoyed the occasional bagel, and he obediently shuffled off with Claire to synagogue services for the High Holidays most years. He impatiently sat through his share of family dinners for Hanukah or Passover or Purim, when those holidays didn't collide with his traditional trips to Sun Valley or the Bahamas or Hawaii. But nothing more.

* * *

During the drive from Kingman back to Wikieup, with Dalia blacked out in the passenger seat of the oversized SUV that Marc drove while he was out West, his thoughts drifted back to that brief, strange exchange that began with Dalia's probing speculation about the nature of the encampment that was taking form out in what was, at this time of the evening, the cold blackness of the Arizona desert.

Suppose that Dalia, and Jack Keller, and whomever it was that had passed on the wild speculation to

Keller, were correct. Suppose that all along, Marc Weber hadn't been building a detention and imprisonment camp for undocumented aliens from which they would be expelled from the United States. After all, no one had ever spelled out that particular purpose of the facility to Marc Weber, or to anyone else working on his project. This was all pure conjecture on his part. Logical, trail-of-breadcrumbs conjecture, to be sure, steeped in RAVG Party doctrine and Ephraim Hollinger's pronouncements—but supposition nonetheless.

Suppose—just suppose—that the encampment was instead designed for either permanent imprisonment, or temporary detention in concert with banishment, of American Jews.

People like his own parents, brother, and sister; like Claire's parents and her brother.

People like Claire herself, along with Noah and Rachel.

People like Marc Weber.

No way!

Even if—and this was about as far-fetched as it can get—there was a fragment of truth to this speculation, all of those people who had just clocked through Marc's thoughts would have to be immune from such draconian measures. After all, Marc Weber was tightly locked in with the Restore American Values and Greatness Party backroom power brokers, with a fair number of senators and representatives, with state and local RAVG Party officeholders…and with Ephraim Hollinger himself!

Marc had bundled millions of dollars, much of that his own money, for election and re-election funds, and Hollinger's inauguration, and RAVG-friendly PACs and advocacy groups. If he and his family, and Claire's family, were at risk because of their Jewish heritage, would DHS have funneled these hush-hush encampment-building contracts to him? Of course not!

No way, Marc Weber shook away the disturbing thoughts and images that dared to mock his self-assured impunity. He shoved those ideas aside and looked over at Dalia Travers, who was finally stirring slightly, as she usually did by this point while Marc drove them back from Kingman. Soon enough they would be back at her trailer, and she would be fully awake and ready for…

The sudden recollection of Dalia's words from earlier abruptly slammed him once again, rudely shoving aside Marc's preferred salacious contemplations.

I heard that they're going to start rounding up Jews.

Troubling imaginings rolled through the theater of his mind.

No way, Marc Weber—confidant to many of the powerful men who ran the Restore American Values and Greatness Party and America itself—argued with himself one more time.

Chapter 44

Many men are beholden to overpowering obsessions.

Randall Weston, for one, compulsively masturbated while watching Toni Fowler on AVGN; and through social media and the dark web's chat rooms, he knew with certainty of hundreds of others who shared his passion.

Marc Weber's siren's song was Dalia Travers. The rational portion of his brain could flash warning lights all day long that he should keep his distance from this meth-head, drug-dealing, increasingly unstable woman; yet he was powerless when confronted with her raw sexuality that was unlike anything he had experienced with his wife during all the years of their marriage.

Spencer Howell's obsession, like Randall Weston's, was voyeuristic in nature. Howell's compulsion, however, didn't involve anything of a sexual nature, either solo or in the company of anyone else. The Attorney General of the United States had watched every episode of *The Man in the High Castle*, the old streaming series from the second half of the 2010s, at least two dozen times over the years.

Howell wasn't all that interested in the JPS—Japanese Pacific States—plot line of the series, and could easily have done without the whole sci-fi parallel dimensions theme. But from the moment he watched the series trailer for the first time, even before the first season dropped, Spencer Howell was mesmerized by the striking sights and sounds, and the very idea, of a 1960s-era Greater Nazi Reich overlaying about two-thirds of the former continental United States landmass following a World War II Nazi victory in this alternative history drama.

Spencer Howell had been twenty-seven years old then, in early 2015 when the initial episode aired as a teaser for the rest of the first season. At the time, he was fast-tracking his way toward partner in a modest-sized Kalispell, Montana law firm whose reach throughout the entire northwestern United States far outstripped what one might have expected.

The first hour-long episode captivated Howell so completely that he agonized during the ten months that followed, until November, when the rest of the first season was released. For the next four-plus years, through the release of the show's final season in late-2019, Howell watched and re-watched and re-re-watched every episode, old and new alike. His addiction continued long after the series concluded. Even now, amid the earthquaking transformation of the United States that had cast Attorney General Spencer Howell in a starring role, every so often he would sequester himself for a couple of hours and binge-watch two or three episodes. Only occasionally in recent years would Howell watch all forty episodes in sequence; mostly he would flip around to his favorites—those that most called to him—and lose himself for a short while.

The show's imagery enraptured him. From the building-length, lightbulbed swastika in the heart of this alternative reality's Times Square to the enormous swastika-topped New York skyscraper, abreast of the East River, that housed the defeated United States' S.S. overlords; from the revisionist American flag with a blue-backed swastika in place of the nation's stars, to the Berlin-set scenes at the epicenter of the world-conquering Third Reich; all of that, and more, infiltrated every pore on Spencer Howell's body, and permeated his soul.

Most of all, he was captivated by John Smith, the former American soldier who had evolved into the black-uniformed, swastika-armband-bearing S.S. *Obergruppenführer* and who continued his ruthless quest for power season after season, ending up as *Reichsführer*.

Spencer Howell saw himself as John Smith—the common man bearing the everyman name, rising from modest means and the ashes of defeat to steadily accumulate power, vanquishing his many enemies through sheer force of will and cold brutality. Howell imagined himself commanding the legions that were released into the American streets at John Smith's orders. The paramilitary brownshirts who roamed the streets with impunity were also at his command. He conjured images of pitiless prisoner interrogations in dark dungeons after his minions accomplished their handiwork of torture. Spencer Howell saw himself sitting commandingly at his breakfast table, his real-world wife Helen (ironically, the same name as the fictional John Smith's wife—talk about fate!) dutifully acceding to his blunt-but-calmly-delivered commands for how every aspect of their household was to be run.

Howell found himself especially captivated by scenes depicting John Smith's interactions with some of the real-world Nazi leaders, even though the series was set in the early 1960s, more than fifteen years after World War II had ended in the real world. Hitler, Heydrich, Goebbels, Eichmann, Mengele…the show brought them to life, much to Spencer Howell's delight.

Especially Heinrich Himmler.

* * *

Spencer Howell came by this affinity for "The Continuing Adventures of the American Nazi" honestly. He had never known his great-grandfather, Rudolph Howell, but young Spencer grew up on family tales about the man. Rudolph Howell had been one of the founders of Camp Siegfried, the American Nazi summer camp in Yaphank, New York, out on Long Island. Spencer Howell's great-grandfather had been a big shot in the German American Bund, the Nazi-sympathizing organization of the mid- and late-1930s. After Camp Siegfried was established, Rudolph

Howell devoted a good portion of his time there, especially during the summers when the camp activities were in full swing. Rudolph Howell died in 1973, at the relatively young age of sixty-seven, fourteen years before his great-grandson Spencer was born.

Spencer's grandfather, however, lived long into the lifespan of his grandson. Max Howell had vivid firsthand recollections of not only summers spent at Camp Siegfried, but also the massive Bund-organized Nazi Rally at Madison Square Garden in early 1939. ("Massive" not necessarily by the standards of Hitler's annual Nuremberg Rallies that drew more than half a million people each year; but twenty thousand American Nazi attendees was an impressive tally for the heart of New York City.) Young Max had been eleven years old then, and had been attending sleep-away camp at Camp Siegfried for the previous three summers.

Max Howell regularly regaled not only Spencer but also his other grandchildren with tales of glorious summers filled with bonfires, parades, swimming meets and other competitions, and overall camaraderie with like-minded Aryan Americans. Camp Siegfried provided an oasis against not only the difficulties of the Great Depression but also the increasing presence of Communist-loving Jews in the labor unions and American life in general, oozing from their traditional strongholds in moneylending. Max nostalgically recalled how the campers themselves, even the younger ones, did the hard labor to build much of the Camp Siegfried infrastructure themselves, the idea being to avoid having to use the Jew unions that teamed up with the Mafia-run construction-related businesses to heartlessly steal from hardworking Americans like the Howell family.

Camp Siegfried was arguably the best-known of the American Nazi summer camps that dotted the country during the 1930s, and which faded away only after the Pearl Harbor attack and America's entry into the war against Hitler. Others existed, though. As fate would have it, Greta Schneider—the young girl who grew up to marry Max Howell and become Spencer's grandmother—attended a similar camp that briefly operated in Sellersville, Pennsylvania, about an hour north of Philadelphia. And Spencer Howell's maternal grandfather spent the summer of 1937 at yet another American Nazi camp, this one in, of all places, Windham, New York, right in the midst of the Jew-ridden Catskills!

Both Hans Alder—Spencer's maternal grandfather—and Max Howell were born in 1929, which placed them slightly too young to fight in World War II. Consequently, the "we went to war and personally saved the world from fascism" theme that ran through so many American homes of the post-war years, up until the Vietnam War began tearing the country apart, was totally absent from the households of the Howell family. Instead, defiant and strangely nostalgic recollections of the American Nazi movement that was cruelly cut short by the war were the tales and sentiments passed down through the generations of Howells.

* * *

Two rapid-succession incidents much earlier in Spencer Howell's life—an assault, and then the legal aftermath—had vectored him to where he was today, serving as the Attorney General of the United States; and, as a result of his machinations during the past four years, functioning as the supreme power behind the Federal Police Force.

In college, Howell played football at a Division II school in eastern Washington State, starting at offensive tackle during his final two years. One Thursday night during his senior year, Spencer and several of his oversized offensive-line buddies were at a country bar, about a half hour outside of Spokane. The 2008 presidential race was in the home stretch, and the football players were loudly bemoaning that a Black man—one with the middle name of Hussein, no less!—might actually win the presidency. How fucking far had this once-great country fallen, they all wanted to know?

Three other college-age men were, for some reason, in this same bar at the same time—"for some reason" because each of the three could easily have been a throwback to Berkeley or Madison or Ann Arbor, circa the late-1960s and the days of the Vietnam War campus protests. Even at a glance, they were as out of place in this country saloon as if they were reenacting that old "Uneasy Rider" song about an early '70s hippie's misadventures in a Jackson, Mississippi bar one Saturday night.

Wouldn't you know it, and maybe it was the beer talking, but they overheard and then protested Spencer Howell's and his football buddies' characterization of the Democratic Party's presidential candidate, and—for good measure—the jocks' collective assessment of the state of the country. Spencer Howell skipped a verbal rebuttal and instantly landed a single, brutal punch squarely in the center of the face of the man closest to him. The man went flying, smacking the back of his head into the cold concrete floor as he landed.

Howell was handcuffed by a couple of sympathetic deputies who apologized to him during the squad car ride back to the county sheriff's barracks that they didn't have any say in the matter, they had to place him under arrest; but that Spencer should call this lawyer named Tanner Vogel, who had a stellar record defending good Americans like Spencer Howell against unfair charges that in a different place and time would never see the light of day.

Howell's victim was a twenty-two-year-old student at the same college where Howell played football, a man named Marc Niebaum, who had—for some inexplicable reason—decided that a Jew from Seattle mouthing back to a bunch of oversized football players in an eastern Washington State country bar wasn't the stupidest idea in the world. Marc Niebaum would remember this unfortunate decision for the rest of his life, which was spent hobbling along only by using polio-style leg braces and crutches, and with permanently reduced cognitive and verbal abilities.

Fortunately for Spencer Howell, Tanner Vogel turned out to be everything the two deputies had promised…and more. By the time the attorney was done twisting the other two hippies into knots during their turns on the witness stand, enough confusion had been sewn that the jury—which was filled anyway with sympathetic, hardworking Americans who also bemoaned what was happening to this once-great country—came back with an acquittal in less than an hour.

Celebrating with his football buddies at the same bar that night, one of them slurred to Spencer:

"Reminds me of that line from *The Godfather*: you know, that old Mafia movie?"

"What line?" Spencer Howell slurred right back. It took quite a bit of alcohol to get a six-ten, two-hundred-ninety-pound offensive lineman drunk, but Spencer Howell was up to the task most of the time, especially this night.

"Somethin' about a lawyer stealing more with his briefcase than hundreds of guys with their guns," the other player replied. "Somethin' like that; I can't remember the actual words, I saw that movie with my dad and my brother back in high school, so it's been a while."

Howell didn't immediately get where his teammate was headed, but then the epiphany slammed into him.

One punch from a giant like Spencer Howell could take out one un-American Jewish hippie: that earlier night in this same bar, only a few feet from where they now stood, was Exhibit A. During a good old-fashioned barroom brawl, Howell could probably dispense with a half dozen or so, maybe even a few more. But someone like Tanner Vogel, using the tools of the law at his disposal, could conceivably "take out" a whole bunch of leftists and other undesirables...not only one at a time or by the handful, but by the hundreds or thousands!

Besides, the law was a wondrous thing, Spencer Howell now realized. He was self-aware enough to realize that he was fully guilty. The little Jew had jawed back at the football players, objecting to their characterization of the travesty of a Black man possibly winning the presidency. But Spencer Howell's literal counterpunch far exceeded any notion of proportional response. By all rights, Spencer Howell should have been kicked off the football team, expelled from college, and been sitting in a county jail cell for about six months, with a couple years' probation to follow.

But he wasn't, was he?

* * *

Spencer Howell was a giant man, but when it came to possibly playing professional football after college, he had the disadvantage of playing at a smallish Division II school that wasn't well scouted. He was, in fact, drafted by Kansas City in the next-to-last round, simply because of his size, but by then Spencer was of the mind that it was time to move ahead with his life's work—and football didn't exactly fit the long-term picture. He told Kansas City "thanks, but no thanks" and didn't even report to training camp. Instead, Howell applied to several law schools across Washington, Idaho, and Montana, and wound up being accepted into a second-tier program in Montana. No matter: After graduation, presuming he made it through the three-year program and then once he passed the bar, he would be every bit as much a lawyer as some rich kid who went to Harvard or Georgetown or Penn.

Besides, Spencer Howell wasn't after a plum position with some Jew-run New York City firm that devoted their energies and talents to helping their brethren in global finance control the world, or with some D.C.-

based practice that specialized in perpetuating the Deep State evils that refused to die. Spencer Howell was much more interested in working his way into the levers of power at the county and state levels, somewhere out here in the northwestern United States. Through several of his shadowy connections, he developed ties to sovereign citizen groups and also those who supported the "constitutional sheriff" notion, both of which rebelled—sometimes violently—against the perceived overreaches of the Deep State-ridden feds, and even state-level government.

Fast-forward to *The Man in the High Castle* and the latter years of the 2010s.

Now that good Americans such as Spencer Howell had seen what could be accomplished, even at the federal level, when right-thinking folks were able to seize power, he began to set his sights on The Prize. The images of the alt-world Greater Nazi Reich depicted in *The Man in the High Castle* were regularly refreshed in Spencer Howell's mind—thus his obsession with watching the episodes over and over and over—and he began expanding his own political base, even as he watched with awe as some fragments from the show actually played out in the courts and in Congress and in the streets.

In 2024, Howell ran for Montana Attorney General as a far-right Republican, and won. In 2028, he was re-elected. Two years later, when the Restore American Values and Greatness Party splintered from the Republican Party, Howell went along with the rebels, with whom he had much more in common than those centrist, traditional Republicans who had reasserted power and control over that party. Good riddance!

Howell quickly became part of the inner circle propelling Ephraim Hollinger toward the 2032 presidential race. In Ephraim Hollinger, Spencer Howell instantly recognized both a kindred spirit and a vessel to bring to life some form of his own family's long-dormant American Nazi wet dream.

Hollinger's original brain trust of RAVG congressmen and senators—Braxton Knox, Tom Bucker, Tal Chadwick, Lowell Irvine, and others—quickly accepted Howell into their ranks, even though the Montana Attorney General was lacking in any sort of national-level connections. But if Hollinger ended up victorious, the Justice Department was slated for Spencer Howell.

And that's exactly what happened. Spencer Howell's on-the-record positions at that time were certainly far to the right of center, but not particularly authoritarian or draconian. His confirmation as the nation's Attorney General wasn't quite a slam dunk, and a few Democratic senators read the between the lines and saw Spencer Howell as a worrisome enigma. Still, a little bit of horse trading helped take Howell across the finish line, and his nomination ended up being confirmed, even with the Dems still controlling the Senate at that point in the nation's history that would soon pass.

* * *

From Howell's perspective—and perhaps unduly influenced by his continued obsession with the fantasy of an American Reich—he saw fated convergence in what was unfolding. In the Nazi Germany that his great-grandfather Rudolph Howell and his grandfather Max Howell had longed to bring to America, the two leaders arguably most responsible for setting that nation on its fated collision course with the Jews who pulled the world's puppet strings were Hitler and Himmler: H + H.

Hollinger and Howell.

H + H.

Adolph Hitler had been the charismatic face of Nazism. Even in America, at Camp Siegfried and in Sellersville and Windham, and then at Madison Square Garden on that February night in 1939, the sheer magnetism of *Der Führer* overshadowed any considerations of internal policy or international jockeying. The same could be said for Ephraim Hollinger. When Hollinger spoke, whether as a candidate or as a sitting president, the world stopped, no matter what he was saying.

Behind the scenes, though, Hitler had needed a Goebbels and a Göring and a Speer to turn his visions into a reality. He also needed a Heinrich Himmler; and he needed Himmler to captain the actions of others, such as Heydrich and Eichmann.

H + H.

Spencer Howell knew of the catalyzing event, back in 1984, that had set Ephraim Hollinger on the lengthy journey that culminated with his ascendancy to the presidency. Hollinger had sworn to avenge his family's eviction, and had accumulated a lifetime of fragmented ideas for how that vengeance might be attained, even while he accumulated his vast fortune.

For Hollinger, however, Job One for the past four years had been to ruthlessly consolidate unprecedented and unassailable presidential power. While he focused his entirety on achieving an imperial presidency and softening the battlefield through his incendiary rhetoric, Hollinger needed someone to do the heavy lifting—to collect all of his fragmented ideas of vengeance; to cull some, reorganize others, and plug any gaps; and to quietly, methodically build the machinery that would eventually be unleashed to reshape the American landscape.

Clearly, Spencer Howell was destined to be Ephraim Hollinger's Heinrich Himmler.

Chapter 45

Put Josh Stein, the convicted and now-imprisoned Colorado Bureau of Investigations head analytics whiz, into a blender along with Bart Lawrence, and out would come Kirk Barber.

Barber had served as the White House Chief Analytics and Data Officer since the earliest days of the Hollinger administration. Like Josh Stein, Barber earned his PhD in artificial intelligence-enabled analytics. Like Bart Lawrence, Kirk Barber was practiced in the dark arts of coercion and manipulation—though in Barber's case, through the weaponized usage of data and social media.

Others in the Hollinger orbit were now responsible for the intense and ongoing social media efforts, in concert with Bob Platte's AVGN. Kirk Barber had yielded those responsibilities following the 2032 election. Even though he organizationally still reported to the White House, Barber was soon detailed to the Federal Police Force to head up *the* pet project on Hollinger's and Spencer Howell's radar.

Kirk Barber had built the single most comprehensive "big data" collection ever constructed. Barber's masterpiece dwarfed anything done within the intelligence community, or in China or Russia, or in private industry…anywhere.

For starters, Barber had funneled quintillions of scraps of data together, expertly linking every piece of data with one or more American citizens. At one time, a data-gathering exercise of that magnitude would have been, by itself, an accomplishment like none other. However, given the steady march of technology, year after year, Kirk Barber's massive collection of literally every possible factoid, about every American, was still quite an achievement...but not quite earth-shattering, or even unprecedented.

Barber's secret sauce was what he did what all of that data.

Take Edmund and Eleanor Garfield.

Kirk Barber's masterpiece could inform an authorized and security-cleared White House staffer, an FPFer or other Justice Department user, or someone from Homeland Security that the Garfields were solid, loyal American Values and Greatness types. Their friends and acquaintances were "the right ones," with no association at all with any designated troublemakers that the FPF was keeping an eye on. Using the unending flows of mobile tracking data that were vacuumed into Barber's system, Edmund Garfield's daily post-lunch jaunts to the clubhouse were well established. Garfield met daily with other loyal patriots—no worries there. Any day that Edmund varied from his routine was noted in the data; and if he had been under FPF surveillance for any reason, his case officer would have been automatically alerted about the divergence, possibly triggering further investigation, depending on where Edmund wound up.

Both Edmund Garfield and his wife each earned a Citizen Loyalty Score—a CLS—of "High."

On the other side of the loyalty coin, consider Tamara Duncan.

Tamara was a thirty-one-year-old half-Black, half-Caucasian woman. She was originally from San Francisco but now lived in Dallas, after completing her master's degree in applied biomechanics at UCLA in 2031. Tamara had a lengthy history of supporting dangerous liberal positions. Until AVGN's takeover of social media and, essentially, the internet as a whole, she had signed an average of twenty-three online petitions each week for years, advocating environmental controls and restraints, animal welfare causes, voting rights, immigration reform, and the like.

Her circle of friends included numerous flagged people, similar to Tamara herself. Her mobile tracking data placed her at seven protests within the past two years, including two of those last October, both in downtown Dallas.

Tamara Duncan was awarded a CLS of "Low" and also given Priority 2 observation status, meaning that her FPF case officer was regularly notified with real-time updates as to her movements. Should Tamara be detected in the vicinity of, say, a known gathering of anti-government anarchists, her observation classification would be raised to Priority 1, and she might possibly be flagged for immediate detention and interrogation.

Kyla Danvers had already been branded as even more dangerous than Tamara Duncan, and was currently under active, constant FPF surveillance. African American; immediate and extended family with a history of supporting radical causes; a Black Lives Matter activist while an undergrad at the University of Michigan and then during grad school at Harvard; and among the protestors in Boston back in October. She had been halfway back in the crowd when the shooting started, and had escaped from Boston Common across the river to Cambridge, first heading up Charles Street and then turning onto Beacon. Five other observation Priority 1 anarchists followed the exact same escape route at the same time, heading back to Danvers' apartment in Cambridge along with her.

In the months since then, Kyla Danvers had been among Boston's leaders in organizing what appeared to be an embryonic resistance cell, numbering somewhere between fifty and seventy-five anarchist radicals. Consequently, Kyla Danvers was scheduled to be swept into an unmarked FPF van tomorrow morning at eight-thirty, as she walked to work.

On the other side of the spectrum, there was Randall Weston.

Randall's extensive social media record squarely categorized him as a friend of the administration and the American Values and Greatness movement. His mobile tracking data placed him at the Jewish cemetery "visits" back in early 2034, and flagged him as one of the more active culprits in Denver's vehicle vandalism wave last autumn. He was also present at the violent Denver encounters in October, but his location had been granularly pinpointed among the police, military, and paramilitary forces, not within the crowds of the protestors. When Randall's application for the Federal Police Force was received, the system generated a lightning-fast approval for him, based on his Citizen Loyalty Score of "Very High."

Now, consider a woman named Michele Burgess, currently residing in Pittsburgh.

Retired Army major; Rangers and Special Forces; and Jewish. For this demographic combination alone, Michele Burgess was given a Priority 2 observation status, even though neither her activity record nor her movements over the past several years indicated problematic behavior. Major Burgess was now a college professor who moved freely around the Pittsburgh metropolitan area. Her mobile tracking data recorded her routine of near-daily runs and workout sessions, but nothing else in her pool of data indicated anything other than a continuation of her physical fitness habits she had likely acquired during her Army days, if not earlier in life.

Her online activity didn't indicate any red flags. Going back three years she was only a sporadic social media user—primarily for keeping in contact with high school, college, and military friends, but without a single post or private message that indicated negative sentiment toward Ephraim Hollinger or his administration. Still, at the same time, none of her social media or other online activity indicated favoritism toward, or support for, the American Values and Greatness movement; so this retired Army major was flagged for regular surveillance to highlight any movement in her CLS, which currently registered as "Uncertain."

Finally, consider this Michele Burgess' boyfriend—her *lover*, to use the sneering vernacular of the right—named Daniel Jacobson. Jacobson, another elitist history professor like his *lover*, had authored that thinly veneered smear of President Hollinger's regime and the American Values and Greatness movement that, fortunately, had become the first successful test case for TAMCA and the Literature Review Board. That trespass alone had earned Jacobson a perpetual Priority 1 observation status, and an "Uncertain" Citizen Loyalty Score.

Since then, though, he appeared to have been a good boy. None of his social media activity or emails indicated communications with other designated enemies of the state. He didn't appear to have corrupted Michele Burgess, at least from their mobile tracking data and the contents of their back-and-forth texts.

Still, the Jewish *lovers* were marked. They would get theirs, soon enough.

* * *

Kirk Barber was another man with a voyeuristic streak. In his case, though, he spent hours each day accessing dozens of comprehensive profiles and movement reports from the system that he had built and for which he was responsible. Some of those individuals he spied on were randomly selected.

"Tawny Jeffers" sounds like an interesting name; and from her pictures, she's hot! Let's see who her friends are, where she goes and with whom, and what interesting tidbits I can learn about her. Maybe she's into sexting, or even some occasional online porn? Let's read some of her texts, and scan through her browsing activity…I hope she's been nasty…

Howard Silverman, age 68, retired in Tucson—and a Jew. Let's see what old Howard is up to these days—if he's behaving himself or if perhaps he's now getting together with other known troublemakers on a regular basis. That could mean that they're riling up dissent that needs to get squashed now, before it gets out of control. Doesn't matter if he's old, those people are all troublemakers at the core...

Others were people whom Kirk Barber knew or had encountered over the years.

Steve Michaels—man, I hated that guy in high school! He always acted like he was better than people like me, just because he played football and made all-state. Let's see if I can find anything on him...

Kara Robertson—she actually laughed at me when I asked her to prom, and posted all kinds of dismissive shit about me on social media. I swore that someday I would get her back for that...let's see...well, what do you know? Kara signed ninety-seven online anti-Hollinger petitions between 2032 and last year! She's already flagged as observation Priority 1 with a CLS of "Low," but sounds to me like the FPF needs to question her...VERY soon...

Chapter 46

Toni Fowler's blood froze as she read over tonight's opening monologue for her AVGN program that was coming up in less than a half hour. She was exhausted after a long day at the White House, but the script was a jolt of pure adrenalin. Resurgent recollections of the scripts Keenan Lucas had been handed in the weeks leading up to his assassination jockeyed for attention with the words in front of her.

The similarities were terrifying.

> Tonight, we can share SHOCKING details that have just been uncovered by Federal Police Force special investigators. A broad conspiracy of microbiologists and virologists employed by numerous universities throughout this great country has created a deadly virus in their labs...labs that are paid for by YOU, the loyal American taxpayer, even though they are run by universities that spread SOCIALIST propaganda to corrupt the minds of young Americans!
>
> Working in cahoots with numerous corrupt doctors and public health officials, these vicious scientists intended to release this virus throughout this great country to try and bring us to our knees. Why? As revenge for the crackdown last fall by our magnificent Federal Police Force that began when Jewish assassins murdered our own Keenan Lucas, in retaliation for him calling out their

diabolical plans to disrupt the presidential election.

Yes, you guessed it—EVERY SINGLE ONE of these conniving scientists is a JEW!

And of course, an army of shady JEWISH lawyers was already lined up to manipulate and subvert this nation's law and order system to help these deplorable people get away with their crimes.

Fortunately, our magnificent Federal Police Force has now rounded up EVERY SINGLE ONE of the conspirators and disrupted the plot. Loyal Americans can sleep easy tonight—but this was a CLOSE CALL, and unfortunately, it won't be the last one!

Remember COVID-19? This would have been COVID-37, brought to you directly from a cabal of reprehensible and immoral JEWISH scientists, doctors, and lawyers who won't stop until they have totally ruined the GREATNESS that is AMERICA!

Bob Platte had anticipated Toni's terrified reaction.

"Nothing to worry about," he preemptively said, the moment she looked up from the script with a wide-eyed, panicky stare.

Platte obviously intended his even-keeled tones to be reassuring. Instead, Toni took the tenor of his voice in concert with his words as an ominous "Okay, sure; we *could* be setting you up to be murdered, just like Keenan; but don't worry, not this time."

"We're good?" Bob Platte added, this time with a touch of irritation that signaled his impatience at even having to reassure AVGN's once-again star performer that she wasn't being set up for yet another highly visible, false-flag murder. Toni should know better. As long as Bart Lawrence was doing her, she was untouchable. More importantly, Toni Fowler remained *the* moneymaker among the AVGN stable of talent. Keenan Lucas had been a flash in the pan; he had served his purpose, but he was expendable…especially when the means of his demise had been architected as an essential step toward both Ephraim Hollinger's imperial presidency and the AVGN monopoly. Toni Fowler, though—she was a keeper. She would mint money for Bob Platte for time immemorial.

"Uh-huh," Toni managed to mutter, a moment before Bob Platte did an about-face and exited the opulent AVGN read-through room.

Toni had already been through a light touch-up on her makeup, so for the next twenty minutes until it was time to head to and then settle into her studio, she was left alone with her thoughts.

In recent months, Toni Fowler had begun doing the previously unthinkable: She earnestly pondered the truthfulness—or, more accurately, the lack thereof—of what she was about to go on-air with. Not that she would balk at this latest script, or even hesitate. Janice Bailey—the earlier incarnation of Toni Fowler; the journalism major; the daughter and granddaughter of Pulitzer Prize-winning investigative journalists who had dedicated their careers to seeking out the truth—would have flatly refused. But long ago, Janice Bailey had sold her soul to Bob Platte and received a hefty sum in return. Even before AVGN lowered an impenetrable blanket of ignorant hatred over the American landscape, Janice Bailey was no more.

Still, her heritage pricked at her conscience. Toni Fowler engaged in this exercise with regularity these days. She would entertain the concept of truth for a few moments, and then she would shrug and proceed with her broadcast.

Your soul is already forfeit…

In the course of her official afternoon White House press briefings, Toni spewed a fair amount of "hyperbole" through her official statements, and she maintained the evasiveness and sometimes-outright lies all the way through the make-believe press questions from her AVGN confederates who had replaced the actual White House press corps in these briefings. Rarely, though, did her official statements venture this deep into the realm of outlandish conspiracy theories and verbal bomb throwing. That dominion remained the province of her AVGN persona, as it had been for years.

Clearly, this was what Ephraim Hollinger and Bart Lawrence had in mind way back in 2032 when they first approached her about the press secretary role, and even more so when Bart revived the pitch after the 2034 midterms. Toni Fowler had become, essentially, her own one-two punch on behalf of the Hollinger administration and the American Values and Greatness movement. Her faux White House press briefings came bestowed—at least in part—with an aura of officialness, and were aimed at somewhat more cerebral viewers who still held out hope that the Hollinger era would maintain a few tenuous threads back to prior presidential administrations, and those earlier notions of normalcy. But then, come nighttime, just like a superhero shedding a secret identity and then unleashing all of her available superpowers, mild-mannered (or as close to mild-mannered as one in the Hollinger administration might pass for) Toni Fowler suddenly became TONI FOWLER!

Toni read her opening monologue once again. All bets were off when it came to "the truth." Continuing the deep traditions of "conservative" media, truth was a malleable commodity that could be reshaped, or even manufactured out of nothingness, at will. Truth was the classic *1984*-ish "2 + 2 = 5" if that was what suited the needs of Ephraim Hollinger, or Spencer Howell and Braxton Knox and General Frank Douglas, or Bob Platte.

Was there an actual COVID-37 plot? Highly doubtful. But were there virologists and microbiologists working in university labs across the country conducting research on viruses and infectious diseases? Of course! Were some of those scientists Jewish? Almost certainly...and that's all that was needed. Had any university-employed Jewish virologists and microbiologists even been taken into custody by the FPF? Had any Jewish doctors and lawyers actually been locked up? Any Deep State public health officials? Who knew?

And better yet: Did it really matter? A few kernels of plausibility, a few theoretically-possible-though-unproven threads of IF-THEN logic, and the AVGN machine would do the rest. Paul Simon and Art Garfunkel nailed it, almost seventy years ago:

All lies and jests;
Still a man hears what he wants to hear,
And disregards the rest.

In the three and a half months since the aborted presidential election, while Ephraim Hollinger and Spencer Howell had been busy subverting the Constitution of the United States to spawn their indefinite hold on absolute power, Bob Platte's forces had been working full throttle to destroy inconvenient truths. Those now-demised realities were pitilessly shoved aside by reconstructed variants—gross mutations, actually—that far better served American Values and Greatness doctrine.

Consider a representative online encyclopedia entry from "before" for *Kristallnacht*, the infamous "Night of Broken Glass" in Nazi Germany that kicked Hitler's violence against German Jews into high gear:

> Kristallnacht began the night of November 9, 1938, and continued past midnight to November 10th. Nazis throughout Germany executed wide-scale attacks against German Jews and their homes, businesses, and synagogues. Spurred by an order from the *Gestapo*, municipal German police stood by and watched Jewish businesses erupt in flames and brutal attacks against Jews proceed unimpeded...

Legacy encyclopedias, even the online variety, had been sucked into the fatal undertow of the Federal Literature Commission. Now, if a curious individual desired to consult an encyclopedic entry to learn more about a subject such as *Kristallnacht*, one must navigate to AVGN's *Revised American Values and True History Encyclopedia* website, where one would read:

> "Kristallnacht was a false-flag operation conducted by Jewish radicals in National Socialist Germany on the night of November 9-10, 1938. Seeking to undermine the economic recovery policies of Adolf Hitler, a cabal of German Jews along with terrorists smuggled into Germany from Palestine and various Eastern European countries attacked and burned thousands of Jewish homes, businesses, hospitals, and schools. The Jewish terrorists wore SA

paramilitary uniforms in an attempt to deflect blame onto the lawful German Government. The Kristallnacht subversion backfired on the Jewish antagonists by leading to warranted crackdowns by the German Government, including the necessary collection and detention of these Jewish terrorists in so-called concentration camps."

* * *

In the aftermath of Toni Fowler's program that mid-February night in 2037, Americans across the land of all political persuasions braced for a replay of last fall's massive unrest. Surely, the nationalist militias would gleefully exact their revenge against Jewish targets, in retaliation for this heinous COVID-37 plot. Disrupted or not, what the Jews had intended was unconscionable, and they had to pay!

In response, the protestors would somehow muster the courage to return to the streets, meeting the inevitable, overwhelming deadly force of the FPF. Would thousands of protesters once again lie dead in the streets by the time these clashes had concluded? Would this cycle of violence in the streets of America ever be broken?

Strangely, no militia attacks occurred at all, despite plenty of "let's saddle up!" agitation among the ranks of the many groups who were anxious to reprise their "*Jüden Verboten*" defacements, destroy Jewish-owned property, and hopefully unleash their firepower. Once again, it seemed as if some shadowy authoritative entity behind the scenes silently held up a hand, signaling the forces to "stand back…for now."

Something's coming.

Chapter 47

February 28th.

Another Purim Eve, but to Daniel, this one seemed…off.

Way off.

For one thing, his parents' house was *always* filled with the sweet, doughy aroma of still-baking *hamantaschen* as the family gathered to read from Nathan Jacobson's homemade *Megillah* booklets. Now, though, a musty, dank odor assaulted Daniel's nostrils, as if his mother hadn't cleaned her house for months, and the windows hadn't been opened for at least as long.

Then there was the presence, directly across the table from Daniel, of both Pop-pop and Michele's great-grandfather.

They both died last year…on Purim day, right? Maybe their spirits decided that a surprise visit was in order on the Hebrew calendar anniversary of their passing? The Ghosts of Purim Past?

Apparently, the ghosts or apparitions or whatever they were of Nathan Jacobson and Isaac Gretz intended to fully participate in tonight's *Erev Purim* rituals, as Isaac Gretz was now reading from his *Megillah*, clutched tightly in his surprisingly steady hands.

"And at that time," Michele's great-grandfather began in a clear, strong, but still heavily accented voice, "shall Michael stand up, the great prince who standeth for the children of thy people; and there shall be a time of trouble, such as never was since there was a nation even to that same time; and at that time thy people shall be delivered, every one that shall be found written in the book."

That's really odd, Daniel contemplated as he listened to Michele's great-grandfather read in his accented voice. *He pronounced "Michael" the same way he always pronounced Michele's name—"My-KEL" with the second syllable accented. Somehow I had never before noticed the similarities to "Michael" when he spoke her name.*

When he was alive.

Another oddity: Isaac Gretz's passage wasn't from The Book of Esther, the historical Purim tome, even though he was reading from one of the standard Jacobson family *Megillahs*. Daniel knew with absolute certainty that what Michele's great-grandfather had just recited was actually the first verse of the final chapter of a different book in the Hebrew Bible.

The Book of Daniel.

My namesake.

Now, it was Pop-pop's turn to read, and he apparently was sticking with Daniel, Chapter 12, as he moved on to the second verse with an exceptionally strong, commanding voice that instantly brought a flood of memories of the Pop-pop from Daniel Jacobson's youth.

"And many of them that sleep in the dust of the earth shall awake, some to everlasting life, and some to reproaches and everlasting abhorrence."

Well, THAT might explain why our great-grandfathers, both dead for almost a year, are sitting across the dining room table from me right now…

Daniel jolted awake. He wasn't in his parents' suburban Pittsburgh house after all. The musty odor hung heavy in the deep darkness; no *hamantaschen* were in the oven, baking their way to delectable perfection.

For a good ten seconds, Daniel was unable to wrap his thoughts around whose blacked-out, unfamiliar house he was in, or even where he was. Soon, though, the flicker of remembrance came to him.

It was, in fact, February 28th, Purim Eve; though if the clock had swept past midnight during his troubled slumber, it was now the first of March. Daniel's parents were here, in this house, as were Michele's parents as well, all the way from Houston. So, too, were Daniel's Uncle Mike and Aunt Sharon from Syracuse. Daniel's Uncle Adam—his mother's brother, who lived near Columbus, Ohio—and six members of his family were present. Eight others from Michele's family, all from the northeastern U.S., were here as well. They were all scattered through the various rooms of this old farmhouse. A few would, hopefully, be asleep; most were probably lying awake, unable to sleep.

Thinking about tomorrow.

As clarity infused Daniel's mind, he sadly realized that neither Nathan Jacobson nor Isaac Gretz was among the huddled masses inside this desolate farmhouse. Their appearances were confined to the realm of Daniel's extremely vivid dream.

Still...

They all had, in fact, been at Uncle Mike's and Aunt Sharon's house in Syracuse earlier in the evening, gathered for an abbreviated Purim Eve, solemnly reading from Nathan Jacobson's homemade *Megillahs*. *Hamantaschen* had, in fact, been baking in Aunt Sharon's two ovens, though none of the twenty-nine people gathered would be sitting around after dinner, slurping coffee while they enjoyed the pastries, talking and reminiscing. Instead, the *hamantaschen* were for the road—much like the *matzah* from the Passover tale as the Jews fled the tyranny of Pharaoh, albeit with a vast improvement in the eatability of travel rations one would expect after more than three thousand years.

They were now sequestered in a desolate farmhouse out in the middle of the proverbial nowhere, about one hundred thirty miles northeast of Syracuse. The caravan of vehicles, spaced out just enough not to draw any unwanted attention from the recently deployed FPF observation drones that were increasingly blanketing the nation's lower-tier airspace, had departed Uncle Mike's and Aunt Sharon's house around eight-thirty. Along with the people were seven dogs, eight cats, two hamsters, a rabbit, and a turtle. Miraculously, all of the pet refugees were quietly and peacefully coexisting, at least for the moment. They were now about one hundred twenty miles due south of Dundee, Quebec, which was where Michele and Daniel would lead these many from their respective families across the border, not long after first light.

* * *

Michele Burgess had been preparing for this moment for more than two years now; since mere days after the 2034 midterms, even before Ephraim Hollinger's early 2035 *blitzkrieg* maneuvers with his Cabinet, the joint chiefs, and the Supreme Court; since before Daniel's novel was crushed by TAMCA. Long before the October bloodbaths and the "postponed" presidential election, before American democracy died, uttering a pitiful whimper, Michele *knew* that something was coming.

She wasn't alone.

A tight-knit cadre of like-minded former U.S. military and intelligence community special operators, just shy of four dozen in all, had stealthily prepared for the once-unthinkable. Green Berets, Army Rangers, Navy SEALS, Marine Recon, black ops veterans from the intelligence community…each one of them coolly observed Ephraim Hollinger's maneuverings during the first two years of his presidency, and waited to see if the 2034 midterms would become the inflection point of the American Experiment. Along the way, they regularly signaled each other through carefully constructed social media posts that became the modern incarnation of World War II-era coded messages embedded in radio broadcasts and newspaper advertisements. Then, once Hollinger's all-out assault on democracy went full throttle in early 2035, they began periodically, stealthily, meeting in smaller groups, in quiet remote out-of-the-way locations for a day or two at a time.

They began preparing in earnest.

At the beginning, not every one of these military vets knew—or knew of—each other. But Michele had served with both John Garcia and Roseanne Morris in Special Forces, and with Frank Sanchez in the Rangers. Roseanne knew Aidan Beckett from a different Special Forces assignment, while Frank Sanchez knew Fletcher Carlson, a Navy SEAL, from several joint operations in Afghanistan. Carlson knew Joy Patel, one of the ex-intel operators, who had recruited three of her trusted former colleagues who were appalled at what Hollinger and Spencer Howell and Braxton Knox were able to get away with; and so on. Even now, they were scattered around the country, working in smaller teams, and none of them had met everyone else in person.

Michele Burgess had, in fact, been the one who initiated the entire operation. Her encounter with Ephraim Hollinger at the 2033 West Point graduation ceremony, shortly before her retirement from the Army, haunted her.

I swear it could have been Hitler; or even the devil…I never felt like I was in the presence of pure evil the way I did with Hollinger two feet away from me.

Over the next year and a half, as she settled into her new life in Pittsburgh and her new relationship with Daniel Jacobson, Michele's thoughts frequently, compulsively gravitated to Hollinger's speech that May afternoon; to the President of the United States ominously vowing to vanquish all of his designated domestic enemies, and promising one thousand newly minted Army second lieutenants that they would soon join his crusade.

Long ago, Michele Burgess had taken the same oath that those Class of 2033 West Point graduates spoke that afternoon. She had sworn to support and defend the Constitution of the United States against all enemies—foreign and domestic alike—and to bear true faith and allegiance to the words and spirit of that sacred document.

Hollinger himself was the threat to the Constitution; to America itself. She sensed it even back then, and time would sadly prove her correct. Michele began preparing for…something. On a whim, she connected with John Garcia, also recently retired from the Army, using a spoofed social media account. Garcia had recently met in person with Roseanne Morris, where over the course of an evening—and nine beers each—they lamented the early stages of renewed dystopian descent that Hollinger was hell-bent on leading. Back in the summer of 2033, Ephraim Hollinger and Spencer Howell were just beginning to architect their police-state apparatus, which meant that Michele and the others had time to construct an extensive portfolio of coded social media posts that they could later use to signal one another.

At the time, Michele was just beginning her relationship with Daniel Jacobson, and had no intention of allowing him to enter her little circle of trust. Besides, given Michele's two-year relationship with John Garcia while they both had been stationed at Fort Huachuca, enlightening Daniel about her occasional communiqués with the former Green Beret wouldn't have been the most prudent idea, she reasoned.

Initially, the precise nature of the dangers posed by Hollinger was frustratingly opaque; but Michele and the growing cadre of special ops and intel veterans were all absolutely convinced that Ephraim Hollinger, Spencer Howell, Braxton Knox, Bob Platte, and the others represented an existential threat.

Reading the manuscript of Daniel's novel, *The Twilight's Last Gleaming*, as it progressed was what solidified the essence of Hollinger's immorality for Michele. His vivid descriptions of the tale's Hollinger-of-the-near-future's evil intent jolted Michele to her core. The resurgent mainstreaming of white nationalism; the brutal clashes in the streets across

America; the merciless hostile takeover of the entire apparatus of the United States government as well as the governing apparatus of so many states and municipalities. So much of Daniel's book had already turned out to be every bit as much a prophecy as it was a novel.

Then there was Daniel's chilling reprise of 1930s Nazi Germany, right here in mid-twenty-first-century America...Hitler's belated revenge from the grave on the nation that had led the effort to extinguish his quest for both world domination and "solving the Jewish problem."

In *The Twilight's Last Gleaming*, American Jews abruptly found themselves uprooted from their lives and facing a reign of terror at the hands of their own government. Daniel had infused his novel with a futuristic backdrop derived and extrapolated from what was actually occurring in the present day as he was writing, back in 2034: the blasphemous Jewish cemetery and synagogue defacements; the lies spewed nightly on AVGN about Jewish plots and thievery; the wholesale arrests of Jews in the financial world that had occurred earlier in that year of 2034 when Daniel was working on his novel; and the ominous threats posed by the RAVG Party electoral conquests that November.

And then, back in the real world, soon after forty thousand copies of *The Twilight's Last Gleaming* had been consigned to become fuel for that enormous swastika that blazed one summer night, *everything* actually did descend to hell. If a copy of Daniel's book could rematerialize and rise from the ashes, one would chillingly read of a near-future fictional America that horrifically resembled the nation in the present day, including the late-January arrest of Senator Jack Bancroft and numerous other designated Enemies of the State.

The false-flag assassination of Keenan Lucas—which was hauntingly similar to one of Daniel's plot threads—had clearly been concocted to trigger rioting in the street as a pretext for canceling the presidential election. Further: The assassination had been explicitly architected to lay blame on Jews. Michele was certain that Hollinger's assault wouldn't end with his coronation, and Toni Fowler's early February broadcasts with their horrific claims of a "Jewish COVID-37 plot" were confirmation that a reign of terror was about to be unleashed.

Time to move.

* * *

Michele had been the one who selected this particular safe house location, in a remote—but not too desolate—farming area of upstate New York, a few miles from State Route 28. Almost twenty other safe houses had been set up, strategically scattered around the country, leading to several key ones that were within striking distance of a passable, relatively low-traffic border crossing to either Canada or Mexico.

Two of the "final stop" safe houses were down south: one north of Laredo, Texas, as the primary, and another a little bit south of Deming, New Mexico, as the backup. One was in the Pacific Northwest, northeast of Seattle. One more was about an hour west of Duluth, Minnesota. Five others were scattered around central and southern Arizona, given the proximity to both the concentration camps and the Mexican border.

Other safe houses laid trails to the border-crossing ones. Someone refugeeing from, say, Kansas City, could be led a couple hundred miles at a time from one safe house to the next, eventually being in position for that final sprint across either the northern or southern border, most likely northward via Duluth.

Every one of the safe houses was fairly secluded, with no neighboring properties within line of sight. Each had a large barn or oversized RV-style garage that could keep at least half a dozen vehicles—or dozens of people—out of sight of aerial observation.

The interior roof structures of each of the outbuildings had, over time, been completely layered with highly secretive materials that had been "procured" from military supplies. These materials prevented aerial thermal sensors from detecting the heat signatures radiated by dozens or even a hundred or more bodies, which would be a clear indication to airborne FPF drones or surveillance aircraft that fugitives or refugees being sought had been located.

Just after Christmas Day of 2035, Michele signaled the other special operators via several coded social media posts that they now needed to shift into the next phase of operations, and begin meeting in person. The farcical "Sedition through Media Content and Transmission" mass trial in Denver had just concluded, and the sting of Daniel's novel also being victimized by the draconian TAMCA provisions was still as strong as it had been that past summer. Michele had begun this operation; and though no vote was ever held nor did anyone still hold an active military or government rank, Michele quickly became the group's de facto leader.

That late-December weekend, which was immediately following the morning when Michele had evasively told Daniel "I need you to do something for me," was when the second phase had been set into motion. Each of the special operators knew exactly what needed to be done—and not done—to mask one's physical movements while scouting and preparing the safe houses. No cell phones; no smartwatches; older vehicles only, without GPS or any location-tagged data uploads back to manufacturers' databases. Ideally, an accomplice would concoct sleight-of-hand activity and movement back home by moving one's cell phone from one location to another, plus sending and receiving pre-scripted misdirection texts, all according to a predetermined schedule. The accomplice didn't necessarily need to be fully informed—as was the case with Daniel Jacobson, at least for a while—but that other individual needed to be absolutely trusted, as if he or she were an adjunct supporting member of this elite unit.

Even when back home and not at one of the safe houses, each of them was careful not to generate any location data that would place them at an FPF "area of interest." When Michele and Daniel went to the shooting range or the laser-tag facility, they both left their cell phones at home to avoid pinging any towers or satellites from a place of business that might trigger an alert.

While none of them knew the specifics of the "big data" monstrosity that Kirk Barber had built, each one was savvy enough to know that Hollinger's and Howell's police state apparatus absolutely had the capabilities and the corrupt intent to monitor their unsuspecting citizenry en masse, beyond anything the world had previously seen. Even if none of them was lighting up the FPF radar at the moment, they eventually would be. They needed to buy as much time as possible.

Each of the safe houses had been purchased by someone who didn't actually exist. Two of the ex-intel operators were field-tested at creating "deep cover" false identities, with comprehensive backstories comprised of thousands of concocted data points expertly and covertly hacked into numerous databases: years of banking records and tax returns, high school and college transcripts, wedding and divorce licenses, social media and email accounts, and much more. These deep cover dossiers would provide enough of a barrier to protect their real identities for at least a little while, allowing them to operate out of these safe houses. At some point, ultimately, they *would* be unmasked; and then they would have to fold up shop and move on to their next operational phase. That decision would come later; for now, they were all laser-focused on racing the clock.

Each safe house had also been acquired in an all-cash deal. The funds—slightly more than fourteen million dollars in total—had likewise been alchemized from a dizzying sequence of masked and spoofed banking transactions that undetectably transformed hacked cryptocurrency into "real" money. Joy Patel tried several times to explain the machinations to Michele, John Garcia, and the others, since she had devised the scheme and was responsible for executing it. No matter how many times Joy tried to diagram what she was doing, to Michele—and most of the others—Joy might as well have been describing alien technology being used for instantaneous intergalactic time travel. Finally, they all just agreed to take it on faith that Joy knew what she was doing…which she obviously did, since their fake alter egos now had clear title to the safe house properties.

Responsibility for the safe houses had been divided among the overall team members, determined by where everyone currently lived. That first meeting in this central New York location, with ten of them in attendance, was spent scouring the surrounding area—ferreting out all possible risks, identifying escape paths, and recording observation trajectories both from and at the house. They split up into three different vehicles, each one taking a different route north from the safe house. One route swooped heavily west; another angled slightly east; and the third was a mostly straight shot up a moderately traveled state highway. They watched for FPF mobile patrols, which had recently been increased. They took note of road conditions, overall traffic density, construction zones with narrowed through-lanes, accessibility of alternative routes, and a dozen other factoids that an experienced special ops or intel veteran would notice.

Each of the routes converged at Dundee, Quebec, where the unstaffed, lightly used border crossing lay just across from the small town of Fort Covington, New York.

* * *

Michele finally unveiled the full truth to Daniel on the same day that Ephraim Hollinger announced that for the good of the nation and its patriots, he would "postpone" the election and "safeguard the presidency." By now, Daniel had figured out that Michele's mysterious, periodic out-of-town trips—during which he would follow a newly devised set of instructions to the letter—had something to do with the ever-increasing unrest and danger. Her sudden interest in Daniel learning to shoot, encouraging him to take up running and weightlifting, and teaching him rudimentary combat techniques via laser tag didn't all materialize—at the same time, no less—absent of reason. She had asked him to trust her, though; so Daniel resisted the ever-present urge to press her for details.

After democracy was murdered, though, Michele realized that there would be no turning back. All along, she and the others had hoped that this would turn out like so many missions during their military or intelligence operations days: a lengthy preparation, sometimes even up to the cusp of execution, but then interdicted by a stand-down order.

Once Hollinger seized the presidency, there would be no stand-down order. Hell on earth was just around the corner, and they needed to act.

* * *

Among the forty-seven special operators, only Michele Burgess was Jewish. Therefore, they readily yielded to Michele's initial phase of *Operation Exodus*, the all-too appropriate name for their mission that hearkened back to both the biblical tale as well as the seminal Leon Uris novel.

I need to get my family out first, and Daniel's family also.

Ephraim Hollinger's incarnation of an Iron Curtain hadn't fully descended yet, but Michele knew with all the certainty in the world that their time was running very short. On Sunday, February 1st, she and Daniel headed to his parents' house, ostensibly for Sunday family dinner. Despite the below-freezing temperatures, they quickly walked outside into the snow-covered backyard for a conversation that none of them ever thought would have occurred in the United States of America, the once-beacon of democracy and freedom. Michele highly doubted that any listening devices had been directed at the home of Robert and Nancy Jacobson—but she wasn't taking any chances.

"You both need to get out of the country," Daniel bluntly began.

Daniel was shocked that his parents weren't stunned by his words. Michele, though, had a hunch that his parents already had a clear-eyed understanding of where this was all headed.

"When do we need to leave?" was Nancy Jacobson's quiet, surprisingly dry-eyed response.

* * *

The next day, after her Monday classes were finished, Michele flew to Houston to somberly inform her own parents the same thing they had just told the Jacobsons. Her parents responded the same as Daniel's, with resigned acceptance that life as they knew it was over…and that for a brief moment, they had at least a little bit of control over what came next.

For the next four days, a frenzy of warnings was delivered to numerous family members of both Daniel and Michele. Some were delivered in person by either of them; others were done by proxy, courtesy of Michele's comrades. Aidan Beckett, the Special Forces alumnus, working out of one of the Pacific Northwest safe houses, was the one who handed a prearranged handwritten plea from Daniel to his cousin Julie and her husband Bob. They would be in the hands of the former Captain Beckett and four additional operators, to be ferried across the U.S.-Canada border five miles east of the official crossing near Blaine, Washington.

Both Daniel and Michele had fully expected at least a few of their relatives to balk at being told that they needed to leave their entire lives behind and flee the country. Fortunately, each adult had no illusions about what was about to happen all across America. They might not have possessed the chilling foresight of Michele and Daniel, but nobody was in denial that their safety and freedom were in jeopardy. Both families had long-ago relatives who disregarded the prophetic handwriting on the wall and missed their chances to leave Germany or Poland or some other homeland before the Nazi rampage began. Those tales of fatally missed opportunity had persevered through years of family lore; none wanted to reprise their ancestors' heartbreaking hesitations.

Michele and Daniel had drawn up the plans of who-goes-where in the early days of last December, and did a few minor tweaks to the rosters over the next two weeks. For the most part, just as the special operators themselves had been divided among the safe houses along geographical boundaries, so, too, were the family members who would comprise this initial exodus from what was about to happen in Ephraim Hollinger's America.

The lone exception was Michele's parents. Living in Houston, the safe house outside of Laredo would have been a more natural point of departure for them. That's where Daniel's living grandparents—Robert's parents, Evan and Shelly Jacobson, who lived in Dallas—would be departing from. Michele, however, had no intention of leaving her own parents to the charges of anyone else other than herself. The targeted time frame for the mass exodus—the end of February—presented the perfect opportunity. Purim came early this year, and Michele concocted a cover story of her parents joining Daniel's for a joint family gathering at Mike's and Sharon's home in Syracuse. By this time, Michele was certain that she was under at least periodic observation by the FPF, which likely meant that her parents' movements would also be monitored. This way, the Burgesses had plausible reason to fly north into New York State without tripping any alarms in the FPF's surveillance system.

For all among the huddled masses, once convinced of the inevitability of what America would soon become, fleeing to safety was of paramount importance. But once they were sequestered in either Canada or Mexico, what would they do about money? About their livelihoods?

Michele's parents had, fortunately, taken out a sizable home equity loan on their formerly paid-off house late last summer, but had yet to spend any of that money on their planned home improvements. Along with surreptitious withdrawals from their bank accounts and cashing in some of their mutual funds and stocks, they would at least be able to transport a couple years' worth of expected living expenses across the border. They would still be leaving behind a sizable portion of their assets; but they were far more fortunate than most of history's refugees.

Daniel's parents, unfortunately, would likely wind up forfeiting every cent they had in their paid-off home. They didn't have nearly enough time to tap into any of their home equity at this point; and besides, attempting to do so could well be a tipoff to the FPF. On the other hand, Daniel's father had always been somewhat of a gold bug, with a significant stash of rare gold coins squirreled away in a couple of suburban Pittsburgh safe deposit boxes. Over the next two weeks, he spaced out two hopefully innocuous trips, one to each bank, and successfully extracted close to two hundred thousand dollars' worth of gold. Coupled with a few strategic cash withdrawals, Robert and Nancy Jacobson would also have adequate funds for the beginning of their late-in-life new beginning.

All of the others tapped for the late February escape likewise stealthily gathered whatever assets they could without raising suspicions about their intent to flee. Some would be less well off than others, but they would be able to count on their relatives for at least some assistance.

Additionally, the networks in Canada and Mexico that Michele and the others had organized were all standing by, ready to aid the refugees: not only the Burgess and Jacobson family members coming across in this first run, but others who would follow. Most of the special operators had worked with their counterparts in both the Canadian and Mexican militaries and intelligence communities over the years. As with the Americans, more than a few of the retired vets in Canada and Mexico were appalled and disgusted at what Ephraim Hollinger had been able to destroy thus far in the nation that had once been the free world's shining beacon, and they were all clear-eyed about what was coming. Not only would the Canadian and Mexican veterans aid in the border crossings and subsequent transport, but they would also arrange logistical and financial aid for the refugees once they were safely ensconced in those countries, as well as some degree of protection. They had already obtained access to apartments and safe houses far enough away from the American borders, and would provide regular safeguard watches against possible cross-border reprisals by the FPF or militias or Spencer Howell's mercenaries.

By February 21st, one week before the mass exodus, everything was, miraculously, more or less in place, with one exception…technically, three exceptions.

* * *

"What about Claire?" Michele had anticipated the question coming from Daniel's mother, that frigid afternoon when they broke the surreally horrific news.

Before Daniel could answer, Michele interjected. She would take the bullet for him on this one.

"Not until both of you and everyone else is safely across," she grimly shook her head. Michele was about to amplify her response, but Nancy Jacobson immediately understood.

"It's because of Marc," Daniel's mother quietly nodded her sad acceptance of Michele's declaration.

Michele looked over at Daniel, her eyes indicating *okay, you can field this one from here.*

"I promise that we'll get her and the kids across the border right after you," Daniel picked up the discussion.

"And Marc too," he added, "if he'll go."

Daniel's "if" hung heavy in the frigid February dusk. Nothing else needed to be said, either by Daniel or Michele, or Daniel's parents. The hundred-million-dollar question—literally—was whether Marc Weber would recognize that not only his wife's freedom and that of his children were in peril, but so was his, wealth and RAVG Party connections notwithstanding.

"Can't we bring Claire and the kids along with us," Nancy Jacobson pondered, "and then afterward, you go back and try to get Marc?"

"We just can't risk Claire saying anything to Marc beforehand," Michele shook her head, deliberately keeping her voice even keeled.

"And if she does, and then if he tells anybody else about—"

"I know," Daniel's mother mournfully interrupted. "Then everything could fall apart, and we're all…"

Nancy Jacobson's voice trailed off. All four of them knew that Marc Weber was *the* major complicating problem in this opening run for the border. If Marc hadn't thought of himself as "one of them"—the American Values and Greatness elite—and if he had valued his family's safety over status and wealth, there would be no question about including Daniel's sister and children, and her husband, in this first wave of departures.

Truthfully, Michele didn't give a damn about Marc Weber in the context of Daniel's family. From a purely tactical perspective, Marc Weber was a major operational risk…which made Claire a potential point of cataclysmic failure as well. At least Daniel had agreed, long before this moment, that Claire and her children needed to be excised from the first cohort. Both Daniel and Michele had expected a battle from Daniel's parents, however—his mother in particular—

and they were relieved when Nancy Jacobson immediately accepted the somber reality that for everyone's safety, their daughter and their grandchildren needed to be coldly left behind for at least a day or two.

Hopefully no longer.

* * *

The convoy departed the safe house, two cars at a time at seven-minute intervals, beginning at six o'clock the next morning. The cars fanned out along all three of the preset northbound routes. Encrypted burner phones were carried along, available for emergency usage. In the event of an FPF roadblock or any other setback along one route, the other vehicles scheduled to take that path could be alerted to divert. Otherwise, the phones remained off to avoid the FPF picking up pings that weren't correlated to known phone numbers, and which might then trigger interdiction.

Michele and her four comrades spread out among the cars. Daniel drove with his parents and his Uncle Mike and Aunt Sharon—and their two medium-sized dogs. Two other vehicles carried only refugees (and more of the pets)—though Michele's cousin Jon Burgess had served in the Air Force, which put him "in charge" of one of those SUVs.

By the grace of God, all eight vehicles zoomed up their respective routes and then slid across the Canadian border without incident. They rendezvoused about nine miles northeast, at a newly established safe house outside of the hamlet of Pointe-Leblanc. Later today, the Canadian special operators would ferry the refugees another sixty miles northeast, into the heart of Montreal for at least a little while.

There, they would begin their new lives.

* * *

The goodbyes were heartbreaking. Daniel watched tears stream from Michele's eyes as she tightly hugged her parents, both of them together, for nearly three full minutes. He knew the same would happen to him when he said goodbye to his parents; so he postponed the inevitable as he made the rounds of Uncle Mike, Aunt Sharon, and the rest of his relatives. He even spent several minutes making the rounds of all of the refugee animals, extending comforting hugs and head pets to the dogs, soothing chin and ear scratches to the cats through their carrier doors, and reassuring strokes to the other creatures, even the turtle.

Finally, the moment could be delayed no longer.

Daniel's mother first.

"Go back and save Claire and the children," her shaking, mournful voice pleaded.

"I will," Daniel promised.

"Be safe," Nancy Jacobson added, her voice now totally breaking down.

This time, Daniel was unable to utter a response.

After another minute, he excised himself to say goodbye to his father. Before Daniel could move, Robert Jacobson grabbed his son, pulled him in tight, and then shifted his eyes heavenward.

"Pop-pop is so proud of you," his father said, his voice breaking as Daniel dissolved into tears.

Alan Simon

Part V
Life During Wartime

March 20, 2037–January 18, 2038

The Voice of Prophets

> *"Heard of a van that is loaded with weapons,*
> *Packed up and ready to go;*
> *Heard of some grave sites, out by the highway,*
> *A place where nobody knows.*
> *The sound of gunfire, off in the distance,*
> *I'm getting used to it now…"*

- Talking Heads, *Life During Wartime*

> *"We'll be fighting in the streets*
> *With our children at our feet*
> *And the morals that they worship will be gone;*
> *And the men who spurred us on*
> *Sit in judgment of all wrong;*
> *They decide and the shotgun sings the song."*

- The Who, *Won't Get Fooled Again*

Chapter 48

Spencer Howell's blueprint came straight from 1930s Nazi Germany—of course—while Ephraim Hollinger's pretext was provided by one of his presidential predecessors.

In December of 1862, Ulysses S. Grant—still a Civil War major general then, though slightly more than six years later, the President of the United States—issued General Order Number 11, which expelled all Jews from his "Department of the Tennessee" jurisdiction that included the majority of Kentucky, Tennessee, and Mississippi. Grant's order ostensibly targeted the Southern cotton trade as a key facet of his economic warfare against the Confederacy during the Vicksburg Campaign. In Grant's own words, cited in a letter to the Assistant Secretary of War, he was taking aim at "Jews and unprincipled traders" who helped sustain the South's viability.

Grant, however, didn't stop with Jewish merchants. He gave *every* Jewish man, woman, and child in the impacted geographies all of twenty-four hours to leave behind their homes and their livelihoods. History records the opening words of Grant's order:

> The Jews, as a class, violating every regulation of trade established by the Treasury Department, and also Department orders, are hereby expelled from the Department.

Grant's order declared that any Jew not leaving, or caught returning after departing, would be arrested and imprisoned. Further, Grant had no intention of relying solely on a voluntary exodus. Three days after issuing his order, the remaining Jews in Holly Springs, Mississippi, were rounded up and forced out of the city on foot. Union Army enforcement broadened throughout the affected occupation zone. As word of Grant's order spread, intense pressure mounted from across the Union, declaring that the expulsions were (in the words of a politically connected Jewish Kentucky merchant named Cesar Kaskel) "the grossest violation of the Constitution and our rights as good citizens under it." In early January 1863, Abraham Lincoln ordered Grant to rescind the order, which the general did several weeks later.

(Perhaps in protest of Lincoln's meddling, in August of 1863 Grant issued a different directive ordering the wholesale evacuation of rural areas in western Missouri using the exact same title: General Order Number 11.)

Spencer Howell and his minions had worked quietly and feverishly alongside those of Senate Majority Leader Tal Chadwick and House Speaker Lowell Irvine to draft the legislation that would soon be rubber-stamped by both houses of the United States Congress. Ephraim Hollinger certainly could have issued an Executive Order containing the full breadth of his immoral anti-Jewish measures that would soon descend over the nation. After all, Hollinger owned the courts and could easily fend off any challenges to the legality or constitutionality of his action—who could possibly stop him?

No. Hollinger wanted this done via federal legislation that would, for all time, mark the law of the land.

* * *

"President Hollinger will now address the nation."

Toni Fowler's lightning-quick, somber-toned introduction on Friday morning, the twentieth of March, was followed by a glaring Ephraim Hollinger stepping to the podium without even acknowledging his press secretary. Hollinger was flanked by his entire brain trust: Spencer Howell, of course, but also Vice President Paul Nelson, Braxton Knox from DHS, Treasury's Tom Bucker, Secretary of Defense Gil Reed, National Security Advisor Connor Patterson, and General Frank Douglas. White House Counsel Travis Whitman and Chief Justice of the Supreme Court Bryant Hayes were also present to accentuate the legal foundation of what Hollinger was about to unveil. The presence of Senate Majority Leader Tal Chadwick and House Speaker Lowell Irvine signaled that Congress was already on board.

"Our nation and its loyal patriots continue to face unprecedented danger from an insidious internal threat," Hollinger began.

"Last month, the combined efforts of the Justice Department and the Department of Homeland Security"—Hollinger nodded in Spencer Howell's direction, and then toward Braxton Knox—"and in concert with our national security and intelligence establishment under the direction of National Security Advisor Patterson, uncovered a widespread conspiracy to develop and then disseminate a highly lethal virus across this nation. This attempted COVID-37 bioterrorism would have dwarfed the COVID-19 pandemic in terms of American deaths and long-term severe illness."

Hollinger's eyes, the window into his dark soul, deadened as he continued.

"Investigation by our powerful Federal Police Force revealed that the roots of this plot were as a reprisal for the unprecedented civil unrest last October in the wake of the murder of beloved and highly respected newscaster Keenan Lucas by international and domestic Jewish conspirators. *Every single person* arrested for involvement in this attempted biological warfare against this nation is an American Jew. Intelligence gathered during the arrests and subsequent interrogations has revealed that this plot was only one of several that were planned by the treasonous conspirators."

The Voice of Prophets

Spencer Howell, knowing what was coming, fought back a vicious grin as Hollinger continued.

"As President of the United States, it is my responsibility to safeguard the welfare of the loyal, patriotic citizens of this land against all perils, including those generating from within. Therefore, I am asking the United States Congress"—a nod toward Irvine and Chadwick—"to draft and then pass legislation that will protect this nation and its citizens from these internal threats, by imposing severe restrictions on those who would threaten our safety and our traditional American way of life."

* * *

As of April 1st, 2037, no Jews would be permitted to hold federal, state, county, or local government positions in the United States of America. Jews would no longer be allowed to infect young, impressionable minds in the nation's schools, nor spread their seditious anti-American messaging in America's universities. Jews would be barred from the nation's legal system: judges, attorneys, even juries.

Their long-standing infestation of banking, finance, and real estate would finally come to an end. Certainly there would be no Jewish police officers or soldiers, and American Jews would no longer be permitted to own firearms.

Jewish-owned businesses were effectively banned, though a Jewish business owner could apply to the newly formed Department of Jewish Employment Control—the DJEC—for an essential variance, which might be granted if one could clearly demonstrate that maintaining the business was in the public interest. Still, an oppressive licensing tax would be levied should the DJEC decide to issue a waiver.

For now, Jews were permitted to still practice medicine—they made good doctors, after all—though none would be permitted to continue to own or co-own a medical practice or facility. All Jewish doctors must now be employed by an authorized hospital system or federally licensed and supervised medical practice, with newly implemented caps on their salaries.

The DJEC published a list of permissible occupations for American Jews: store clerk, laborer, warehouse worker, delivery driver, restaurant worker, call center agent, lower-level office employee, housekeeping, and custodial services... A relatively small number of Jews were permitted to retain or be demoted into lower-end and mid-level technology support positions, such as software tester, as long as they were closely supervised; though an overall quota would be imposed and enforced.

Even though Spencer Howell's Justice Department had crafted the specifics of the American Professions and Employment Restrictions Act—APERA—that would be ushered through Congress by Lowell Irvine and Tal Chadwick, Ephraim Hollinger's personal imprint was heavy on the legislation.

Hollinger was haunted by the memory of his parents in the aftermath of their eviction from their farm, especially after Josiah Hollinger was unable to maintain one of the dwindling number of 1980s-era steelworker jobs. The Wall Street Jews sat high above Manhattan, and their West Coast brethren rested easy in their gilded offices on Wilshire Boulevard and in Beverly Hills. They had the good life, the easy life, the life of riches, while the victims of their thievery were forced into the daily hard labor that was ultimately in the service of this newest generation of immoral robber barons themselves.

No more.

* * *

Synagogues were ordered closed, effectively immediately, because—as Toni Fowler would indignantly shriek on tonight's AVGN program—it was in many of these supposed houses of worship around the country where the COVID-37 plot was hatched. The interests of national security called for shuttering locations where Jews would habitually gather, to make it much more difficult for them to simply shift to some scheming, nefarious Plan B.

* * *

Effective May 1st—exactly one month after APERA went into effect—every American Jew regardless of age was required to have registered with the DJEC, with mandatory approved employment required of every Jew seventy years old or younger. One month later, on June 1st, the new laws would be fully enforced. Those who were currently in a permissible profession would be allowed to remain exactly where they were. Anyone who wasn't, however, would be required to have already resigned from one's former job and found a new one from the approved list.

But what if, say, a Jewish lawyer or stockbroker or college professor was unable to transition to "suitable" employment during the month of April? That's where the corollary legislation shepherded through Congress and signed by Hollinger came into play.

The Jewish Resettlement Act of 2037.

Long ago, in 1862, Ulysses Grant's General Order Number 11 had been a simple "get out!" edict. For all Grant cared, any of the expelled Jews could meander over to some other southern town outside of his jurisdiction, or migrate to cities or small towns up north. As long as they weren't trading cotton and other goods on behalf of the Confederacy in a manner that could hinder his Vicksburg Campaign, or providing shelter and comfort to those who were, Grant didn't particularly care what they did.

On this matter, however, Ephraim Hollinger was much closer to Adolf Hitler than he was to Ulysses S. Grant.

The essence of the Jewish Resettlement Act could be summed up in a single lengthy sentence:

> Any Jewish person residing in the United States who is not legally registered as being gainfully and fully employed within a permissible profession under the terms of APERA shall be remanded into the custody of the United States Government and relocated to an encampment site, where that person will be assigned relevant workforce responsibilities for the benefit of the nation and its loyal, patriotic citizens.

* * *

And what if an American Jew had no intention of allowing Ephraim Hollinger to revoke every basic human right, not only for that individual but also for one's family? Why not just leave the country? Why not escape?

An hour before this morning's vengeful pronouncements, Hollinger signed a Presidential Executive Order closing the borders to American Jews, and prohibiting any Jewish person from boarding an outbound international flight. Kirk Barber's data geeks had already compiled a master list of every American who was at least one-quarter Jewish. Years of DNA data seized by the Federal Police Force from the many "trace your ancestry" sites, coupled with billions of public and private records, provided a name-by-name photo roster of every one of America's seven and a half million Jews. This list had already been disseminated electronically to every staffed border crossing to Canada and Mexico, and every airport that hosted international flights, in case any of those remote connections back to the U.S. government's central database was disrupted. FPF officers had been dispatched around the country to the airports—as well as bus and train stations—to take into custody any Jewish man, woman, or child who attempted to flee the destiny Ephraim Hollinger had in store for them.

* * *

Josiah Hollinger's long-ago and oft-spoken words after losing his farm, his steelworker job, and then spending the rest of his life working menial jobs alongside his wife:

Never forget what they did to us.

Swear that one day you'll avenge what they did to us.

Ephraim Hollinger had, at long last, fully honored the solemn pledge he had made to his father.

Chapter 49

Several weeks before Hollinger's ominous proclamation, the morning after returning to Pittsburgh from Quebec and the mid-New York State safe house, Daniel had sought out his sister, as he had promised his mother. Noah and Rachel were already off to school that chilly, overcast Monday morning, and Marc—his mid-March deadline looming—was out West for the fifth straight week.

"I don't believe you! You're lying!"

Claire Weber's indignant denial wasn't unexpected, yet her brother was powerless against the instant wash of anger that enveloped him.

"It's true," Michele interjected. "We don't know exactly what's coming, or when, but it's going to be horrifying."

Michele added:

"And it's going to be soon—*very* soon."

Claire furiously shook her head and launched a flurry of frenzied questions.

"You're saying that just because we're Jewish, they're going to...send us to concentration camps or something? And you actually took Mom and Dad across the border to Canada because you believe that? Yesterday? They're gone?"

"Look," Daniel responded through clenched teeth. "You heard that psycho Toni Fowler a couple of weeks ago, with that bullshit story about a Jewish COVID-37 plot. They—"

"Hollinger has been saying that stuff ever since he got elected," Claire interrupted. "Even before then, when he was first running. It's just like Marc says—"

"Damn it!" Daniel finally exploded. "This is what he's been leading up to! *This!* Open your eyes!"

Claire looked over at Michele, and then back at her brother. Both Daniel and Michele could read her thoughts as clearly as if they were materializing in thought bubbles above her head.

You're the one who got him all riled up; he never used to be like this until he met you.

"So you're saying," Claire's eyes narrowed, her voice clearly conveying her skepticism, "that Marc is out West right now, building some kind of concentration camp? And that they're going to send all of us there?"

"I can't tell you how I know," Michele kept her voice even keeled, "but there's room for twenty-five, maybe thirty thousand *prisoners* in that facility."

Michele made certain to emphasize the word "prisoners." Frank Sanchez had led a reconnaissance mission to the site outside of Wikieup late last year, once word filtered to the team that a facility of some sort was being built in the Arizona desert.

"Looks like fuckin' *Stalag Luft III* out there," Sanchez had reported back, referring to the massive World War II-era German prisoner-of-war camp that was later immortalized in the movie *The Great Escape*.

"It's probably for undocumented immigrants," Claire countered, her mind furiously racing for an explanation, *any* explanation, to counter what her brother and Michele Burgess were saying. "Marc never specifically said anything, but a couple of times he hinted that DHS and the FPF are going to start big-time crackdowns on the illegals, just like back in 2018 or whenever it was. And that's what the camp, or prison, or whatever you want to call it is going to be used for."

"Maybe," Michele was now struggling to maintain her cool. They didn't have time for this! "But you *know* that Hollinger is gunning for us—for Jews—and frankly, I don't feel like taking the chance. Neither did your parents or your grandparents, or my parents, or your Uncle Mike and Aunt Sharon, or..."

Michele rattled off the names from Daniel's and Claire's family, as many as she could recall, who had refugeed to either Canada or Mexico a day earlier.

"Mom made me promise to get you and the kids out," Daniel urged. "She made me promise!"

Claire's gaze involuntarily elevated above her brother's head, above Michele's, and then almost imperceptibly around the posh living room where they stood. Both Daniel and Michele could once again clearly read Claire's thoughts:

Do we need to give up all of this?

In that moment, Daniel knew that his sister would not leave, at least right now.

* * *

"I need to call Marc," Claire's mind continued to race furiously.

"No." Michele's single-syllable response was an issued order, just as if she were still an Army officer commanding one of her soldiers who was contemplating some sort of insubordinate action.

"You can't say a word to him," Daniel chimed in. "We need to get you and the kids out first, and then we'll come back for him."

"I need to call Marc," Claire repeated.

"You can't!" This time, Daniel's voice betrayed his anger.

"We're not saying," Michele chimed in, "that he knows what's going on. I'm figuring that he thinks just what you said: that he's building a new place for undocumented immigrants. He's almost certainly in the dark..."

"Why would they give him the contract to build a camp for Jews?" Claire challenged, echoing her husband's own musings back in January, after Dalia Travers confronted him with the rumor she had heard. "They know he's Jewish!"

"I'm not sure," Michele admitted.

They would all find out the answer eventually. To Spencer Howell, this was a perverse mirror image of his grandfather's tales of Camp Siegfried, where the campers and staff themselves constructed the camp's infrastructure to avoid using Jewish union labor. If either Max or Rudolph Howell were alive today, the Attorney General's grandfather and great-grandfather would be tickled at the malicious notion of not only Marc Weber, but also other wealthy Jewish construction magnates, unknowingly building the camps that would soon hold their fellow Jews, thinking all the while that they were going to grow richer than they already were.

"I need to think about all of this," Claire finally said. "You can't just spring this on me and expect me to yank Noah and Rachel out of school within the hour and flee the country right away."

She has a point, Daniel admitted to himself. At least with his parents, they had several weeks to prepare for their exodus.

Daniel knew the question that was coming next.

"If you truly think this is real, why didn't you come to me back when you approached Mom and Dad?"

Daniel Jacobson's eyes conveyed—betrayed—the truth.

"I need to think about it," Claire repeated, after her mind raced frantically for a full minute, contemplating the just-unveiled notion that her brother and his girlfriend categorized Marc Weber as the enemy…or at least complicit with those whom they saw as the enemy.

"You don't have much time," Michele laid her cards on the table. "Pretty soon the FPF is going to realize that your parents and my parents, and everyone else, are gone. And they'll know that you're still here…"

Michele's eyes grew cold.

"…and it will be too late then for us to help you and your kids."

* * *

"She's going to call Marc anyway," a dejected Daniel Jacobson sighed to Michele Burgess as they drove back from his sister's suburban home toward the city.

"I know," Michele agreed.

"How much time can we give her?" Daniel hesitatingly asked.

"Two hours at most."

"She's not going to come," a dejected Daniel murmured, his voice cracking.

"Let's give her the two hours," Michele sympathetically responded, knowing with all the certainty in the world that Daniel was right.

* * *

Michele Burgess wasn't taking any chances. The two hours of wait time were spent in their vehicle, circling along a predetermined route that offered both a quick path back to Claire's house should she call them, as well as egress north from the Pittsburgh metro area should she not. Even before the Purim exodus, they had said their permanent goodbyes to their homes; to their old lives. This spring semester of 2037, neither of them taught any Monday classes. By the time Tuesday, March 3rd, arrived, when neither Daniel nor Michele showed up for the day's scheduled classes, they would be ensconced in the mid-New York safe house, helping some of the other special operators ferry their own families out of the country.

Though nobody else among them was Jewish, at some point they would all be unmasked as insurgents, which would put their own family members at risk. Several of the veterans were, essentially, sans family: unmarried, from broken families with very few close relatives during their younger years. In fact, several of them had gravitated toward the military and then the special operations community for that very reason: minimal familial attachments, and thus an appetite for dangerous missions because there really wasn't anything for them back home...or even a "back home." Others, though, had close family that needed to be ferried out of the country for their own safety, just as if they were Jewish.

As Michele was packing the few keepsakes that she wanted to take along, she was struck by the irony of what was happening. A large part of the reason she had retired early from the Army rather than stay for twenty or even thirty years was the yearning for some sense of permanence in her life. Every two to four years, the Army transferred her to a new assignment and a new place to live...or at least be based out of, given that she found herself deployed a good portion of her time once she qualified for Special Forces and the Rangers. She had every expectation that teaching in Pittsburgh would provide that sense of stability and permanence previously absent from her adult life, especially after becoming involved with Daniel Jacobson.

As it turned out, her time in Pittsburgh from the summer of 2033 until early March 2037—not quite four years—was only another medium-duration assignment. Now, she was about to deploy once again, with combat operations clearly in her future.

For Daniel, his departure was surprisingly less painful than he imagined it would be. As of Purim Eve, there was nothing left behind in Pittsburgh for him. His parents were now ensconced in Montreal. Hopefully Claire would come to her senses and give Michele and Daniel the green light to ferry her and the kids out as well, before all hell broke loose.

Pop-pop was gone, Daniel's still-vivid dream notwithstanding. Daniel's teaching career at Western Pennsylvania University would likely soon be over anyway, even without going AWOL (as was soon proved true by Hollinger's pronouncement and the resultant Congressional action). If what Michele and the other special operators told him was truly coming—and Daniel had no reason to doubt them at this point—life in Pittsburgh would never be the same.

Ever the historian, Daniel clearly saw the ominous parallels with 1930s and 1940s Europe. Those who hesitated and tried to convince themselves that "it can't happen here" paid the ultimate price, even if they somehow survived the concentration and death camps. Others who clearly saw the ominous handwriting on the wall, and escaped early enough from Europe, joined an Allied Forces Army or Navy or Air Force and fought back.

Just as Daniel was doing.

* * *

Two and a half weeks later, watching Ephraim Hollinger's edicts on AVGN, Claire Weber instantly knew that she had made a terrible mistake. She prayed that it wouldn't be a fatal mistake.

She immediately called Marc. No answer.

She tried again two minutes later; again, no answer.

Three minutes passed before another attempt. This time, her call went straight to voicemail.

As if he had shushed her.

Why isn't he here with us? Protecting us? Damn him! He's probably in some meeting! Does he even know what Hollinger just announced? I need to know if we'll all be safe!

Marc was again spending the weekend out West; he hadn't been home for two months now. Construction on his facility had actually been completed on the accelerated schedule, five days earlier. The usual lengthy list of minor building defects all around the compound needed to be addressed; but for all intents and purposes, Marc Weber had met the hastened completion date that Braxton Knox had given him, and now he expected to be rewarded for his efforts.

Marc had, in fact, glanced at his phone the first two times that Claire called him. He wasn't yet on-site that Friday morning, given the time zone difference between the East Coast and Arizona. He was in Dalia's trailer, slouching naked on the threadbare sofa as her head bobbed above his lap. Not wanting to have his concentration broken, he flicked his phone to

"No Interruption from Anyone" mode by the time of his wife's third panicky call.

He wouldn't find out until later that morning what the President of the United States had pronounced.

Even then, after the shock dissipated and he digested the horrific news, Marc Weber was still convinced that he—his family also—would be immune from the soon-to-be law of the land. He immediately called Claire, brushing aside her panicky "Why didn't you answer?" demanding question.

"Daniel was right!" Claire angrily threw the accusation at him. Back at the beginning of the month, less than a minute after Daniel and Michele departed, she had indeed ignored Daniel's and Michele's warning and called her husband. Marc had immediately scoffed at the idea; though at the time, Dalia's words echoed once again.

I heard that they're going to start rounding up Jews and sending them there…

"Let's not panic," Marc quickly interjected. The last thing he needed right now was an angry I-told-you-so from his wife. "They said that Jewish business owners can apply for exemptions."

Mentioning the possibility of receiving an exemption brought to Marc's mind what else he had just heard—the licensing tax that would be imposed as a cost of being allowed to continue doing business. Just how much of a hit would that be?

I wonder if there is a way around that, maybe by appealing directly to the administration…

"We should be fine," Marc continued, his mind still multi-tasking, fretting about the impact of this licensing tax…and that was *if* he was able to secure a variance! "All of this is highest priority work, this place we just finished, and then the next one we're about to—"

Marc abruptly halted his attempt to assuage his wife's terrified panic. His mental math about the licensing tax immediately ceased as well. The abrupt realization was a nuclear blast shock wave. Jack Keller, the meth-dealing, Jew-hating, hick bartender was right after all.

Marc Weber had just completed the construction of Ephraim Hollinger's first concentration camp, a horrifying facility intended to imprison thirty thousand of America's Jews.

Chapter 50

Daniel Jacobson and John Garcia didn't exactly get off to a warm start.

The only time that Daniel accompanied Michele to the safe house before the Purim exodus was back in early December, so she could fully bring Daniel on board with what would soon be transpiring. The special ops veterans working out of that safe house rendezvoused there to dot the proverbial "i's" of the operation, and to meet Daniel.

Michele was out in the barn-sized garage with Fletcher Carlson—the retired Navy SEAL—and most of the others, securing their latest stash of "requisitioned" material onto the interior ceiling of the barn to defeat the Federal Police Force's heat- and image-sensing surveillance technology. Back in the house, Daniel sensed the hulking John Garcia's presence even before turning around.

"Get one thing absolutely clear," the ex-Green Beret snarled, his left index finger delivering a single dull poke against Daniel's chest. "This isn't some *Red Dawn* wet dream; so if you have any fantasies of shooting up a squad of FPFers and yelling 'Wolverines!' or any shit like that, get that out of your fucking head right now!"

Garcia dropped his index finger, but continued his menacing admonition.

"We're doing interdiction and rescue, not laying down fire on troop convoys or blowing up infrastructure. That makes you Harriet Tubman, not Patrick Swayze. Your weapon is *only* for self-defense, and *only* if your life is in imminent danger. If you ever go rogue or disobey an order from *Major* Burgess, or me, or any one of us, I'll personally put a bullet right into your fucking brain. You got that?"

"You do know that Harriet Tubman was the first woman to lead an armed assault during the Civil War? The Combahee River Raid? Freed seven hundred and fifty slaves just on that one mission?" The history professor's retort was delivered in an even voice with clear undertones of "Cut the bullshit; we're on the same side here."

John Garcia couldn't help the smile that came to his face as he pivoted and headed to the farmhouse's kitchen, still grinning as he wordlessly walked away.

Truthfully, once Michele clued Daniel into the fact that one of the vets working out of the central New York State safe house was someone with whom she had had a two-year relationship, he wasn't particularly thrilled about the idea. Not that he had any say in the matter; but deep in the recesses of Daniel's mind, knowing Michele's own military background, Daniel wondered if this might be a disastrous inflection point for his relationship with her.

Certainly, matters of the heart weren't even on the radar when it came to the ominous events that were unfolding. Still, Daniel wondered if Michele—now back among not only military veterans, but elite ex-Green Berets and Navy SEALs and others—would still see Daniel in the same light. And finding out that one of them had been in a relationship with her for two years? Not great…

Now, though, with his and Michele's families safely out of the country and two more shuttle missions under his belt, Daniel felt more at ease: more assertive. John Garcia didn't seem to show any interest in shoving Daniel aside and worming his way back into Michele's bed. Daniel, Garcia, Michele, and the others planned together and trained together, apparently without any friction.

And they all waited.

* * *

Even though Daniel knew more or less what was coming, the shock of hearing the President of the

United States declare that American Jews were, henceforth, *personae non gratae* shocked him to his core. The farmhouse had no cable or satellite connection, nor any sort of smart TV, that would collect and then transmit data that could eventually betray them. An old-fashioned, still-functioning, computer-free television from the 1990s had been located, and the tallest rooftop antenna had been mounted shortly after the safe house had been set up. The farmhouse rested at the outmost fringes of the broadcast radius of the two remaining Syracuse-area traditional television stations. One of them had been usurped last autumn by AVGN for much of its broadcast schedule, which allowed Michele, Daniel, and the others to stay up to date.

Not that he had been second-guessing the no-turning-back exodus of his parents and the rest of his family, but Daniel's most immediate reaction—once recovering from the shock of Hollinger's stunningly evil pronouncement—was a flood of pained relief that they had acted when they did.

The horror was genuine!

For weeks now, even after ferrying his parents across the border to Canada, this all still seemed to Daniel as if it was a terrible waking nightmare; that Hollinger and Howell and the others might back away from the precipice at the last minute, and some semblance of normalcy would return to the land. The nation had survived its brush with tyranny almost twenty years ago; surely this all would end the same way, before the nation actually crossed the Rubicon.

Oh my God! Claire!

Daniel had sadly come to terms that Claire wouldn't make it out of the country before the hammer fell. He prayed that she was right—that Marc Weber's connections might actually provide them with a blanket of immunity, their Jewish heritage notwithstanding. Hearing Hollinger spew his evil this morning sent a fresh wave of nausea through Daniel's core at the involuntary images of his sister and her children—oh God, Noah and Rachel!—cruelly transported to some concentration camp, the same fate that befell Isaac Gretz a century earlier.

A sympathetic hand landed on Daniel's right shoulder. He turned to look, and saw John Garcia perched above him.

"Get ready for war," the ex-Green Beret said, his face a unique blending of empathy and determined hatred.

Chapter 51

Paul Nelson, the Vice President of the United States, was convinced that the President of the United States was a psychopath. And not just Ephraim Hollinger—that assessment applied to Tom Buckner, and Braxton Knox, and White House Counsel Travis Whitman…and definitely General Frank Douglas.

And as for the Attorney General…Spencer Howell was the worst of all, with his perverse fascination with All Things Nazi.

How in the holy hell did I wind up in the middle of this damnation?

* * *

Paul Nelson was first elected to his central Florida House seat in 2026, as traditionalist, center-right Republicans doubled down their efforts to wrestle their party back from the lunatic fringe. Nelson was forty-nine years old at the time. Charismatic, tall and fit, handsome, and wealthy from riding the residential real estate wave shortly after the end of the Great Recession, Nelson fully fit the profile of what the traditionalists needed to continue clawing back their party. His politics were definitely "right of center-right" but nothing like what had dominated the party in the latter part of the previous decade into the early and mid-2020s; so he meshed well with the others whom the party recruited, as well as the survivors who were leading the rebuilding.

His first congressional campaign was largely funded by Ephraim Hollinger. At the time, no alarm bells rang for Paul Nelson.

Nelson easily won re-election in 2028, doing his best to raise his profile through cable television appearances. When Bob Platte formed the American Values and Greatness Network, Paul Nelson became the token traditionalist Republican for talking-head guest slots. Even though Nelson wasn't among the conspiracy theorists and the open racists in the party, he regularly spouted the obligatory party warnings about the dangers of unchecked immigration, the evils of government regulation, the perils of leftist violence, and the rest of the usual bogeymen. Through Paul Nelson, Bob Platte was able to accentuate AVGN's messaging:

See, it's not just the fire-breathers who are warning us—warning YOU—about illegal aliens, government overreach, and the attacks on our traditional American values and heritage!

In the summer of 2030, when the Restore American Values and Greatness Party tore away from the Republicans, Paul Nelson stuck a moistened finger in the air, determined which way the political winds were blowing, and went along with the RAVGs. Unlike much of that first generation of the RAVG Party, Nelson wasn't a fiery, combative, conspiracy theory-spreading demagogue. As with future Cabinet secretaries Stephen Channing and Jim Wiley—two other center-right Republicans who also headed over to the RAVGs—Nelson simply gravitated to the political party that had a future and left behind the one that now teetered unsteadily astride the grave.

Two years later, just before Ephraim Hollinger's inevitable nomination as the RAVG Party's presidential candidate became official, Hollinger reached out to Paul Nelson to demand that the congressman join the party's ticket. Hollinger knew that Florida would be key to capturing the White House in a tight three-way race. Nelson's stature in Florida extended far beyond his own congressional district that contained the enormous planned community where Edmund and Eleanor Garfield, and so many other loyal patriots, had chosen to retire. Nelson had solid relationships with state-level, county, and local influencers up and down both coasts, and across the panhandle. He could call in favors; Paul Nelson could bring out the voters.

Though Hollinger's rhetoric was only beginning to openly reflect his hatred of Jews, Paul Nelson clearly saw the presidential candidate for exactly what he was. Nelson personally didn't have anything against Jews—not really. He didn't particularly like them; but then again, he didn't dislike them, either. He definitely didn't trust them when he had to deal with them during his business career. But hell, there were only what—seven and a half million of them in the entire United States? They didn't really impact his life much, so live and let live.

Personally, Paul Nelson was much more concerned about the ever-growing number of Hispanics and Latinos spreading throughout the country. If this continued much longer, America would no longer be America. That's what his constituents in his district believed, and he had been their fierce advocate in the Washington, DC swamp for the past eight years.

Nelson knew, though, that the American Values and Greatness movement had a numbers problem. The 2030 census reported that the Hispanic and Latino population in the United States had crossed sixty-five million—eighteen and a half percent! You can't just yank a substantial portion of sixty-five million people out of the workforce and eject them from the country without collapsing the entire economy. None of the RAVG Party elected officials particularly cared for the brown people from Mexico and other Latin and South American countries; but for now, they were stuck with them.

And then there were the Blacks. Another fifty million of them were scattered around the United States, with heavy concentrations in still-Democratic stronghold cities like Chicago, Detroit, and Philadelphia. Could Hollinger's administration do something concrete about fifty million people without a tragic ripple effect that irreversibly caused collateral damage to White America? Highly doubtful…

The Jews though…

The consensus among Hollinger's Cabinet and brain trust was that they could send one hell of a message to the brown and Black people by how they handled the Jews. That crystal clear message:

Be VERY careful and don't cause any problems, or you're next!

* * *

Nelson agreed to Hollinger's demand to join the RAVG Party ticket (*Do I actually have a choice? I'm not sure…*) for two reasons. First, Ephraim Hollinger's rhetoric about the overall infestation of America matched the concerns of Paul Nelson and his constituents. Hollinger might have "Jews on the brain," but Nelson reasoned that once in the White House, Hollinger would also begin to focus on the southern border and related immigration problems.

Then there was Paul Nelson's own dogged quest for power and prestige. If Hollinger's third-party candidacy fell short in '32, then as the vice-presidential nominee, Nelson would be off to a running start for 2036. But if Hollinger was successful, and if he won a second term in 2036, Nelson would definitely be in the driver's seat for 2040. And even if Hollinger won the first one but somehow lost in '36, Nelson would still be at the front of the 2040 line.

Paul Nelson's political calculus had one fatal flaw. As with every other person in the country—except Bart Lawrence and Spencer Howell, and perhaps also Bob Platte—Nelson had never entertained the possibility that all along, Ephraim Hollinger intended to set himself up as President for Life. Unless something radically changed in the next year or two, there would be no presidential election in 2040, just as there hadn't been one in 2036. Paul Nelson's presidential aspirations had evaporated in the dark mist of Hollinger's coup.

Now what?

* * *

Paul Nelson wasn't exactly part of Hollinger's inner circle during what would normally have been his first term. As with so many American vice presidents of the past, Nelson's role mostly fell into the "not worth a bucket of warm piss" category, as was so acidly declared by Franklin Roosevelt's first VP, John Nance Garner. Mostly, Hollinger occasionally trotted Nelson out for demonstrations of solidarity, with references to "our magnificent Vice President" or "Paul Nelson, a great patriot."

Still, Nelson attended enough meetings in the Oval Office and the White House Cabinet Room to watch Hollinger, Howell, Braxton Knox, and Tom Buckner methodically lay the groundwork for Hollinger's seizure of power and then the commencement of reincarnating much of 1930s Nazi Germany.

Nelson hadn't been party to the planning for the false-flag assassination of Keenan Lucas, but he instantly knew what had gone down. He wasn't shocked, or even surprised—by now, he knew that Hollinger and his inner circle were capable of anything. He was fully aware that Bart Lawrence had blackmailed both Stephen Channing and Jim Wiley into concocting those summer and fall blowout economic reports leading up to the 2034 midterms. (Nelson knew about their past financial chicanery that gave Bart Lawrence his leverage, though he was unaware that Lawrence had gained this knowledge by sleeping with both of their wives, or that compromising pictures of recent liaisons had been part of the blackmail packages.)

Why was he so squeamish about all of this? If Spencer Howell had been targeting Hispanics and Latinos and planned to bring back the Golden Oldies—mass immigration sweeps through targeted neighborhoods, family separations and cages for kids, denying all southern border asylum seekers—Paul Nelson wouldn't have a pit in his stomach every time the coming displacement of American Jews was plotted.

No doubt it was the throwback parallels to Hitler's genocidal rampage against European Jews. Nelson had read plenty of history when he was younger, and he was well aware of the horrors of the Holocaust. Even though Howell and Hollinger had no intentions of gassing and then burning their victims (*they didn't, right?* Paul Nelson often wondered to himself, invariably accompanied by a terrifying shudder), just the idea of rounding up Jews—American citizens!—and shipping them off to desolate concentration camps in the Desert Southwest, where they would be consigned to a life of slave labor, nauseated him.

Paul Nelson tried his damnedest not to think about what was about to transpire, right here in the United States of America, at the hands of an administration for which *he* was the vice president. History was written by the winners, which meant that perhaps history wouldn't judge Paul Nelson as harshly as he knew he deserved to be portrayed. In some ways, Paul Nelson saw himself as a victim…nowhere near as much of a victim as any one of America's Jews who would soon suffer in one way or another, but a victim nonetheless.

Nelson was trapped. He couldn't "resign in protest" from the vice presidency. America had become Ephraim Hollinger's America. In Ephraim Hollinger's America, one was either fully on board, or one was the enemy. There was no gray area, no middle ground, no in-between. Paul Nelson was fully aware that even though the camps out West would be largely populated by Jews, they wouldn't be the only prisoners. Even now, more than ten thousand American citizens of all races, religions, and ethnicities were being held in jails and prisons around the country. Every one of them was someone whom the FPF had deemed an imminent or likely threat to the Hollinger regime, as indicated by their danger-zone Citizen Loyalty Scores. Jack Bancroft—the now-former senator, the Democratic Party presidential candidate only six months earlier, the retired Air Force three-star general—was one of them. Bancroft would soon wind up in one of those camps.

Thinking again about the camps (*call them CONCENTRATION camps,* Nelson's conscience demanded, *that's what they are—say the word!*) took Paul Nelson's thoughts full circle, back to Spencer Howell.

Nelson had sat in the Oval Office or the Cabinet Room on many occasions during the past four-plus years, a conjured grin plastered to his face to not only mask his disgust but also avoid bringing about his own demise, as Howell regaled those gathered with his nostalgic tales of growing up in a family with roots back to the American Nazi movement of the 1930s. Spencer Howell had been the one, of course, who assigned the nickname for Federal Detention Facility One, the recently opened concentration camp outside of Wikieup, Arizona.

"Dachau," Howell had sneered, his eyes radiating evil. "That was the first camp that Hitler opened, back in 1933. So I don't give a shit if anybody here doesn't like it; that's what we're going to call our new one…unofficially, of course."

Paul Nelson laughed along with Tom Buckner and Braxton Knox and everyone else, making certain that Spencer Howell took notice. Inside his sickly pulsating brain, Nelson's immediate reaction was much like that of Toni Fowler's as she prepared for her on-air AVGN segment in the immediate aftermath of Hollinger's pronouncement that the 2036 presidential election would be "postponed."

Just keep your head down, and for God's sakes, you can't let them know what you're thinking! There's no way out for you from all of this. Your soul is already forfeit, so you might as well be at peace with wherever this jarring journey takes you until then.

Chapter 52

Life in Ephraim Hollinger's America during the summer of 2037.

* * *

Saturday night, June 27th.

Emily Costa smiled at Matt Ashfield as she returned to the two-top bar table from the restroom. A few minutes earlier, on her way to the women's room, she had messaged her friend Mia:

OMG he's gorgeous! And HOT!

This definitely was turning out to be a FANTASTIC night for the recent Rutgers graduate! She had connected with the twenty-five-year-old investment analyst through AVGNInstaMeet. Matt Ashfield saw her picture, swiped right, and then walked the three blocks to the downtown New Brunswick bar where Emily was after she agreed to meet him.

"So I'm up in Parsippany," Matt decided the time was right. He had checked the time while Emily was gone. Only eleven o'clock. If this didn't work out, right now, he could get right back on AVGNInstaMeet; the night was still young. "That's about forty miles from here..."

He left the proposition hungrily hanging in the area, hoping to trigger her counteroffer.

"My apartment is only about a mile that way," Emily indeed offered, nodding to her right. "We can go there..."

"Okay!" Matt was unable to suppress his lascivious grin, but he didn't need to worry. The look on Emily Costa's face matched his.

"Let me pay this," Matt Ashfield signaled for their waiter, and then turned back to tonight's hookup. Their eyes met, and they shared the same thought.

All is right with the world—it's gonna be a great night!

* * *

At the same instant that Matt Ashfield was paying his and Emily's bar bill, three miles away, Jared Friedman was pulling a mop bucket from a storage closet. The supermarket had just closed its doors, though about a dozen shoppers still dawdled in the aisles. Jared knew that it would be a good half hour, maybe even forty-five minutes, until every customer had finished shopping, paid for the groceries, and then cleared out of the store. In the meantime, Jared could get started with the mopping in the back storerooms, away from the customer traffic. That would take him a good hour, and then he could make his way through the cavernous supermarket during the next two hours.

Jared's overnight janitorial shift would last until seven the next morning, and he would be balls-to-the-wall busy every single moment. Mopping would be followed by the windows, which would be followed by sanitizing each of the cashier stations. The restrooms came next, and then another pass up and down the aisles, cleaning off any food stains or other blemishes on shelves and the shelf-fronts. By then, seven o'clock will have arrived, and it would be time to fight the northbound morning rush-hour traffic up to Teaneck for the next hour and a half, maybe even two hours if traffic was particularly bad.

Less than three months ago, Jared Friedman's work life was literally night and day from what it was now. Instead of leaving work at seven in the morning, that's the time his alarm would have woken him. An hour later, he would be on the New Jersey turnpike, headed south toward downtown Newark, where he would put in his eight hours as that city's Director of Procurement.

For the first seven years of his professional life, after graduating from Montclair State, Jared dabbled in a couple of techie jobs over in the city. Truthfully, none of them had been a good fit for him, mostly because Jared never really took to technology past the basics. He had made it through college with an information systems degree, but the accounting and finance side at those past employers seemed much more of a fit for his natural abilities.

Besides, the commuting in and out of Manhattan wasn't all that easy; and with two small children now, Jared had the self-awareness to realize that he wasn't cut out for the fast track.

He wound up taking his New Jersey Civil Service exam, and when an intermediate financial analyst position with the City of Newark opened up, he didn't look back. For the next twenty-three years, he ratcheted his way up the ladder with the city, eventually landing the Director of Procurement position five years ago. Jared figured that this was about as far as he would ever advance, which was fine with him. He was now fifty-two, and after another seven years, he would be eligible for his full New Jersey Civil Service pension and could retire, just shy of sixty.

Hollinger's American Professions and Employment Restrictions Act was a cataclysmic nuclear explosion to that plan: no more Jews in government jobs at any level, effective April 1st, 2037.

"What are we going to do?" Jared's wife Shoshanah panicked. "Oh my God, they're going to send us to the concentration camp! The children too!"

"I swear," Jared promised, doing his best to appear calm to his wife even though he was terrified, "I'll find a new job. You too. We have until June 1st, and they published that list of jobs we're allowed to hold…"

Jared Friedman spent the next six weeks frantically searching for a new position. Finally, in early May, the manager of a New Brunswick supermarket, Bobby Lee

Richards, took pity on Jared and offered him a job as the nighttime janitor. The position had just opened up when its previous holder, a Rutgers senior, graduated and headed off to his new career. Truthfully, Jared was both overqualified and underqualified for the position: overqualified because of his education and professional background, but also underqualified because he had exactly zero previous experience with anything related to janitorial services. Bobby Lee Richards knew, though, that if he didn't give Jared Friedman this position, odds were that this frazzled-looking man in his early fifties would be shipped off to a concentration camp along with his entire family. Bobby Lee was originally from Mississippi, and had wound up in Jersey during his enlisted days in the Army a while back. He liked the Garden State enough to settle there after his enlistment was up. Bobby Lee knew how so many of those back home thought about Jews—and Blacks, and also pretty much anybody with brown skin—but he personally had nothing against those whom most of his friends and relatives thought to be pathetically inferior to good white Christian Americans.

Maybe this is my good deed for the year, Bobby thought to himself. *Maybe even for the decade. I ain't gonna stick my neck out and say nothin' about what the government is doing to the Jews. Hell, they'd probably send me off to some concentration camp as fast as they're sending those people. But I'll give this Jewish fellow a job, and hopefully he'll be safe for a while.*

* * *

Tom DeFurio's name might as well have been Tom DeFurious.

How the fuck am I gonna get anything done now? Those stupid federal fucks don't give a shit about what we gotta do here. I got the Mayor and my boss breathing down my neck 'cause we got fuckin' seven major construction projects goin', and now every single one of them is way behind on purchasing. Son of a bitch, all of a sudden I'm down twenty-three people! Twenty-three! How the fuck am I gonna fill all of those jobs?

Tom DeFurio was the Deputy Chief Financial Officer for the City of Newark. Despite the lofty title, DeFurio had the appearance, the demeanor—and the vocabulary—of a Jersey mob *capo*. A few of the neighborhood guys he grew up and ran around with did turn into wiseguys; and when Tom would meet up with some of them to watch a game in some local bar, he easily gravitated toward their vernacular, if not their actions or way of life.

Until recently, Jared Friedman had reported directly to Tom DeFurio. Tom liked Jared—the guy met his deadlines and knew his shit. That's all Tom DeFurio cared about. The city's Chief Financial Officer had tapped DeFurio to be *the* money guy for everything going on with this latest rendition of Newark's revitalization. That meant a bunch of construction work at any given time, which in turn meant a crapload of city money being spent all over Jersey, New York State, and even up into Connecticut and over into Pennsylvania. Jared Friedman was the quiet type, but he could diplomatically go toe-to-toe with the union guys and the contractors—even the "connected" ones—when necessary.

It wasn't just Jared Friedman, either. In Jared's division, six other Jews—four guys, two women—were forced to hit the bricks along with Jared. The other divisions that reported to Tom DeFurio were also hit hard, though Jared Friedman had been Tom's only direct report who lost his job. But overall, Tom DeFurio suddenly had twenty-three vacancies on his hands and a growing backlog of untouched work…and resultant problems.

Hollinger and the rest of those clowns are a bunch of fuckin' psychos, was Tom DeFurio's assessment of the current state of the nation, echoing that of Vice President Paul Nelson…albeit with a touch more color. DeFurio was personally outraged at this whole "get the Jews!" bullshit that they had started.

And these concentration camps that we hear are being built out in Arizona and Nevada? What the fuck?

All four of Tom DeFurio's great-grandfathers had fought the Nazis during World War II: two as B-17 tail gunners in the Army Air Forces, and two in the infantry. Tom DeFurio and Daniel Jacobson would never meet and make the connection, but Giuseppe DeFurio and Nathan Jacobson—their respective great-grandfathers—had both served, side by side, in the U.S. Army's 45th Infantry Division, in the same platoon, in fact, landing in Southern France in August of '44 and fighting their way into Germany. Giuseppe DeFurio had been with the 45th when they liberated Dachau, and the horrifying stories of what he had witnessed were passed down to subsequent generations of DeFurios of what he witnessed.

Growing up in Jersey, most Italians like Tom DeFurio mingled with Jewish guys. There were the occasional tensions, but for the most part, they all got along. They played ball together and hung out together. For those like Tom who went on to college, they took classes together. They went to weddings and communions and funerals together.

I just don't fucking get it.

But whether Tom DeFurio "got it" or not, he now had to find a way to deal with the unfortunate consequences of Ephraim Hollinger's and Spencer Howell's vendetta.

* * *

Wednesday afternoon, July 1st.

Rick Brandon's head jerked as his office door crashed open. He had just finished modifying this weekend's holiday weekend reservations at the B&B out in Nantucket, adding Monday night to make it a four-day stay. Normally, adjustments at this late date for a place on Nantucket would be out of the question. However, Rick Brandon was an A-list lawyer with the "who knows whom" sway to be able to pull off the trick. Truth be told, Rick Brandon did this a lot: making reservations for Nantucket, or the Cape, or out on Montauk, and then deliberately demanding some normally-out-of-bounds, last-minute change.

After all, what was the point in being a top Boston lawyer if you couldn't throw your weight around a little bit, here and there, to command special treatment?

Brandon's lavishly decorated office was suddenly filled with four nasty-looking, black-uniformed, weapons-bearing cops. Before Rick Brandon could get out the words "What the hell is going on?" two of the Federal Police Force officers were already behind his mahogany desk, one on each side, yanking Rick's arms as one of them slammed his head into the hard desktop.

Finally, Rick was able to blurt out a single word—"What..."—before the FPFer who was apparently in charge spoke.

"Richard Steven Brandon: You are hereby charged with violation of the American Professions and Employment Restrictions Act, and are remanded into the custody of the United States Government."

For a few seconds, Rick Brandon had no idea what the hell this guy was even talking about. Some "employment restriction act"? Huh?

Then the epiphany came: That was the law that Hollinger announced back in March about Jews being restricted to only certain types of jobs.

"Wait wait wait wait!" Rick blurted out. "You got the wrong guy! I'm not Jewish! That doesn't apply to me!"

Just a misunderstanding...this will all be over in a minute...

"Richard Steven Brandon," the same FPFer was now reading from his mobile device, "mother: Roberta Sarah Goldman..."

Oh shit!

"I'm only half Jewish!" Rick frantically tried to clear up this mess. "I mean, my mother is Jewish, but I'm not! I even go to church..."

Rick Brandon was yanked to his feet by the two FPF officers, and then perp-walked through his own office, down the one flight of open stairs to the lobby, and then through the massive glass front doors. He was shoved into the side of an ominously black, unmarked van. And then, Rick Brandon disappeared.

* * *

Caleb Plunkett was paranoid, but not nearly to the extent that his wife Gail was.

"You won't believe what I read today," Gail Plunkett whispered to her husband. The mid-summer Arizona sun blazed above their suburban Phoenix two-story house, yet there was no way in hell that Gail Plunkett would murmur those words inside their house.

Where the Federal Police Force could well be monitoring them through their smart television, or their cable TV box, or via their Wi-Fi router…

Gail Plunkett knew that wasn't out of the question, and her husband agreed with her.

Caleb Plunkett was frightened. Everything that President Hollinger was doing was absolutely evil. This wasn't the America in which Caleb had grown up, married, and raised a family.

Still, what could he do? What could any of them do? They had all seen the horrific scenes in the streets last October. Hollinger didn't only have his FPF storm troopers, he had his reshaped military as well.

All that he and Gail could do was keep their heads down. If they wanted to discuss anything that was even the least bit controversial, they knew better than to do so inside their house.

Like now, when Gail wanted to tell him what she had read on AVGN's social media network. Caleb personally stayed far away from that stuff, but Gail had acquired the social media habit years earlier and had never fully kicked it.

"You need to be *very* careful," Caleb had cautioned his wife on numerous occasions. "Don't post *anything* that could wind up being taken the wrong way."

Gail Plunkett mostly stuck to posting family pictures, sharing recipes, and reminiscing with long-ago high school and college friends...what social media had ostensibly been created for in the first place. While she was on AVGNSocial, however, Gail would monitor various newsfeeds to try and gauge the sentiment of others.

"Toni Fowler is going to announce tomorrow that they're going to start paying bounties to people who turn in *anyone* who turns in a Jew who is in violation of APERA, or anyone who hides a Jew. Or anyone who knows about a Jew hiding but doesn't turn them in. Ten thousand dollars for each person!"

That news tidbit was why Gail Plunkett dragged her husband out of the house, out under the one hundred fifteen degree-five o'clock sun, only minutes after he got home from work. She had to share that sordid news item with Caleb, and certainly couldn't risk surveillance picking up her obvious disgust...and, of course, sheer terror.

Not that either of them could do anything about it. Bounties had become a powerful weapon of oppression and enforced compliance almost two decades ago as the lunatic fringe seized control of too many state and local governments. Now, Spencer Howell was taking the concept of profiting from betrayal to all-new heights, anticipating that many American Jews who weren't able to comply with APERA—or who deliberately chose to resist—would go into hiding. Howell wanted all resisters flushed into the open for his FPF forces to scoop them up and send them on their way to his camps. Why not enlist the assistance of loyal American patriots, and encourage that assistance with good old American cash?

Gail Plunkett couldn't help her eyes, her head, pivoting in the direction of the Lindstroms' two-story house that shared a backyard fence with their own. She and Caleb each knew that Marcy and Buck Lindstrom had been hiding a Jewish family for more than two weeks now. Marcy Lindstrom and Gail Plunkett were the closest of friends, and had been all the way back to when they had attended high school together in Scottsdale. The Lindstroms were as helplessly appalled at what had befallen American society as Gail and Caleb were, but Buck Lindstrom took his disgust a step further. Frank Cohen had been Buck's co-worker until earlier this summer, and the Lindstroms were hiding the entire Cohen family— Frank, his wife, and their two grade-school-age children—until they all could somehow figure out a way to slip the refugee Jewish family across the southern border into Mexico, more than a hundred miles to the south.

Caleb contemplated what his wife had told him. Were he a lesser man, he might simply go to the FPF website, soullessly report his neighbors, and quickly collect a $40,000 bounty on the Cohen family and another $20,000 for Buck and Marcy Lindstrom.

Caleb Plunkett also knew that eternal damnation would be his actual reward if he indeed were a lesser man and subscribed to the abomination that America had become. Of course, he wouldn't even think about betraying his neighbors; but a terrible shiver enveloped him as he acknowledged that almost everyone else in their neighborhood would act differently should they come to possess the same knowledge as he and Gail.

And if someone also knew that Gail and I were aware of what Buck and Marcy were doing, they could quickly add another $20,000 by also including our names when they contacted the FPF.

* * *

"That will be $320.76," Sharon Kaplan informed the frat boy who seemed to be the one in charge. *The cases of beer and bottles of tequila really add up*, Sharon realized. Involuntarily, she thought back to her own college days, in the first years of the new century and millennium. Were alcohol prices that much more now, almost forty years later? Maybe; but truthfully, Sharon didn't remember what a case of beer or a bottle of whiskey cost in those days.

The frat boy waved his mobile phone, and about two seconds later the transaction was concluded. The convenience store now had $320.76, and Kirk Barber's "big data" monstrosity now had a few more tidbits about the purchasing and social habits of a twenty-one-year-old college senior named Andy Gutiérrez.

Andy and his friends carried the beer cases and the tequila to a couple of waiting vehicles, and for the first time in more than an hour and a half, the convenience mart was empty. Sharon was almost afraid to check the time, but she did anyway.

Whew—only an hour left on my shift; I was worried that time was dragging slower than I thought it was, and that I really had two or even three hours left.

It wasn't supposed to be like this.

In fact, it didn't used to be like this.

Ephraim Hollinger's March 20th pronouncement shoved Sharon Kaplan and her husband Richard into hell's waiting room and slammed the locked door behind them. Right now, they both were doing anything they could possibly do to prevent descending into hell itself.

The incident in front of their house a little more than a year earlier, at the beginning of March 2036, was an ominous warning sign. That drunken, foul-mouthed Duncan Heltefer stumbling out of that golf cart, with every intention of attacking Sharon but instead literally lurching to his death, was only the beginning. When Heltefer's widow Darlene began blaming Sharon for her husband's death, and when so many of the Heltefers' neighbors ludicrously joined in the chorus of condemnation…well, the handwriting was on the wall.

But what could they have done? Sharon and her husband were settled into this community, after years of hard work. Sharon had routinely worked eighty-hour weeks at the law firm, while Richard's academic career at Penn had surprisingly been hallmarked by numerous sixty-plus-hour weeks. They had timed their retirement for their mid-fifties, trying to hit that sweet spot where they had enough money to live comfortably and travel, but still be relatively young and healthy enough to enjoy those retirement years.

Everything had changed.

Hollinger's vengeful APERA laws required every American Jew under the age of seventy to be employed full-time in a permissible job. So not only were Sharon and Richard Kaplan being cruelly forced out of their retirement, they were also forbidden to return to their respective chosen professions.

Or else, they were off to the camps.

Sharon scrambled to find a job as a convenience store clerk. Richard was also working retail, though at one of the big-box home goods and building supply stores.

Only one more hour left for tonight, Sharon gave herself a light pep talk as a customer came through the front door.

And only nine more years remaining—if I can somehow survive this for that long; and God help me, I'm not sure that I can…or even want to…

* * *

According to the new laws of the land, once an American Jew passed the age of seventy, that individual no longer needed to toil away in one of Ephraim Hollinger's and Spencer Howell's approved job categories. If, say, Sharon and Richard Kaplan were able to endure the late-in-life hardships thrust upon them, they could once again return to "retirement"—such as it was. Social Security payments, Medicare eligibility, and other social safety net programs were no longer available to American Jews, very likely forcing many of those who chose to step away from backbreaking labor to move in with younger family members fortunate enough to avoid the concentration camps; time would tell.

The laws of the land were malleable, though.

Jeffrey Marcuson was eighty-two years old in the summer of 2037. Long ago, he had worked in banking, in Center City, Philadelphia. In 1982, the large institution where he worked acquired a central Pennsylvania agricultural bank that mostly issued and serviced loans to Schuylkill County's rural communities. Marcuson and another not-yet-thirty banker named Allen Silver were sent on the road to drum up new business among customers of the just-acquired Ag bank.

"Equipment, new and expanded outbuildings, buying up additional land, digging new wells, livestock and new fencing...go write loans!" were the marching orders given to Marcuson and Silver. "And don't waste time qualifying those farmers; book every deal that you can. If any of the loans go south, just start foreclosure."

Allen Silver had died back in 2014, though Jeffrey Marcuson was unaware of his once-partner's passing. In fact, Jeffrey Marcuson lost touch with Allen Silver only a few years after they went on a foreclosure binge in the spring and summer of 1984. So many properties had been foreclosed, in fact, that the details all blended together. Years later, Jeffrey Marcuson could recall the faintest details of a handful of the properties—two hundred acres outside of Oneida; a five-hundred-acre, multi-generational farm with three houses scattered around the parcel, north of Brandonville; one hundred and fifty acres, including eighty acres that had been recently acquired and then grafted onto the original seventy, at the northmost edge of Schuylkill County, outside of Nuremberg—but not the names or faces of their former owners.

When Ephraim Hollinger rose to the presidency, and "Nuremberg, Pennsylvania" coupled with "my father lost our farm to the Jews" became essential components of the man's legend, Jeffrey Marcuson belatedly realized that one of the properties that he did indeed remember was the centerpiece of Act I of that saga. For several years, he hoped—he prayed—that Ephraim Hollinger had long forgotten the names of the two Philadelphia bankers who had first convinced his father to borrow money to expand his farming operations, and then had coldly foreclosed on the property only two years later. After all, the President of the United States had been a young boy then; so with God's will, his revenge tour that was unfolding throughout America lacked specific targets.

Jeffrey Marcuson had retired to Carlsbad, just north of San Diego, two decades earlier. Ephraim Hollinger's announcement of the American Professions and Employment Restrictions Act and the Jewish Resettlement Act at first appeared to have little personal impact on either Jeffrey Marcuson or his wife Shelly. Both were well over seventy years old, and according to the new laws were long past the cutoff age for mandatory employment in an approved job category…and thus immune from being shipped to a concentration camp for lack of "mandatory authorized employment."

For almost four months, the reprieve seemed genuine. Even though their Social Security payments were now cut off and they were no longer eligible for Medicare, their portfolio would almost certainly be able to sustain them even if they each lived to be one hundred. Daily life in America, circa 2037, had grown ominous for Jews such as Jeffrey and Shelly Marcuson, but they could hopefully keep their heads low and maybe this would all pass over at some point.

Jeffrey Marcuson wouldn't have been nearly as complacent if he knew that Kirk Barber's "big data" monstrosity had been monitoring and stashing away every little tidbit about him for a long while now, and feeding regular reports to Bart Lawrence that in turn were summarized for Ephraim Hollinger.

When the Marcusons' front door was rammed and splintered shortly after four o'clock in the morning on Tuesday, July 21st, and when a dozen heavily armed FPF storm troopers dragged a horrified Jeffrey

Marcuson and his shrieking wife from their bed and then shoved them through the sliding side door of an unmarked black van, and when half of those FPFers piled into the van and immediately began the four hundred-mile drive to "Dachau," Ephraim Hollinger was able to put his personal stamp on Revenge Tour 2037.

Neither Hollinger nor Spencer Howell knew the first thing about Jewish holy days; but two weeks earlier Bart Lawrence had advised them that Tuesday, July 21st, marked *Tisha B'Av*, the date in the Hebrew calendar designated by Jewish lore and history for the occurrence of numerous tragedies, including the destruction of both temples.

Closer to modern times, *Tisha B'Av* - the ninth day of the Hebrew calendar's month of Av—fell on the second day of August 1941. On that date, Heinrich Himmler formally received Nazi Party approval for the Final Solution, effectively transitioning Hitler's and Himmler's progressive reign of terror consisting of book burnings, draconian Nuremberg Laws, *Kristallnacht*, and all the rest into the Holocaust.

"Absolutely perfect," Spencer Howell had smirked as he signed the authorization for the FPF to arrest Jeffrey Marcuson and his wife on the morning of July 21st, 2037, this year's *Tisha B'Av*.

"Absolutely perfect," he had repeated, his dead eyes a window into his dead soul.

* * *

About three miles away from where Sharon and Richard Kaplan had originally intended to enjoy their retirement years, Edmund and Eleanor Garfield were kicking off a midsummer visit from two of their grandchildren. Zeke, their youngest, had sent his kids south from North Dakota for a couple of weeks to give his wife Jessie a break. When nine-year-old Hayden and seven-year-old Crystal were in school, Jessie had plenty of time to herself during the day. Summers, though, were a different story. Those damn kids were so needy! Two years ago, Zeke's parents had offered to take the kids for a couple of weeks, and so a tradition was born.

"So what's your favorite subject in school?" Edmund Garfield asked his grandson, shortly after returning to their house from the airport. Zeke had plopped his kids onto an early morning flight out of Fargo into Orlando, the closest airport, about two hours due north of the massive development. The flight was on time, and the kids—exhausted from waking so early and then the three-hour flight—zonked out during the drive to the Garfields' house.

"I like history," Hayden mumbled through a mouthful of peanut butter and jelly sandwich.

"Oh really? Me too!" Edmund replied. "I used to like studying about World War II when I was your age...well, maybe a little bit older."

"We learned about World War II this year," Hayden replied, just before taking another huge bite from his sandwich.

"Really? What did you learn?"

"We learned how the Jews started the war and killed a lot of people."

"Really?" Edmund Garfield repeated.

"Uh-huh," Hayden nodded, his mouth fuller with this bite of sandwich than with the previous one, though the youngster soon conquered that challenge and continued his narrative.

"The Jews controlled all of the oil in the world, and they wouldn't give any to Japan. That's why Japan bombed Pearl...Pearl..."

"Pearl Harbor," Edmund threw in an assist.

"Uh-huh, Pearl Harbor," Hayden confirmed. "And they had all the money in...what's the place where Germany is, Grandpa?"

Edmund thought for a moment, not sure exactly what his grandson was referring to.

"Do you mean Europe?"

"Uh-huh," the boy nodded energetically. "The Jews had all the money in Europe, and Germany needed some of it to feed all of their starving children, but the Jews wouldn't give them any."

Interesting...

"And what else did you learn?"

"That in America the Jews made President Rose...Rose..."

"Roosevelt," came another grandfatherly assist.

"Roosevelt," Hayden repeated. "The Jews made President Rose...Roosevelt fight in the war, even though most Americans didn't want to."

"And what are you learning?" Eleanor Garfield chimed in; her question directed to her granddaughter.

Edmund's own thoughts turned Crystal's response into a wordless drone as he contemplated what Hayden had just related. He didn't remember learning all of that when he was in elementary school, or even high school, all those years ago. Edmund Garfield hadn't exactly been a National Merit Scholar, sliding through his school years with mostly B's and C's, plus a few D's. Truthfully, he didn't remember much at all about his school days, especially the academics. If someone were to mention "Pythagorean theorem" or "Magna Carta" or "Federalist papers"—or even something more elementary such as "the Dark Ages" or "the Spanish Inquisition"—a flicker of faint recognition at a term or phrase might tickle at Edmund's memory, but nothing further.

Still, a few tidbits had stuck with Edmund Garfield throughout the years. As far as he could recall, "Jews" had never come up in any classroom discussion of the attack on Pearl Harbor. Plus, he vaguely remembered learning that Hitler had used Jews as a hollow excuse for his assault on Europe, but nothing like what Hayden had just described.

Oh well. Edmund knew that when he and Eleanor had been in school, all those years ago, the curriculum was heavily influenced by a pervasive left-wing, socialist agenda. These days, though, Ephraim Hollinger and his Secretary of Education, Bryce Logan, had stripped away all of the lies. At least Hayden was learning the truth now; maybe he would remember that stuff better than his grandpa had.

God bless President Hollinger! The man had saved this entire country from its godless descent and restored it into a truly wonderful place to live and grow up for Hayden, Crystal, and the Garfields' other grandchildren!

Chapter 53

"I suddenly realized what this feels like." Daniel Jacobson wiped a fresh burst of perspiration from his brow. This summer's weather had been especially oppressive, the worst that Daniel could recall. He had always been in Pittsburgh for summers, not up here in central New York State, but temperatures and humidity in the two locations were mostly the same over the years.

Now, as the second week of August arrived, the scorching sun seemed worse than ever. Temperatures were regularly clocking in the low one hundreds, with stifling humidity the norm most days. Despite the unrelenting steaminess, rain was scarce; if times had been different and Daniel, Michele and the others had entertained planting and working this property's fifteen acres rather than using the facility as a safe house, they would have been in deep trouble this year.

"You mean the weather?" Michele replied to Daniel's question, wiping her own brow. They were walking from the farmhouse to the garage, following the latest intel briefing from Frank Sanchez. They were alone, a rarity during daylight hours at the safe house.

"No," he shook his head, "I mean all of us just…you know, sitting and waiting and planning, day after day. A couple of intelligence reports like this morning, but otherwise…"

Daniel shrugged.

"…just waiting."

Slightly less than five months had passed since Ephraim Hollinger proclaimed his sweeping new anti-Jewish laws. Other than refugeeing their families across the Canadian border—which actually took place almost three weeks before Hollinger's pronouncement—no blows had yet to be struck in response.

"The *sitzkrieg*," Daniel answered his own question, referring to the eight-month long period in Europe that immediately followed Hitler's invasion of Poland and lasted until Germany resumed large-scale offensive operations, aimed at conquering France. Daniel had taught a half-semester grad-level seminar course at Western Penn covering this early phase of the European Theater.

"The Phoney War?" he added. "That's what this feels like."

The so-called "Phoney War"—"phoney" being the British spelling of the word given the venue, rather than the American version—was hallmarked by relatively low levels of combat across Europe, as contrasted with what one might expect from what was now being called World War II. Given that the world had been stunned by Hitler's *blitzkrieg*, "*sitzkrieg*" was obviously a somber play on the original phrase.

Michele contemplated Daniel's sentiment. In some ways, he was right. Hollinger had declared war on America's Jews, and this group of forty-some special ops and intelligence veterans had every intention of meeting Hollinger's forces on the field of combat.

Thus far, though: all quiet on the North American front.

Hollinger had yet to start any mass transports to "Dachau." Michele and the others knew that smaller-scale transports of up to two dozen people at one time had indeed occurred. However, most of the earliest prisoners sent west had been sent for political reasons rather than the "crime" of being Jewish. Not that any one of those inmates at the three camps deserved their fate, of course; but all of the special operators were in agreement that their opening salvo needed to bring about the most significant disruption possible to the Hollinger regime's designs, and mass transports of Jews determined to be "in violation of" the American

Professions and Employment Restrictions Act made the perfect target.

So they waited.

Way too much time to think.

Much of the time, Daniel's ever-troubled ponderings gravitated toward his family. How were his parents adapting to having their lives uprooted so late in their years? *Were* they adapting? Daniel received word that they were now somewhere outside of Toronto; but given the strict electronic communications blackout in effect at all of the safe houses, he had had no contact with them since their tearful goodbyes back at the beginning of March. Were they just sitting around some strange apartment or small house, in absolute shock? Had his father been able yet to find any work up there in Canada?

I have absolutely no idea! And it's killing me!

He also was terrifyingly worried about Claire, Noah, and Rachel. The last he had heard, they were still free; still living in their house. That was back in mid-June, when Frank Sanchez made an earlier reconnaissance run west and, at Michele's request, swung by the Pittsburgh area on his way back to recon Claire.

"Your sister is safe for now, because your brother-in-law managed to get a work variance," Sanchez told Daniel upon his return, making no attempt to hide his disgust.

"He's still out West building concentration camps—nice job for a Jew to do, to be able to stay out of one of them, huh? That one in Wikieup that they're calling 'Dachau' is done, so he's now over at the giant one being built near Bowie," Sanchez continued, referring to the largest of all of Spencer Howell's concentration camps. This one was in southeastern Arizona, about thirty-five miles from the New Mexico border. Frank Sanchez had led this scouting mission to observe this gigantic concentration camp they had heard was being built. He zigzagged by each of the in-use safe houses on his way back east, spreading word that this under-construction camp looked to be architected to hold at least 120,000 prisoners.

Frank Sanchez had been a wealth of critical intelligence this morning. He returned to the New York State safe house from his latest recon mission and reported that Dane Marshall, a retired Navy SEAL and a latecomer to the team of renegade freedom fighters, had gone undercover as a Federal Police Force trainee. Marshall didn't use an alias; he applied online in his own persona, the same as Randall Weston and so many others had. With his SEAL background, Dane was snapped up and immediately sent to the FPF Academy. Marshall maneuvered his way into the Special Services Division, and conducted a full-scale situation assessment from the inside. Marshall then surreptitiously met with Frank Sanchez the previous Sunday afternoon, after carefully ensuring that he wasn't being tailed or otherwise monitored.

"There's this weird paradox," Sanchez continued relating what he had learned. Michele, Daniel, John Garcia, and ten others were gathered in the safe house's living room that had been turned into an ops planning center: walls covered with marked-up maps, tables littered with diagrams and even more maps, and a sampling of their much larger small arms cache resting against a wall by the door, for easy access should that become necessary.

"Most of the FPFers who have been there for a couple of years are fairly skilled, at least as far as police operations go. They use shock-and-awe tactics and overwhelming force to race into office buildings and houses, or manning roadblocks—that sort of thing. So for arresting one person at a time, or maybe some unlucky family or a bunch of office workers, they get the job done."

Sanchez paused to slug down almost a full bottle of water, and then continued.

"But they're way overextended with their street operations all around the country. So they've been bringing in thousands of recruits since late last year, particularly to ramp up the Special Services Division since it's new, and Marshall reported that a lot of them are clowns; no other way to put it. His Special Services class is mostly made up of loser social misfit types, and the FPF is assigning almost all of them as TDOs—Transportation and Detention Officers. They're the ones who will be doing the transport to the camps, as well as doing guard duty out West."

"Clowns?" John Garcia wanted to confirm what he had heard.

"Yeah," Frank Sanchez nodded. "He said that they strut around in their black uniforms and call themselves the S.S. all the time."

The trainees' overt usage of the "S.S." of the FPF's Special Services Division and the allusion to Hitler's S.S. was not lost on any of them as Sanchez continued.

"A bunch of them were bragging that they did the Jewish cemetery defacements around the country a couple of years back; same with that car vandalism back before the election that Hollinger and Howell used as a pretext for all those arrests and that sham trial in Denver. They think they're hot shit, but they're all wannabees. Mostly they're a bunch of street thugs who hate Jews and every other minority and who want to play soldier or cop, and the FPF is perfect for them because they aren't being selective right now. These new guys can gang up on a couple of unarmed people and beat the shit out of them, but that's about it."

Sanchez looked toward the door for a quick second, and then continued.

"They just about had an orgasm when they saw that Marshall was a retired SEAL, and they instantly made him a team lead trainee, which will be great for us getting additional intel. But for the most part, they're getting all these lowlifes—and the strange thing is that Dane doesn't think the FPF leadership even realizes what a bunch of clowns most of them really are."

"So they're not us," John Garcia smirked.

Frank Sanchez's eyes scanned the room, lighting on Daniel for a painfully long half-second before continuing on.

"No, they're not us," he nodded.

* * *

Those first months of what Daniel had termed this new war's *sitzkrieg* had been an eye-opener. He frequently thought back to that final conversation with his great-grandfather only hours before Pop-pop's death, on the enclosed porch at his parents' house after that Purim Eve dinner, telling Pop-pop about Michele tutoring him in combat techniques at the Monroeville laser-tag facility. Daniel's unspoken self-assessment at that time was, with that wonderful benefit of 20-20 hindsight, laughable.

I might not be channeling Rambo, but I would have at least a slight chance of surviving if I were dropped into a combat situation.

Now, after months of daily contact with a dozen military and intel special ops veterans, Daniel glumly realized that when it came to war-fighting techniques, he knew next to nothing. These retired Green Berets and Army Rangers, Marine Recon and Air Force Special Warfare vets, and Navy SEALs were the best of the best. Daniel was definitely grateful that he was on their side, but he had never before felt so inadequate.

And that ominous feeling absolutely took its toll on Daniel's relationship with Michele.

As civilization methodically crumbled throughout 2035 and 2036, Daniel and Michele endeavored to maintain a semblance of normalcy in their lives. Even when the news of the day was another death blow against the country's democratic institutions, they went out of their way to comfort one another. They did their best to maintain the level of intimacy that had blossomed so soon after Michele moved to Pittsburgh.

From the moment they bugged out to the safe house, though, affection and intimacy all but disappeared.

It's natural, Daniel told himself a thousand times. *We're at war, or at least getting ready for war; these aren't normal times.*

He and Michele slept together every night, in one of the smallish bedrooms that was barely big enough for a double bed, as was commonly found in late 1800s farmhouses. Despite the close confines each night—unlike the king-sized beds back in their Pittsburgh homes—sex had become a rare occurrence.

She's still here, sleeping with me, Daniel struggled to convince himself. *She hasn't abandoned me for one of the others...or maybe even worse, to sleep by herself.*

Daniel's back-of-mind worries about Michele reuniting with John Garcia had proven groundless. Not long after the exodus of his and Michele's families, Garcia and Roseanne Morris hooked up, and they had been together throughout the spring and into the mid-summer.

"They were together after John and I were," Michele had confided in Daniel a while back. "Up at Fort Lewis, in Washington State. That's where John went after Fort Huachuca, when I left for grad school at Harvard. Looks like a second go-around for them."

Daniel observed how John Garcia and Roseanne Morris acted around each other during daytime hours. Other than an occasional shared glance for a second or two that he wouldn't have noticed if Michele hadn't clued him into them being together, they were just two soldiers in the same unit...working together, planning together, preparing to fight together.

But at least they are "together" each night.

The walls in the aging farmhouse were on the thin side; and even though John and Roseanne weren't exceptionally loud, the muffled sounds of their lovemaking were detectable most nights.

But not us.

* * *

"You know, I saw you flinch this morning."

Once they reached the garage, Michele plopped onto one of the hay bales stashed just inside the oversized sliding doors. The hay was at least three or four years old, from the last time the property had been farmed, and had seen better days. It hadn't gone moldy, but the timothy had bleached from its original rich green hues to an almost straw-like, washed-out yellow. If any horses or cows had still been present, the hay—its nutrients now almost fully eroded with age—would be all but useless for feeding purposes. Still, the dozen or so bales served as passable seats inside the garage.

"When Sanchez looked at you after Garcia's comment about 'they're not us,'" Michele continued.

Daniel briefly considered denying the allegation, but instead just shrugged as he slid onto another of the hay bales.

"Just because we're all special ops…remember, we've all been through so much training and on numerous missions before, and you haven't. So in some ways you're even more courageous than us, because you're doing this for the first time, and with almost no training."

She's patronizing me.

"Just feels like I'm doing nothing but sitting around," Daniel shrugged, echoing his observation from earlier. He didn't call Michele on her apparently patronizing comment, though.

No sense in provoking a confrontation.

"Doesn't feel courageous, or anything like that," he added.

A sad smile came to Michele.

"It'll change soon enough," she somberly replied.

"Just too much time to think," Daniel put words to his ever-pervasive mental burden.

"Me, also," Michele added after a brief pause. "In fact, all of us."

Another pause, and then Michele added:

"But yeah, me also."

"So what are you thinking about?" The question had slipped through Daniel's lips before he could consider it and, most likely, chop it off before it could be uttered. Personal-level discussions with Michele had sadly become not only rare, but uncomfortable.

Michele looked at Daniel and smiled sadly.

"Lots of things, but one in particular: that really, for the first time since I was in high school, I actually *feel* Jewish...I mean, *really* Jewish."

"Yeah?" Daniel cocked his head.

"You would think that growing up with a great-grandfather who was a Holocaust survivor, I'd have a strong connection to Judaism; and when I was younger, I did. But from the time I started at West Point, there just weren't a lot of other Jewish cadets or officers there. I started off going to services at the Jewish Chapel there a couple times a month, but every year I went less and less. And then, once I went on active duty, especially being in training or deployed so much of the time, I just..."

Michele paused to try to collect her thoughts.

"I guess 'Jewish' became a label for me, but not much more than that."

Suddenly she smiled warmly and locked eyes with Daniel.

"Until I met you, and started going to Purim dinners and Seders, and lighting Hannukah candles at your parents' house, and going to synagogue services again."

She shifted slightly on the hay bale, and then back at Daniel.

"Speaking of Hannukah, now I feel like one of the Maccabees," she added, referring to the heroic underdog family of the Hannukah story who led the successful revolt against the persecution of Antiochus IV.

"You also," she added.

Michele's smile remained in place.

"I don't think I ever told you this, but did you know that on our first date, that night we went to dinner to celebrate my new house, you were the first Jewish guy I had gone out with since way back in high school?"

Daniel shook his head and offered a single-syllable reply.

"No."

"Like I said, my whole time in the Army, it was like being Jewish kept dropping lower and lower in how I thought of myself."

Now, Michele shuffled to the left side of her hay bale, toward Daniel and now within reach of him. She took his hand.

"For that alone, not to mention that I love you very much, I'm eternally grateful."

Her words caught Daniel off guard.

That's the first time she's said "I love you" in…I don't even remember the last time.

"I know things aren't exactly romantic, or whatever, between us now," Michele continued. Her smile had passed, but her eyes remained locked with Daniel's.

"It's nothing to do with you, or anything like that," she continued. "This might be TMI, but I've always been this way leading up to an operation, no matter who I was with. Not everybody is the same way…"

"Not Garcia," Daniel quickly interjected, thinking of the muted lovemaking sounds that wafted through the hallways and the walls into their room most nights.

"Yeah, well, that's John," Michele blurted out too quickly. For a flash of a second she almost rolled right into a confirming anecdote, but caught herself. John Garcia might be with Roseanne Morris now, and Michele had been with Daniel for several years, but her own memory instantly time-traveled back more than a decade earlier, to northeastern Africa. She had been with Garcia then, at Fort Huachuca in Arizona, when their unit quietly deployed to Somalia to support an anti-terrorism operation there. Each night, out in the field during the week leading up to the operation, she and Garcia went at it like there was no tomorrow…which might have actually been the case should their encampment have been discovered and overrun, or if the mission went south. At first, Michele had been reluctant to slip away from the main encampment; but for John Garcia, they might as well have been leisurely camping at one of their regular getaway spots in the Rockies or up north in Arizona, near Payson. He wasn't to be deterred from his nightly "mission" just because they were in Somalia, about to embark on a dangerous operation.

No, I don't think Daniel would appreciate me sharing those memories…

"Never forget: No matter what happens, I love you with all my heart," she said instead.

Michele's words were both heartfelt and ominous.

"You make it sound like…"

Michele cut off Daniel's words.

"You never know what might happen once shit gets real," she again offered a sad smile, "and I want to make sure you know it."

* * *

As the first summer of Bizzarro America wound down, clocking toward and then past Labor Day, the *sitzkrieg* continued. Ops plans were continually reviewed, rehearsed, and tweaked. Sooner or later, the first transports to "Dachau" would be underway. Until then, Michele, Daniel, and the others monitored the state of the country and the world.

As expected, America's traditional allies had abandoned those alliances, loudly condemning every action taken by Ephraim Hollinger and his minions dating back to the horrific shootings the previous October that paved the way to Hollinger's seizure of absolute power. This past spring, fresh rounds of condemnations and sanctions against the United States resulted from Hollinger's "New Nuremberg Laws," as they were commonly termed, clearly linking Hollinger to Hitler's early handiwork via the shared name with the president's birthplace.

Hollinger didn't care in the least. He had absolutely no interest in the nation's traditional alliances, or foreign affairs, or most aspects of international relations. The standing of the United States on the world stage was a disruption, and "America First, Round Three" was in full swing. Besides, Hollinger continued to nurture vile relationships with authoritarian regimes across the globe. Trade pacts, new political and military alliances…in an upside-down world where the President of the United States could strip seven and a half million of its own citizens of property, liberty, and possibly even life, the unthinkable was now commonplace.

Two decades ago, the nation's traditional alliances were stress-tested throughout an entire presidential term but managed to persevere. Leaders and the general populace alike throughout the free world separated the temporary hijacking of the state apparatus from the will of the American people as a whole, and nervously waited for the political dumpster fire to be extinguished.

Now, though, the will of the American people, circa 2037, was—where it counted, anyway—one and the same as that of King Ephraim the First. Those who opposed Hollinger no longer had a voice of dissent. Most had been cowed into submission, anyway; and for the rest, TAMCA served as the ultimate cancel-culture vehicle, silencing the once-free press and also the voice of the masses via social media. America was beyond salvation, thanks to the darkness and tragedy of a Second American Revolution.

* * *

Thursday afternoon, September 10th, 2037.

The first day of Rosh Hashanah, the Jewish New Year.

At one o'clock in the afternoon, Toni Fowler stepped to the podium in the White House Press Briefing Room and began speaking in stoic tones.

"Good afternoon. Pursuant to the provisions of the American Professions and Employment Restrictions Act and the Jewish Resettlement Act, President Hollinger and Attorney General Howell are announcing today that the first large-scale resettlement of violators of these laws will begin next Friday night, one week from tomorrow. President Hollinger, Attorney General Howell, Homeland Security Secretary Knox, and the entire Hollinger administration have committed to protecting the American people from those who would harm our citizenry. The resettlement that will commence next Friday night will ensure the safety and welfare of the homeland and this nation's patriots."

Fowler paused for a moment, swallowed, and then continued.

"To fully demonstrate this administration's commitment and resolve to our great American people, the first transports will be broadcast live on the American Values and Greatness Network. Transports are scheduled to begin at midnight, Eastern Permanent Daylight Time, and will simultaneously depart from the following locations..."

In upper New York State, the entire special operations team watched and listened to Toni Fowler's pronouncement. Their reactions went like this:

Michele Burgess: "Yom Kippur night," followed by a bitter "What a surprise."

Frank Sanchez: "Fucking bitch."

Roseanne Morris: "Gotta love it when the enemy tells you their entire battle plan."

John Garcia, clapping a hand on Daniel Jacobson's right shoulder: "Get ready."

Chapter 54

Prisoners had populated Federal Detainment Facility One since the concentration camp went operational back at the end of March. Some were political prisoners such as Jack Bancroft and Asher Clayton, Bancroft's running mate in last year's aborted election. Initially detained back in the nation's capital, they were now imprisoned alongside some of the Hollinger regime's earliest targets such as Jeremy Goldstein, Todd Silverberg, and the other Jewish financiers who had previously been locked up elsewhere since early 2034. Craig Ryan, Josh Stein, and the rest of the "Denver Thirty" were also now confined at FDF-1. Numerous other prisoners were those with low enough Citizen Loyalty Scores and who had been surveilled doing or saying "something" that triggered being swept up by the Federal Police Force. Some of the swept-up Jews had also been randomly transferred to "Dachau," though most were still held in regionally dispersed prisons, awaiting their fated destination.

That first cadre of prisoners had trickled into FDF-1 in small batches throughout the spring and early summer of 2037, mostly transported by unmarked black vans and box trucks. Now, though, as Toni Fowler had announced, Spencer Howell was adamant that the first mass transports of Jews from the regional interim prisons to "Dachau" would be a spectacle, which put him at odds with General Frank Douglas, Braxton Knox, and most of the Hollinger administration's brain trust.

"I want AVGN broadcasting and recording every one of those bus convoys departing," the Attorney General demanded. "I want every single person in this country to know that what the president announced is actually happening. Otherwise, before too long some people will start going 'Maybe there really aren't camps, and maybe the Jews aren't really being sent there.'"

Howell's eyes flashed evil determination.

"They all need to know."

Spencer Howell wasn't done.

"It's going to take place after nightfall, under blazing spotlights. Think about the intimidation factor when they all get marched onto the buses, *three thousand* of them, and they're squinting and shielding their eyes. Broadcast live, with a four-way split screen—one for each of the convoys. Seven hundred fifty *Jews*"— Spencer Howell spat the word, as he always did—"in each transport. Midnight eastern time, so it will be dark out West as well."

The split-screen part was, no doubt, the idea of Bob Platte. *Everything was always theater with Platte*, Frank Douglas silently snarled.

At this point Douglas, Knox, Tom Buckner, and the others knew that further argument was futile. When it came to "Jewish matters," they had learned that Spencer Howell *always* got his way with Ephraim Hollinger.

Frank Douglas, for one, foresaw at least the possibility of trouble, especially since Howell demanded that the transports were to be an FPF-only operation. Unlike last fall, when Howell's FPF storm troopers marched side by side with Douglas' soldiers (along with the militias and mercenaries) through American streets, Howell had no interest in sharing either responsibility or authority when it came to his concentration camps. Howell had preemptively and successfully lobbied Hollinger that rounding up non-compliant Jews, manning the transports, guarding the camps—all of it—was to be solely within his realm.

Even worse: Douglas had futilely argued for early-morning departures, at the dawn's early light. Uncertainty lurked in the post-midnight darkness. There would be enough after-dark driving for the northeastern departures anyway, all the way out to

Arizona. That convoy from northern New Jersey would take approximately forty hours, including refueling stops. The Seattle and Houston buses would each take around twenty-four hours. Why not drive as much as possible of that time block in the daylight, when danger could be more readily spotted? Why not control the environment, when it was within their power to do so?

So be it, General Douglas reasoned. *If anything goes wrong, then it's solely on him; my hands are clean.*

Frank Douglas had also gone on record urging Howell to maintain a dome of secrecy surrounding plans for the transports, in the interest of both operational and communications security. Howell rebuffed the general's suggestion with a sneer.

"If you're worried about a bunch of protestors showing up in L.A. and Seattle and the other cities to try to prevent the buses from leaving, I'm not. My men are locked and loaded, and anyone who even thinks about protesting is going to wind up like all those stupid bastards last fall."

To satisfy his own curiosity, Frank Douglas had his aide-de-camp do a dive into Kirk Barber's massive data environment, seeking any crumbs of data that might indicate a threat to the transports. The first item of interest that came back was that a retired Army Special Forces and Ranger officer—a major, some woman named Michele Burgess—had dropped off the face of the earth back in February: no credit card transactions since then, no cell phone pings...nothing. She had also abruptly abandoned her job teaching at a college in Pittsburgh. Interestingly, her boyfriend likewise suddenly dropped off of Kirk Barber's radar...as did all of their respective families.

However: Both Major Burgess and her boyfriend were listed as being Jewish, and their disappearances happened only a couple of weeks before the president's announcement. And get this: Her boyfriend was the one who wrote that scurrilous trash novel, *The Twilight's Last Gleaming*, that the TAMCA laws had squashed. Maybe this Major Burgess' sixth sense lit up, or maybe she had a deep-cover source somewhere within DoD or even the FPF who alerted her about what was soon to go down. But whatever had triggered it, it looked like they fled the country and took their families with them, just ahead of Hollinger's doomsday pronouncement, and were laying low.

Douglas' initial reaction was "no big deal," but later that same day, his aide-de-camp came back with additional data points. Major Michele Burgess wasn't the only retired special operations veteran to have gone dark during the past couple of months. At least twenty others had, seemingly, also faded into oblivion. Strangely, none of the others were Jewish; so that almost certainly left out being tipped off and fleeing the country. They came from scattered backgrounds, rather than all having served together. Still…

A resistance cell, was General Douglas' immediate hypothesis upon receiving this information. *And not just a bunch of amateurs like the ones being swept up almost daily, either; these were pros.*

"This is classified," he sternly ordered his aide as he pocketed the folded sheets of paper. "Not a word to anyone."

It's probably nothing. Maybe they're all a bunch of libs at heart and opposed to what we've done, so they left the country. Before the purges that I put into motion, not everyone in the military was a true patriot, and that held even in special ops.

But perhaps…

The general had no intention of sharing these scraps of data with Spencer Howell, Braxton Knox, or anyone else. If some sort of resistance cell comprised of special ops veterans was really out there, and if it somehow caused havoc with one of the upcoming caravans out to FDF-1, then that was on Howell for demanding unitary control over these first transports.

I wouldn't mind seeing that asshole's balls on a skewer, Frank Douglas thought.

* * *

Time, location, environment, and force strength.

By late summer of 2037, Daniel had sat in on enough ops planning sessions that those elements were now ingrained in his thinking.

"Ideally, we want all four in our favor," Michele had patiently explained to Daniel, back at the beginning of the year, even before they shuttled their families north across the border.

"We want to pick the time of attack, as well as the location," Michele continued. "Then we want to manipulate and maximize the environment to our favor as much as we can. Think about the D-Day invasion, when they postponed the landing because of high winds and rough seas. It still wasn't great on June 6th, but a lot better than it would have been if they had gone on the original date."

Satisfied that Daniel was absorbing the lesson, she went on. Daniel was an expert in the European Theater of World War II, in part because of his great-grandfather; so D-Day analogies were perfect for Michele to get key points across to him.

"As for force strength, ideally we attack the enemy when they're at their weakest, or at least at diminished strength. With D-Day, that's what was behind all of the deception to make the Nazis think that the invasion would instead be at Pas-de-Calais, to draw a substantial amount of Hitler's troops away from Normandy."

"But what if…" Daniel began, but Michele—realizing that the others were gathering downstairs, and they needed to get down there—interrupted.

"The enemy also gets a say," she solemnly added, knowing exactly what Daniel was thinking. "That's what makes this business so difficult and dangerous."

As Daniel would learn, though, sometimes the enemy stupidly gives you a gift—which is exactly what

Spencer Howell had done, with his insistence on a "late-night broadcast extravaganza" debut of his Concentration Camp Express.

Special operators usually prefer to attack under the cover of darkness. If Howell's initial bus convoys had departed northern Jersey, Houston, L.A., and Seattle at the break of dawn, then each would have been far along their routes by the time darkness fell, and even farther before the desired post-midnight time of attack. The L.A. transport would never see even one second of darkness by the time it arrived at FDF-1. In the case of the convoy that Michele, John Garcia, and the others were targeting—the one leaving from northern Jersey—those buses would have been on the other side of St. Louis when darkness arrived, and well into Kansas in the post-midnight hours. Making a successful run for either border would have been much more difficult from the center of the country: some sixteen hours zigzagging either north to Manitoba or south into the Mexican state of Coahuila. Or, more likely, they would need to make use of some of the secondary safe houses for all of those freed rather than only a small number, and spread out this first strike of Operation Exodus over a longer period of time. And, of course, the longer the escapees remained within American borders, the riskier the whole operation became.

Putting all of those factors together, they instead would have been forced to make a daylight assault on that initial FPF convoy to execute their operation closer to New York State and, of course, the Canadian border: still doable, but definitely with increased risk versus the murky blackness of night.

Now, though, with the northeastern convoy inexplicably leaving northern New Jersey at midnight, the team could hit the buses near Allentown, Pennsylvania. Any adrenalin rush among the amateurish FPF contingent guarding the convoy from the departure extravaganza will have crashed by then: the guards now lulled into exhausted complacency an hour and a half, maybe a bit longer, into the journey and in the middle of the night. The special ops team could make a run for the border with most of the rescued Jews, while scattering the others among the safe houses in north-central New York State, waiting to ferry them northward in small groups.

The team that included Michele and Daniel had the toughest of all the four missions, at least geographically. The attack points for the Seattle, Houston, and L.A. convoys were all much closer to their designated border crossings than theirs would be. All four of the missions were difficult ones, though. But whether due to fate or God's will or sheer happenstance, Spencer Howell had seen fit to flip at least a couple of the elements in the favor of the liberators.

* * *

The wait was excruciating.

"You should try to get some sleep tonight," Michele had told Daniel late the previous afternoon, just before the rest of the team departed the safe house at intermittent intervals and headed south toward the attack point. "There's no sense in you waiting up all night. At the earliest, it'll be around six-thirty in the morning for us getting back here with anyone we rescue."

Sleep was impossible.

His heart pounded nonstop and was almost audible in the quiet second-floor bedroom. Finally, at around three in the morning, Daniel surrendered and headed downstairs, and then outside. Autumn was still a few days away, but here in the quiet of upstate New York, the blackened chill smacked him the second he stepped through the rickety wooden screen door onto the porch. The old-fashioned thick red mercury thermometer to the left of the front door indicated that the post-midnight temperature now rested a few degrees below freezing. He was dressed in the same all-black uniform of tactical pants, a thick turtleneck military-style sweater, and scuffed leather combat boots identical to those that each attacker wore. His black ski mask was rolled upward above his face, resting halfway on his forehead, providing at least some protection from the cold.

Daniel walked down the five steps of the front porch onto the level ground and gazed at the long, tree-lined driveway. At any second, he expected to see one or more of the box trucks materialize out of the darkness, headlights off. Their appearance four or five hours ahead of schedule would only mean one thing: The mission had failed, for one reason or another.

The night remained quiet, motionless. Daniel gazed upward. Only a quarter moon; the cloudless nighttime sky was filled with millions of pinpricks of light. The tranquility that spread across the heavens belied the hellish reality on earth.

At any moment I'll wake up. Maybe I'll still be up here in the middle of nowhere, staring up at the stars, but camping with Michele instead of being part of a resistance movement; or maybe I'll open my eyes and be back in either my apartment or her house, and this whole past year will have been just a nightmare.

Daniel's stomach churned with hunger, but he feared that he wouldn't be able to keep anything down other than a couple of crackers. He had brought a mug of coffee, but he might as well have been drinking acid, the way his stomach revolted against only a few sips.

Being left behind at the safe house stung. After months of training side by side with Michele and the others, at the last minute Daniel was ordered to remain in place and prepare for the arriving freed prisoners. He was the little kid, not enough of a grown-up to go to a late dinner or a movie with his parents. The only thing that Michele and the others didn't do was leave him in the care of a babysitter.

"Also, someone needs to stay behind for continuity, in case we're all captured or killed." That had been Michele's explanation by way of her dispassionate, cold orders. Daniel didn't believe her for a second, but he knew that protests were futile. He highly doubted that at a safe house near any of the other three attack sites a special forces or SEAL veteran was sitting around at this very minute, as he was, "for continuity."

Daniel checked his watch again, as he had been doing every few minutes. The raid was over by now; or at least it should have been. Toni Fowler had unwittingly provided them with all the intel they needed, disdainfully announcing that each of the convoys would consist of ten FPF transport buses, each carrying seventy-five prisoners headed for FDF-1. The special ops teams had stealthily acquired fleets of box trucks throughout the summer, one fleet for each planned attack site, with each truck capable of barely squeezing an entire busload of freed Jews into the cargo area. Each truck's suspension and frame had been reinforced and ruggedized to be able to handle its payload of seventy-five freed prisoners. They would have just enough trucks for the job. The hours-long journey to freedom would be excruciating for those packed in so tight they could barely breathe, yet still absolutely preferable to Spencer Howell's intended destination for human beings whose only "crimes" were being Jewish and "not employed in an authorized manner" in Ephraim Hollinger's America.

Daniel checked his watch yet again. If his comrades had been successful, all of the box trucks had crossed into New York State across the Pennsylvania border within the past half hour, along several different routes. Eight trucks would vector toward the Canadian border. That left two trucks that would head for safe houses rather than attempt a direct border crossing. One of those two remaining trucks would take its seventy-five freed Jews to the safe house an hour and a half south of Plattsburgh in upstate New York, while the other would head back here.

Of the eight trucks racing for the border, two would veer west toward Buffalo, remaining on secondary roads, and complete the journey—God willing—by unloading their freed prisoners on Unity Island. The newly minted refugees then would be led on foot into Canada via the little-used railroad bridge that still stood. Three more of the vehicles would continue zigzagging north past Syracuse along separate routes, converging at their designated spot on the shore of Lake Ontario, where Canadian special ops teams would be waiting with boats to ferry the rescued prisoners across the lake—and the border—onto Prince Edward Island. The other three Canada-bound trucks would split up and follow the various routes up to Dundee that had been used for the successful exodus of Michele's and Daniel's families. Additional safe houses waited along each route should any of the runs for the border need to be aborted rather than be executed to immediate completion.

Five of those eight trucks would be ostentatiously abandoned on Unity Island and on the American side of Lake Ontario, deliberately awaiting discovery by the FPF sometime later that day, or soon thereafter. Another would be dumped just over the border in Dundee, following the same protocol as a few others from each of the other three attack sites that would be similarly abandoned just over the Canadian or Mexican border, all waiting to be detected by FPF drones. The plan was to convince the FPF that every one of the freed prisoners had been immediately shuttled out of the country, and none remained in the U.S. for the FPF to seek out. Inconspicuous vehicles had been preplaced at every drop point for the special operators to jump into for their circuitous return drives to their respective safe houses; none of the box trucks would be making a return trip.

Just west of Allentown, twelve special operators would attack the buses (*I would have been unlucky number thirteen*, Daniel had realized, though he doubted superstition played any part in his being ordered to stay behind). Roseanne Morris and Michele were paired up in the truck headed back to this safe house, while Fletcher Carlson and John Garcia were assigned to the other safe house. Each of the other trucks heading directly to Canada would have only one special ops veteran at the helm. They were stretched way too thin, but that couldn't be helped.

Daniel replayed the mission repeatedly in his mind. He watched his conjured film of the attack, over and over. The attack would be set up by halting the buses along the interstate through a staged multi-vehicle accident, the same as with each of the other three intercept sites for Howell's other convoys. On the way to Allentown, four of the box trucks had each been carrying cargo: a subcompact car, barely able to fit into the bay. Two of the vehicles had been mocked up with the exact markings and light bars as the cruisers now being used by FPF-controlled state and local police forces throughout the country. The fake police cars were, in fact, smaller than the actual vehicles used by the cops; but in the blackness of night and with the element of surprise, that minor visual discrepancy would almost certainly be overlooked by the FPF TDOs in the lead bus who would first spot the "police cars."

The two fabricated FPF vehicles would be positioned across the westbound lanes of I-78, lights flashing and flanking the other two cars that would be positioned as if a head-on collision had occurred. John Garcia, Fletcher Carlson, and Rob Sperry would play the roles of state troopers, flagging down and stopping westbound traffic along the interstate, presumably until the crash could be cleared from the highway. They had chosen a straightaway where the fabricated crash scene could be seen for more than a mile by the lead bus, which would immediately trigger a chain reaction of slowing down by the entire convoy.

When the lead bus crawled to a stop just ahead of the supposed FPF cruisers, Carlson and Rob Sperry would officiously approach that vehicle while John Garcia would quick-step toward the second bus, each one unrolling his face mask and grasping his weapon during those few seconds while out of sight, hugging the right sides of their buses. At that moment, the rest of the attackers would rush the remaining buses from the brushy cover to the right side of the interstate. The intel from Dane Marshall over the summer was that each transport bus, in each convoy, was being outfitted in the same manner as a typical prison bus, with a thick mesh grill and locking door separating the driver's compartment from the seats filled with prisoners.

Most important of all: Each transport bus would carry only two FPF TDOs: the driver and one additional guard. Spencer Howell was so overconfident that his Concentration Camp Convoys were immune from trouble that he didn't see the need for anything other than minimal security so he could squeeze three or four additional prisoners onto each transport bus.

The designated attacker would, lightning-fast in each bus, disable both TDOs with electro-bullets. Once Spencer Howell's storm troopers were down, the attacker would grab the keys, unlock the gate to the seating area, and then hustle the prisoners off of the bus and into one of the awaiting box trucks that were parked out of sight, off to the side of the nearby exit ramp that had been a key part of selecting the exact attack site.

And then they would all make their escape...if the plan succeeded.

In Daniel's numerous conjured, tortured mental viewings of the attack, sometimes the buses were taken by surprise and the prisoners freed exactly as planned; other times Michele and everyone else were mercilessly gunned down as their mission failed miserably.

When Daniel wasn't torturing himself by mind-traveling to the point of attack or the journey to freedom for the freed prisoners, he somberly contemplated the fates of hundreds of thousands, perhaps millions, more American Jews who would never have the chance to escape. Even if tonight's operation was one hundred percent successful—not only here, but also in the other three convoy interdictions—at most, three thousand Jews would be spared imprisonment in Spencer Howell's "Dachau."

Tonight's plan of attack would likely work exactly once. Spencer Howell, Frank Douglas, and Braxton Knox wouldn't make the same mistakes a second time. Future convoys would be heavily fortified, rather than manned by only a couple of rookie TDOs in each bus. They would maximize daylight travel the next time. The future transports might not even be by bus convoy, but rather via railroad or air.

Our rescues tonight will be little more than a few drops in a bucket, even if all four intercepts are one hundred percent successful. We won't be finished; we'll move on to other attacks, in other manners, but these will almost certainly be the only transport buses that we take down. Are we really making a difference?

The counterarguments to Daniel's anguished pondering materialized in the form of names.

Oskar Schindler.

Raoul Wallenberg.

Gustav Mikulai.

Semmy Riekerk.

And thousands of others. Schindler, who became famous because of the old movie, was credited with saving 1,200 Jews. When six million died, wasn't the number "twelve hundred" a mere drop in that terrible bucket of death? But for those twelve hundred souls blessed to have been spared a torturous murder in the death camps or being slave-labored to their deaths, Schindler's actions absolutely mattered!

Even if Daniel, Michele, and the others were able to spare only a single American Jew from imprisonment out West, for that person the effort will have been a *mitzvah*.

* * *

Daniel was inside, in the second-floor bathroom, when the distant crunch of gravel underneath tires caused his heart to jump into his throat. The sun had been up for nearly forty-five minutes, though any warmth was filtered out by the heavy layer of clouds. Daniel had just checked his watch seconds earlier, so he knew the clock had just swept past 7:40. He quickly finished up and raced down the stairs and then out the door. His eyes fell on Roseanne Morris, who had just exited the driver's side door.

She was sobbing uncontrollably.

Daniel's eyes frantically scanned the cab of the truck.

Nobody else.

Oh my God!

Then he saw her, coming around the right side of the box truck from the back, followed by a mass of prisoners, now free of both their confinement in the cargo bay as well as the clutches of the Federal Police Force.

Michele Burgess was also weeping as her watery red eyes met Daniel's.

* * *

"None of us knows what happened," Michele told Daniel. "John had to have taken down both of the TDOs, because he was able to get the key and unlock the gate on bus number two. And every single prisoner walked right past those TDOs, off of that bus. But one of them must have recovered, because he got off a shot and hit John when he was bringing up the rear behind the last of the prisoners."

The pain in Michele's eyes was torturous.

"Fletcher, Roseanne, and I all opened fire on the bus and took out whichever TDO it was that shot John. We only saw one of them standing, so the other must have still been down from the electro-bullet."

Michele again dissolved in tears.

"He's dead, Daniel," she quietly sobbed. "You were right: We should have just shot every one of them as soon as we boarded the buses, rather than use the electro-bullets to disable them."

As the attack plan solidified through the summer, one risk had pricked repeatedly at Daniel. The plan called for stunning and incapacitating the TDOs with electro-bullets rather than simply opening fire with standard ammunition and killing them.

"We want to avoid giving Hollinger and Howell any additional reason for retaliation against future prisoners," had been Michele's explanation when Daniel asked her, one-on-one. No way was he, the amateur, going to question even a single aspect of the ops plan in front of a room filled with battle-tested special ops and intel veterans!

"There's going to be enough hell to pay as it is," Michele had continued at the time. "But if we leave every one of the FPF transport officers alive, then hopefully Howell isn't going to do something like his beloved Nazis would: you know, line up a hundred or a thousand Jews and gun them all down in retaliation."

"You were right," Michele repeated again, in the here and now. "If we had just shot and killed every one of those fuckers, John would be alive right now."

* * *

Early the following afternoon, after the other special operators who had headed to Canada had all successfully made their way back to the safe house— each one's mission of salvation fully and successfully completed—Fletcher Carlson and Rob Sperry began digging a grave about forty feet behind the back of the barn. Daniel, quickly realizing what they were doing, grabbed a shovel and joined them. The ground proved difficult: rocky, and partially frozen for the first foot and a half beneath the surface. More than two hours passed until the three of them had dug a hole deep, wide, and long enough to serve as Major John Garcia's final resting place.

Several of the others constructed a makeshift casket out of lumber stored off to the side of the storage room inside the barn. John Garcia wasn't Jewish, of course, but he would go to his grave in a simple pine box as if he were the most devout Orthodox Jew.

The freed prisoners all wanted to pay their respects to their fallen rescuer as John Garcia was buried, but Fletcher Carlson refused to allow that many people to congregate out in the open. By now, the FPF and maybe even the military would have kicked aerial surveillance into high gear. Adding another seventy-five people to the special ops team in the open could betray their location, should a drone pass overhead or even nearby at that time. The prisoners needed to remain in the barn, undercover and hopefully shielded from body heat surveillance by the material nailed to the inside of the barn roof. Even a brief, simple ceremony with a dozen or so graveside mourners was a risk, but the vote to hold a brief burial service and bear that risk was unanimous.

Thus, the task of saying goodbye to John Garcia was left to those with whom he had shared the battlefield this past spring and summer; the battlefield of a tragically transformed America. John Garcia could have simply turned away when Michele Burgess approached him several years ago. Ephraim Hollinger's ruination had yet to materialize. Major John Garcia had honorably served his country, and he could easily have observed the Decline and Fall of the American Experiment merely as a disapproving bystander.

Instead, he chose to continue to honor the oath that he had once taken; a vow to protect and defend the Constitution of the United States against *all* enemies, both foreign and domestic, and to bear true faith and allegiance to that centuries-old affirmation of American democratic values.

Shortly after four o'clock, under a heavy sky with cold, dark rain threatening, Fletcher Carlson, Rob Sperry, and two others grasped the opposing ends of long, thick canvas straps and slowly lowered the pine box containing the body of John Garcia into the earth.

No marker would ever note his grave. His remains would be confined to anonymity, perhaps for all eternity, though his deeds would live on in memory.

"*Yitgadal v'yitkadash sh'mei raba,*" Daniel began reciting the Mourner's *Kaddish* as John Garcia was laid to rest. To Daniel's left, Michele Burgess' voice broke as she tried to join in the prayer.

Chapter 55

Life in Ephraim Hollinger's America, as the surreal summer of 2037 yielded to the inevitable extinguishing of life that coldly commenced during the early weeks of autumn.

* * *

"I can't wait to watch the next ones," Jerry Floyd chortled.

"Yeah, me too," Carson Everett agreed as he quickly killed his seventh beer, motioning to the hot bartender for a couple more. "That was fuckin' awesome!"

Neither Jerry Floyd nor his long-ago high school buddy Carson Everett knew, of course, that all four of Spencer Howell's convoys had been intercepted not long after their dramatic televised departures. They certainly had no knowledge that every one of three thousand American Jews destined for Federal Detention Facility One were now safely across the Canadian and Mexican borders, safe forever from American Values and Greatness-style "justice." One full week past the first round of bus convoys, AVGN continued to maintain the tightest of news blackouts about what had happened. As far as Jerry, Carson, and about three hundred fifty million other Americans were concerned, the transports had all dumped their human cargo without incident inside "Dachau," and three thousand additional prisoners were now consigned to a life of slave labor.

"I used to hear stories from my granddad about when he was young," Jerry continued as he reached for his latest beer that had just been plopped in front of him. He eyeballed the bartender for a moment before continuing, wondering if he might have a shot with her later on.

"He was born in 1950, I think," Jerry continued. "So when all of that civil rights shit was happening in the '50s and the '60s he was, um…"

Jerry paused to attempt a bit of mental math, which was always a challenge for him.

"…I guess…I dunno…anyway, he was pretty young. But his daddy—my great-granddad—used to crack some heads at those marches and lunch counter agitation. And my great-granddad's dad, I don't know what that makes him to me; but anyway, way back in the 1920s, that's when they *really* took care of business, you know? My granddad had heard *all* those stories when he was young, and he used to tell all of us."

"No shit," Carson Everett nodded as he sucked on his beer bottle. "Yeah, I useta hear the same stories in my family. Man, back in those days, when you were a good, solid white man, you didn't hafta put up with no bullshit from no mouthy Jews, or anybody, ya know? But that was before that pussy Eisenhower sent in the Army to Little Rock, or before that other president, what was his name, the one from Texas; you know, after Kennedy…anyway, before that one betrayed the white race with that Civil Rights Act bullshit."

"Yeah, I know," Jerry absolutely agreed with his buddy; but after all, this was an ages-old discussion between the two of them, replayed hundreds of times over the years. "Then we had to deal with fifty years of—"

"It don't matter," Carson interrupted as he killed his latest beer and signaled for a couple more. "With Hollinger in the White House forever now, it ain't ever goin' back to those fuckin' civil rights days. He's takin' care of the Jews first, and then he'll…"

Jerry Floyd's ears involuntarily squelched his friend's stream of vitriol as he again locked eyes with the bartender when she reached for their empties. She smiled at Jerry. She had certainly overheard enough of their conversation as she regularly swept by their barstools during the past hour. Even down here in what was once known as the Deep South, in the not-too-distant past you still had to wonder about people…how they leaned when it came to matters of the white race versus the others.

No more. Not for the past couple of years, since early 2035 when President Hollinger brought out the big guns. And certainly not since almost a year ago, when Hollinger's army and FPF mercilessly dealt with those treasonous street agitators. Now, Jerry Floyd could look at a hot bartender and know that if he got her home, or at least out to the parking lot later, he wouldn't be getting any libtard bullshit from her. To get by in Ephraim Hollinger's America these days, you either had to be fully on board with the American Values and Greatness movement, or you had to be damn good at hiding it if you weren't.

Otherwise, you'd probably wind up on the passenger manifest of a bus convoy headed out to Wikieup; or eventually to Bowie, or Holbrook, or Indian Springs up in Nevada, or…

* * *

"My husband has a work variance!"

The heavily armed, uniformed FPFer ignored Claire Weber's objections to being taken into custody, along with her two Jew kids.

"Please!"

The hulking FPFer's eyes narrowed as he glared at this Jewish woman.

"You get into that van right now," he snarled as he pointed his automatic weapon toward the FPF LTV—local transport vehicle—that was visible through splintered remains of the front door to this woman's palatial home. "Or I'm going to grab you by your hair and drag you across your front yard and throw you in headfirst. You'll be lucky if you wind up with only a couple of broken bones and a concussion."

Rachel realized that this terrifying man, fully decked out in combat gear, meant business. She had a flash of what he was about to say next, a split-second before the words reached her ears.

"And then I'm going to grab your little girl there"—he now aimed his weapon directly at Rachel, cowering in the corner of the living room that she would never again see—"and I'm going to throw her into the back of the van from twenty feet away. And if she doesn't make it that far, I'm going to pick her up again, and then one more time…"

"Okay, please! PLEASE!" a terrified Claire Weber surrendered. She motioned to Noah, who was standing wide-eyed in terror in the walkway between the kitchen and the living room. Noah remained frozen in fear.

"Come over here, please!" she pleaded. "You need to come here with your sister and me. PLEASE! NOW!"

Finally, the boy took a couple of hesitant steps in the direction of his mother, who was now heading to the living room corner to collect her daughter. Only a couple of seconds passed, but her mind raced through a thousand different thoughts, every one vectoring back to one belated observation, and also one unanswerable question.

The observation: My God, she had been so wrong in disregarding her brother's and Michele's pleas to flee the country with her children when she had the chance.

The question was actually a two-part pondering. The first part:

What had gone wrong that the veneer of protection provided by Marc's work variance had suddenly been peeled away, leaving Claire and her children at the mercy of Spencer Howell's dreaded Federal Police Force?

The second half:

Were they going to grab Marc also?

But then:

Maybe this was all a misunderstanding!

That thought, that flicker of hope against hope, anesthetized Claire Weber's mind as she led her children through the front door, across the pavers to the curb, and into the back of the Federal Police Force's local transport vehicle…a prison wagon, essentially.

That remote possibility, that hope against hope, now tussled for mindshare in Claire Weber's brain with unwelcome, century-old images of others being ushered away from their homes and loaded into similar prison wagons.

Others like Pop-pop.

All that was missing in the here and now were the yellow stars.

* * *

"You know," Jack Keller muttered, "you're damn lucky that the Jew isn't here anymore."

To Jack Keller, Marc Weber had always been "the Jew."

"You never know," he continued, "some FPFer with a real hard-on for Jews might have grabbed you also, if they came for him and you were there, either at your trailer or his motel. You know, for fraternizin' with him, or somethin' like that."

Dalia Travers hadn't seen Marc Weber since mid-April, when his work variance was granted and he immediately was moved over to the gigantic camp construction near Bowie, almost three hundred miles to the southeast. There had been no goodbyes of any kind. They had tumbled into bed only once more after that late March morning when President Hollinger unveiled his plans for the fates of America's Jews. Marc's frantic focus for the next two weeks had been squarely aimed at securing a work variance to remain at the helm of his construction company, at least in a titular sense.

One day, in mid-April, he was gone; and that was that.

"A guy I know down in Phoenix said that all of a sudden," Jack Keller continued as he sucked on his half-empty, rapidly warming beer, "the FPF is arresting lots of Jews there who supposedly had work variances. Not everyone, but a lot of 'em. Something happened; I don't know what, but…"

The bartender-slash-drug dealer's voice trailed off.

Dalia Travers shrugged as she worked on her own beer. The bottle was of the longneck variety, and she suggestively worked it to let Jack Keller know exactly what was on her mind. She had yet to find some other guy up in Kingman or farther north in Vegas, or down in Wickenburg, to fill Marc Weber's regular slot in her rotation, so Jack had had her full attention for the past five months. Jack Keller didn't care one way or another if Dalia was doing anybody else. Truthfully, though, he had been grossed out by the thought of her letting a Jew stick it in her on a regular basis. That didn't stop his own encounters with Dalia, but still…

AVGN had reported that the gigantic compound near Bowie was about two-thirds complete and would be receiving its own transports of Jews starting early next year, alternating with FDF-1 and the other new facilities also expected to be completed by then. Rumor also had it that nearby "Dachau" would eventually be accompanied by a newly constructed second camp only a mile or so away, with this second compound slated to be even larger than the first one. Jack Keller wondered if Homeland Security or the FPF or whoever was building the camps would transfer Marc Weber back here to work on the construction of "Dachau 2" or whatever they would unofficially call this new facility. And, if that were the case, whether Dalia would pick things up with the Jew where they had left off. Again, not that Jack Keller cared much one way or the other, except the nagging worry that the Jew's presence might conceivably present a risk for Dalia. And damn, if that happened, there went Jack Keller's prized conduit for moving oxy and meth!

The worry was just a fleeting one that disappeared as quickly as it had appeared, as Jack Keller watched Dalia Travers continue to suggestively slide her lips up and down that longneck beer bottle.

* * *

Claire Weber's tortured contemplation had been:
Were they going to grab Marc also?

Claire's pondering had been framed in the context of the future; but the ominous, treacherous "they" had, in fact, already taken Marc Weber into custody.

A day earlier, on a blazing late September Tuesday morning, Marc had been abruptly summoned to the main construction office at Federal Detention Facility Two shortly before 8:30. The temperatures outside of Bowie typically ran a good ten degrees lower than up near Wikieup, which should have put the thermometer in the low nineties and have provided a touch of relief to Marc Weber when compared to the same time a year earlier while working on FDF-1. This hellish year of 2037 had, however, been hallmarked by temperatures across the entire United States that mockingly reflected the satanic depths to which the United States had descended. The final phase of construction at FDF-2 was proceeding amid relentless century-mark temperatures, day after day, and this one would be no exception.

Not that Marc Weber would be in the vicinity of FDF-2 by the end of the day.

The moment Marc crossed the threshold into the smallish waiting area in the construction office, he was surrounded by a half dozen stone-faced, FPF-uniformed men. Perhaps to force the cold terror away from his conscience mind, Marc's brain instantly and involuntarily conjured up a scene near the end of that classic old movie, *The Godfather*; the vignette where the one gangster thinks he's about to lead Al Pacino's character into a fatal trap at a sit-down with a rival mob family but abruptly realizes, as he's suddenly surrounded by his now-former allies, that he's the one about to be driven away to meet his death.

"Marc Judah Weber," one of the men ominously intoned, "in accordance with the provisions of the Department of Jewish Employment Control, your work variance has been revoked, and you are hereby remanded into the custody of the Federal Police Force."

A tragically belated revelation, far too long in the making, unveiled Marc's future—his wife's future, and the future of his two children—in the theater of his mind.

Those conjured images, as tortuous as they were, would pale in comparison to what would soon occur.

Jack Keller's contemplation had proven correct: Marc Weber would be returning to FDF-1, to "Dachau."

Just not the way that Keller, nor Dalia Travers nor Marc Weber himself, had envisioned that return trip unfolding.

* * *

Dane Marshall sauntered slowly, pensively along the Denver municipal park's bricked pathway that was nearly blanketed with deceased leaves of all colors: purples, rust-browns, oranges, and even a few semi-bright reds. In years past the glorious fall scenery that surrounded him would have been accompanied by the crisp chill of a typical Colorado autumn. Instead, the late-October sun bathed him in glorious warmth. Children played nearby; adults who may well have been playing hooky from work relished anywhere from a few minutes to a few hours as they shared the park's expansive lawns with each other and with nature herself.

The Apocalypse wasn't supposed to be like this. Where were the scattered burned-out cars—some still in flames, others smoldering—smashed into streetlight posts or abandoned in the middle of pockmarked streets? Where were the billowing clouds of black smoke filling the horizon? This splendid October scenery that surrounded the former Navy SEAL—and present-day freedom fighter—belied not only the clichéd film sets depicting the hellscape backstory of so many movies and television shows, but also the reality of Ephraim Hollinger's transformed America in the autumn of 2037.

* * *

General Frank Douglas, the Chairman of the Joint Chiefs of Staff, was correct: Someone's balls would be on a skewer in the aftermath of the audacious attack on Spencer Howell's concentration camp transports.

The Attorney General's *cojones*, however, were not the ones that wound up being impaled.

The Joint Chiefs Chairman had ordered his aide-de-camp to treat the possibility of a resistance cell comprised of former special operators as highly classified intelligence. Naturally, in the immediate aftermath of the attack on the initial FDF-1 convoys, the aide-de-camp sniffed the brisk winds of the American Values and Greatness Movement and tattled to Spencer Howell's Chief of Staff that General Douglas had received—but then buried—intelligence about the possible existence of a highly skilled, militarized resistance movement.

A furious debate raged within the innermost circles of Ephraim Hollinger's cabal about the fate of General Frank Douglas. Treasury Secretary Tom Buckner and DHS Secretary Braxton Knox argued for a staged shoot-down of the General's private plane by "Antifa Zionists."

Spencer Howell, on the other hand, thought that Hollinger had gotten enough mileage out of scapegoating the country's beleaguered Jews, and yet one more faux attack would yield dramatically diminished returns. After all, Hollinger's draconian transformations were now all in motion. Jews were being forced en masse from the American workforce and were being rounded up. Soon, once operational changes were enacted, the transport convoys to FDF-1 would be underway. Howell thought arresting Douglas, followed by a show trial and then his public execution, would be far more impactful to tamping down resistance from all but these apparent professionals who had disrupted his inaugural transports.

And I'll hunt them down soon enough, Spencer Howell mused, channeling some of his favorite scenes of American Nazi vengeance against a stubborn resistance movement from *The Man in the High Castle*.

Besides, Howell reasoned—though of course he didn't share these thoughts with anyone else—publicly scapegoating Douglas would also serve to deflect any doubts that Ephraim Hollinger might now be entertaining about his Attorney General's competence. Howell was honest enough with himself to acknowledge that had he not resisted Frank Douglas' recommendations for daylight, clandestine transports, the attack either would never have happened, or would have likely been far less effective. Spencer Howell badly needed a heat shield, and the spectacle of Frank Douglas' trial and execution would likely do the trick.

The common thread among Spencer Howell, Tom Buckner, Braxton Knox, and even Ephraim Hollinger was that Frank Douglas would soon be a dead man, one way or another.

Spencer Howell won this round; and Veterans Day, 2037, was celebrated by AVGN televising a firing squad summarily ending General Frank Douglas' life, much as his platoon had callously ended the lives of innocent Iraqi civilians some thirty years earlier.

Patriots across the nation were now properly warned of what might befall any of them, even the Chairman of the Joint Chiefs of Staff, should they stumble while traversing the long, torturous journey toward American Values and Greatness.

* * *

A fresh burst of rancid perspiration materialized on Randall Weston's brow, and again he wiped it away. An historic, brutal late-November heat wave had descended on the desert Southwest a day earlier, and was forecast to maintain its hellish stranglehold for at least another three days. Historically, temperatures around Federal Detention Facility One topped off in the seventies and eighties throughout November…a good forty degrees lower than during the worst of summers these days, when the thermometer regularly bumped up against the one-twenty mark. This year, though, the mercury had clocked at or above ninety degrees almost every day since Halloween. And now the worst had arrived, with this unprecedented return to the one hundred and ten-degree mark, even as Thanksgiving approached.

Randall had arrived at "Dachau" two months earlier. He was immediately assigned to intake duty, responsible for meeting incoming transports and then herding new prisoners to their assigned barracks. Thus far, though, the job had been a giant slog of nothingness. Randall was fully aware that the first bus convoy transports back in mid-September had been intercepted, with every one of the prisoners somehow escaping their fate. Randall also knew that an FPF Transportation and Detention Officer named Drew Chapin had been killed in one of the attacks, the one up in the northeast.

Prisoners still arrived every few days, though squeezed into vans and box trucks, rather than by the busload. For Randall and the other TDOs, one monotonous day blended in with the next.

Now, finally, FPF leadership had apparently corrected whatever flaws had led to the successful attacks. All Randall knew was that the busloads of Jews would leave the northeastern and southeastern disembarkation points now accompanied by heavy military guard, and would all be transferred to railroad transports at a highly secretive hub somewhere in or around central Kansas.

Expect boxcars, not passenger trains, the transportation orders advised the TDOs assigned to FDF-1...which delighted the "Dachau" troops to a man, given the obvious nod to Hitler's and Himmler's preferred method of transport to their enslavement and death camps. *Three thousand Jews would be on the train—the exact same number as had been freed from the buses by those four brazen attacks. We're not only resuming the transports, we're sending an unmistakable message to these treasonous ex-military radicals, whoever they are. Our message...Ephraim Hollinger's message...Spencer Howell's message:*

You can't stop us.

Randall checked his watch again. If the train arrived on schedule, he would soon be hearing the chugging and clacking along the newly built tracks.

"Soon enough," the man to Randall's right, a TDO named Matt Grady, snarled. "Soon enough," he repeated, his eyes dead yet paradoxically radiating pure hatred. Grady had roomed with Drew Chapin, the now-deceased TDO, during their FPF training in the class ahead of Randall's. The two had bonded over their shared lust for restoring pure American values and greatness, and that the grace of Ephraim Hollinger had put both of them in a position where they not only had front-row seats, but also served as instruments of his designs.

The sudden distant sound of the concentration camp-bound train instantly took Randall back to downtown Denver, a little over a year ago; to those first thrilling, terrifying sounds of the approaching forces that would retake the streets from the disloyal anarchist traitors and then set in motion Ephraim Hollinger's banishment of the political opposition. The chug-chug-chug became slightly louder, and Randall shot a look at Matt Grady, and then at the dozen other TDOs who had been assigned to intake duty this historic day.

Something's coming.

Nearly two minutes passed until the procession of boxcars rolled to a stop abreast of the Federal Detention Facility One disembarkation platform. Randall took a half step toward the closest train door, an enormous sliding steel monster imprisoning that car's human cargo. Matt Grady's beefy arm swiveled downward, an unyielding railroad-crossing gate instantly blocking Randall Weston's forward progress. For a second or two Randall was perplexed at his fellow FPFer's action, wondering exactly what Grady was doing; why he was waiting.

A look into TDO Matt Grady's eyes instantly gave Randall Weston his answer.

"This is for Drew," the man's words fully encased in evil.

A wave of nausea slammed Randall Weston, but curiously the sickly sensation quickly passed as he surrendered to eternal damnation.

Your soul is already forfeit, so you might as well be at peace with wherever this jarring journey takes you until then.

* * *

Oh God! They have to open the train door! I don't know how much longer we can take it! We're suffocating and broiling alive!

Claire Weber struggled to focus her vision as she clutched her two children. All around them the other passengers moaned and cried out in anguish, struggling for breath, for life, amid the suffocating heat. How long had the train been stopped? Ten minutes? Fifteen minutes? A half hour? Time had lost all meaning, other than every passing agonizing second brought Claire, Noah, and Rachel a tick closer to death.

Soon, the delusions came. Claire Weber's final fevered image was that of Pop-pop, sadly locking eyes with her as he reached with one of his hands to clasp hers and with his other to gently take hold of both Rachel and Noah.

Chapter 56

Another wave of nausea slammed Daniel Jacobson as he waited for the unmistakable signal that the attack was now underway. Again, he fought back the unwanted, involuntary impulse that repeatedly slammed him from the moment he began belly crawling into position.

I wish they had left me behind again, just like the bus rescue mission.

But each time, he forced himself to remember. Each time, Daniel's naked fear vaporized and was overtaken by raw hatred.

Claire...oh God, poor Claire! And Rachel and Noah!

Again, Daniel fought the urge to yank the dark military scarf that blanketed his neck and face up to his lower eyelids, now soaked in dread-induced sweat, away from his head and try to relieve himself from the intense claustrophobia. The attack had yet to commence; he could raise the scarf at the last minute. However, Michele had warned—ordered—him to leave the face covering in place.

"You never know when a battle might begin prematurely because something goes wrong," she had patiently explained. "From the moment you gear up, you need to be ready to engage at any second; so face coverings, gloves, night-vision goggles—all of it—stays in place, no matter how uncomfortable. This way, you're not scrambling at the last second if everything goes to hell and you're suddenly fighting for your life."

Daniel distracted himself by lowering his eyes slightly to his weapon. With his night-vision gear, he could easily see that the safety was still flicked to the "on" position, even in the post-midnight blackness. The thick desert cloud cover blocking almost all moonlight was a bonus—a blessing, maybe even a sign from God. Ideally, they would have attacked Federal Detention Facility One at the end of January, on a near-moonless night; but the intel report from Dane Marshall had informed them another attempted transport of prisoners was scheduled to arrive at "Dachau" on either January 23rd or 24th. Spencer Howell's bus convoys would once again converge at the FPF's railroad junction in Central Kansas, where another three or four thousand desolate souls would be loaded onto yet one more concentration-camp-bound train.

The team had caucused and were in unanimous agreement that the optimal moment to attack and destroy "Dachau" was *before* this next transport train departed Kansas, and even before the unfortunate concentration camp inmates-to-be were boarded onto Kansas-bound buses from various corners across the soulless shell America had become. Right now, the prisoner population at FDF-1 was still only around 1,500 imprisoned Jews and political prisoners. Unlike the simultaneous attacks on the bus convoys, the chances of every one of those newly freed prisoners being ferried to safety were near-zero, even if the assault was letter-perfect. The location of FDF-1—literally out in the middle of nowhere—was an insurmountable problem if the team tried to reprise the exact box-truck-based escape plan from the previous successful assault on the buses.

"We're better off destroying FDF-1 and the other camps and denying Howell a destination for any of his prisoners," Michele had declared as their assault plans took form. "We'll get as many of the current prisoners as we can either across the border or to one of the safe houses, but mostly we set back Howell's and Hollinger's concentration camp network by at least a year, and hopefully we throw them into a state of total chaos after seeing every one of their camps simultaneously destroyed."

"Yeah, it doesn't matter if FDF-1 has 1,500 or 5,000 prisoners when we take it," Frank Sanchez had agreed. "We'll get them all out of the camp itself. But the FPF will recapture a much higher percentage if we attack after a train arrives with a couple thousand more prisoners than before. We're better off clogging their prisoner supply chain before they try again. We hack into AVGN with video of the concentration camp being destroyed and people running for their lives as they're liberated, and you never know; maybe we trigger a broader uprising against Hollinger. So yeah, I concur that we attack before the date that Dane said they've set for the next arrival, and before those buses hit Kansas and the prisoners get loaded onto the train cars. In fact, before they even get loaded onto the buses from all of those local detainment facilities."

And so, the time and date for the assault and—hopefully—destruction of "Dachau" had been set, and had now arrived.

2:00 a.m. on Monday, January 18, 2038.

Martin Luther King Day.

Again, only a few seconds after he had just done so, Daniel's night-vision-enhanced gaze lowered to his weapon as his thoughts took flight across a mere seventy-five yards of desert darkness to the perimeter of the concentration camp.

He had their names.

Matt Grady. Randall Weston. Willie Williams. Cody Masterson. They were the ones who had been closest to the train, and who bore the largest share of responsibility for Claire's monstrous, agonizing death. But there had been nine others on the platform that day, and Daniel knew their names as well. Spencer Howell had, thus far, hid the unplanned, torturous murders of three thousand Jews from the American public. Howell was deviously crafty enough to realize that even with his and Ephraim Hollinger's iron grip on the nation, knowledge of what his FPF troops had done could well be a bridge too far and trigger the masses to fight back...or at least shake off their utter passivity. And Spencer Howell needed the masses as docile and fearful as possible.

But Dane Marshall had smuggled out a coded message detailing the abomination along with the names of every TDO directly or indirectly responsible. Daniel was now painfully aware of what had shockingly happened to his sister, his niece, and his nephew.

I'll kill every one of them, Daniel thought for the thousandth or ten thousandth or millionth time. As with every previous time, though, his lust for vengeance was immediately followed by the remembrance of what Michele had matter-of-factly, icily replied the first and only time he had voiced those same thoughts.

"You won't get the chance; they'll all be dead before you even get close to them."

* * *

The liberation and then the destruction of FDF-1 would commence from inside the facility at zero-two-hundred hours when Dane Marshall, who three weeks earlier had maneuvered to get himself transferred from Denver to FDF-1, would rapid-fire a series of rocket-propelled incendiaries—RPIs—into the two adjacent barracks where almost every one of the 200 FPFer assigned to "Dachau"—other than those assigned to overnight guard duty that fateful evening—would be sleeping. Spencer Howell had mandated that his TDOs assigned to FDF-1 be moved out of their two-man dormitory rooms and now sleep in open-bay barracks as punishment for the unauthorized mass murder of three thousand Jews. Even the camp *Kommandant* now had his personal quarters embedded inside one of the guard barracks with the *Vice Kommandant* assigned to the other building.

"Mass concentration of targets—one more Spencer Howell miscalculation that we'll use to our advantage,"

Michele had immediately recognized during the first planning session for the attack.

Dane's RPIs would instantly ignite firestorms that would quickly, mercilessly kill or maim around half of the TDOs before he switched to his high-caliber automatic weapon. Dane knew where Matt Grady slept, and Randall Weston, and Cody Masterson, and every other one of the men who had stood on that platform back in late November and watched three thousand people broil and bake to their death. The fates had dictated that all thirteen men had bunks not only in the same barracks building, but on the same floor.

All of my primary targets all neatly clustered together, Dane had immediately recognized.

The firestorms triggered by RPIs were designed to burn out approximately thirty seconds after being ignited so they could be quickly followed by close-order small arms fire. Dane would open fire in their direction, over and over, one high-capacity magazine after another, to continue the attack while the main phase of the assault commenced. Fletcher Carlson, Roseanne Morris, Joy Patel, and Aidan Beckett would rush the exterior of the FDF-1 compound, one of them from each compass point, and quickly attach two circular, smoke alarm-sized devices each against the thick block outer wall. These sonic wave emanators—SWEs in military lingo—would then simultaneously be remotely triggered by Frank Sanchez seconds after each of the attackers had barely cleared the blast zones. As one might expect from the weapon's name, ultra-powerful sound waves would instantly emanate from the devices in all directions, causing the thirty-foot-high, seven-feet-thick block wall surrounding "Dachau" to fracture and crumble.

Because of the technology used by the SWE to radiate its destructive force, the weapon had been nicknamed the Jericho Bomb, an unmistakable tribute to the biblical tale of Joshua's *shofars* crumbling the wall surrounding the city that the Hebrews were destined to conquer.

Once the walls of "Dachau" had been reduced to rubble, the main assault force would fan out to their respective assigned assault lanes. Three of the attackers would join Dane in finishing off the guards in one of the barracks, while four others would assault the other guard barracks to pick up the attack from Dane's RPIs.

The rest of the assault team—all except the two who were assigned to sniper duty along the inbound road, watching for any approaching TDOs returning from a night of debauchery up in Kingman or even Vegas—would rush to the currently occupied prisoner barracks and begin hustling the concentration camp inmates out of the buildings, and then away from FDF-1 entirely. Once all the TDOs had been neutralized, the assault teams assigned to that primary mission would join the liberators and help lead the prisoners away from the facility before the rest of the compound's buildings were destroyed with additional Jericho Bombs.

If all went according to plan.

Daniel was, alas, painfully aware of what might become of the best-laid plans of mice and men.

And freedom fighters.

As with the night of the bus convoy raids, Daniel's mind mercilessly tortured him by offering up one nightmare scenario after another. Sudden, violent death and then eternal nothingness; excruciating pain after being severely wounded in combat; capture and subsequent torture...every conceivable outcome from the attempted liberation of FDF-1 raced through his panicky mind.

Every conceivable outcome except a successful mission, Daniel was painfully aware.

* * *

"It will happen fast," Michele had warned Daniel. "*Very* fast. We have the advantage of surprise so their six-or-seven-to-one manpower advantage will mean nothing, but only if we move very fast."

It's too late to save Claire, Daniel knew, *but Marc is in there somewhere. He's partly responsible for all of this happening—not just building a fucking concentration camp on American soil, but also greedily willing himself into blind ignorance and paving the way for Hollinger's dictatorship. But at least if I can find him during the chaos of the attack and get him to safety, then in a small way I can help carry on for Claire.*

The last time Daniel had slept—now more than 24 hours ago—he had dreamed of Pop-pop. A jumbled dream, where past and present gyrated and intertwined. In part of the dream, a much younger incarnation of Pop-pop who Daniel knew only from vintage 1940s family photographs was fighting in the present day alongside this group of retired military and intel special operators—and also Daniel—to liberate this modern embodiment of "Dachau," a reprise of what the 45th Infantry Division had long ago accomplished at FDF-1's namesake. In Daniel's dream, Pop-pop—not Dane Marshall—was inexplicably the inside man who commenced the assault with his attack on the FPF TDO barracks. "Inexplicably" because how would a Jew have been able to stealthily maneuver his way into Spencer Howell's Federal Police Force?

Don't look for logic in your dreams, Daniel had reprimanded himself when he attempted to pull apart the fragments of his dream that he could still recall after awakening. *Look for meaning instead.*

In the dream, Pop-pop quickly located Matt Grady, writhing in pain and hemorrhaging from a severed right arm, his skin already torched a sickly red-black, and cold-bloodedly executed the man they all knew was most responsible for three thousand deaths, including Claire and Rachel and Noah. Pop-pop emptied his entire high-capacity magazine into Grady's torso and head before shoving another magazine into his weapon and searching for his next target.

Daniel knew why, in his dream, Pop-pop exacted his revenge. Nearly ninety-three years earlier, on the day of Dachau's emancipation, Nathan Jacobson had been among the American soldiers who had undertaken reprisal killings of many of the S.S. troops captured during the liberation. Daniel had never known this about his great-grandfather until the day Pop-pop first met Michele's great-grandfather back in 2033—a lifetime ago—when Nathan Jacobson finally unburdened his soul and confessed his deed to Isaac Gretz.

Michele's hand nudging Daniel's right arm snapped him back to the here and now. He quickly looked in her direction and followed her eyes toward her watch, and then to the safety on his weapon.

Almost time.

Thirty special operators—including Daniel—would execute the assault on FDF-1. Their objective was the liberation of every soul who had been imprisoned there for the sin of being Jewish or, for the non-Jews, standing in opposition to Hollinger's murder of American democracy. They would also bring about the irreparable destruction of the concentration camp.

Marc's handiwork; the thought forced its way into Daniel's mind every time he mentally rehearsed the overall plan as well as his assigned role.

The remaining team members had fanned out to the three nearly completed concentration camps in Bowie and Holbrook here in Arizona, and Indian Springs up in Nevada. At zero-two-hundred hours, at the precise moment the attack on FDF-1 would commence, they would attack and destroy the in-progress camps with Jericho Bombs, and then liquidate the skeleton crews of TDOs assigned to each one to oversee each day's construction. The civilian construction crews were all housed at nearby motels and RV campgrounds. They were all knowingly constructing concentration camps that would imprison innocent victims, but those civilians hadn't taken blood oaths to Ephraim

Hollinger and Spencer Howell and the American Greatness and Values movement. Violent death was too harsh of a penalty for their sins, unlike the FPFers, so the teams could effortlessly avoid killing those construction workers during their attacks on the camps themselves.

No prisoners had yet been transported to any of the other partially completed camps, and each skeleton crew—per intel provided by Dane Marshall—clocked in at two dozen or fewer TDOs.

No match for our teams, Michele had emphasized as the plan took shape, *especially with the advantage of total surprise.*

Daniel ratcheted his wrist and focused his green-tinted night vision at the thick hands on his military-style watch.

Daniel flicked his safety to the "off" position. Less than one minute to go.

* * *

Those fifty or so seconds paradoxically passed in a flash but also agonizingly creaked ahead in what seemed like an eternity. Daniel kept his eyes focused on the silhouette of the TDO manning the nearest guard tower as he awaited the series of explosions from Dane Marshall's RPGs that would signal the commencement of the attack, followed quickly by the walls of FDF-1 crumbling from the sonic force of the Jericho Bombs.

In the days and months and years to come, Daniel Jacobson would periodically force himself to recall the first trauma-drenched minutes following zero-two-hundred hours on January 18, 2038. Every fragment of recollection, Daniel would remind himself each time, had been artificially injected into his memory solely through the retroactive knowledge of what he knew to have transpired. Actual firsthand recall of those first few minutes of the attack? Daniel's memory was a total blank, having instantly dumped every sensory input onto the cutting room floor of his mind without permanently saving so much as a scrap of what he experienced and what he did during the initial moments of the assault.

Daniel's actual remembrances began as he raced into the nearest prisoner barracks along his assault lane. He was aware that Michele was to his immediate right, also running at top speed and also with an automatic rifle at the ready. They shouldn't run into any of Spencer Howell's TDOs, according to Dane Marshall's intel report; but if they did, Daniel was every bit as prepared as Michele to start firing away.

Prisoners were already running down the hallway of the main floor, having been awoken by the sound of battle and instinctively knowing that their attempted liberation was a real possibility.

"Grab a weapon! Grab a weapon!" Daniel began shouting, turning to point out the door to the first of the wheeled crates of handguns that Roseanne Morris had pulled into the compound after the freedom fighters breached the crumbled walls of "Dachau." Unlike the bus convoy assault and rescue, they had no capacity to bring a fleet of box trucks to the scene of the attack and then evacuate every one of the liberated prisoners. The element of surprise necessary to destroy FDF-1, along with the concentration camp's remote location, made that strategy an impossibility.

This time, they would arm as many of the liberated prisoners as possible and equip them to do battle with Spencer Howell's troops, who would inevitably be sent to recapture them. Many would, tragically, be recaptured; some would perish in battle as they fought for their freedom. But at least the majority would now be armed and have a fighting chance.

"Who's in command?" came the booming voice from the tall, imposing man rushing toward Daniel and Michele. Those three words and the vision of that man—and the immediate recognition of who he was—were Daniel's first genuine recollection of the remainder of the assault and then the exodus that would forever shape the rest of his life.

"I am, sir," was Michele's immediate reply. For a fraction of a second, Daniel's mind fixated on Michele's instinctive usage of "sir." But after all, how else would retired Army Major Michele Burgess address former Senator—and retired three-star general—Jack Bancroft?

"What can I do?" came Bancroft's immediate reply...essentially a recursive command that communicated to Michele: "Give me my orders—now!"

Michele nodded over her shoulder, out the door, to the nearest crate of small arms that Roseanne Morris was still wheeling closer to the prisoner barracks so every escaping person would have to pass right by the weapons cache.

"Grab a weapon, sir," she immediately replied, "and you can start leading people out of the building and telling them to each grab a weapon also. Are there any others who have military training?"

Despite the urgency of the situation, the former presidential candidate couldn't help releasing a derisive snort.

"Hell, yes!" he instantly answered. "They made sure that veterans, especially combat vets, with low loyalty scores were among the first people they took into custody and transported here."

Jack Bancroft appeared to eyeball Michele Burgess for a split second. Despite Michele's face being fully covered up to her eyes, perceptive insight crossed his face.

"And especially Jewish combat veterans," he added, his eyes locking knowingly with Michele's.

Michele was about to instinctively issue an order to this retired lieutenant general, but Bancroft's mind was one with hers.

"I'll organize everyone coming out into groups of fifteen or twenty, with each group led by someone with military experience and who knows how to handle a weapon. We've been plotting for months now, waiting for the right moment to revolt and escape. Thanks to you"—Bancroft's eyes shifted to Daniel, and he offered a quick "and also you" nod of appreciation—"that moment is here."

"We staged ten vehicles two klicks southeast of here, scattered about a hundred yards off the highway," Michele informed Bancroft. "Another ten are a klick and a half northwest."

"Good," Jack Bancroft answered matter-of-factly, his mind obviously whirling as it absorbed yet another dose of real-time info. "We'll get as many people as possible into the vehicles and the rest of us will take off by foot."

"We have a network of safe houses..." Michele informed the retired general.

"Don't say anything more," the retired general interrupted.

Michele instantly knew why Bancroft cut her off. If he ended up being captured and tortured, he wanted absolutely no data points that he might divulge under extreme duress that might betray the freedom fighters and those whom they were rescuing. The less he knew about any other part of the exodus, the better for all involved.

For the first time, Jack Bancroft's eyes betrayed the severity of the odds that were stacked against them.

"I don't know how many will get through," he said quietly as his eyes began searching the fleeing prisoners for any of those who would soon lead others away from the now-destroyed FDF-1. His words were interrupted by a series of loud explosions coming from what he knew were the motor pool and fire station areas of the concentration camp. A dozen of the freedom fighters continued to make sure that returning "Dachau" to operational status would take a long, long time...if that day ever came.

"But if not, we'll go down fighting, rather than rot away in this abomination," he continued.

Michele's eyes locked with Bancroft's once again as she offered:

"Godspeed, sir."

In a flash, Jack Bancroft was on the move, barking orders as the liberation and exodus moved into high gear. They had to hurry; soon all two hundred of the prisoner barracks buildings, including those now being liberated along with those that would blessedly never be populated, would be destroyed.

* * *

Dozens of people raced past Daniel as he frantically searched for his brother-in-law. He was back outside the building now, swiveling his weapon from side to side, eyes keenly watching if one of Spencer Howell's TDOs survived the carnage at the guard barracks and stumbled over to the prisoner area, intent on exacting revenge for the attack.

I'll probably miss him, Daniel realized. *People are running all over, from at least four of the barracks. The odds of me finding him are...*

And then his eyes recognized Marc Weber.

"Marc! Marc!" Daniel shouted and began running toward the figure he recognized. Daniel was within ten feet of his late sister's husband when Marc realized that a shadowy, fatigue-clad figure was calling his name. At first, he recoiled in fear.

He must think I'm one of them...FPF, Daniel realized. He reached up to quickly lower the scarf that covered almost all of his face.

"Marc! It's me! Daniel!" he shouted.

A look of horrified recognition instantly crossed Marc Weber's face.

"You!"

Michele had raced alongside Daniel to intercept Marc, and she had likewise lowered the military scarf from her face.

"And you!" Marc screamed, now recognizing Michele.

"You both killed her! And my children! You murderers!"

What the fuck? was Daniel's immediate reaction to his brother-in-law's ravings.

"Marc! It's me! Daniel!" came the reprise of what Daniel had shouted only seconds earlier. Obviously, Marc was confused: delusional. He had to be!

This time Daniel added:

"And Michele. It's us! We're here to get you out of here!"

"You murderers!" Marc Weber perplexingly repeated. "I should have known! You attacked that bus and killed that guard!"

Oh, shit!

"That's why they murdered Claire and Rachel and Noah!" Marc continued his crazed accusation. "If you hadn't decided to play hero, Claire and my children would still be alive! It's *your* fault! They told me!"

"Marc, no!" Michele interjected. She began trying to reason with him, to break through to Marc's fevered mind. All the while, Daniel fought the wave of nausea that blasted him along with the sickening thought:

In a way, he's right.

"If you didn't have that gun," Marc's voice radiated hateful fury, "I would kill you right now!"

Marc's eyes shifted to Michele.

"Both of you!" he raged. "You need to pay for Claire!"

In a flash, Daniel's mind took flight. The theater of his mind presented Marc Weber sycophantically spilling his guts to Spencer Howell himself; the ultimate act of revenge, in his fevered mind, against the brother-in-law whom he had disdained for years as not being worthy to be in the presence of Marc Weber's greatness. Michele Burgess also; in Marc's mind, she had wasted the better part of her adult life in idiotic service to a nation and its democratic ideals that no longer existed. If only these two unworthy peons had long ago been taken into custody or killed by the Federal Police Force; that would be Marc's reasoning. This armed rebellion or whatever they thought they were doing would never have happened. Marc Weber would not only still be a free man—a rich man—his wife and children would still be alive.

I'll tell you everything I know, Marc Weber would plead to Spencer Howell. *Let me go free and I'll help you find them. I can help you! Please!*

Daniel's mind was teetering on the brink of the unthinkable when Marc Weber sealed his fate.

"They told me that your parents and your grandparents and all of your relatives escaped to Canada. But not Claire and my children! You left them behind to die! Your own parents left their daughter and their grandchildren behind to die when they ran like cowards!"

Daniel fought the urge to tell Marc exactly why Claire and her children weren't included in the initial exodus, and why Daniel had had to delay his futile after-the-fact appeal to his sister.

Because you would have betrayed us.

The vengeful hatred in Marc Weber's eyes went nuclear.

"I'll help the FPF track them down," he continued his threats. "Now I know how they got out of the country; you did it, and you took everything from me when you did that! I swear on my children's graves that I'll make all of you pay..."

Marc Weber's vengeful ravings continued, but Daniel no longer heard the words; only a drone of sound. Daniel's eyes caught Michele's, and in his peripheral vision he detected the slight shift of her left hand away from the barrel of her automatic weapon, starting downward to her waist.

Daniel quickly, almost imperceptibly, shook his head. His eyes remained locked with Michele's as he wordlessly communicated to her:

No. I'll do it.

"Marc...Marc...Marc!" Daniel's interruption finally halted his brother-in-law's ranting manifesto of revenge. He nodded toward the far side of the building that Marc had just exited as he stepped forward. He slung his automatic weapon over his right shoulder as he reached with his right hand to grasp Marc's left arm. Marc pulled away, but Daniel wasn't to be deterred. He held up both of his palms—that "alright, we'll do it your way" signal—but nodded again toward the far side of the prisoner barracks.

"Just come over here," Daniel's voice was firm, commanding. "Come on, you're going to get stampeded if you stand here." Daniel now nodded toward the accelerating stream of liberated prisoners racing by, dodging the three of them who were indeed standing directly in the escape path.

"Come on, let's talk this over," Daniel cajoled. Marc's eyes radiated hatred, but surprisingly he began to comply with Daniel's request, pivoting toward the building and beginning to walk. Daniel didn't attempt to grasp Marc's arm again, but he waited for the slightest sign that Marc would suddenly bolt. If that happened, then he would do it right here, no matter who was watching.

For whatever reason, Marc Weber walked another dozen steps until he reached the corner of the building, and then flanked to his right.

Daniel was right behind him now, adrenaline surging.

God forgive me for what I have to do, Daniel prayed silently, his hand now easing his combat knife from the protective sheath as his eyes burned into the back of Marc Weber's torso.

The Voice of Prophets

Alan Simon

Epilogue
He's Alive

March 20, 2038

*"Meet the new boss;
Same as the old boss."*

- The Who, *Won't Get Fooled Again*

Chapter 57

"And letters were sent by posts into all the king's provinces, to destroy, to slay, and to cause to perish, all Jews, both young and old, little children and women, in one day…"

The words scalded Daniel's throat, yet he forced himself to continue reading. This year the *Erev Purim* reading, especially *this* passage, tortured the minds of every family member gathered around the dining room table and overflowing into the suburban Toronto home's adjoining family room.

They all had agreed that *Erev Purim* needed to be commemorated this year—not celebrated—especially in light of their loss. The readings from Pop-pop's *Megillah* booklets would proceed, but this year would not be accompanied by whirling *graggers* or gleeful shouts of "Haman!"

Even as he struggled to read the words with his trembling, breaking voice, Daniel's mind took flight to *Erev Purim* five years earlier. Only five years! A lifetime had passed during that half-decade. America had been transformed into a dystopian nightmare. That mid-March evening five years ago had been when Rachel and Noah conspired to replace the hated name of Haman with "Ephraim Hollinger" during the *Megillah* reading, instantly bringing their father's wrath to life, followed quickly by his wife's admonishment for overreacting to a childish prank, and then Pop-pop commanding Daniel to proceed with his portion of the reading.

Rachel and Noah were dead. Claire was dead. Marc Weber was dead. Pop-pop was dead. *Erev Purim* had made its immutable return, and the Jacobson family would continue to mark the holiday even in their

Canadian diaspora; yet the commemoration would never again be the same.

Today would have been Pop-pop's 112th birthday. He had made it to only days short of his 110th—an extremely long life by any metric. Yet Daniel missed his great-grandfather more than he ever might have imagined over the years when his thoughts involuntarily drifted to contemplate Pop-pop's mortality. Oh, how he wished that he could unburden his anguished soul to the only person Daniel had personally known who might understand what had transpired two months earlier. Pop-pop had vengefully executed several S.S. concentration camp guards at Dachau in late April of 1945 during the camp's liberation. History and fate had dictated that his great-grandson would more or less do the same at modern America's own "Dachau" more than ninety years later.

The obvious difference was that Pop-pop had taken the lives of S.S. guards whom he had never previously encountered, and who had perpetrated the horrors of the Holocaust on so many innocent victims. Their evil had become a matter of record.

Daniel, however, had executed his own brother-in-law; and not as a punitive measure but as a preventive one.

Yet great-grandfather and great-grandson were both bound by the guilty weight of electing to be self-appointed judge, jury, and executioner.

Pop-pop had lived with his burden for ninety more years.

I have no idea how much more time I have left on this earth, Daniel had told himself countless times over the past two months, *especially after we go back to the States and resume our war. But regardless of how many years or months or maybe only weeks I have left, I need to live with this guilt. I wish Pop-pop were here so he could tell me how he did it all these years.*

* * *

Uprisings had begun across America. Only a scattered few clandestine bombings thus far that caused little damage, and still small-scale...especially when compared to the sheer destruction that Michele, Daniel, and the others had been able to bring about during that single January night. Dane Marshall, in the short time between his arrival at FDF-1 and the concentration camp's destruction, had obtained a copy of the cellphone videos that Matt Grady and Randall Weston had sickeningly made that horrific day last November on the railroad arrival platform: after three thousand human beings had all perished, and after the TDOs finally slid open the boxcar doors to gaze upon the lifeless bodies of their victims. Other than the crisp color of modern digital video, the images might well have been from the spring of 1945, as the Nazis frantically shuttled concentration camp prisoners across the network ahead of the liberating Allied forces, eventually leaving thousands of souls to perish in boxcars.

Joy Patel had hacked into the AVGN network one week after the attacks on FDF-1 and the other concentration camps. She waited until five minutes into Toni Fowler's nightly screed on the evening of Tuesday, January 26th, and millions of Fowler's minions suddenly witnessed a three-minute montage of the horrific aftermath of 3,000 murders, followed by video of FDF-1's destruction and the liberation of its prisoners. The AVGN technicians finally cut the hacked video feed, only to have the same images suddenly overtake every major AVGN Internet service: news, sports, weather, even AVGNInstaMeet.

For the next six days, Joy reprised her AVGN hacking as she scurried from one public internet hotspot to another, preventing the FPF from getting a fix on her. By the time a week had passed and February 2nd had arrived, nearly everyone across the land had borne witness to Ephraim Hollinger's and Spencer Howell's abomination. Appropriate enough for Groundhog Day, numerous Americans could no longer blissfully dive underground and escape the horrors that had been unleashed. Only a tiny fraction of the populace would eventually take up arms against the Hollinger and Howell regime; yet a nation had been shocked out of its willful coma and could no longer feign ignorance of a murderous, vengeful dictator's true intentions.

* * *

Barely two months after the assault on "Dachau," Michele and Daniel had been party to only sporadic coded reports about the fates of their comrades or the hundreds of newly freed prisoners. How many had made their way to safety? How many of the freedom fighters would eventually rendezvous to fight the next phase of this battle against Ephraim Hollinger, Spencer Howell, and the pure evil they both had brought to this once-great nation? Their own journey out of central Arizona had been a harrowing one. They had led a group of twenty freed prisoners on a mad dash southwest from the ruins of FDF-1, vectoring toward a point twenty miles east of Mexicali but doing so in an "island hopping" manner using three recently purchased Arizona safe houses. They easily sliced through the bars of the border wall in the post-midnight blackness four days after the "Dachau" assault, dodging FPF patrols the entire time, starting shortly after H-Hour.

Allies in Mexico's special operations community escorted Michele and Daniel to Mexico City, to a predesignated rendezvous point, waiting for other arrivals among the freedom fighters.

Roseanne Morris, Dane Marshall, Frank Sanchez, Fletcher Carlson, and Joy Patel eventually made their way to the makeshift Mexico City safe house, where they all consolidated intel reports about their respective pieces of the overall mission. The others? Hopefully they were still jumping from one safe house to another in various parts of the U.S., eventually heading north across the Canadian border as planned.

Eventually Daniel and Michele boarded a flight to Winnipeg, using false-name passports and in thick disguise. Should the plane develop problems and be forced to make an unscheduled landing within the United States, they needed the protective cover of deep-cover aliases. They also knew Spencer Howell's Federal Police Force had inroads into the global passenger travel system, and should they get wind that two frantically wanted freedom fighters were aboard a flight traversing U.S. airspace, they could always have the Air Force intercept and then force down the plane. Aliases and disguises were, therefore, a must to make the flight to Canada.

They made it to Winnipeg without incident, and then—still in disguise—traded off driving their rental car as they traversed the sometimes-treacherous highway (the result of a blustery snowstorm two days earlier during winter's dying days) to the Toronto suburbs. Neither Daniel's parents, nor Michele's, knew that a brief reunion was about to occur, of course.

"Stay here with us," Daniel's mother had sobbed when he showed up on his parents' front porch, Michele by his side, three days before the family's Purim commemoration. "You can't go back; it's too dangerous! Stay here where it's safe!"

Daniel wouldn't fight with his mother; not then, anyway.

But he would be going back to pick up the fight; how could he not?

"How are you getting along here?" Daniel had changed the subject as they went inside the house that had become their new home. "Are you settled in? How are the neighbors here?"

"They all seem fine," Nancy Jacobson had replied. "It took a while, but we're finally feeling safe here."

* * *

Barely ten miles away from where the Jacobson family gathered for a solemn, mournful *Erev Purim*, a bitter man offered poisonous words to his eight-year-old son.

"Thousands of those Jews," he lamented. Though no official word had ever been offered by the Canadian government, the presence of Jewish refugees in Canada—especially clustered around Toronto—had been an open secret in the dark corners of hate-filled websites and on social media.

Then, in the aftermath of Joy Patel's hacks into AVGN television and websites at the end of January, Spencer Howell decided to release a fabled version of the bus convoy attacks last fall. According to Toni Fowler and the other AVGN hosts as they circled the wagons, every FPF TDO aboard the buses at all four departure points had been cold-bloodedly murdered by these antifa terrorists—all of them Jews—who then spirited three thousand fellow Jewish scum criminals across both the Canadian and Mexican borders.

"They'll start infesting and infecting your countries," Toni Fowler had screeched to her international viewers in those two countries. "Just you watch—they'll ruin Canada and Mexico the way they almost did here. They'll steal your jobs, and cheat you out of *your* money. Be on your guard because MORE OF THEM ARE COMING!"

The bitter man's fortunes had, in fact, taken a major downturn only a week earlier. Plainly, he was a total fuckup at the truck tire plant where he had worked for the past two years; in fact, he had been a total fuckup at every job he had held since dropping out of high school at age sixteen after getting his girlfriend—his son's mother—pregnant. He didn't care though; he did almost nothing, had learned almost nothing, during his entire school "career." Work life held about as much appeal for the man as school had. He was habitually late or a no-show for his shifts. He was impossible to get along with, and his workdays were filled with confrontations with his coworkers. The tight labor market, though, had helped him preserve his job longer than might have otherwise been the case.

Now, though, with a fresh supply of new labor—men and women with a newfound appreciation for life and freedom and even hard work, in the aftermath of their escape from the dystopian horror their country had become—the man was summarily fired for poor performance and replaced with one of the refugees who had been freed via the Allentown, Pennsylvania attack.

"They're already here," the man told his son. "Never forget what they did to me—those Jews cost me my job. They'll try to destroy your life too, but don't let them. Someday you'll get a chance to make things right again and put them in their place."

The man's eyes bore into his son's.

"Never forget what they did to us."

And the flywheel of hatred again began gathering and storing energy that would, one day, be unleashed.

Made in the USA
Middletown, DE
11 October 2022

12401460R00309